THE SYNECTIC SNARE
BOOK TWO OF THE CELESTRIAD

Marise Morland

THE SYNECTIC SNARE
BOOK TWO OF THE CELESTRIAD

DOUBLE DRAGON

Chapter One

A pleasant but persistent chime echoed across the slum quarter of Alda Mexa. Idenion stirred, turned instinctively toward the other half of the bed, then sighed as he found it empty. Of course, he was no longer Arnalta's partner. Strange that his body could still miss her after his mind had lost interest. Resolutely, he pushed back the oddly-assorted covers and went to wash and dress. Then, yawning, he went into the kitchen, spooned two tiny helpings of cereal into unmatching bowls, and poured out two measures of liman.

As usual, Dena had not woken. Idenion went quietly into her room and shook her gently. "Dena? Dena, wake up. You'll be late."

"I'm so tired, Idenion," she murmured.

The chime sounded again, more rapidly.

"Do hurry, Dena," Idenion pleaded, but her reply, whatever it was, went unheard. A relayist had contacted him, saying simply: +Idenion, First Poet, you are excused from work today. Your presence is required at the akron. A flitter is on its way to you+

+Who originated this message?+ Idenion asked. Dena sat up apprehensively.

+Tralvar+ came the reply after a few moments. +He's there already. The Narvellans want you to attend the resignation of their Governor+

"Curious," Idenion remarked to his sister. "Still, I suppose anything's better than factory work, even their interminable ceremonies."

"Could I come with you?" asked Dena.

"Better not." He patted her shoulder apologetically. "You weren't invited. Where's my decent tunic - the white one? I'd better make myself presentable."

5

Dena found it for him. He had scarcely changed out of his overall and finished his meagre breakfast when the flitter arrived.

"At least you have an excuse for being late today," he said lightly. "Make the most of it."

She smiled, but her eyes remained troubled. "Idenion... don't quarrel with anyone, will you?"

"Don't worry," he reassured her. "Tralvar will keep me in order."

The Narvellan pilot was not in the mood for conversation, but Narvellans seldom were. Idly, Idenion wondered why Governor Grevin was leaving so suddenly, and so early. Then, as the flitter neared the plaza adjoining the akron, he began to realise that all was far from well. Tension and disquiet assailed his acute perception.

"What's going on?" he demanded of his silent companion as they came to land.

The latter deliberated for a moment, then said: "Do you know Isylla?"

"Grevin's wife?" said Idenion, carefully respectful as one always had to be when speaking of high-born Narvellan women. But his mind, caught off guard, was more precise. +Grevin's beautiful young wife+ he elaborated.

"So you're familiar with her?" said the Narvellan. "I wonder *how* familiar? No matter; such details are irrelevant. Ah, I see your First Citizen in conversation with our new Governor. They will explain everything to you, poet. Now be on your way - I have other duties."

Idenion disembarked hastily. Tralvar was standing outside the main portal, looking worried and self-conscious. The Narvellans, finding that the First Citizen of Celestra had no distinctive costume, had insisted on providing him with one - a tunic and leggings of pale blue with a contrasting indigo belt. His status, in

6

Narvellan script, was embossed on each sleeve above the elbow. As Idenion approached, Tralvar surreptitiously signalled him to be cautious. Idenion wasn't in the mood to obey.

"What in chaos is happening? Where are the Governor and Isylla?"

"I am your Governor now," said the gaunt Narvellan beside Tralvar. Idenion found himself looking into a pair of mesmeric green eyes, and flinched a little. "My name is Axmiol tyl Thuuvin," the Narvellan continued. "Tralvar knows me already, and he will verify that I am a far less indulgent person than Grevin tal Prelix. You will address all questions to me."

"What's happening?" repeated Idenion more quietly.

"You have been brought here as an observer," Axmiol stated. "You, the First Poet - defender of the wrongdoer and champion of free love. You have steadfastly maintained that we Narvellans live by one set of rules and seek to impose another. Today you will see this is not the case. Isylla has abused her position and disgraced her husband, and will be punished accordingly."

"Please be more specific," Idenion requested. How he hated Narvellan rhetoric!

"She gave birth to a hybrid son," said Tralvar. Axmiol glared at him.

"Very succinctly put, First Citizen. Never let it be said that Celestrians waste words, whatever else they waste. You look distressed, poet. Could it be that you actually comprehend her wantonness?"

Idenion was indeed shaken by Tralvar's pronouncement. He could acknowledge the social misdemeanour, if not the moral one. "Why do you wish to involve *me*?" he asked.

"You are to narrate this morning's events on the radio," Axmiol explained. "Here, as they happen. Your participation will ensure a good audience."

"I could refuse," Idenion said tentatively.

"Then you would have your work quota doubled," Axmiol said coldly. "But somehow I think you'll find plenty to say. Remain in this exact location: a microphone will be brought to you. The First Citizen will keep you company." Then he turned swiftly and stalked into the akron, leaving Idenion to stare resentfully after him.

"I'm sorry I couldn't forewarn you," Tralvar said apologetically. "I'd no idea *he* was going to be running things. Axmiol's contingent has been trying to oust the tal Prelix family for years, and poor Isylla's played right into their hands."

"Who's the father of her child?" Idenion asked.

"Her personal relayist," Tralvar replied. "And as far as I can gather they're not interested in him, even though he owned up. They say Isylla has to take all of the blame."

"What will they do to her?" Idenion said, almost to himself.

"Whatever it is, they've taken three octals to arrange it," said Tralvar. "I was with Grevin the night she went into labour."

"Do they intend any harm to the baby?"

"No; I have their word on that. But they'll stigmatise him, of course, as only they can."

The sky was becoming overcast, as if in sympathy with the city's mood. Idenion could discern the thoughts of various relayists announcing that he was to speak. Presently, a Narvellan youth came dutifully toward him and handed him a tiny instrument no bigger than a writing stylus. "Remain facing the akron, or you will block the signal," he said. "My lord Axmiol will notify you when to start."

Very soon afterward, a small procession began to emerge from the akron in single file. At the same time, Axmiol commanded Idenion to begin. The new Governor's thoughts were as chilly as his gaze, and twice as implacable. It was like being showered with icewater.

"This is possibly the strangest broadcast I've ever made," Idenion commenced. "I'm outside the akron, with the First Citizen next to me, and we're here to witness the ritual judgement of Isylla, wife to Governor Grevin. Her firstborn child is, so I've been told, half Celestrian - and if I may be allowed to comment on this - " He braced himself for another blast of ice. Nothing happened.

"Consider Isylla's isolation," he continued. "Most of her friends have been sent home, her husband is often busy, and she's forbidden to seek contact with Celestrian minds. Every message, whim, or request must be vocalised to her relayist. Is it any wonder, then, that she turned to him in her loneliness? The Narvellans find this behaviour untenable. Perhaps they should try to be more realistic.

"While I've been speaking, six of the Narvellan elite have formed a line nearby. They wear the regulation grey, plus sleeveless over-tunics and gauntlets. And in the square, to either side of me, groups of black-clad Moderators have appeared. I see there are a number of children about: would anyone who's close enough please take them to safety?"

Just then the main doors of the akron opened again, and Isylla stumbled out as if she'd been pushed. She wore a voluminous grey gown with a cloak over it, but no shoes. Idenion duly reported her presence, adding that she looked dazed or drugged. He had forgotten how unusual her eyes were - not the brilliant Narvellan green, but pale greenish-blue like the sea. Today, as she'd been crying, they resembled the sea after rain. He repressed a foolish urge to run to her side and comfort her. Instead, he spoke his reflections aloud, sadly and slowly. He'd once written a poem called Isylla's Eyes, and he wondered if Rinyi, the young relayist, had ever read it.

Two of the six men remained guarding the doors, possibly to prevent Isylla running back inside. The other four suddenly surrounded her and wrenched off her cloak and gown. The seams tore so easily that Idenion guessed they had been loosened in advance. And, as he also guessed, the intention was not to strip her naked, but to destroy the symbols of her respectability. She still wore an opaque shift which covered her from shoulder to ankle; and thus, as Idenion was quick to point out, was fully clothed by Celestrian standards.

His complacency didn't last long. Steel blades flashed in the air, and several people cried out, including Tralvar. But the Narvellans were wielding shears, not knives.

"They're cutting her hair!" Idenion whispered disbelievingly. "All of it! Her lovely long hair..."

+Speak up, poet+ Axmiol prompted. +This is the interesting part+

"They're cutting off her hair," Idenion repeated, furious and helpless. "Fistfuls, in chunks, as clumsily as they can. Throwing it at her feet. She doesn't even look down, but stares at the horizon. Now Grevin's been sent out to join her: she doesn't look at him either. They've finished with her now; she's just standing patiently, arms at her sides. One of the officials goes back indoors and the remaining three start on Grevin, pulling the epaulettes and ribbons off his tunic and throwing them on the ground with Isylla's hair. He has tears in his eyes as he looks at her. Tears ... and a great love." Idenion paused, frowning. "The fourth man has reappeared, carrying something metallic and circular. He's putting it round Isylla's neck..." Idenion's voice trailed off in fresh outrage.

+Well done, versifier. Prolong the suspense+ Axmiol's thoughts tweaked maliciously at his consciousness. +But don't wait too long, will you?+

"In harmony's name, must I go on with this?" Idenion cried. Tralvar gripped his shoulder sympathetically. He too was lost for words.

Before Axmiol could reply, there was a scream from behind Idenion and a distraught young man rushed past him. It was Rinyi, the relayist. "Don't hurt her any more!" he sobbed. "Punish me instead! Punish *me*!" He had addressed Isylla's captors, but it was Isylla herself who answered.

"I'm not worth it, Rinyi," she said tonelessly. "Go away."

Startled, he fell back. Idenion, turning to see how far he would retreat, remained looking anxiously across the plaza. There were too many bystanders - students, retired people, a few archivists, and many workers who'd ignored the call to duty. Just the sort of gathering the Narvellans hated, without the addition of Rinyi, who was trying to muster some active support.

At Axmiol's wrathful prompting, Idenion shakily resumed his narrative. "Forgive the delay, citizens. I was ... still am ... very grieved by what I've been forced to witness. Before Rinyi tried to intervene, an iron collar was fastened around Isylla's neck and locked in place. The key was handed to Grevin. Attached to the collar is a short chain; attached to the chain is a heavy lump of stone. Isylla must hold on to that stone or risk injury. And at last, an attendant is bringing the baby to her. She accepts it with difficulty. It seems to be asleep - conveniently perhaps - and is dressed like any infant of ours would be. To give a better description I'd have to go closer, which I've already been forbidden to do; but from here I can see its pale skin, and that confirms the truth of its parentage. It's obvious to me now that the stone symbolises the burden of the child, and that only Grevin can free Isylla from it."

A flitter came to land halfway across the plaza and, flanked by three officials on either side, Isylla and Grevin slowly walked toward it. Isylla struggled to balance the child and the stone, unable to lower her head enough to see either. Idenion was about to elaborate on her difficulties when a tiny click came from the microphone. Axmiol had cut the transmission.

+No more sentiment+ he instructed. +You've said all that's necessary+

Idenion turned angrily and hurled the microphone into a flowerbed.

"Don't let him provoke you," said Tralvar at his elbow. "It won't help."

"*You* were pretty quiet through all that," accused Idenion.

"With good reason. You're allowed to be outspoken at times: just the First Poet plying his trade. If I did it, they'd call it insurrection. I make my complaints privately." His attention abruptly switched to the centre of the square. "That young fool - what does he think he's doing?"

Rinyi and his supporters were blocking the way to the flitter. The air was volatile with their anger. Idenion wasn't surprised to see two heavy stun-cannon being towed out of the akron and aligned in their direction. But as Tralvar had sensed, the demonstrators had no clear objective, and the situation might have been defused if Isylla hadn't tripped. She trod on the hem of her shift, kept hold of the baby, but let go the stone. It swung free, dragging her forward. As she fell, she managed to twist her body so that the child was uppermost, but her left arm was trapped painfully beneath her. The child began to cry. Her escorts paused and watched silently as she struggled on the ground. No-one, not even Grevin, made any move to help her up.

Rinyi suddenly sprang forward, shrieking something incoherent. Idenion heard 'parasites' and 'barbarians' before his voice was lost in the general uproar. The relayist and his friends were soon grappling with Isylla's captors, while the Celestrian onlookers reacted with verbal and non-vocal encouragement. The Moderators began to move purposefully forward.

Tralvar kept a wary eye on the stun-cannon. There were plenty of Narvellans in the line of fire, but he wasn't sure that would stop Axmiol. A more pertinent consideration was the time it took for the weapons to recharge themselves after firing: almost a day, or so he understood. The current unrest probably didn't warrant their use. The Moderators, accustomed to a homeworld driven frantic by famine and natural disaster, would make short work of a few inept young Celestrians.

Then the scuffles came to an abrupt and premature halt. Tralvar, peering through the shifting crowd, saw that Grevin had taken charge of events. Quietly and deliberately he raised Isylla to her feet, embraced her gently, and took the baby from her.

"She has endured her punishment bravely," he declared. "She has erred, but she is still my wife. And this is my firstborn son, whom I acknowledge." Then he resumed his progress toward the flitter, Isylla stumbling by his side.

The group of six divided again. The quartet who had chastised Isylla went with her, and the other two stood guard over Rinyi. He knelt dazedly on the ground, blood trickling from a cut lip. Three Moderators and two Narvellan civilians, acting on instructions from their unseen superiors, paced solemnly forward to encircle the hapless young man. The two officials moved away.

"We are the appointed Five," announced one of the Moderators. "Rinyi, you are guilty of incitement to riot. We ask your forgiveness for what we must do."

Rinyi shrank from them in sudden awareness of his own peril.

"Tralvar, stop them!" cried Idenion.

"I cannot," he replied bleakly.

"Forgive us," repeated the Narvellan.

Idenion, anguished, made a sudden dash forward. He never reached the circle. One of the remaining elite swung his gloved fist and felled the interloper with an efficient, almost casual blow to the head.

Everything became very quiet. Tralvar felt lost, ineffectual, and in desperate need of a strong drink. The flitter was departing with its passengers. Most of the spectators had run off. Rinyi, smiling vacantly, was led away by the appointed Five.

"We were only carrying out our duty, First Citizen," said their spokesman.

Tralvar didn't trust himself to answer. Once again he'd been left to face the Narvellans alone. There had been other such confrontations, and each time his people had lacked the strength or resolve to finish what they'd started. Wearily he turned and walked towards Idenion, who lay unconscious. His attacker was standing over him and, to Tralvar's surprise, seemed rather dismayed.

"I'm Administrator Narad zyl Pereth," he said as Tralvar drew close. "I'm sorry I hit him so hard, but there was no time to do anything else. The Five's concentration was already building, and if he'd got any closer we'd have had a First Poet with only half an intellect. I couldn't let that happen."

"I'll have to take him home," Tralvar said uncomfortably. He wasn't used to apologetic Narvellans, and suspected an oblique form of sarcasm.

"Some of us admire his work," said Narad, obviously aware that Tralvar did not. "My quarters are close by. Will you permit me to give him healing?"

"Very well, just enough to bring him round," Tralvar replied. "Leave his bruises alone. He needs some reminder of his stupidity, and a black eye will do nicely."

"That's just the type of answer I'd expect from you, First Citizen," said Narad with the merest hint of a smile. He lifted Idenion with ease and carried him into one of the apartment buildings which bordered the square. "This Isylla business makes me ashamed," he said to Tralvar once they were inside. "Grevin would have taken her away quietly, but Axmiol wouldn't hear of it."

"I can imagine," Tralvar said, carefully neutral.

Narad settled Idenion onto a low couch and placed a cushion under his head, gently brushing aside the poet's long fair hair. Tralvar, now that he had a chance to observe his friend more closely, realised he looked concussed - probably due to striking his head on the flagstones.

"What happens to people you *don't* like?" he asked Narad.

"I dealt with him as if he were Narvellan," Narad said unhappily. "But I think I can undo most of the damage." Removing his gloves, he knelt and placed his fingertips on Idenion's forehead. Tralvar said nothing, but continued to watch narrowly. He mistrusted psychokinesis almost as much as he mistrusted Narvellans in general - possibly because, to a Celestrian, it was indiscernible save for the effects. Narad himself became still as he concentrated exclusively on his task.

"So fragile," Tralvar heard him say wonderingly. The comment did little to reassure him.

Idenion's return to consciousness, when it happened, was sudden. He shuddered away from Narad, putting up his arm as if to deflect another blow.

Narad stood up regretfully. "Without his co-operation, I can do no more," he stated.

"I can take over from here," Tralvar said levelly. "I'll require a flitter, of course."

Narad gave him a cold stare. "Shouldn't you be at the investiture?" he inquired. Idenion, behind him, looked imploringly at Tralvar.

"Now listen, Adjudicator, Minister, whatever you are," Tralvar said, dragging the injured poet to his feet and looking rather surprised when he stayed on them. "Idenion was coerced into making that broadcast. He was given no warning and no time to prepare. It's Axmiol's fault he over-reacted and it's Axmiol's fault he's hurt. He's coming home with me, this instant, and you'll have to explain that any way you can."

In a trice, Narad was his former conciliatory self. "Very well, First Citizen," he said quietly. "You already know my views on our new Governor. If, at any time in the future, there is anything I can do to smooth the way - anything that's within my jurisdiction - I'll be willing to oblige." Tralvar thanked him formally, then led Idenion outside. The latter stood swaying and drawing deep breaths like a drowning man regaining the air.

"What became of Rinyi?" he asked hoarsely.

"He was reduced," said Tralvar. "And you almost joined him, you cretin. Don't you realise I need you with all your faculties intact?"

"Everyone needs me today," said Idenion, and began to laugh painfully. Tralvar put out an anxious hand to steady him.

Narad, who had followed them out, watched Idenion intently. His look was wistful, almost envious. Tralvar, uncomprehending, filed the strange expression in his memory for future reference.

Then the expected flitter arrived and whirled the two Celestrians away from the plaza. They passed low over the spot where Isylla's black tresses still lay; and Idenion, glancing at Tralvar, suddenly regretted accusing him of indifference. Out of the public gaze, his whole demeanour changed alarmingly. He buried his face in his hands and his shoulders began to shake.

"Don't you think I'd have given anything - *anything* - to save Rinyi?" he cried. "He was just a boy. I'd have sacrificed my own reason if I'd thought they wouldn't take his as well. We can't fight them - don't you understand? None of us can, so don't try." When the little craft touched down outside his villa, he said more quietly to the pilot: "Wait here. I'll be back in a few moments." Then he propelled Idenion indoors and went straight to the study, where he systematically downed three glasses of resnay. Idenion, who normally didn't touch the potent drink, sipped cautiously at a tiny measure.

"Do you think I convinced him?" Tralvar said at length.

"You were acting!" Idenion marvelled. "Well, you certainly convinced *me*. Why the pretence?"

"Because I don't want anyone guessing I'm up to something." Tralvar took one more drink, then straightened his tunic and brushed his lank hair. "I've decided to go back to the investiture. No sense in starting off on the wrong foot. Rest up, bathe your eye, and get some food inside you. There isn't much here, but it'll be more than you've seen for a while. When I come back, I want to see you recovered, alert, and ready to commit a treasonable act."

"And what might that be?" Idenion asked.

"I want you to fetch Laura," Tralvar answered calmly. "No, don't ask questions. I'll explain later."

"But I've begged and begged - "

"I know. It wasn't an easy decision, just an inevitable one. So take comfort, First Poet, in the knowledge that you'll see her again soon."

Idenion, left alone, expected to feel elation or apprehension. Instead, he merely felt hungry. In the larder he found liman, cakes and dried fruit; taking exactly half of everything he returned to the study, ensconced himself in Tralvar's favourite tattered armchair and switched on the radio receiver. Axmiol, or someone very much like him, was pontificating about the role of the Celestrian in Narvellan society.

"You work for Narvella: we have endowed your lives with purpose and virtue. It does not matter what kind of work you do, but how you go about it. Work is not degrading, but ennobling, irrespective of whether it is accomplished with the mind or with the hands..."

Lulled by the monotonous voice, and more replete than he'd felt all year, Idenion slept.

Three ilden or so later, the slam of the front door woke him. The daylight in the room was subtly altered and the radio hissed quietly to itself. He stretched, and immediately wished he hadn't.

"Oh, discords, I ache all over," he groaned as Tralvar came in.

"You'll survive," said Tralvar with scant sympathy. "Ah, good, the eye's turned an interesting colour."

"There's no need to sound so pleased," Idenion muttered.

"Oh, but there is," Tralvar contradicted, "for two reasons. Firstly, no-one will think it strange if you don't go to work tomorrow. Be ashamed of your appearance, hide from everyone. It's a rare chance to get off the

18

planet. And secondly, what was Laura's very first reaction to you?"

"She wanted to protect me," Idenion said hesitantly.

"And so she will again, when she sees you looking like that."

Idenion was suddenly dubious. Tralvar, seeing him waver, decided to challenge rather than reassure.

"Can you handle it, Idenion? It's been ten Earth years. You'll have to find her, convince her she's needed, lie to the Narvellans and harbour her under your roof. If you get caught, I won't be able to help."

"I know. I won't let you down."

"Just make sure you don't. Your role will be crucial, and that means no more hot-headed behaviour."

"I understand."

"Since you're not making flowery speeches, I believe you *do* understand," said Tralvar, smiling. The smile was totally unexpected, like a brief glimpse of the sun through storm-clouds.

Idenion, emboldened, asked only one question. "Tralvar - why did you relent?"

"I made a promise," Tralvar said solemnly. "When I was inaugurated, I vowed I would defend Celestra always. And I haven't done it. That outburst on the flitter was credible because it was a half-truth. I can't free my people single-handed, and I don't command enough loyalty to recruit help other than yours. And with respect, Idenion, poets aren't much use in the current climate. I need scientists." He located his half-empty resnay bottle, took a lengthy swig, and continued: "Look at what happened today. Rinyi's friends ran off and left him as soon as things got rough, and no-one seemed too bothered about you either. We need someone who can inspire, motivate, lend cohesion. That someone is Laura. And if I seem less than happy at the prospect of her return, it's because I don't like admitting failure." He stared moodily out of the window. "The plans will still be mine, but the leadership will be hers."

"What about Earth's defence network?" Idenion asked, but then realised Tralvar wasn't listening. Of course, even thinking of bringing back Laura would resurrect some painful memories: the poisoning of Tristell, the death of little Tioni, the torments inflicted by Alendis. As always when stressed, Tralvar hadn't merely shielded his thoughts, but barricaded them. The message was unequivocal: keep out, or else. This man, thought Idenion pensively, is like theridolyte; strong but inflexible. He'll break sooner than bend. Always he falls back on his own resource rather than seeking comfort from others.

Patiently, he waited.

"Don't worry about Earth's defences," Tralvar said suddenly as if no time had elapsed. "I've written a new programme with added safeguards. It's here, ready and waiting. Now all we have to do is decide the best way of getting you to Treva."

"That could take a whole day," Idenion objected. "There are always spheres at Communications. Why can't I use one of those?"

Tralvar's expression became as icy as anything Axmiol could produce. "Because," he snapped, "you'd get caught before you could set foot on the spacefield. Discords, Idenion, how could you even consider anything so stupid? Sit down, featherbrain - I see I shall have to take you through your movements step by step."

***

Tralvar returned his protégé to the slum quarter just before sunset.

"I'll never convince Dena I'm ashamed," Idenion declared just before they set out. "She knows me too well." But, to his genuine embarrassment, he'd no sooner alighted from the flitter than he was surrounded by an

20

inquisitive group of factory girls. He soon learnt from a reproachful Dena that his broadcast had been heard by the workers, along with a fairly accurate account of subsequent events. In vain, he protested that his actions had been hasty and ill thought out; to the young women he was a hero, the only person brave enough to try and save Rinyi. Finally, as twilight deepened, the girls wandered off, puzzled that he hadn't chosen a partner for the night.

It was widely assumed that Idenion was an indiscriminate lover - a belief the Narvellans readily subscribed to. But aside from a few youthful indiscretions, he'd never favoured transient partnerships. He only wrote love poems to women he considered unattainable - such as Isylla. And, of course, Laura. During the last three years, he'd written over a hundred odes to her under the collective title of Clemoridys -"star begotten." Arnalta had left him whilst he was in the middle of composing one of them, declaring that she was tired of competing with a dream. Now that he was on the brink of fulfilling that dream, he had no need for unity with anyone else.

After he'd changed his extremely grubby tunic Dena innocently picked it up, intending to wash it. Quite uncharacteristically, he yelled at her to leave it alone. Her little face crumpled and she retreated to her room and slammed the door. Idenion didn't go after her straight away, but seized the tunic and rescued two programme crystals from its pockets. One for Earth, one for the planet Myrma - all part of Tralvar's careful scheme, now etched into his memory. The computer crystals looked identical, but Tralvar had made sure the carrying pouches differed slightly. "If you download the wrong one you can replace it, but you'll be stuck on the ground for an extra five astallen," he had warned Idenion. "So get it right."

Idenion transferred the crystals to one of his overalls and then went to comfort Dena. "It's been such a harrowing day," he apologised. "I didn't expect to get home and find myself propositioned from all directions. I think I'll stay off work till the fuss dies down." There; he'd turned the situation to his advantage, just as Tralvar had taught him.

"I'm sure Chisrin will excuse you," Dena said, referring to their Narvellan overseer. "He was quite upset about Isylla, and he called Axmiol some filthy names."

"Such as?"

Dena blushed. "Ask him yourself. I'm sure he wouldn't mind repeating them."

Idenion laughed and ruffled her hair. "Am I forgiven?"

"Of course," Dena said. "Need you ask? But I wish you'd try to behave."

Poor Dena, Idenion thought. She's going to be dragged into a conspiracy once again, just because she's my sister. I wish I could tell her about tomorrow. I don't even know how long I'll be away.

Too keyed up to sleep, he spent most of the night reading. When the chime sounded he feigned slumber, hoping that Dena wouldn't have time to check on him. Fortunately, she didn't. As soon as she'd left, Idenion donned his overall and pocketed their entire supply of grain cakes. It wasn't fair to Dena, but she could always borrow more. He, on the other hand, would have to be self-sufficient for an indeterminate time. The morning was chilly, which suited his purpose well. He put on a hooded cape to hide his hair, then, after mentally inspecting the area to ensure there were no more workers about, quit the house.

Walking casually, stopping frequently to shake pebbles from his shoes, he traversed three rows of tattered dwellings. "Don't hurry," Tralvar had warned.

"Workers never hurry." But he was finding it difficult not to. When he reached some woodlands he felt less exposed, but knew that his safety was illusory. The wooded hills bordered the river; Alda Mexa's generating station lay immediately to the east and was doubtless crawling with Narvellans. The undergrowth was too dense and thorny for him to consider leaving the ridge straight away, so he continued cautiously along it. As he progressed, he heard the roar of the waterfall which powered the turbines, and saw a cluster of squat white buildings on the forest floor to his right. He was about to turn aside when a faint shriek from below brought him to a halt. A solitary Narvellan came running from somewhere in the power plant, stumbled, then continued to run, swiftly but aimlessly. He was pursued by several other Narvellans who did not trouble to run. The valley walls were sheer, and the fugitive would soon find himself trapped.

Frightened yet intrigued, Idenion hid behind a tree and watched. He counted the number of pursuers; there were ten. Five psychokinetic minds could reduce a man's intelligence by half. Ten Narvellan minds could kill, and did, whenever they had to eradicate one of their own people. Idenion continued to watch in horrified fascination as the victim darted helplessly onto one of the stone walkways encircling the complex. From there he could only run straight back to his executioners. There was a terrible inevitability about it all.

Too late, Idenion remembered that Celestrians were urged to close off their perception should they be witness to such an event. His mind had been drawn in sympathy to the man's distress, and indeed, there was nothing very harmful in that; but then the fear and panic were gone, to be replaced by ... nothing. The soft, seductive void of non-being. Not darkness, but something cold and cloying which refused to let go of him. Hardly aware of his surroundings Idenion slid to the ground, still clinging to the tree. Part of his mind fought against the not-darkness, but he knew that he was losing the struggle, simply because he was no longer interested in winning. He had absorbed the dying man's defeat.

How long he lay there he never knew. Something, a voice perhaps, began to summon him back to reality. An alien voice with melody in it. Laura. Laura? Gradually, he again recognised the cool bark beneath his hands, the dim green daylight, and the sound of the distant river.

"Restore thyself, Celestrian!" said the voice; it was female, and spoke High Narvellan. Idenion looked up blurrily and saw a woman, cloaked and veiled, standing alone on the path. He blinked stupidly. A Directress? Alone?

"You are fortunate to have broken your trance so easily," she said. "It is folly to meddle in the affairs of the Ten."

"Your voice woke me," Idenion whispered.

"Is that so strange? I am not permitted to touch your thoughts nor your person, but there is no law against speech."

Idenion stood up shakily. He was grateful for the intervention, but from a Directress? Discords, it was the worst luck In the world. These women never went anywhere without a bunch of lackeys in tow. Any moment now he'd be caught and searched.

"Are you wondering about my retinue?" the Directress asked. Idenion suspected she was smiling beneath the profusion of veils. "They formed part of the Ten, and until they have purged their minds, they cannot return to me. If you would rather not encounter them, leave now."

"Thank you for ... for your concern," Idenion stammered. The woman stood aside to let him pass.

"Concern? Yes, I suppose that is the right word. For me, only the land lives, and you people seem insubstantial as clouds. Had you not been carrying aldacite crystals, I would never have noticed you." So saying, she walked serenely away. For a moment, Idenion stared after her in astonishment; then, against all orders, took to his heels.

He half scrambled, half fell down the westward-facing slope, and scarcely stopped running until he'd reached the monorail sidings about a silmos beyond. A goods train was just pulling out. He managed to haul himself into the last truck, and kept his head down until Alda Mexa was left behind. Then he found some sacking and made himself as comfortable as he could amongst the boxes of sphere components. It would be a long, thirsty ride to Treva.

***

After the near-abortive start, the rest of Idenion's journey was uneventful. He had plenty of time to reflect on the events of the morning, despite not wanting to. He could have managed to doze, except that his mind still conjured echoes of the not-darkness. He was afraid, not of nightmares, but of the trance itself returning. For the moment, he dared not sleep. He wondered if he'd ever have the nerve to tell Tralvar what had happened.

He didn't quite know what he'd expected to find at the Treva spacefield. Rows of spheres perhaps, stretching as far as the eye could see. In fact there were only about thirty, unattended, not too far from the railway. Of course, most of the fleet had already been taken to Narvella Prime. This would be the latest consignment.

The train had slowed to a mere crawl, and it was easy to step off. In the distance he could see the outline of many hangers and sheds, steel structures flung up in haste and shimmering in the heat of the afternoon sun.

He also saw tiny figures milling about, but there was a distinct lack of vigilance. Tralvar had known this would be so, but at the same time had warned against complacency. "They're engineers, not bureaucrats," he'd said. "But they're still Narvellan, so don't let them challenge you."

The field and its environs were absolutely flat, and there was no cover. Trying not to look furtive, Idenion walked briskly to the sphere nearest him, entered, secured the hatch and checked the life support. There were, he noted thankfully, food concentrates and drinking water on board; and, just as Tralvar had promised, a remote guidance unit - a small white wafer - nestling in its locker. All correct so far. Next, he hunted in his pocket for the crystals and, after scrutinising them minutely, presented the correct one to the logic circuits. Then, leaving the data to be assimilated, he went to indulge in a thorough scrubdown. In these straitened days, the sphere's meagre hygiene facilities seemed luxurious. When he emerged, the pre-flight setup was nearly complete, and a display screen was giving details of the projected course and destination. As he watched, a simulation of Earth and its continents appeared, followed by the British Isles, then a section of England with precise co-ordinates overlaid. Tralvar had not relied on the vagaries of the poet's memory.

All was now in readiness. Idenion, eyes bright with anticipation, seated himself in the command chair and pressed the activation key. Someday, he thought as the sphere lifted off, he'd have to persuade Tralvar to go into space just once. There was really nothing to it: nothing at all.

Chapter Two

Superficially, Cheveney was unchanged, although an ugly arterial road had been carved across the nearby countryside. That much Idenion had noticed on the final vertiginous descent. But now that the sphere was safely in orbit and he was trudging towards Laura's house, he detected sombre overtones in the minds of the villagers. It seemed that here, as on Celestra, the people were oppressed by something. Everywhere he sensed worry, loss and despondency. Ten of Earth's years ago, there had been a most pervasive optimism which he still remembered. What had happened to it?

The sun was not far past its zenith, and the sticky heat burdened him, as did his increased weight. Belatedly he began to worry about the next stage of his mission. He'd still no idea what he was going to say to Laura - all his attention had been focused on simply getting here. How would she receive him when, by her reckoning, he was five years overdue?

Soon he realised, with a further stab of apprehension, that Laura wasn't at Windbourne. But Nathaniel was in the summerhouse, reading. The oppression was in *his* mind too. Suddenly impatient beyond all measure, Idenion summoned his remaining energy and hurtled down the garden, almost forgetting that the Earthman would not have sensed his arrival.

"Nathaniel," he called breathlessly. "Nathaniel, why's everyone so miserable? Has there been another war?"

Nathaniel put aside his newspaper and looked up with only a trace of surprise. "*You* took your time," he remarked after Idenion had tumbled into his presence. "No, there's been no war. The word is recession, though I doubt if you'll understand what that means." Idenion, sensing that the explanation was centred around the (to him) incomprehensible subject of money, probed Nathaniel's surface thoughts to gauge his true reaction. "Looks like he's been in the wars himself... thinner than ever ... there's trouble, obviously. I hope he wants Laura for himself and not just as peacemaker. She can't take any more disappointment - "

"Celestra needs her; I *love* her," Idenion said solemnly.

As always, there was no disbelieving him. Nathaniel had forgotten the burning clarity of the young man's gaze, the strange mixture of artlessness and omniscience.

"I cannot read you well," Idenion continued. "I never could. But I perceive that Laura is still in the neighbourhood and that she is married. Perhaps I would not be welcome."

"Listen to me, son," said Nathaniel. As always, the term made Idenion a little sad; he had never met his natural father. "I'm none too adept with sentiment, as you know, but when you appeared I could have wept for joy. And believe me, Laura will do just that. Can you spare a few minutes to talk with a tired old man?"

Idenion hesitated for a moment, then gave assent. He'd squandered so much time on his way to Treva that Tralvar's plan was getting out of phase, but he couldn't confront Laura without first hearing what Nathaniel had to say about her. Silently, he followed his host into the study with its rows of leather-bound books and high-backed armchairs. The room looked dusty and little-used. Nathaniel poured a glass of sherry for himself and a lemonade for Idenion, then went over to the mahogany writing bureau and took up a tiny brass key. With a hand that trembled slightly, he unlocked one of the drawers and took out a sheaf of yellowing paper.

"Music," he announced.

"I can't read it," Idenion said.

"Oh, I forgot - you only read Greek." Nathaniel smiled fractionally. "Laura wrote these songs soon after she came home. She says they're from your planet. That's as may be. All I know is, she teamed up with a pop band - some lads she met at Stonehenge - and on the strength of these items they managed to get a recording contract. They called themselves the Celestrians." He delved into the drawer again and brought out a photograph. Idenion gazed at it thoughtfully. Laura, pale of face, eyes heavily made up, in the company of three longhaired young men.

"1968 was a strange year," Nathaniel continued. "Laura was caught up in the flower power movement. You'd have enjoyed that, Idenion – youngsters with flowers in their hair, songs about peace and love. Laura revelled in it - and common-sense, of course, went out of the window. She signed away the copyright on her work and lost the chance to make any real money. Even in retrospect, she wasn't too concerned . She said the songs weren't hers anyway." He paused to marshal his thoughts. "As usual I was too preoccupied with the financial side of her career to notice what was happening to *her*, but at last I found out. She came in, sat exactly where you are now, and said she was pregnant. Once I'd finished slandering the absent father and the music business in general, I asked what she intended to do. She'd already made up her mind, of course: she wanted an abortion. I arranged it for her."

Idenion made a tiny sound in his throat. He looked shocked and sorrowful. Of course, such destruction was normal - even necessary - here, but... Laura's child?

"There were no complications," Nathaniel added. "She can still have children. As I said, 1968 was an odd sort of year."

"I should never have let her go," Idenion said unhappily.

"You had no alternative," Nathaniel contradicted. "She hadn't attempted to live here as an adult, and she needed time to establish exactly where she belonged. After the termination, she quietened down – a little too much. She spent hours gazing at the photographs we took of you in '66. She'd speak your language aloud, over and over, to stop herself forgetting it. And she took up singing lessons again, working her way through the higher grades. Her voice is much improved."

"When did she decide to get married?"

"She didn't. Peter decided for her. He came along just as she'd convinced herself that you were gone for good." Nathaniel put away the mementos and locked the drawer carefully. "These things stay here. He knows nothing about any of it."

"If she didn't trust him with her past, how could she trust him with her future?" Idenion asked sagely.

"A good question – I wish I'd thought of it myself. Peter was a calculated risk that didn't pay off. He had the makings of a good husband: well-educated, but dull. He wanted Laura because she was remote and mysterious, but he didn't expect her to stay that way. Once he realised she'd never change, he became overbearing and sarcastic - and, I suspect, unfaithful."

"Then why hasn't she moved back to Windbourne?" Idenion asked.

"She never really left," Nathaniel said. "It wasn't Peter's idea to stay in Cheveney. I daresay she's been getting ready to send him packing, now that he's lost the ability to make her feel guilty."

Idenion's brow furrowed as he tried to imagine himself linked to Arnalta by guilt alone.

"Complicated, isn't it?" Nathaniel said drily. "Don't worry - it will all be resolved the moment she sees you."

"You're already aware," Idenion said, "that my reason for returning isn't purely personal."

"That's fairly obvious."

"We're under occupation," Idenion continued. "There is hardship. It's only fair that you should know."

"Save the details for Laura," Nathaniel advised. "Not that she'll care. Your troubles never deterred her in the past, did they?"

Idenion stood up. "Then - will you direct me to her?"

"Of course," said Nathaniel, faintly surprised at this lapse in perception. He wasn't aware that his own mind was creating a barrier. He'll take her so far away, he lamented. So unthinkably far ...

Aloud, he said: "Do you remember the way to the church? The little path by the stream? That's the shortest route to Laura's house. Once you get past the church, you'll see it. Battleship Cottage, it's called - Battle*field* would have been more appropriate."

"You realise," Idenion said hesitantly, "that I must leave Earth as soon as I can?"

"Prolonged goodbyes would upset Laura *and* me," Nathaniel replied with dignity. "I entrust her to you. Now get along and rescue her, my boy."

Idenion thanked him with simple sincerity, and left. Nathaniel, after lengthy deliberation, picked up the telephone and dialled Laura's number. He intended to give some spurious reason for the call, simply needing to hear her voice for what he was sure would be the last time. But the telephone in Laura's house just rang and rang.

Idenion had only gone a few yards when an attack of dizziness, a vagrant echo of the not-darkness, made him stumble. More irritated than alarmed, he suppressed it and continued walking. Further down the lane, he encountered Mrs. Moffat. Her hair was a startling shade of red, but she was otherwise unchanged. "Hello, lovey!" she greeted him, smiling broadly. He blessed her for that smile.

"I'm glad *someone's* cheerful, Mrs. M."

"Mustn't grumble," she began, then paused as she noticed his eye. "Gracious, who did that?"

"I was in a demo," he replied truthfully.

"I thought you were going to say Laura's husband did it," the woman chuckled. "Oh, don't look so nervous! Peter couldn't knock a hole in a wet lettuce. Have you been... *seeing* Laura, then?"

"I've come to take her away," Idenion replied with unhesitating candour. "If she's willing."

Mrs. Moffat's smile faded. "Doesn't she know you're back?"

"Not yet. I've been at Windbourne." Idenion scanned the road ahead for a trace of Laura's thought patterns, without success. Maybe his perception was still skewed. Or maybe he simply wasn't recognising her mindset. It *had* been ten years.

"Worried about what to say?" asked Mrs. Moffat shrewdly.

"Very," Idenion admitted. "Do you know if she's home?"

"She was, an hour ago. She doesn't have a job at the moment," Mrs. Moffat explained. "She used to work in a record shop but that didn't suit Mr. High and Mighty. Why she married him I'll never know. He doesn't even like music, and he's that rude...!" She launched into a character assassination of the unfortunate Peter. Idenion let her continue a moment, then gently interrupted.

"Am I likely to bump into Tracey Wyatt?"

Mrs. Moffat switched subjects without seeming to draw breath. "Tracey surprised us all. She changed completely - stopped being a little tart and went to train as a social worker. She helps boys and girls who've been, you know, interfered with. Her parents got divorced and left the village, so she doesn't come back here any more."

So she *did* reclaim her life, Idenion thought. That's something I managed to accomplish, at least. He was about to say his goodbyes and move on when he noticed Mrs. Moffat's cat on a nearby wall, asleep in a dappled patch of sunlight. Remembering how devoted the animal had been to him, he went across and stroked its head gently. The cat opened an eye, then returned to its dozing. There was no recognition in its mind, just tired indifference.

"Tib's always asleep these days," Mrs. Moffat said dolefully.

"Why? Is she ill?"

Mrs. Moffat directed a puzzled glance at him. "She's just old, Denny. Nearly fourteen."

"Oh - of course." Idenion felt a tinge of regret. He hadn't realised the little creatures' lives were so short.

"Denny," said Mrs. Moffat, her voice suddenly ominous, "I really ought to be cross with you. All this time without a word to Laura, and then you turn up casual as you please, wanting to take her away. And look at you! Dreadful shiner, scruffy old overall - what's she going to think?"

"I'm sorry I abandoned her," said Idenion contritely. "It was unavoidable."

"I don't know what happened before," the woman hurried on, "but please don't let her down a second time. It would break her heart – and it'd kill Nathaniel. Promise you'll take care of her, no matter what."

"I promise," Idenion said softly, dazzling her with the intensity of his eyes. A little perplexed, she watched him depart. There was no earthly reason why she should believe him, yet suddenly she did. Implicitly.

***

"Mrs. Meredith?"

Laura, sweeping the front porch with a twig broom, took no notice.

"Excuse me," the voice persisted. "Are you Mrs. Meredith?"

Laura paused and looked up. When people called her by that surname, it didn't register straightaway. "Laura Meredith" was a cipher, a shadow, a near-stranger who for the past four years had existed alongside her. She was Laura Gilcoyne, and always would be. She'd kept that name for her stage appearances, much to Peter's annoyance.

"Can I help you?" she asked the two men at her gate.

"I hope so," said the one who had spoken. He had fair hair, freckles, and was aged about thirty. His younger colleague was short, bespectacled, and carried a ringbinder crammed with papers. "We're investigating UFO sightings, and wondered if we could ask you a few questions. I'm Chris, by the way, and this is Darren."

"Ask away," Laura said wearily. There had been a seasonal influx of UFO hunters for several years, so she was used to such inquiries.

Darren handed her a business card which identified him as Darren J. Gillett, UFO Chronicler and Historian. "As you doubtless know," he began, consulting his dossier, "there have been several sightings in the area of Wickens Clump, mostly in 1966. We also have a leaked document describing an aerial pursuit over Cheveney."

"What does this have to do with me?" asked Laura.

"We've been speaking with your neighbour Mrs. Stretton, and she tells us that you and her son James spent a lot of time in the Clump."

Wickens Clump. How ugly that name is, thought Laura. I prefer what Jimmy called it - the Cradle of the World.

34

Darren and Chris waited expectantly.

"Yes, we went there a lot," she said at length. "And we *weren't* looking for UFOs."

"Later, James Stretton disappeared."

"There's nothing mysterious about that. He ran away to London."

"And you also went missing, for three days."

Damn you, Caitlin Stretton, Laura thought fiercely. "Teenage rebellion," she said aloud, with her sweetest smile. "And now, if you'll excuse me - "

"Are you sure you've never seen anything odd in these woods?" persisted Darren.

"Don't you people ever share your research?" Laura countered. "You aren't the first UFO spotters to come calling - the entire village must have been interviewed by now. I can only tell you what I told the others: Jimmy and I never saw anything weird in the Clump. Ever."

Darren looked disappointed but duly noted it down. Chris, meantime, had been scrutinising Laura closely.

"I know you from somewhere," he mused. "Pub gigs. Weren't you a singer?"

"I was lead singer with the Celestrians," she admitted. He beamed delightedly.

"I remember now! Great sound. Psychedelic, but with a difference. What was that number you always ended with? - Total Unity, that was it. Pity you never made the charts."

"We didn't get much airtime."

"Do you think you'll perform again?" Chris asked.

"No, I don't think that's very likely. Artistic differences: you know the type of thing."

Darren had been thumbing through his notes. "It's very strange," he said, "that none of the locals have seen anything. All the reports are from people passing through. It's almost like a conspiracy of silence."

"Oh, don't start on your conspiracies!" laughed Chris.

"I have to make dinner," Laura announced. "My husband will be home shortly." If he bothers, she added under her breath.

"Thanks for your time," said Chris. "Oh by the way, we're organising a skywatch on August Bank Holiday. If you want to attend you'll be very welcome."

"I'll think about it," Laura promised.

"Shall we have one more look at the Clump?" asked Darren.

"No point. It won't have changed since this morning," said Chris, gazing longingly at the Green Man Inn, which had just opened its doors.

Laura bade them an affable farewell and watched them stroll away. Chris glanced back once. "I like your dress," he called cheekily.

Laura's dress was of white cheesecloth with a pattern of marigolds. It was bias-cut and swirled gracefully as she moved. It was also, she remembered belatedly, semi-transparent in sunlight. With a shrug, she continued her desultory sweeping. Dinner could wait.

How many more saucer enthusiasts do I have to lie to? she wondered sadly. All this denial seems to diminish what happened to me. The most precious year of my life, and I can't discuss it with anyone except Uncle Nat. *He* knows what I threw away.

Familiar anger welled within her. What an idiot I was, she raged silently. An inhibited little schoolgirl, scared of healthy sexuality and embarrassed by the idea of free love. No wonder Idenion lost patience with me. Then the Narvellans came, and instead of staying to fight my corner I ran away because I felt inferior. And what did I find when I got back here? Flower children and free love! What an irony.

36

She put down the broom and perched disconsolately on a garden bench, attempting to re-live the sights and sounds of another planet. Some time ago she'd asked an astronomer friend if it were possible to see Sun-like stars at a distance of three hundred light years. Not with the naked eye, he'd said. She'd been so disappointed, having thought she might at least be able to locate Alda in the night sky.

She wouldn't admit it, but her memories of Celestra were starting to lose their immediacy. The more she tried to hold on to them, the more distant they seemed to become. Even her love for Idenion was becoming muted, less painful. But some events hadn't faded. She vividly remembered standing on a clifftop in Virda, beneath a gold and purple sky, talking to the young relayist Kyrin. Taken from Virda in infancy, he'd spent years being homesick, but once he was back there had soon realised he didn't belong. He was too changed by his experiences. There'd been a lesson to be learnt from that, but she hadn't heeded it.

Inexplicably, her most abiding memory was of sad gentle Tyvian. "Oh, First Singer, what am I taking you back to?" he'd lamented as they neared Earth for the final time. He'd referred, of course, to the images of war he'd seen in Laura's retrace; but his words held a different meaning now. If I could have had one tiny glimpse into the future, she thought, I'd have asked him to turn the sphere around.

Turn the sphere around. All so casual. She'd never been able to visualise the distance involved - the pristine interior of the Celestrian spacecraft had hidden the enormity of it. There was a viewscreen, but it had nearly always been switched off, leaving no other way to see out. Transposal, as the Celestrians called their stardrive, meant nothing more to her than a pattern of lights on a panel and a strange tingling silence. She still couldn't believe she'd been spirited across the galaxy in a couple of hours.

"But you were," said a familiar voice.

She looked round and froze in blank incredulity. Then, released, she flew down the little path and flung herself into the newcomer's arms. Tears of joy coursed down her face, fulfilling Nathaniel's prediction.

"Idenion!" was all she could say, over and over. "Idenion, Idenion...."

He embraced her wonderingly, noting how slender she'd become. More than ever, he regretted the youthful selfishness which had caused him to miss Laura's progression into womanhood. At last he disentwined her, holding her appraisingly at arm's length, and thus enabling her to take a proper look at him. She touched his eye with light, tremulous fingers.

"Who did this? And what's this you're wearing? It makes you look like a convict!"

As she spoke, another wave of dizziness hit him. "Oh...discords," he muttered, and grabbed at her outstretched arm for support. An instant later he recovered and apologised, but Laura's loving gaze had already become a concerned frown.

"Someone's roughed you up mentally, haven't they?" she asked shrewdly. "You've got that dazed look about you. I saw it after Alendis had - "

Across the lane, Caitlin Stretton's net curtains twitched.

"Let's go inside," Laura suggested, propelling Idenion across the narrow threshold. She then sat him in the inglenook and poured him a generous measure of Peter's best brandy.

Idenion tasted it carefully, then with more enthusiasm, focusing his mind inward and observing with satisfaction as the not-darkness fled before the sustaining glow of the liquor.

"Who attacked you?" repeated Laura.

"It wasn't an attack exactly," Idenion began. "I strayed too close to an execution - "

Too late, he remembered Tralvar's instructions: "There's no need to mention the Ten. It would only scare her. After all, they don't execute *us*, do they?"

"I'm getting this all wrong," he concluded lamely.

"Just tell me what's going on," Laura prompted gently. "Take your time."

"Time is something I don't have," said Idenion gravely.

She raised her eyebrows. "That sounds very un-Celestrian."

"We've all been forced to make changes." Idenion finished the brandy and reluctantly set aside the empty glass. "That was quite - therapeutic. Tralvar would love it."

"How *is* Tralvar?"

"Much the same," Idenion said with a degree of affection that would have startled the First Citizen, had he been there to hear it. "Laura - please don't think I only came back looking for help. I'm here because I made you a promise."

"And what promise was that?" Her smile was provocative and profoundly beautiful.

If she were Celestrian, Idenion thought with a trace of sadness, there would be no more words spoken at this point. We would have unity. But that, of course, can never happen. Words are all I have. Once again, Tralvar's voice spoke in his memory. "As soon as you're alone with her, find out if she remembers our language. It's important that she does." Accordingly he made his reply in his own tongue, gently taking Laura's hands and drawing her down to sit next to him.

"I still love you," he said simply. "And as I'm still First Poet, I wanted to say something more elaborate than that. But it will have to wait."

"I don't mind waiting," she replied in Celestrian, accented but tolerable. "Now tell me why time is so short."

Idenion sighed, partly with relief. "Tralvar made a plan which I'm supposed to be following, but I was injured and delayed, and I'm worried I'll miss him at the rendezvous point. Laura, my only love, if you come to Celestra with me, you'll have a difficult and dangerous time. The Narvellans rule us."

"I knew it. I *knew* it!" She was speaking English again, righteously indignant. "Didn't anyone listen to Tralvar? He knew they were up to no good."

"It wasn't as simple as that," Idenion began.

"Is that why you didn't show up five years ago?"

He bowed his head. "The Narvellans monitor all spaceflights - no one goes anywhere without their permission. I didn't dare ask. They'd never have given it." He didn't mention that Tralvar, the one person who could conceivably have helped, had opposed his wishes. And had gone on doing so until recently. "In the end, I stole a sphere," he added.

"You didn't run into any jets, did you?" asked Laura anxiously.

"Tralvar modified the programme," Idenion replied confidently. "At the first sign of pursuit, safety protocols will cut in and take the sphere to safety."

"You hope."

"Tralvar is our *only* hope," Idenion said quietly. "He's determined to get rid of the Narvellans. You can help him devise a scheme."

"*Me*?"

"Of course. You can help Celestra as you did before."

"Now just a minute!" Laura began.

"Speak Celestrian," Idenion ordered.

"I *didn't* help you," she said haltingly. "I didn't do anything except sing, get myself into a jam and have to be rescued by Tralvar. Twice."

"You destroyed Alendis."

She shook her head vehemently. "It was an accident. Idenion, it was all happenstance. And what's more, there were only three people trying to rule the roost. How do you expect me to contend with a whole planetful?"

"We'll find a way," Idenion said staunchly.

He hasn't changed a bit, thought Laura in a mixture of fondness and exasperation. All that unshakable idealism. It's frightening.

"You'll do what you can," Idenion added. It was a statement, not a question.

"Of course. Just don't expect miracles," Laura said, reverting to English again.

"How would you say 'miracle' in Celestrian?" inquired Idenion.

Laura pondered a moment. It didn't translate, of course: they had no religious symbolism. "A superhuman deed," she said at length. "I take it there's some point to these language lessons?"

"Tralvar wants to pass you off as Celestrian - at least for a time."

"But how? Everyone will know I'm not telepathic."

"He says he has the answer to that," said Idenion. "He didn't explain further in case the Narvellans caught me."

Laura was silent, realising for the first time what risks he'd taken.

"It won't be as you expected," Idenion pursued. "No fame, no luxury, and above all, no singing."

"But I'd still have you."

He embraced her fiercely. "Yes, you'd still have me. Celestra's your home, Laura. Will you come back to it?"

"Just try and stop me."

"Then let's go. Tralvar will be waiting." Idenion was already halfway to the door, and would possibly have reached it had he not become entangled in Peter's angle-poise lamp which sat on the floor like a large ungainly insect.

"Wait," Laura said irresolutely as he righted the lamp. "I can't just leave - not if..." She faltered. "Not if I'm never coming back. I have to ring Uncle Nat."

"I've been to see him. He didn't want any protracted farewells," Idenion said with the simple candour that Laura remembered so acutely.

"If you're sure," she conceded reluctantly. "But there's one call I *have* to make. It would be unprofessional of me not to." She picked up the trimphone receiver and dialled. "Hello, is Gus there? Then could you page him, please? It's important."

Idenion mooched round the tiny, overcrowded living room, trying not to knock anything else over. He knew, now, that Nathaniel had told the truth about this house. There was nothing of Laura in it, for she'd never relinquished Windbourne. He found himself staring at a poster depicting the Earth as seen from the arid surface of its own moon. Laura, still waiting for the eponymous Gus to respond, commented with a degree of pride:

"We've been busy in the past ten years."

"Your people have reached the moon?" Idenion queried. Laura thought he sounded dismayed, but her call was put through before she could quiz him.

"Gus? Laura Gilcoyne. I'm sorry, but I'll have to cancel my spot on Saturday. And the rest of my bookings. I'm going away for a bit."

"More trouble with your husband?" asked the unknown man sympathetically.

"Yes. I'm putting some space between us," Laura replied. "I'm really sorry to let you down - I loved the atmosphere at the club, and it's been good experience for me."

"There'll always be a job for you at the Firelight, if you want to come back anytime," Gus said. "You're a talented girl, Laura. Don't neglect your singing."

"I'll try not to," she said, and hung up.

"So you've been singing professionally," Idenion commented.

"Not really. Gus used to be sweet on my mother, and that's why he gave me the job," Laura explained. "I've been singing the same songs she did - torch songs. It was something I promised myself I'd do when I was mature enough. Speaking of songs, I'd really like Tralvar to hear my recordings from '68. Is that possible?"

Idenion hesitated. "He said you were to come empty-handed."

"But we're seeing him as soon as we arrive, aren't we?" Laura persisted. "I just want to take a radio cassette player, only a small one, and some tapes. I could give them straight to him."

Idenion still didn't think it was a good idea, but there wasn't time for a debate. "All right, bring them," he said.

Laura hastily began locating cassettes. "Uncle Nat's got the originals, but I made copies for myself," she said. "A lot of this material was never released, but it was all taken from Celestrian sources, and since Tralvar taught me most of it - "

From outside came the scrunch of tyres on gravel followed by the slam of a car door. Laura glanced out of the window and uttered an epithet which Idenion had never heard her use before. The occupant of the car, a stocky young man with receding hair, had been waylaid by Caitlin Stretton, who pointed meaningfully at the cottage.

"Peter," Laura said dispiritedly. "And he's early. Damn it, he's *never* early!"

"I can deal with him," Idenion said calmly.

"Idenion, no! Don't say anything if you can help it. I don't want him interrogating Uncle Nat."

Peter opened the door somewhat cautiously. Caitlin had uttered one telling phrase: "There's someone here out of Laura's past." That selfsame past which had done nothing but cause trouble...

"Just what is going on here?" he inquired.

"I'm leaving you," Laura answered distantly.

"Running off to Windbourne again?"

"No. This time I'm *really* leaving." And indeed, Laura spoke as if she were already far away.

Peter glared. There was much he didn't know - would never know - about Laura, but he knew her moods well enough. He'd never seen her so alive. Well, once perhaps: he'd visited the Firelight Jazz Club without telling her, and watched while she sang "Invitation". She'd had the same look then: radiant, introspective. That song had put her in mind of someone, and there were no prizes for guessing it wasn't him.

"I hope you're not going to make a scene," Laura was saying.

He hadn't intended to. Cool sarcasm always worked best. But he was incensed that she could stand there exuding love for some emaciated hippy. If she'd ever looked at *him* like that, he might not have felt so insulted; but she never had. So he snapped at her, and when she wouldn't be drawn, yelled. Then, when she tried to push him aside, he hit her on the shoulder - not a

44

hard blow, just a desperate attempt to make her take notice of him.

"I forbid this!" said the longhaired young man, turning a piercing gaze in his direction: and suddenly Peter couldn't focus his own eyes. The room seemed full of darting lights.

"Now perhaps you'll let us go," said Laura's lover.

Peter often had migraines, but had never known one to manifest itself so instantaneously. The aura settled into a barbed pinwheeling sunburst, obliterating half his vision - just as it had the previous Thursday. He leant heavily on the doorjamb and, through a distorting haze, watched Laura and her companion join hands and run down the path like a couple of children. She had taken nothing except her cassette player.

"To the Cradle of the World?" he heard her ask.

"To the Cradle of the World," came the equally obscure reply. Then they were gone. And seconds later, so had his migraine.

***

"I had to intervene," said Idenion as they picked their way through the wood. "You weren't going to defend yourself."

"It isn't his fault I couldn't forget you," Laura said quietly, bunching up her skirt to avoid snagging it in the undergrowth. "What did you do - give him a headache?"

"No, I gave him the memory of one," Idenion explained. "It's a little technique I learnt from Lydion when we were on Myrma - very useful if you're in a tight corner."

"Such as being caught with someone else's wife?"

"In Lydion's case, yes," affirmed Idenion, holding a branch aside for Laura to pass. "But until today I'd only used it to prove my origin. I gave Nathaniel a moment with Ida, remember?"

"How could I forget? He was a changed person after that," Laura reflected. "I'm glad you never tried your technique on *me*."

"You weren't hostile," Idenion reminded her, and she laughed.

"Tralvar gave me a dreadful headache once. He didn't retrieve it from my memory, though. I've never had a headache like that before or since."

Idenion stopped walking. "When did this happen?"

"The night you were in prison."

"And I'd closed off my perception to write poetry," Idenion recalled. "That explains why I didn't sense anything at the time. But why didn't I see it in your mind later?"

Laura shrugged. "I don't know. You didn't see me till the following day, and then I'd just been retraced."

"I shall have words with Tralvar," Idenion said ominously.

"Oh, let it go," Laura urged. "It's ancient history. I was being a brat, and he finally ran out of patience."

"Perhaps," Idenion said thoughtfully.

"Definitely. Now come on, we mustn't stop here. Unless the gravity's getting to you?"

"I can manage," he assured her as they continued down the track. "I remembered to change the environmental controls during the outward journey. And I daresay hauling boxes around all day has helped too."

"Is that what the Narvellans make you do?"

"I'm a factory worker. A packer," he told her. "This overall is standard work issue, and this - " he pointed to some lettering on the upper sleeve - "is my work designation. Light industrial. Like many others, I'm helping the Narvellans build their space fleet."

"But you're First Poet!" Laura exclaimed in outrage.

"They don't have a symbol for that," he replied flippantly.

"I mean," Laura went on stridently, "you should be exempt from factory work."

"I was assigned to clerical duty at first, but I didn't last long at it," Idenion explained. "I had to write endless lists, and I kept missing things out. Packing doesn't require much concentration."

"All the same," Laura began, but they had reached the little clearing at the heart of Wickens Clump. Idenion searched his capacious pockets and drew out the device that would summon the sphere. Laura gazed curiously at the object he held. It was smaller than the one she'd seen him use ten years ago, although it still resembled a tile. Idenion slid its cover aside and keyed in a standby code.

"A lid?" Laura observed. "What happened to your trickle technology?"

"Theridolyte is in short supply and is reserved for the spheres themselves," explained Idenion.

"But Tralvar was using it to make gramophone records. Did the Narvellans stop him?"

"Not only that, but they reclaimed all the records for salvage," said Idenion regretfully. "You can imagine how angry he was, but they were remorseless. Our record industry never got off the ground."

Laura was so dismayed by this news that she failed to congratulate him when he landed the sphere without mishap. Nothing had challenged the peace of the glade: unconcerned birdsong continued on all sides and the layer of long-dead leaves had scarcely stirred. The little sphere's white hull seemed luminous in the shadows. Idenion went forward and, after an anxious pause, entered a second code on an almost invisible panel.

"The Narvellans changed the entry sequences," he explained.

As Laura watched, an eerie schism appeared in the smooth whiteness and the surface flowed apart to form a hatchway. Another section rippled outwards, touched the ground, and settled into the shape of a ramp.

"I don't think I'll ever get used to seeing that," she murmured.

"But it doesn't scare you anymore, does it?" Idenion returned softly.

They went inside, Laura wishing she could think of something significant to say as the wall flowed soundlessly back into position. After all, she might never see Earth again. But instead she concentrated on practicalities.

"Will the soundsweep work before lift-off?" she asked.

"I believe so," Idenion said.

"Then could you scan Windbourne? Peter's no fool; he must have realised his headache was induced. He'll go straight to Uncle Nat and demand to know more about you - in fact he's probably there already. Just what I *didn't* want to happen."

"I have every confidence in Nathaniel."

"Please, Idenion. It's bad enough that I'm leaving without saying goodbye. Can I at least find out how he deals with this?"

Idenion looked doubtful. "We shouldn't stay here. Those two investigators - "

" - are in the pub. And if they saw the sphere they'd probably think it was a hoax. Just two minutes - please?" She continued to gaze at him beseechingly, and eventually he gave in.

"Very well, I'll make a soundsweep. But unless Nathaniel has the windows open, we won't hear anything." Tiny clusters of lights appeared on the pilot's console, augmenting the gentle pink glow of the cabin interior. As Idenion's fingertips explored the display, tantalising fragments of sound hovered in the air around Laura. A lawnmower; a radio; children playing. Then, suddenly, Peter's voice:

"Do you expect me to believe that Laura was on the road with a rock 'n' roll band for *two years?*"

"See for yourself," Nathaniel replied. "This is her scrapbook." A pause.

"And - those tapes she kept playing - that was *her?*"

"If you hadn't been so indifferent to your wife's voice, you'd have realised that."

Another pause. Laura could almost hear Peter fuming. "But nobody in the village knew about this," he protested at length.

"We let everyone think Laura had gone back to school."

"We?"

"Margaret Moffat and I."

"So *she* was in on it, was she?" said Peter resentfully. "That figures. She always hated me."

"Less of the paranoia, if you don't mind," Nathaniel said briskly. "And stop playing the injured innocent. Your marriage was over long before Denny reappeared."

"But who *is* he?" Peter persisted. "Caitlin said he came here as a student. I don't see him in these photos of the rock band."

"He was their lyricist," Nathaniel said gravely. "But he never could sing. You wouldn't want to hear him try. I gather he's joined one of these punk groups - the ones who scream and yell and insult the audience. That's probably where he got the black eye."

Laura chuckled delightedly. "Oh, Uncle Nat, that's priceless!"

"And you were worried he couldn't handle it," murmured Idenion, holding her close as they listened.

"What's the cradle of the world?" Peter was continuing.

"I believe that's the name of the group," Nathaniel said with utter seriousness.

Peter gave an exasperated sigh. "What's wrong with you, Nathaniel? This is your niece we're talking about. I can't believe you'd condone such a lifestyle, not now nor in the past."

"She's where she wants to be," Nathaniel replied in the same measured tone.

"With him?" Peter sounded a little shrill. "I'm telling you, there's something *wrong* about him. He gave me that migraine. Some sort of hypnosis - "

"You gave yourself a tension headache," returned Nathaniel irritably. "Now if you don't mind, I'm going for my evening walk - alone."

"I'd like to remind you, Nathaniel, that you once told me Laura needed peace and security. Now you tell me she'd rather be a groupie. Since you've misled me, the least you can do is help me divorce her!"

"I believe there are legal contingencies if the respondent can't be found," Nathaniel stated.

"In other words you're not going to help me trace her."

"That's *your* responsibility," said Nathaniel. "Personally I don't believe you'll succeed, but if you do, be sure to let me know. Good day!"

"But you can't - "

"Good*bye*, Peter."

Laura could imagine her uncle's expression: implacably set jaw, pale sardonic eyes. There was a momentary silence before the conservatory door slammed. Laura expelled the breath she'd been holding.

"It's time we weren't here," she said.

"It's way past time," Idenion answered quietly. The computer screen lit - long strings of symbols in a language Laura still couldn't read.

"There's so much I need to learn," she mused.

"There is. But you're equal to it, Laura - you know you are."

Nathaniel waited a couple of minutes until Peter was out of sight, then took up his walking stick and strolled to the front gate. He didn't go through it, however, but stood gazing in the direction of Wickens Clump. The evening sky was streaked with pink, gold and palest blue. And above the clustered trees a long line of light, bright as a sunbeam yet needle-thin, slanted toward infinity.

"Goodbye," he whispered.

"Goodbye Mr. Gilcoyne," responded a voice. He turned with a scowl, thinking that Peter was still skulking about, but instead saw the two UFO hunters passing by. They had their backs to the Clump.

"I thought you boys had gone," he commented.

"We've finished our research," said Darren.

"We've just been for a pint in the Green Man," added Chris. "A pity we couldn't find any concrete evidence of UFO visitations, but there'll be other days."

"Perhaps," said Nathaniel, turning back toward the light-trace just as it contracted to a point and vanished. "Perhaps."

***

Whenever Laura had imagined making love to Idenion, her chosen setting had been Windbourne or the Lyricon. She'd never been close to the eventual truth - that they'd be on board a sphere in flight, lying on an unyielding slab of a bunk with the cabin lights dimmed and an incomparable starscape blazing from the viewscreen. Not once did she think of total unity, its absence, or whether Idenion would be dissatisfied. She simply knew that she needed him, and was only faintly surprised when his gentle skill took her effortlessly toward one climax and then another. Hitherto she'd

51

never experienced even one. She'd never trusted anyone enough.

Later, lying contentedly by his side, she almost wished she didn't feel so happy. At such times, something always came along to spoil things.

Idenion, too, was introspective. His dream, which had sustained him throughout the writing of Clemoridys, had finally materialised. And as he'd anticipated, the joy was bittersweet, because part of Laura's wonderful spirit would always be denied him. But that didn't mean his love was any less profound. He'd made his choice years ago, in the full knowledge of what he could never attain. And he would never, after today, allow himself any regrets.

Unconsciously Laura closed her fingers around the Parthenon pendant that she still wore. She'd worn it every day for years, as a souvenir of her Lyricon debut. Perhaps, once she was on Celestra again, she'd be able to dispense with souvenirs.

"Do you remember how embarrassed I was when I first saw you naked?" she asked, breaking a silence which had lasted a fraction too long. "I'd just discovered we weren't on Earth anymore, and you came prancing out of the shower cubicle..."

"You turned scarlet," he recalled.

"How could I have been such a ninny? You were so beautiful!"

"And still am, I hope."

She dug him in the ribs.

"And now," he said airily, "I want to reacquaint myself with your singing voice."

"You want me to sing? Now?"

"No, I want to hear the songs on your little machine. I'm curious about that side of your life."

"We...e...ll..." She sounded dubious.

"It's either that or another language lesson."

"Oh, please, not that!"

"Then let me hear the tapes."

She stood up reluctantly. "All right, just a few tracks. I don't want to run the batteries down before Tralvar's heard my songwriting efforts." She moved unselfconsciously across the cabin, took the cassette player from a locker, placed it on the floor a short distance from the bunk and returned to Idenion's arms.

For two or three astallen they reclined in mutual languor, listening to the eighteen-year-old Laura singing earnestly of peace, love and total unity. Then, suddenly, the viewscreen went dark and the panel lights changed their pattern once. The sphere was in transposal. And as it crossed that incomprehensible boundary, the music faded and died.

Laura got up to see what was wrong. The tape was still turning smoothly and a faint hiss emanated from the speaker.

"It isn't the batteries," she said, perplexed.

She tried another cassette, which was as silent as the first. As was the third and fourth.

"They're all blank!" she cried. "Unless something's happened to the heads. Could transposal have done this?"

"I don't know. You'll have to ask Tralvar."

"And I did so want him to hear my songs," she lamented.

"You'll have to sing them yourself," Idenion smiled. "He'd probably prefer that. Now come back to bed. I'm getting lonely."

She obeyed, with one uneasy glance around the still cabin. The guidance system had ceased its soft chittering, leaving only a barely audible ringing from the crystal array - something she'd always compared to distant mocking laughter. It seemed more baleful than she remembered.

"I hate that sound!" she whispered.

"There's nothing to fear," Idenion said comfortingly. "It'll get us home. It always does."

They lay sharing each other's warmth while the tiny sphere pursued its infinitely lonely journey. Presently they made love again. Then they slept.

Chapter Three

Idenion woke to the sound of a chime. For a moment he thought he was back in Alda Mexa and being summoned to work. Then, with a surge of remembered pleasure, he saw Laura by his side and realised where he was. The programmed flight had ended and the sphere was safely in orbit round Celestra.

He made landfall at the co-ordinates Tralvar had given him: an area due south of Alda Mexa where the meandering river Lisir joined with a tributary, the Etys. He opened the hatch and looked out. The air was still and sultry, and there was no sign of Tralvar nor anyone else. Fields of liman plants extended in every direction as far as the eye could see, and kyffu - plump ungainly waterfowl - uttered discordant squawks as they settled down for the night. The sun had just set, although daylight would persist for an ild or more.

Laura was still asleep, and Idenion let her remain where she was while he began to destroy the evidence of his illicit voyage. He removed the Symerid Three programme crystal and substituted the one for Myrma, then deleted the contents of the flight log. He lobbed the incriminating crystal into the river. Then, struck by a sudden thought, he took a tiny blade from a tool kit, picked up Laura's clothes and carefully cut out the makers' labels. He also scored out some wording on the inside of her espadrilles. He hadn't been instructed to do this, and was pleased at having thought of it.

It was now nearly dark outside, and he could no longer pretend to himself that Tralvar was on his way. Obviously he had been and gone. The original plan had been for Tralvar to arrive in a flitter and spirit Laura off to the city, leaving Idenion to justify the theft of the sphere - an act of defiance, he would have said, brought about by his shabby treatment the previous day. But if he couldn't meet the rendezvous, he'd been given a second slightly more risky plan to follow. Hastily he began to revise the details. The Narvellans would have tracked the sphere as it came in, and would know his approximate position. Any moment now, someone would locate him.

Laura hadn't woken. Idenion carefully re-arranged the soft metallised blanket which covered her, partly to keep her warm and partly to afford her some modesty. Then he stood watchfully by, once more hearing Tralvar's cynical instructions.

"And while you're on your way back, I shall expect you to have sex with her. I'm sure you'll cope well enough with *that* part of your assignment. If the Narvellans find you before I do, I want them to see a recently serviced, satisfied woman. Your average official will be so embarrassed he won't attempt to pry into her background."

"Supposing I can't persuade her?" Idenion had asked.

"If you've persuaded her to leave Earth, I'm sure you'll find her compliant," Tralvar had replied blandly.

In fact, Laura had made the first move. Idenion had been glad of that. He wasn't quite sure if he could rely on Tralvar's tact, and he certainly wouldn't have wanted Laura to think that their lovemaking had just been part of the plan.

The sound of a motor interrupted his reflections. It wasn't the whirr of a flitter engine, however, but the chug of a river craft. He went to the hatch again: in the distance, he could see the boat's running lights approaching. He ventured a mental sweep and encountered one shielded mind - rigidly self-contained and indubitably Narvellan. The steersman wasn't using a searchlight, but he didn't need to. The Narvellans had excellent night vision.

Idenion checked the sphere's cabin one last time to ensure all was in order. He still had one item to dispose of - the redundant cassette player. He'd deliberately left it till last, not wanting to destroy it, but there was now no choice. He waited until a bend in the river temporarily hid the boat from view, then reluctantly hefted the machine and hurled it into the dark water, aiming for the centre where the current was strongest. He threw the remaining cassettes after it, then settled down to await his visitor.

The Narvellan was young, officious and just a trifle nervous. "A sphere was stolen from Treva earlier today," he began. "I assume this is the one."

"Stolen no longer, since I've returned it," Idenion said casually.

"Why land here, and not at a spacefield?" the Narvellan asked peevishly.

"Sheer ineptitude," Idenion said with a cheerful smile. "I, in case you don't recognise me, am First Poet Idenion. And this - " gesturing at Laura, who was beginning to stir - "is my partner in unity, Lisset."

"I know who you are," responded the Narvellan, unimpressed. "You were seen taking the sphere. I am Quon zyl Apteris, overseer at Etys Point liman mill."

Idenion didn't recognise the boy's lineage. Highborn enough to win him a passage to Celestra, he thought, but lowly enough to find himself stuck in this dreary spot. "Let me guess," he said. "The spaceport tracked my landing, the flitters were all at their charging stations, and you happened to be closest. So sorry for the inconvenience. What are you required to do with us?"

"I expected to find only you," Quon said pointedly.

"Lisset was stranded on Myrma," Idenion replied in the same equable tone. "That's why I took the sphere. I had to bring her back."

"But you didn't have to indulge your carnal appetites on the way," Quon retorted sharply. "How typically Celestrian! No self-discipline, even when in charge of a valuable spacecraft."

Laura opened her eyes. "Idenion...?"

"I'm here, Lisset my love," he said hastily. "This is Quon. He's come to arrest us."

She regarded the young Narvellan through heavy-lidded eyes. "Why? What have we done?" she asked huskily, remembering to speak Celestrian.

Tralvar, thought Idenion grudgingly, was absolutely right. It was impossible to see whether Quon was blushing under his golden skin, but he certainly looked uncomfortable.

"Clothe yourself, woman!" he snapped. "I'm taking you both to Etys Point, where you will remain until you're fetched."

Laura picked up her clothes and sauntered to the shower cubicle, giving Quon a long level stare.

"I *could* just take the sphere back to the Alda Mexa spaceport," Idenion offered.

"The sphere will stay where it is until it can be inspected. Then it will be returned to Treva," Quon informed him. "And tomorrow you will present your lamentable excuses to the city elite, who will decide what restitution is necessary."

"I will answer only to First Citizen Tralvar," Idenion said with a sudden show of anger.

"You will answer to the Narvellan Protectorate," Quon returned icily.

"I intend to in due course," Idenion continued more calmly. "However, I wish Tralvar to intercede for me. It is my right as a citizen."

"Perhaps he will choose not to intercede."

"Perhaps so, but are you qualified to predict what he'll do? I suggest I contact him. He may even be able to take us off your hands."

Quon hesitated only a moment. If there was a chance of getting this immoral pair off his territory before morning, he wouldn't balk at it; but he was careful not to show too much enthusiasm. "Very well, you may try to locate him," he said.

Idenion went to the radio, trying to maintain his casual air.

"If anyone should ask me, I did *not* give my permission," Quon added.

Idenion called the Communications tower in Alda Mexa. Someone would hopefully be able to relay a message to Tralvar from there. In the old days he could simply have contacted the akron - but Tralvar no longer resided at the akron. Much to his surprise, his call was answered by a Celestrian, so he was spared the haranguing he'd expected. After an amused comment about the First Poet's navigating skills, the unknown operator told him to stand by while a relayist was contacted. Laura emerged from the shower just as the reply came through.

"Tralvar says, do you think he has nothing better to do than sweet-talk the authorities on your behalf? But he has agreed to hear your case and will collect you at first light. In the meantime, please wait at the liman mill."

Idenion was disappointed, but managed not to show it. Tralvar was playing his role correctly. Hurrying to the rescue would have focused too much attention on the First Poet and his runaway lady. They would just have to brazen it out till morning.

"It seems I'm to be your host after all," said Quon resignedly. Then, to Laura: "Don't you have anything more modest to wear?"

"Sorry, no," she replied edgily.

"I will see what I can find you at Etys Point," said Quon in an attempt at kindness. "You cannot walk about in that outrageous Myrmian garment."

"You'll disrupt the work effort," Idenion put in.

Quon saw that as a statement, not a joke. "I'm glad you understand my position, First Poet. I will turn the boat around. Please secure the sphere and wait on the riverbank."

He went out. As soon as the boat's engine started up, Laura said: "Idenion, this isn't good. Someone's going to find out who I am."

"Quon didn't try to read you, did he?"

"The poor lad's embarrassed," Laura said. "His friends might not be."

"They still wouldn't probe your mind," Idenion reassured her. "The Narvellans have all kinds of taboos concerning women, and when not to use perception on them. It's a sexual misdemeanour to read the highborn, and bad manners to read the rest. And none of the elite would risk reading a Celestrian woman, not even superficially."

"Why not?"

"They consider us depraved - our women in particular," Idenion explained. "They don't want to be dragged down to our level."

Laura didn't know whether to be indignant or amused. "Are *all* Narvellan men like this?"

"Yes, if the ones in Alda Mexa are anything to go by - although it's the elite who perpetuate these silly habits. I suspect the average Narvellan doesn't always follow their example."

"But Idenion, where do Tarit and Shann fit into all this? They seemed so liberated!"

Idenion remembered, only too well, the young women brought by Rillan as emissaries from the endangered Narvellan homeworlds. They had enchanted the Celestrians, beguiled them into handing over the stardrive - and driven Laura away.

"Poor Rillan," he reflected. "He thought he was studying the Narvellans, but they were studying *him*. They sent messengers we were bound to empathise with, whose sexual attitudes mirrored our own. Tarit and Shann were prostitutes."

"*What*?"

"Stage performers as well, but prostitutes, nonetheless. On Narvella Prime the two things go together."

"Then you were duped into making that treaty - " began Laura. Idenion silenced her hastily.

"Shh. Quon's on his way back."

"What if we meet any Celestrians at this place?" Laura hissed. "They wouldn't hesitate to read me - and then what would we do?"

"I'll think of something on the way," Idenion promised.

They sat wordlessly in the boat's prow, seeing nothing beyond the feeble circle of light cast on the waters ahead. Quon, in the wheelhouse, steered them upriver at a safe steady speed. Laura had begun to feel cold in her thin dress, but there was little Idenion could do except put his arms around her. Eventually the complex came into view: a cluster of soft white lights at the river's edge revealed three sturdy conical structures, built in the same style as the hydro-electric plant.

"The Narvellans didn't design this, then," commented Laura.

"Oh no, it was here already," Idenion confirmed. "We've had to step up production, but the system's coping."

They reached a mooring point and Quon tethered the boat. "There aren't many workers here at present," he said. "I've ruled that the centrifuge must be switched off every third night for routine maintenance. This is more efficient than sudden shutdowns, which leave the entire workforce with nothing to do. There are a few of your people in the refinery and the despatch depot, but I don't propose to let them know you're here. That would lead to disruption."

Idenion and Laura exchanged relieved glances. Quon had helpfully provided them with a good excuse to stay hidden.

"I understand," Idenion said neutrally. "We won't try to converse with anyone."

They disembarked, Laura almost overbalancing as she tried to contend with the weak gravity. Quon led the way toward the largest of the three buildings, moving with a swift, assured step. Laura clung to Idenion's arm and did her best to keep up. She felt as if she were walking on sponge instead of solid ground.

Quon escorted them to his office, a small but comfortable room with a panoramic view over the main work area. The centrifuge was being scoured with jets of water, but panels of reinforced glass kept out most of the noise.

Quon immediately began tapping on his computer keyboard and appeared to forget he had company.

"Are there any other Narvellans here, or do we remain under your supervision?" Idenion inquired after a few moments.

"There are four others," answered Quon without looking up. "A clerk, two engineers and a cook. And none of us has time to supervise you!"

"A cook," repeated Laura hopefully. "Does that mean we'll get something to eat? I'm very hungry."

"So am I," Idenion put in.

"First, I must radio my superiors to tell them I've found you," Quon stated. "Then I'll find out if there is sufficient food for your needs. And after that, I'd be grateful if you'd stay out of my way. I've wasted half the evening on you already." The printer hummed and ejected the document he'd just typed. "I have to account for the time spent away from my post. Please endorse this statement." He shoved the paper at Idenion, who hesitated.

"Well, what's the matter, First Poet? Is my grammar incorrect?"

"Your Celestrian is very good," Idenion said truthfully.

"Then sign," Quon said impatiently.

Idenion picked up a stylus and dutifully inscribed his signature and birthplace.

"Now you," said Quon to Laura.

Idenion was about to offer some lame apology when, to his surprise, Laura accepted the document and wrote waveringly:

"Lisit of Triva."

Quon glanced at this effort, smiled faintly and laid it aside. Literacy in a woman was of no merit as far as he was concerned, but he'd assumed the First Poet of Celestra would have different ideas.

"Where are we going to sleep?" Idenion asked in a hasty attempt to divert him from these musings.

Quon looked vaguely irritated. "The rest room is unoccupied," he suggested.

"It would be," Idenion muttered.

"In fact," continued the young overseer with a glare, "I'll take you down there as soon as I've made my radio report. I'll have the canteen send whatever they can spare - and I'll personally find you an overall, Lisset of Treva."

Laura gave him her most charming smile.

The rest room consisted of two single beds and a table. A washroom, with basic facilities, was close by. Quon had departed, hastening back to his duties, but Laura didn't feel she could relax while there were Narvellans under the same roof. The room was too hot, as was the entire building away from the centrifuge hall. She assumed that was for the invaders' benefit. Idenion confirmed this was so.

Later an elderly Narvellan, presumably the cook, brought a tray. The meal consisted only of a thin vegetable broth, two chunks of bread and some shrivelled pilif fruits. But there was, of course, a large jug of liman.

"This is more than I expected," Idenion said. "We're lucky to get fruit - there isn't much about. And just to vary the menu - " he dug into his pocket and produced some food concentrate bars, which he laid proudly on the table.

"From the sphere?" Laura inquired. "I'm impressed! You seem to have thought of everything."

"I didn't bring you all this way to let you starve," he declared. "Now eat up."

They soon finished the meagre supper and proceeded to devour the concentrates, leaving one bar each in case there was no breakfast. Then, sitting chastely on one of the narrow beds, arms clasping her knees, Laura recounted the story of her meeting with the flower children and the forming of their band. She spoke only Celestrian, surprised at how readily it was coming back to her. Idenion allowed her plenty of time to search for unfamiliar words, only prompting her when she appeared to be completely stuck.

"Tralvar will be very pleased with you," he commented.

"Tralvar's *never* pleased with me," she replied with more vehemence than she intended. "Anyway, that's enough about my past. Tell me, what became of Tarit and Shann? Are they still here?"

"Not any more. The elite in their gratitude sent them home. I wasn't sorry: Tarit had made a complete fool of me. All she wanted was to get away from Narvella Prime."

" I don't suppose there's much time left, is there? Before the solar flares?"

"Half a year, maybe less."

Laura shook her head sadly. "Poor Tarit."

"She broke us up," Idenion reminded her.

"It wasn't *just* her - those two girls brought out all my feelings of inferiority. It wasn't easy being the only nonconversant. Total unity mystified me: sciesha terrified me."

"I'm not too fond of sciesha myself," Idenion confessed.

"Does it still go on? I thought maybe the Narvellans had banned it."

"They would if they could," said Idenion with a grim little laugh. "Sciesha's a law unto itself: we can't prevent it happening. The Narvellans say it's due to bad mental discipline."

"So you've had one small victory, at least."

"I don't know about victory, but it certainly annoys them," Idenion said with relish. "If only there were more ways to - " He paused, frowning.

"What is it?" asked Laura anxiously.

"Something's happening out there. Something's wrong."

"What do you mean? Have they been reading me after all?"

"It isn't about us," Idenion said distantly, still concentrating. "Quon's just been summoned back to his office. He's wanted on the radio."

"That doesn't sound too sinister," Laura remarked.

"No, but it *feels* sinister. Fear has a certain sharpness - and there's suddenly a lot of it about." He stood up purposefully. "I'm going to find out why."

"Then I'm coming with you."

"Still trying to protect me?" he inquired gently. "There's no need. I only want to get close enough to hear that radio message. I speak fairly good Narvellan; they tend to forget that."

"We stay together," Laura insisted.

Moments later they were edging back along the gallery, noting that the Narvellan maintenance men were no longer working on the centrifuge. A discarded hose dribbled water.

"Everyone's in the office - even the cook," Idenion muttered. "I don't like this."

"Don't go near those windows!" Laura advised in a fierce whisper.

Idenion steered her into an adjoining room. It had a connecting door, which he'd noticed earlier. The radio was clearly audible through the thin panels, and Idenion repressed a shiver as he recognised the voice of Governor Axmiol.

"...another victim of madness, Firessa lyr Raxel. Beware this woman - she is crafty. We prevented her from reaching the Alda Mexa spaceport, but she eluded capture and stole a boat from the marina. You, Quon, will assemble your staff and wait for personnel from the Etys South mill, who are already on their way by river. Together you will form the Ten."

A collective sigh rose from the five Narvellans.

"We believe Firessa is making for the spaceport at Kest. You should be able to intercept her near your location. Any questions?"

"None, Lord Axmiol," Quon answered steadily.

"Then do your duty, Quon zyl Apteris," Axmiol intoned.

Unhesitatingly, Quon and the others turned and left the room in single file. Laura hastily ducked behind some furniture as their silhouettes passed the outer door, but Idenion didn't bother to hide. He could have leapt in front of the Narvellans and called them names: there would have been no recriminations. Nothing would have diverted them from their dreadful purpose.

"Where are they off to?" Laura asked tremulously.

He translated what he'd heard. "They're going to perform an execution," he added bleakly. "Just like the one I witnessed earlier today."

"But," Laura stammered, "those men are just ordinary workers!"

"Individually, yes." Idenion opened the door and went to the gallery's edge. The execution squad was just filing out of the main hall. "They're heading for the landing stage. Come on."

"Surely you're not going to follow them?"

Idenion looked unusually stern. "Know thine enemy. Isn't that what your people say? Who knows when you'll have another chance to observe the Ten in action? You think the Narvellans are a bunch of irritating bureaucrats - and you're wrong, so wrong." Then, as she hesitated: "Believe me, they won't take any notice of us even if we're seen."

"Then what happened to you this morning?"

"That was my fault; I didn't close off my perception. They warn us to, if we're in the presence of the Ten. Always so solicitous of our safety!"

"Who's this woman they're hunting?" asked Laura, falling into step beside him. "Do you know her?"

"I've heard of her. She's a biologist."

"And she isn't mad?"

"No, not mad," Idenion said softly. "Free."

They halted in the shadow of a boathouse. They could see Quon and the others near the water's edge, silent and still. Their attention was fixed on something beyond the pool of light. Presently a small hovercraft came into view: it carried no navigation beacons and its engine was a mere purr. It swirled to a halt before the waiting assembly, and five more Narvellans stepped out. The two rows of men stood facing each other, wordless, motionless.

Laura couldn't read the lethal build-up of power in their linked minds. But all at once she felt leaden and ill, as if every scrap of hope and joy had been smothered within her. The night seemed to grow darker. Idenion drew a shuddering breath and held her very tightly. Then, breaking the tableau, the ten Narvellans boarded their vessel and drifted away in a slow arc.

"Shall we go back now?" suggested Laura in a very small voice.

"You sensed it, didn't you?" Idenion responded equally quietly. "And they haven't yet killed. I hope they're far from here when they do."

They retraced their steps toward the main entrance. Away from the circles of light the unfriendly stars glinted like crystal splinters. Idenion risked a brief scan of the other buildings, relieved to find the Celestrian workers knew or had guessed what was happening. Their minds were closed to him.

"Can any Narvellan be conscripted into a Ten?" Laura asked.

"Anyone. They're not allowed to refuse."

"And the victims are always their own people?"

68

"So far," Idenion confirmed as they neared the threshold. "Although they've used the Five on us enough times, as they did with poor Rinyi. He -"

Suddenly a figure detached itself from the surrounding darkness and clutched at Idenion - a Narvellan woman in a mud-spattered overall that had once been white. She was limping badly, leaving Laura in no doubt that this was the renegade Firessa.

"First Poet!" she cried breathlessly. "Where have they hidden your spacecraft?"

"It isn't here," Idenion stammered, taken aback.

"You lie, Celestrian!" she snarled, raising her hand as if to strike him. "I heard the report. You stole it and landed here."

"I *didn't* land here!" Idenion was genuinely distressed. "The sphere's four or five silmi downriver. I'm not sure where."

"I have to find them!" Firessa sobbed. "Don't you understand - I have to find them!"

He tried to pacify her, then flinched as an icy pall nudged the edge of his shielded mind. The Ten's focus had left the Lisir and swung back in his direction. They were still testing their range, but they knew their prey was close.

Firessa was staring at Laura. "Clemoridys," she murmured incredulously. Then, with more assurance, "Clemoridys!"

The Ten's chilling scrutiny returned, and stayed.

"Run!" Idenion cried. "Firessa, run!"

"I have failed," she said, quite calmly. But she ran, back towards the river. Idenion stared helplessly after her until she vanished into the darkness she'd come from. She was drawing the Ten away, to a distance where their death-bolt would cause him no pain.

"What's Clemoridys?" asked Laura.

"My name for you, in a poem," Idenion said wearily. "Yes, she knew who you were. But it doesn't matter - she's as good as dead."

"And what did she mean, I have to find them?"

"I wish I knew." Idenion resumed walking. "Let's go back inside. We can do nothing for her."

Silently Laura followed him back to the rest room. It no longer seemed too hot. They waited, clinging to one another like lost children, until presently Idenion said:

"It's over."

"Why, Idenion? Why are they doing this?"

He faced her earnestly. "Laura, my dearest love: when you meet with Tralvar tomorrow, when your alias is established, we'll tell you everything. Until then, it's safer not to discuss it." He turned the light-tube down to a dim glow. "We should try to sleep. The morning will come more quickly."

"Will Quon and the others be normal again now?"

"Yes, but they won't be back for a while. There's a cleansing ritual they have to perform."

They climbed into their separate beds and tried to make themselves comfortable under the rough blankets. Laura kept her dress on. It was beginning to look like a dish-rag anyway.

"I didn't get my overall," she reflected.

"He won't have forgotten," Idenion said positively.

They lay holding hands across the divide, convinced that sleep would elude them after the events of the evening. But in a remarkably short time their breathing deepened and their fingers relaxed their grip. And in what appeared to be another brief interval, it was dawn.

***

Laura was surprised she'd slept the night through. Earth days were four hours shorter than Celestra's, and

70

during her previous stay she'd had a tendency to wake early.

As was often the case with Celestrian heating systems, the warmth in the building had dissipated overnight. I'm surprised the Narvellans haven't remedied that, she thought. Or perhaps they have, and someone simply didn't keep an eye on it. They did have other things on their agenda.

She opened the door cautiously; she had no wish to run into Quon and his friends just yet. But everything was silent, seemingly deserted. After a brief chilly visit to the washroom she remained close to Idenion, envying him his ability to enjoy carefree sleep. At least, that was the impression he was giving. Not for the first time, she wondered what in the name of discord he and Tralvar expected her to do about the Narvellans. She was a singer, not a revolutionary.

When Idenion awoke he found her sitting with a blanket round her shoulders, staring out of the window at some angry streaks of pink forming in the sky. He read her concerns, but said nothing to reassure her. Presently there was a light tap at the door. It was the taciturn cook, bringing two beakers of hot liman, but - as Laura had predicted - nothing to eat. They had scarcely finished their drinks when Quon appeared, looking immeasurably tired. He carried a neatly folded overall, which he held out to Laura.

"For you, Lisset of Treva," he said. "I'm sorry I was unable to deliver this last night."

Laura thanked him gravely.

"The First Citizen is on his way," Quon continued. "He will arrive in approximately three astallen. The flitter park is at the northern edge of the complex; you may wait for him there. I'd like you off the premises by the time the day shift arrives."

"Isn't *your* shift over yet?" Laura asked, feeling a tinge of sympathy for him.

"My tour of duty has ended, but I have a report to write before I can leave," he answered.

"Oh. Naturally," said Laura.

"I didn't think I'd ever be part of a Ten," Quon went on unexpectedly. "We're so isolated here. I didn't want...." He checked himself abruptly. "The madness is a contagion. It has to be excised wherever it is found, for your safety as well as ours." Then he was gone.

Idenion made no comment about this brief attack of conscience, and Laura wisely said nothing either. She inspected her overall which, like Idenion's, was coarsely woven and the colour of dirty sand. Making a face, she put it on, buttoning the stiff cloth with difficulty and making sure her Greek medallion was hidden under the close-fitting collar.

"It feels like an old sack," she complained. "What *is* this material?"

"It's called ylur. It's an unrefined version of ytil."

Ytil, silken and durable, had been the most commonplace fabric on the planet.

"And why isn't ytil being used to make overalls?"

"The Narvellans say it takes too long to manufacture, and wastes manpower," Idenion said. "Come on, let's go and find Tralvar."

It took them over an astal to reach the flitter park. Tralvar was waiting for them at the eastern edge of the paved area. He had alighted from his craft and was standing with his back to them, gazing over the liman crop in the direction of the promised sunrise. Low-lying river mist rendered his figure indistinct. The still air was punctuated by the squawks of the kyffu and the uninspired cheeping of other birds. Celestra had no songbirds, just as it had no singers.

As they neared the flitter, Tralvar turned in their direction. Laura was suddenly conscious of her uncombed hair, and the fact that three inches of frilly cheesecloth showed jauntily beneath her overall. Nevertheless, she held her head high and met Tralvar's gaze unswervingly.

The changes in him were subtle. He had the same aura of sinewy strength, but a hint of tiredness had entered his bearing. His hair held no trace of grey, but worry lines were etched a little more deeply into his face.

"So, Laura, you've come back in spite of all your vows," he said. "I'm sorry we've nothing to offer you but our trials and sorrows."

"Would you please get us out of here?" Idenion interjected with less than his normal aplomb.

"You found your errand a little taxing, did you?" inquired Tralvar, opening the flitter canopy and standing aside to let him enter. He then assisted Laura on board and climbed in next to her, closing the canopy with a slam. A moment later they were airborne.

"I've never been so glad to see the back of a place," Idenion declared. "If you hadn't been so determined to do things by the book, we'd have been safely in Alda Mexa when the Ten went into action. I presume you know about that?"

"Of course. I'm sorry you had to witness it."

"So I should think. Two executions in one day! It's terrifying."

"Two?" repeated Tralvar.

"There was one outside the power station this morning," Idenion explained, suddenly hesitant. "I - er - got a bit too close."

"Discord's dreams! Is that why you were late?"

"Partly."

"Chaos give me strength," Tralvar muttered.

"You knew Firessa, didn't you?" Idenion asked, trying to avert a tongue-lashing.

"Oh yes, I knew her. In fact, I believe she tried to get to me before she was chased out of the city."

"Why would she do that?" asked Laura. "Did she wish you harm?"

"Nothing like that. I think she had information."

Laura repeated the sentence Firessa had uttered.

"You *spoke* with her?" Tralvar obviously didn't know the full story.

Briefly, in her far from perfect Celestrian, Laura described their meeting with the doomed woman.

"And she recognised you, you say," Tralvar interrupted before she'd quite finished. "So will everyone else if you don't improve that accent. Not even the Atrisians manage to slaughter our language so thoroughly."

"Now look!" Laura, indignant, reverted to English. "I think I've done pretty well to remember as much as I have. Do you realise how long it's been since I've used Celestrian in conversation?"

"I know exactly how long it's been," Tralvar said drily. "Six years, five octals and four days. And although my life hasn't been exactly restful, it's been blissfully free of any aggravation from *you*!"

"I could say the same," Laura retorted. "Just get it through your head, Tralvar, that I'm no longer a child you can yell at. If you carry on like this I'll probably hit you."

"Patience, both of you!" pleaded Idenion.

Laura glared. "He started it. I'd forgotten how exasperating he could be. Anyway, what does it matter how well or how badly I speak the language? To be a convincing Celestrian I need to be a telepath. And that's something I can *never* learn, badly or otherwise."

74

"Maybe you won't need to," said Tralvar mysteriously.

They headed into the sunrise, following the path of the Lisir. The liman fields had been left behind and they were now above a forested area - but a forest marred in several places by indiscriminate tree-felling.

"We had to extend Alda Mexa in rather a hurry," Tralvar explained laconically. "You'll soon see what I mean."

And indeed, she did. As they neared the outskirts of the city she gave a cry of dismay. The graceful symmetry of the lower laterals was lost in a sprawl of timber hovels extending to the banks of the Lisir and beyond. A shanty town. Here, too, were the factories Idenion had mentioned. They passed close to one of them: long, narrow, single- storeyed, with ventilators and solar panels creating a domino effect on the flat asphalt roof. The houses were already falling into disrepair. Some of them, presumably the oldest, could hardly stand up.

"We used stone at first," Tralvar explained, "but it ran out and the Narvellans wouldn't let us quarry more. They'd rather we built their space fleet."

"They threw you out of your homes and made you live in that slum!" Laura's voice quivered with anger - at the Narvellans for despoiling the city, and at the Celestrians for allowing them to do it.

"They don't all live in the better part of town," Tralvar informed her.

"I bet the elite do."

"The elite took over the running of the planet, so naturally enough they occupy the akron and its environs. But the factory managers have to live near their workplaces, or *in* them, and some of the Moderators live in the poor quarter as well."

"Moderators?" queried Laura.

"Law enforcers," said Idenion. "They spy on us, preach at us and sneak around in the dark. You'll meet them soon enough."

"Is there a curfew?"

"No more than there ever was. We still have to conserve electricity - it's in even shorter supply now. So everything non-essential is shut down at night."

"And frequently, *not* at night," Tralvar put in. "The power supply is liable to interruption without notice, as is the water supply." He directed one of his mirthless grins at Laura. "Better get used to it."

"Do *you* live in the poor quarter, Idenion?" asked Laura.

"Not the worst part. Dena and I live further from the river, in one of the last streets to be built of stone."

"Just you and Dena?"

Idenion hesitated.

"Be truthful now," Laura prompted gently. "I don't expect you to have remained celibate all this time. If you're getting ready to evict someone to make room for me, I think I ought to be told."

"She already left," Idenion confessed. "Her name was Arnalta."

"Nice girl," Tralvar commented. "The long-suffering type, up to a point. She got sick of hearing him recite Clemoridys. I know just how she felt!"

"Have you read it?" asked Laura, though she knew the answer to that.

"No, for the usual reasons," Tralvar replied. "It goes on too long. On - and on - and on..."

Idenion wasn't in the mood to hear his masterpiece derided. "Tralvar," he said abruptly, "did you call on Dena as we arranged?"

"Of course," Tralvar said loftily. "*My* part of the plan went without a hitch."

"And what did you say to her?"

"Naturally I didn't mention Laura. I told her not to worry, that you were doing some work for me, and that she was to disregard the stories that were circulating."

"And?"

"And your sweet-natured little sister told me off. You were in enough trouble already, she said, without my interference. I ought to know better than to involve you in my machinations."

Laura hid a smile and returned her attention to the scene below. Tralvar had flown the entire length of the crowded lateral, probably to increase her sense of outrage. Just before he crossed into the older part of the city, a faint chiming sounded above the purr of the flitter's engines, and she saw people begin to vacate their shabby homes and head for the factories. But they didn't run, didn't even walk briskly. The Celestrians were still resisting the tyranny of time.

The sound was emanating from a white cone atop a tall pole.

"I've promised myself I'll use that as target practice one day," Tralvar muttered.

"You could say it was struck by lightning," offered Laura. "If you managed to hit it."

"Don't encourage him to take risks," Idenion warned. "The Narvellans have to think he's accepted their authority....for now."

Tralvar took the flitter to Lateral Three and landed in front of a pleasant white-walled villa. Laura recognised the area. The retrace laboratory, if it were still in its old location, lay just beyond a curve in the road; and nearby was a steep pathway leading to the akron plaza.

"The Narvellans drew the line at putting *you* in the slums, then," she remarked to Tralvar.

"That wouldn't have suited their requirements," he replied. "They make a show of consulting me on administrative matters, so I have to be on hand."

"Then is it safe to use your house for our discussions?" asked Laura. "We don't want the elite barging in on us."

He gave her a flinty stare. "I've made it clear that no Narvellan is to enter my home uninvited. So far, that rule has been observed. You're as safe here as anywhere."

He disembarked and vanished through the pillared portico, leaving Idenion to help Laura out of the flitter.

"Try not to antagonise him," he urged. "He's in a very difficult position."

"I'm sorry. He just takes everything the wrong way," Laura said, looking about her and shivering. "Why's it so cold, Idenion?"

"We're well into our autumn now," he reminded her. "You've only ever known spring and summer here. It still gets warm at noon - it certainly did yesterday - but early mornings are a different matter." He put an arm round her shoulders. "Come on. Tralvar may be irascible, but he's a good host. He'll give us a proper breakfast."

Laura found it oddly relaxing to sit in Tralvar's study with its untidy bookshelves and precarious stacks of papers, eating grain cakes smothered in syrup. Tralvar had provided her and Idenion with fresh clothes, and they had gratefully exchanged their overalls for conventional ytil tunics. As usual Tralvar ate little, but waited until the others had finished before calling them to attention.

"To business, then," he said. "There are certain things, Laura, which I forbade Idenion to discuss, and now it's time to make them known. I shall use English for clarity's sake, but after today neither Idenion nor I will indulge you in this. *You* may go on speaking it until you have a better grasp of our language, but our replies will be in Celestrian."

Laura wondered which accent was worse - her Celestrian or his English. But this was neither the time nor the place for scoring points.

"While I concentrate on making myself understood," Tralvar went on meaningfully, "Idenion will use his excellent perceptive powers to ensure our conversation remains private. I don't want anyone scanning us, no matter how innocent the reason." He cleared his throat, then continued: "You believe the Narvellans turned on us as soon as we'd given them the stardrive. That wasn't so. Things weren't completely harmonious - we were irritated by their insistence on protocol, and the elite were openly disdainful of our morals. Nevertheless, both sides co-operated for almost a year. The Narvellan engineers were apt pupils and soon there was nothing more we could teach them. They were so full of enthusiasm and hope that I almost regretted speaking against the treaty. And then, within a few moments, everything changed. The entire Narvellan race - all of them, not just those on Celestra - suffered a personality shift. They became, to use your quaint terminology, possessed."

"Possessed?" echoed Laura. "By what?"

"That's what we have to find out," Tralvar pronounced solemnly.

"Let me get this straight," Laura said. "Do you genuinely think they've all been taken over by something? Sorry, but to me that sounds like an excuse for your collective bad judgement. If they changed so suddenly, it must have been planned."

"I'm sure it was," Tralvar said. "But not by the Narvellans."

Laura remained sceptical. It wasn't like Tralvar to give credence to such a silly theory. "How far away is Narvella?" she asked. "Just remind me."

"About a thousand light years," Tralvar replied with some reluctance.

"Just checking," said Laura a shade too flippantly.

Tralvar's anger resurfaced. "Since you refuse to take me seriously, I shan't bother speaking English again. Obviously the message isn't getting through."

"But Tralvar," Laura protested, "you surely don't expect me to believe this possession story? How could anything affect people's minds over a distance like that? *I'll* tell you what happened. The Narvellans realised they could build twice as many spacecraft with slave labour, and co-operated with you only as long as it took to win your trust and put you off your guard. Then they performed their coup. Simple."

Tralvar and Idenion exchanged glances.

"As you predicted," Idenion said. "You were right, Tralvar, to ask Lydion to stand by. Shall I send for him?"

"No, I'll fetch him." Tralvar left the house without another word to Laura. She turned to Idenion in bewilderment.

"What does Lydion have to do with this?"

"You'll see," Idenion said gently. "I realise how odd Tralvar's story may seem, but try to keep an open mind. Would it help if I said I believed it?"

"Not a lot," she confessed. "How could the Narvellans have been got at across a thousand light years? Is it likely?"

"Distance isn't always relevant," he reminded her. "We all take transposal for granted; maybe there are ways for pure thought to bridge such a gap."

"Your people haven't discovered a way."

"No, but the Narvellans' perception is far superior to ours. You've already seen what the Ten can do. Many of the elite can levitate objects and heal simple injuries with a touch, and there are women called Directresses who can actually read the ground for mineral deposits."

"What's your point?"

"The point is, their sophistication may have left them open to attack. And it may be the reason we were spared."

Laura was about to voice more doubts, but decided to wait until she'd heard what Lydion had to say. "I seem to have upset Tralvar yet again," she remarked instead.

"It's easily done," Idenion admitted. "Maybe you'd think better of him if I told you about the concessions he's won for us. He never gives up - just keeps battering at the elite until he gets his way. The workers now have every eighth day off, the Lyricon has been preserved for the people, and the scolia are exempt from factory duties. Also, we've the right to educate our children the way we choose."

Laura raised her eyebrows. "Now that *does* surprise me. You'd think the Narvellans would want to indoctrinate them."

"Yes, it's strange," Idenion mused. "All their propaganda is aimed at the workforce. I suppose they're concentrating on the most useful age-group."

Laura's expression softened. "How are the children taking the occupation?"

"Very well. They're amazingly resilient. We segregate them as much as possible and make sure the little ones are surrounded by older ones, so they only absorb from their own kind."

"Very wise. We don't want any more Alendises."

"We don't want any infant bureaucrats either," Idenion declared. "Not that there's any real danger of

81

that. Many children see the Narvellans as figures of fun - they ridicule the Moderators incessantly."

"Don't they mind?"

"No, that's another strange thing. They don't take any notice."

"Wouldn't it have been ideal," Laura said wistfully, "if I'd conceived a child on the way here? It won't happen, of course: I was on the Pill until yesterday. And by the time *that* wears off, the protections will have asserted themselves. So we've missed the opportunity."

Idenion tried not to look startled. Discord's dreams, hadn't Nathaniel told her there could be no offspring from their union? "It would have been *far* from ideal," he said at last. "There are dangerous times ahead."

"I know," Laura accepted the rebuke with a smile. "I was just dreaming aloud. But I'll make you a proud father one day."

The slam of the outer door and the sound of voices saved Idenion from having to reply.

"I hope you've a good reason for keeping me off work." Lydion's good-natured tones were unmistakable. "Not that I mind. But if anyone complains I'll have to blame it on you!"

"Feel free," Tralvar responded. "And yes, I have a good reason. She's waiting in my study."

Lydion strolled in expectantly. Like Tralvar, he looked drawn, but had lost none of his innate self-confidence.

"Hello," Laura said demurely. "Remember me?"

It took him but a moment.

"First Singer! How you've changed. A promise fulfilled, in every sense. Idenion, you are indeed fortunate."

"Call me Lisset," Laura said.

"If that will please you," he returned, still studying her.

82

"When you've finished admiring the view," said Tralvar, "perhaps you'd tell Laura - or should I say Lisset - about your involvement with Eluthia."

"Ah! I might have known." Lydion was suddenly uneasy. "Will you never allow me to forget how that ended? Not that I ever could."

"Get on with it," Tralvar said impatiently. "And keep it simple. Laura can scarcely recall the basics of our speech."

"I think she understands more than you give her credit for," Lydion said softly.

Laura rewarded him with a grateful smile.

"Eluthia was one of the entertainers," Lydion began. "We had unity on several occasions. Nothing unusual in that, you might think, but it led to the most frightening experience of my life. I was in total unity with her at the very moment the Narvellans suffered their...conversion."

"Then you support this theory?" asked Laura.

"Not theory. Fact," he said gravely. "When the shift occurred, Eluthia's mind was torn away from me. Beyond her I sensed another presence - something immensely powerful, or maybe just immense. For a moment I saw what *it* saw: a universe not of stars but of patterns endlessly repeated, and the Narvellans a lesser pattern it could lock into. As I struggled to free myself, it noticed me. I was picked up, inspected, then cast aside. Then I was falling - across space, or so it seemed. Falling forever into darkness. When I woke I was alone, and nine ilden had passed. I found Eluthia and asked what in chaos had happened. She didn't explain - she couldn't. But when I tried a reconciliation, I knew. Although she was still Eluthia, her mind was veiled and aloof - and that pattern, that presence, was somehow keyed into her."

Laura had never seen Lydion look so serious.

"You know me of old, Laura," he continued. "I'm not the imaginative type. I couldn't invent anything like that."

"No, I don't believe you could," Laura said with a troubled frown. "Have you made a retrace of this experience?"

"I attempted to, but there was so much of my fear in the memory that the prill wouldn't engage with it. At least, that was what Tyvian thought." He forced a smile. "So, I lived to love another day. But only because that thing, whatever it was, rejected me."

"The next day, Grevin and his followers threw me out of the akron," said Tralvar. "By nightfall they had control."

"All right," Laura said after a long silence. "For the sake of argument, let's assume the Narvellans are being manipulated by this life-form. To what end?"

"Survival?" suggested Tralvar.

"Then it's chosen badly."

"It didn't *have* a choice," Idenion reasserted. "If it could have taken us as well, it would have."

"Stay on watch!" Tralvar ordered. Then, to Laura, "It does seem as if we're immune. But we can still be exploited!"

"In that case, why hasn't there been a fullscale invasion? Why aren't *all* the Narvellans over here?"

"Because that would mean their extinction. Our birthrate is only thirty per cent of what it should be, but amongst the resident Narvellans it's a mere two per cent."

"Our ancestors thought of everything!" Lydion put in.

"Of course, the Narvellans have made strenuous attempts to undo our protections," Tralvar continued. "In fact, that's what Firessa was working on. She pretended it was for our benefit, naturally - barefaced as you please. It can do no harm to tell you she was very close to a solution."

"How close?" Lydion was obviously as surprised as Laura.

"She'd determined that the action was twofold. A virus which we all carry, and a co-factor. Something in the ecosystem. She'd isolated the virus, but the co-factor was eluding her."

"Would she have found it, do you think?" asked Laura breathlessly.

"I imagine so."

"And knowing that, the Ten still executed her?"

"She'd broken free," said Tralvar succinctly. "And as you may have gathered at Etys Point, she wasn't the first. I've seen quite a few of these escapees and they've all had one thing in common: the other Narvellans are absolutely terrified of them. And that, First Singer, may be the clue to our salvation." He paused, watching Laura narrowly. "I trust you believe us now."

Laura considered the evidence. Lydion's bizarre encounter; Firessa's murder; and - something she'd only just remembered - Quon's outburst of regret, so quickly stifled.

"I accept your proof," she said. "But what can we possibly - "

"Moderators," Idenion announced. "Two of them, heading this way."

"Are you sure?" asked Tralvar.

"I'm sure," Idenion stated. "They're coming here." He couldn't *read* Moderators - who could? - but he'd learnt to spot the peculiar opaqueness of their minds against the backdrop of city chatter.

Tralvar was obviously prepared for this contingency. "Lydion," he said calmly, "escort Laura to the retracer lab. Tyvian knows what to do. Leave by the cellar door after I've admitted our visitors. And Lydion - don't tell *anyone* that Laura's back!"

"Should I leave too?" asked Idenion.

"I'm supposed to be interceding for you, aren't I? They won't be surprised to find you here."

Lydion hurried Laura down some stairs just as three peremptory thumps were delivered to the street door. Tralvar answered the summons without haste and ushered the two callers inside with exaggerated courtesy. Idenion scowled up at them. They were young, even for Moderators, and their high-collared black uniforms looked fresh and immaculate. New recruits, Idenion thought. Typically over-zealous.

"We seek the woman Lisset," announced one. "She is not listed on our database. She must, therefore, be stateless."

Tralvar didn't bat an eyelid. "That's correct," he agreed. "By travelling from city to city, and occasionally to other planets, she managed to evade your registration system for some considerable time. Unfortunately, your new restrictions on the use of spheres led to her being marooned offworld."

"Why has she not reported for her work classification?" asked the Moderator.

"Because," said Tralvar, "she has a bad case of Myrmian swamp fever, and I've had to quarantine her. She was being most aggressive. That's the nature of the disease."

"We received no word yesterday that she was ill."

"Often, the sudden change of climate brings it out," Tralvar lied smoothly.

"Myrma!" said the other Moderator with a sneer. "I cannot imagine what you people see in that unhygienic planet."

"You wouldn't," muttered Idenion.

"So," Tralvar continued, "I'm afraid it will be several days before Lisset is well. I will ensure that Idenion brings her to the akron as soon as possible thereafter. It would be more efficient to deal with them together, would it not?"

"Indeed," said the first Moderator uncertainly.

"You're both new to Celestra, aren't you?" asked Tralvar with a bright artificial smile. "I thought so. That means your protections aren't fully established yet. Still, you may see Lisset if you insist. You should be safe as long as she doesn't spit at you."

"It will not be necessary to see her," said the second Moderator hastily.

"Why are you so concerned with Lisset's health, Citizen Tralvar?" asked the first.

"She's a valued member of the scolia," replied Tralvar indignantly. "Did you not know?"

"We were not informed of that." The Moderator looked uncomfortable. "Since you seem to have the matter well in hand, it would appear there is nothing more to be said at this time. We will see ourselves out."

Idenion waited until they were well clear of the house before he remarked: "A member of the scolia? That, Tralvar, is a shade too accurate for comfort."

"A little of the truth makes for a palatable lie," Tralvar replied nonchalantly. "You do realise she *is* going to be ill when the protections kick in? *Really* ill?"

Idenion looked blank. "Why? Most people only get mild symptoms."

"Most people haven't been away six years. The longer the absence, the harder it seems to hit you. Remember those archaeologists who spent a couple of years on Alda Four, raking over our lost civilisation? They were laid up for days when they got back. Delirium, dehydration, bad dreams...."

"I hadn't thought of that," Idenion admitted.

"Then I suggest you think about it now," Tralvar said irritably. "I told you Laura would be your responsibility. I can give you herbs and medicines if she needs them, but you'll have to nurse her yourself. And afterwards, you'll need to get her classified as I promised. Thanks to my quick thinking, she's exempt from factory work, but I don't know what they'll give her instead. I was going to say I needed a new secretary, but she's knocked that idea on the head by demonstrating her illiteracy at Etys Point."

"Tralvar," Idenion ventured, "I know you and Laura don't see eye to eye, but will you please stop needling her? You've done nothing but go on and on about her language difficulties. First you insult her accent, then you refuse to speak English. It's gratuitous and unnecessary."

"She has to blend in," Tralvar said stubbornly. "I've seen little evidence that she's even trying."

"Please, Tralvar?"

"Oh, very well." He paced across the room, poured himself a glass of resnay and drained it in one swallow. "I don't enjoy upsetting her, chaos only knows. The truth is, Firessa's execution has left me a little off-balance. She was the nearest thing to a friend I had amongst the Narvellans. Brilliant woman. I'd almost made up my mind to kill her."

Idenion half rose from his chair. "*What*?"

"If she'd found the antidote it would have been the end for us," said Tralvar remotely. "You don't think the Narvellans would have shared it, do you?"

"You'd have sacrificed yourself to buy us more time?" Idenion was horrified. "What would we have done without your leadership?"

"I wasn't planning on getting caught." Tralvar's eyes, sombre and searching, held Idenion's, and the latter felt - momentarily - a trace of disquiet. "This time, I was spared from having to make the decision. But I have to make other serious decisions almost daily: allowing innocents like Rinyi to suffer so that I can maintain my guise of puppet statesman. It wears me out, Idenion. Is it any wonder that Laura's ineptitude tries my patience?"

Before Idenion could reply, a brief communication from Lydion interrupted their grim debate.

+All safely delivered. May I go now?+

+Of course+ responded Tralvar. +Thank you, Lydion+

"What happens next?" Idenion asked.

Tralvar poured himself another drink. "You might as well stay for the result of my little experiment. And then, all being well, you can take Laura back to your home. At least she'll be out of my hair for a while."

***

Lydion, sure-footed, led Laura at a run along a tiny footpath. They traversed a garden and crossed a walled courtyard. Then, to her relief, he slowed down.

"Why were those Moderators after me?" she asked breathlessly.

"Only Lisset, not the real you," he replied. "Don't worry about it. They always panic when someone's been missed off their stupid register." Then, unexpectedly, he continued in English: "Once you get on list, all happy for the time be. Akron penpush works never done with. There are i's to be cross, t's to be dot."

Laura dissolved into laughter.

"There, you see?" Lydion reverted thankfully to his own tongue. "Your Celestrian isn't so bad. The next time Tralvar tries to put you down, laugh! He hasn't told me what he wants you to do, but whatever it is you can't do it if you keep on falling out with one another."

"I'll try to remember that," she promised. They had re-emerged onto the lateral proper and she looked about in perplexity. "Why's it so quiet along here? There used to be all kinds of cottage industries, as I recall. Have the Narvellans closed them down?"

"Not exactly, but there's nobody to run them. Everyone works for the Narvellans," Lydion replied. "And as soon as I've handed you over to Tyvian, I must get back to work myself. It isn't fair on the rest of the team if I'm late."

"Do you still run the weathershield?"

"Sometimes, but my main job is keeping our power grid in repair. Not easy when the system's on permanent overload."

They continued walking.

"Lydion...." Laura ventured after a moment's silence, "this may be a stupid question, but if the Narvellans can't settle here permanently, why doesn't everyone just wait it out? Once their homeworlds are destroyed they'll have to move on."

"We considered that. What if they come here regardless? They might decide that five or ten years without children is an acceptable risk. What do you think *that* would do to us? Or worse still, they - or whatever controls them - might suddenly decide we were expendable. Every Narvellan could become part of a Ten!"

"Is this *your* worst case scenario, or Tralvar's?"

Lydion shrugged. "As I said, I'm not the imaginative type - but I don't fancy waiting to see who's right. Jarras, for instance, thinks they could mount a weapons attack. Today stun-cannon, tomorrow who knows?"

"They have stun-cannon?"

"Yes, for crowd control. We've had a few riots in our time." He halted outside the retracer lab. "Here we are."

"Would you mind explaining why I'm here?" asked Laura.

"Well now," said Lydion conspiratorially, "Tralvar didn't tell me that either, but as I've worked closely with Tyvian I think I can make an educated guess." He paused for dramatic effect. "To all intents and purposes, you're about to become a telepath!"

Chapter Four

When Laura stepped into the laboratory she immediately saw that it too had been subject to change. Previously, the interior had reminded her of a greenhouse; now it resembled a hydroponics farm. Tyvian's exotic flowers and strange trees were gone, to be replaced by row upon row of drab bushes in troughs. The harsh overhead lighting revealed, in addition to the nettle-like leaf structure, some vicious thorns at the base of each stem.

"Tyvian's contribution to the work effort," said Lydion at her elbow. "These are hrilffa. Their sap has industrial uses. Not very welcoming, are they?"

Laura concurred. "It used to be so mysterious in here!"

Just then Tyvian appeared from a side aisle. He looked a little older, a little more stooped, and considerably more worried. He wore a sleeveless black tunic, a waterproof apron and padded gloves. Laura, guiltily recalling how he had begged her not to remain on Earth, ran forward and hugged him.

"It's me, Tyvian! I'm back!"

His eyes misted over and he embraced her very lightly, as if he thought she'd break. "I'm so glad you're here, First Singer."

"She didn't greet *me* like that," Lydion said wistfully.

"You'd only have taken it as encouragement," Laura informed him.

"When did I ever need encouragement?" he countered. "Well, Laura, I must drag myself away - but only for the moment. I can't say it was ever my choice to get mixed up in Tralvar's scheme, whatever it turns out to be, but I've landed myself in it because of Eluthia.

So, be good until you see me again." He departed with a cheery smile. Tyvian gazed after him, frowning.

"I wonder if it's wise to involve him? He's too frivolous by half."

"I think we'll be glad of someone with a sense of humour," Laura said. "Well, Tyvian, don't keep me in suspense. How do you propose to make me telepathic?"

"Come with me." Tyvian laid aside his apron and gloves, and led the way to a shaded area at the back of the lab. There, just as Laura remembered it, was the retracer: a couch, a computer console and a large glass tank, currently empty. Close by was another tank with heat and humidity regulators attached. Within it, basking in the greenish-yellow light which simulated conditions on their planet, were several ugly plants with blistered leaves. These were prill, psi-conversant symbiotes whose unique characteristics made the transcription of memories possible. Laura bent forward and peered through the glass.

"Hello fellas," she said softly in English.

"They're parthenogenetic females," said Tyvian pedantically.

"I'm surprised the Narvellans let you keep all this," remarked Laura.

"There are those who deem it immoral," Tyvian admitted. "Nevertheless, they need it. Their repressed attitude to perception means they make excessive use of our relayists, and, not surprisingly, there have been many casualties amongst the fraternity. Burn-outs, identity crises, or plain overwork. The retracer is a good means of setting their personalities back on track." He made a minute adjustment to the temperature in the tank. "It would please the Narvellans if we were *all* like relayists. Self-disciplined, abstemious - qualities they admire."

Laura watched silently as he opened a panel at the base of the tank and took out a small, insulated box. He carried it carefully to a work surface; then, without warning, groped for the nearest chair and sat down heavily. Laura noticed he'd begun to shiver, although the laboratory was pleasantly warm. With an effort, he raised his head and met her concerned gaze.

"Don't be alarmed - I'm just tired. I'll rest here a moment."

"Have you been running this place singlehanded?" she asked sympathetically.

"I have an assistant, Drusa, who helps with the relayists. She's a healer from Corayn. And my students lend a hand in the evenings, after they've done their stint in the factories. Such boundless energy, the young."

"They do it because they care about you," Laura said.

"Nothing so altruistic," Tyvian answered with the ghost of a smile. "Anyone who does two jobs gets double rations. Now, where was I?"

"The box," said Laura.

"Oh, yes." He seemed to pull himself together. "What do you remember about your retrace, before it actually began?"

"Not much. I was strapped to the couch and everyone went off and left me."

"Precisely. In those days, the attendants had to stand well clear of the subject in case the prill focused on them instead. It was a great drawback. Instead of feeling relaxed and safe, the retracee would typically have feelings of isolation, confusion and fear. Then I realised that I could use the prill themselves as camouflage. Not the actual plant, which couldn't be removed from its habitat, but a seed. If the attendant carried one, the mature prill might ignore him and he'd be able to stay close to the person he was trying to help. I tried it on Drusa and a student volunteer, and it worked."

94

"Surely a seed can't be telepathic?"

"It isn't telepathy as such," Tyvian reminded her. "It's mimicry as a form of defence. A newly germinated seed is just as vulnerable as an adult prill - more so, perhaps - and it will adopt a disguise just as readily. Now do you see what Tralvar's hoping for? When I or Drusa wear the seed, its thought emissions reflect ours, and can hardly be sensed except by another prill. But since you have an enclosed consciousness, there will be only one output. Whether or not it will stand up to everyday scrutiny, we've yet to discover." He opened the little box gently. "I've prepared a nutrient base which should keep the seed alive for seven octals or so. Your body heat will help sustain it."

Laura peered over his shoulder. Inside the box was an even smaller container, lidless, about the size of a thumbnail. In it was a single yellow seed, embedded in a layer of gel.

"How do I wear it?" she asked in a whisper, as if worried it might hear. "Glue? Tape?"

"We considered those, but Tralvar came up with a better idea." From the desk drawer, Tyvian produced a metal disc on a chain.

"That's a scieshanar!" Laura was slightly indignant.

"Not exactly." Tyvian picked clumsily at the disc. Laura, remembering the dexterous care he'd always lavished on his plants, again wondered what ailed him.

"May I help?" she ventured. But as she spoke, the disc clicked open to form the two halves of a locket.

"Tralvar adapted this for you," Tyvian informed her. "Idenion's details are engraved on it, as you might expect. No-one will think it odd if you wear it continuously - some of our young women have taken to wearing the scieshanar as jewellery, much to the Narvellans' annoyance."

Laura's indignation swiftly vanished. "In that case I shall wear mine with pride."

Tyvian picked up a pair of long-handled tweezers and attempted to remove the seed from its tiny cocoon, but his hand was so unsteady that he gave up in frustration. "Chaos!" he muttered. "I don't want to damage it. I'll have to send for Drusa."

"No need," said Laura, gently confiscating the tweezers. Carefully she lifted the seed in its gel plug and transferred it to the locket. "There, how's that?"

"Thank you." Tyvian sounded a little defensive.

"Tyvian....if you're sick, shouldn't you tell someone?"

"It will pass." He reached across and closed the two halves of the locket together. Although there had been no ripple effect, Laura suspected the presence of theridolyte. There was simply no join to be seen.

"Not theridolyte," said Tyvian. "Those tiresome Directresses can spot it at forty paces. This is a stardrive seal."

"How do I open it?" she asked.

"You don't. If the seed dies, I will replace it." He pressed the locket, now a disc once more, into her hand as if vouchsafing a precious gift. "Put it on, First Singer. Wear it next to your skin."

Laura obeyed, removing her Greek pendant to make way for it. The little token, on its long chain, settled snugly between her breasts, and it belatedly occurred to her that scieshanar always had short chains. Tralvar again, she thought wryly. That man thinks of everything. What better way to keep a tiny prill warm?

"Well?" she asked Tyvian expectantly. "What's it doing?"

"Patience, Laura." Tyvian smiled indulgently. "The seed is somnolent at present. Give it time to become aware of you."

"How much time?"

"An astal, maybe longer." Tyvian picked up the medallion she'd laid on the desk. "I remember this. You wore it at your retrace. It's the Parthenon, isn't it, from which our Lyricon was copied? The rule of eight at work in your ancient land."

"Pardon?"

"These eight columns, revered by our architects. Surely you lived here long enough to notice the significance of eight? Our calendar, the scolia, the lattice - and most importantly, the aldacite crystals." He pointed to the retracer tank and the sconces at each corner. "These mirror the atomic layout of aldacite. Each ion has eight equidistant nearest neighbours arranged at the vertices of a cube. A pattern repeated innumerable times in each crystal, of course. And when the crystals resonate, it's...sheer beauty. I can't describe it."

"The music of the spheres?"

"Yes, that's a good analogy. We believe that universal resonance and transposal are linked." He handed the Athenian pendant back to Laura, who put it safely in her pocket.

"Do the Narvellans share these aesthetics?" she inquired.

"Of course not. That's why they never developed starflight," Tyvian said scornfully. "Always so preoccupied with five and its imperfections - like most of your Hellenes. *Eight* is the key. Sometimes, when I'm working with the retracer array, I feel I could step across infinity!"

Laura thought she understood what he meant. When she was being retraced she'd known an intense happiness, a feeling that everything had fallen into place. "Tyvian," she said suddenly, "would you do me a favour?"

"Name it."

"I was bringing some recorded material for Tralvar, but it was destroyed in transposal. If he gives his permission, could you retrace me performing the songs?"

"I'd be glad to, just as soon as I get some new crystals," Tyvian replied. "Only genuine ones will do."

"Are there any other kind?"

"You saw the factories, didn't you? The Narvellans found a way to synthesise aldacite. They had to, as there simply wouldn't have been enough to equip their spheres. All the industry in Alda Mexa is dedicated to the manufacture and refinement of these fakes." His lip curled. "To be fair, I can't tell the difference - and neither, apparently, can a stardrive. But the prill won't link with them."

"Were these fake crystals in the sphere Idenion stole? Only I thought the resonance sounded a bit off-key."

"They would almost certainly have been synthetic," Tyvian said. "But badly tuned or not, I don't see how your music discs could have sustained damage."

"The songs were on magnetic tape," explained Laura.

"Ah! Magnetic." Tyvian was suddenly enlightened. "I'm not an expert on space history, but I know that in the early days we had to redesign our logic systems. Nothing which employs a magnetic medium will survive transposal."

"I thought as much," said Laura dolefully. "The tapes were wiped clean. And my recording machine's at the bottom of the Lisir!"

"Nothing has been lost," Tyvian assured her. "The retracer will - " He paused, his face alight with awe and pleasure. "Laura, the seed! It's beginning to emit!"

Laura waited for his assessment, slightly uncomfortable under his rapt gaze. "Is it going to work?" she asked eventually.

"Wait: let it settle." Tyvian's reply was peremptory, and Laura had the distinct feeling she'd interrupted something.

"Tyvian, I really would like to know what's going on," she prompted after another long silence. Didn't he realise she was completely blind to the prill waveforms?

"All is well," he said at last. "Better than we dared hope. The seed has absorbed your basic self-concept and a hint of your regret at your lost music. But because you're not a sender, it's actually projecting very little. In fact, it's giving a perfect illusion of a shielded mind."

"I can't wait to tell Idenion!"

"I've already contacted him. He'll be here shortly, with Tralvar, and then you'll be free to go anywhere you like within the city. A word of warning - your prill is obviously more sensitive to despondent moods than happy ones. Try not to expose it to strong negative emotion, or it could sustain harm."

"I'll bear that in mind." Hearing a flitter land outside, Laura stood up to leave. "Will you let me know when your new crystals arrive?"

"Assuredly," Tyvian said gravely. "Doubtless Tralvar will want to know also. Once we've retraced your songs, I suspect you and I will be working together under less pleasant auspices."

"You mean at his behest?"

Tyvian bowed his head. "I fear it is inevitable. He will need the retracer."

Laura didn't like the sound of that. "We'll have to trust his judgement," she said uncertainly. "In the meantime, I want you to promise you'll look after yourself."

"Whatever you say, First Singer," the botanist replied wearily.

Just then the door flew open and Idenion hastened in, his step light and jubilant. "This is fantastic!" he enthused. "Tyvian, you've worked wonders. Come on, Laura - we're going to our home!"

He seized Laura's arm and hustled her outside. Looking back, she caught one last glimpse of Tyvian trudging slowly away down the aisle of thorny shrubs.

"He isn't well," she murmured.

"Discords, don't say that!" exclaimed Tralvar from the flitter. "He can't fold on us now. He's the only one who can operate that machine!"

"What about his assistant?"

"He won't let her near it," Tralvar said impatiently. "Now get in, both of you. I'm not discussing this in the street!"

Laura obeyed, still troubled. "You're planning to retrace a Narvellan, aren't you?" she accused when they were in flight.

"Can you think of a better way to find out what's got into them?" Tralvar queried in turn, somewhat defensively. "And before you say another word, I haven't a clue how we'd accomplish anything like that and still retain our sanity and freedom. But somehow, some way, the attempt has to be made."

"Tyvian's fears seem well justified," Laura remarked after a pause.

"It's his own fault for being so proprietorial," Tralvar declared. "If he'd shared his knowledge of the retracer, someone less vulnerable could have taken the risks."

"Lydion offered to learn," Idenion said. "He wouldn't show him."

"You see? The man's obsessive." Tralvar changed course abruptly, nearly capsizing his passengers. "We'll

100

have to hold a conference about our next step. Your role, Laura, is to back me up once I've decided on our tactics."

"Supposing I don't agree with what you decide?" asked Laura.

"You will. I'll convince you." Tralvar sounded utterly reasonable.

Laura wondered if the prill was radiating her uncertainty. It wasn't that she didn't have confidence in Tralvar - she was sure that his campaign, once established, would be sound. Rather, she doubted her ability to unify his flagging followers.

"Of course you can do it!" Idenion assured her. "You inspired us once before."

"So you keep saying." Laura made a wry face. "Life was a bit simpler in those days." Then, suddenly, she had an idea. "Maybe there *are* people out there we can rely on. Has anyone tried to reunite all our original group? Where are Floren, Jarras and Kyrin?"

"Jarras is the foreman of a sphere-building works in Treva," Tralvar answered. "He'd doubtless be willing to help, but his high-profile job might make that difficult. Kyrin is still at the akron, and could well be useful. I'm not sure where Floren is. We weren't on the best of terms when she left the city."

"Personal considerations apart, it would be easy enough to find her, wouldn't it? Don't the Narvellans keep tabs on everybody?"

"There's an archive," Idenion volunteered when Tralvar didn't reply.

"What? Don't tell me they've even tidied *that* up!"

"I think that particular task was beyond them," Idenion said with a chuckle. "They started another."

"Tralvar...?" Laura ventured. "Can we look for her?"

"*You* can look," he answered without much interest. "Get Idenion to take you there once you're acclimatised." He landed the flitter in a street of single-storey dwellings with a factory at one end. "I hate to waste even a few days, but it can't be helped. Out you get. Keep practising your diction. And Idenion, don't forget about her work placement."

Laura gazed after the departing flitter in a mixture of bewilderment and exasperation. "What did he mean, acclimatised?"

"The protections. Don't you remember what happened last time?"

"Oh, of course. The bloom. Well, I can't say it would have been much fun holding councils of war with my face all blotchy, but I'm surprised Tralvar's being so considerate."

"You may have more than the bloom to contend with," Idenion warned obliquely. "That's our house at the far end of the row, but before we go in, I *must* take you to see Dena. She still doesn't know where I disappeared to!"

He took a few steps in the direction of the factory, but Laura hung back. "Idenion, this isn't wise. Can't we wait till she comes out?"

"That won't be for several ilden. I want her to see that I'm safe." He started walking again. "Trust me. There's only one Narvellan, and there's no love lost between him and the elite."

He shoved hard on the ill-fitting wooden doors, which opened with a squeal. Laura winced at the noise, then followed him inside. The interior was dim and dirty, with little or no ventilation. Almost immediately, she began to feel uncomfortably hot. Idenion opened another double door into a large room with rows of identically equipped benches. About twenty girls, their hair tied back with scarves, were unenthusiastically at

102

work on aldacite crystals - poring over them with magnifiers, grinding, cutting, polishing. Their noisy chatter rose above a medley of whirring, tapping and scraping. Perception, Laura was reminded, had its limitations. It wasn't much use in a crowd.

At the far end of the room was an office area. Through the open door, Laura spied a sole Narvellan studying a computer display and making notes. Idenion was making his way toward a small curly-haired girl, probably the youngest present, seated at the edge of the third row. She was leaning on one elbow and talking animatedly to her neighbour, ignoring the pile of crystals in front of her.

"Honestly, it really is possible. You *can* induce sciesha. Malcor and I tried it - yes, of course you know Malcor. He takes all the packages to the monorail. Anyway, we aroused three streets - and we're going to do better next time!"

"Ailsi," said Idenion in her ear.

She whirled around, then treated him to a broad smile. "Well, look who it isn't! Who's been a naughty boy, then?"

"Ailsi, I need a quick word with Dena and I don't want Chisrin questioning Lisset. Do you think you could distract him for a moment?"

"Now *that's* something I enjoy." The girl turned her lively gaze on Laura, pausing expectantly. A moment later, her smile turned to a pout. "Well, *be* like that then."

"Hurry, Ailsi!" Idenion prompted, and she obligingly stood up and skipped toward the office.

Dena was at the far end of the second row, head bowed. At first it looked as if she was intent on her work, but when they drew closer Laura could see she was crying. Idenion reached her first and spoke to her gently. She raised her tearstained face to his.

"Oh, Idenion, it won't go right!" She held up a crystal for his inspection. "This is the third one I've ruined, and Chisrin's due to make his rounds in a moment. Where have you *been*, Idenion? Why did Tralvar - " Then she noticed Laura. Her eyes widened in amazement and she whispered something else which went unheard in the general din.

"Lisset - " Idenion stressed the name - "has come to live with us. I'll tell you everything tonight. I just wanted you to know all's well." And then, under cover of a hug, "Laura's here to help us. Cheer up!"

"Hoi, Idenion!" Chisrin was at the office door, having ejected Ailsi. "If you're back at work, get to the packing department. If you're not, clear out and stop blithering to your sister. She never meets her quota as it is."

Laura was already at the street exit. She leant on the door, thankful to be out of the heat, but after a moment began to feel she'd cooled down too much. The air suddenly seemed very thin, and she coughed.

"That prill disguise works well in company," Idenion said as he caught up with her. "Ailsi thought you were conversant."

"And now she thinks I've snubbed her."

"Oh, she'll have forgotten that by now." Idenion paused to scrutinise Laura as she coughed again. "Are you all right?"

"No, I don't think I am." A rivulet of cold sweat trickled down her back. "It can't be the protections already, surely? I had four clear days last time."

"You weren't a carrier then," Idenion pointed out. "Come on, let's get you inside."

By the time Dena arrived home Laura was running a high temperature. The traditional rash appeared, affecting not just her face but her arms and upper body. On the morrow, Idenion begged more time off to sit with her, and Dena fed her a herb and liman mixture which alleviated the symptoms a little. When she slept she had strange dreams of endless river journeys, or running through deserted streets pursued by the Ten. And once she thought she saw Tralvar at her bedside, regarding her with gentle concern - which, surely, must have been another dream.

The prill seed basked in the increased heat. Even in her troubled sleep Laura was protective of the scieshanar locket, grasping the chain to prevent it from snagging or tangling.

After three days her fever abated as suddenly as it had begun, leaving her weak but clear-headed. She studied her new home in detail for the first time: small, basic, yet kept scrupulously clean by Dena, who had tried to make it look attractive with brightly coloured cushions and pieces of drapery filched from the Lyricon. She was pleased to learn that Dena still found time to choreograph dances for the Lyricon stage.

"Do the Narvellans acknowledge you had a life there?" she asked.

"I'm still the nominal custodian," Dena replied with her customary earnestness. "Tralvar tried to have me released from factory work on the grounds that I was a scolia-sensitive, but the Narvellans decided I wasn't truly scolia because I'd never been in the Guild and couldn't play a musical instrument."

Laura experienced a momentary qualm. Her alter ego, Lisset, was meant to be of the scolia. "I hope no-one asks *me* to play," she said anxiously.

"Don't be concerned. My background was well known before the takeover - you'll find the Narvellans don't monitor our music that closely. But if it would make you feel safer I could ask Tralvar to give you some zirid lessons."

"No thank you," Laura said promptly. "I'll manage."

"That's what I thought you'd say," remarked Dena, and went to check on the progress of their evening meal. Laura followed.

"Was Tralvar here while I was ill?" she asked.

"Yes, briefly. He brought some extra liman for you. And he reprimanded Idenion for taking you into the factory." Dena smiled ruefully. "He thought my reaction might have given you away. Fortunately I was more concerned about the broken crystals."

"I thought it was a bit stupid too, going in there. Prill or no prill, I could have been recognised."

"There was no great risk of that," Dena assured her. "Those young women would only have been small children when you gave your concerts. There are no pictures of you, and the recordings were recycled." She set the table with neat precision. "To many people you are simply Clemoridys, the girl who disdained a poet's love."

Laura thought she detected a faint note of recrimination. "I shan't run off again," she said hastily. "I'm going to stay here and find a way to sort out this mess." Her own resolve surprised her.

"I know you'll succeed," said Dena steadfastly.

Laura, gazing at her child-like face, found it hard to believe that of the two of them, Dena was the elder. "You could be the same age as the factory girls," she opined. "You haven't changed a bit, despite everything."

Dena's wan smile reappeared. "Then I'd better not tell you how old I *feel*!"

Laura returned to a previous topic. "I'd love to revisit the Lyricon and see your dances being performed - but how risky is it? Surely the scolia would remember me!"

"The scolia line-up is renewed every year," Dena explained. "There are so many good musicians, but only one Lyricon. Do come - it's still a wonderful place.

Narvellans are excluded, thanks to Tralvar, so we can be ourselves there. Especially the scolia. It's the only venue in the city where they can form a lattice." She paused to taste the soup. "The Narvellans are mistrustful of the lattice. Idenion says they fear it."

"They don't want you beating them at their own game," remarked Laura, then sighed. "*One* thing will have changed about the Lyricon - I shan't be able to sing in it! That's going to be a problem, actually. It doesn't matter yet, but I shall have to exercise my voice somehow. Somewhere I won't be overheard."

"You should speak to Tralvar about it," suggested Dena. "He's the only one with unrestricted use of flitters and spheres. He'll be able to find you somewhere to practise."

Idenion came home from work a moment or two later. "I'm so glad you're well again," he said in relief at seeing Laura up and about. "I knew the adjustment would be rough on you, but I wasn't expecting anything quite so virulent. Tralvar was so right with that Myrmian swamp story, wasn't he?"

"Don't you just hate people who are right all the time?" Laura muttered, toying with her supper. She didn't have much of an appetite, but that was just as well. There wasn't much to eat.

"It's a rest day tomorrow," Idenion continued. "Shall we go to the new archive and try to locate Floren?"

"I'd like that," replied Laura, pleased at the prospect of some action. "And we'd better see about my work placement as well. We can't put it off any longer."

"I've a small confession to make," Idenion said. "In return for being given time off to look after you, I made an agreement with Chisrin."

"Oh?" queried Dena.

"Apparently," Idenion hurried on, "he's requested more outworkers and not been given any. So I said I'd put Laura's - I mean Lisset's - name forward. I hope that's all right, Laura? It will be for catering or laundering, or something of that nature."

"Just like being a housewife, in fact," Laura said with a wry grin. "Yes, I think I can cope."

When it was time to wash the dishes, they found the water had been turned off. And later, after dark, the electricity failed too. For a time they sat round their one solar tube, talking quietly and drinking wine from their meagre store; then Dena retired for the night, leaving Laura and Idenion to finish planning their day out. After a time the room grew cold, and Laura began to shiver. In unspoken agreement they went to bed, undressing by rushlight in their cramped sleeping quarters.

Laura couldn't remember much about the previous few days, but she did recall that she'd slept alone. "Where were *you*, Idenion?" she asked.

"On the floor, wrapped in a rug," he replied, hushing her apologies. "It tickled. Like this!"

Laura giggled and fought him playfully, then paused guiltily, looking toward the thin wooden wall that separated them from Dena's bedroom.

"She's sound asleep," Idenion reassured her. "She gets exhausted. Anyway, do you mind if she hears us?"

"I'd feel less self-conscious if she had a partner too," Laura admitted.

"She's never had a partner," Idenion said candidly.

"What? But I thought that she and Wemm..."

"No. I - er - chased him off."

"Why?"

"He wasn't serious. I wanted her first experience of unity to be better than that." Idenion sighed. "Only there never was any unity, and she still can't or won't take sciesha."

"Isn't it a bit unusual to be a virgin at her age?"

"Very." Idenion frowned into the near-darkness. "Maybe it's my fault. Maybe I've protected her too much, and it's become a way of life."

"Well," said Laura, climbing into bed, "let's hope she finds someone soon - someone who'll make her see what she's missing!"

***

The following morning Idenion contacted a relayist and sent a message to the akron, audaciously requesting transport to its portals. Much to Laura's surprise a flitter was sent, and Idenion recognised the lugubrious pilot who had escorted him to the shaming of Isylla.

"Tell your woman to hurry, First Poet," the Narvellan said brusquely. "I don't have all day!"

Laura finally emerged, looking the epitome of modesty in a freshly-pressed ylur smock. She'd tied back her hair in a snood, and put on a pair of comfortable boots that Dena had obtained for her. As she made her way to the flitter a noisy group of young people rounded the corner. They were carrying hampers and what appeared to be a change of clothing each.

"Idenion!" called someone. It was Ailsi, twined around her current partner Malcor. "It's a lovely morning, so we're off to Lake Holpen. I thought Dena might like to come with us, but she isn't here, is she?"

"She went to the Lyricon to rehearse her dancers," he replied. "Shouldn't you be with them?"

"I forgot," she said unapologetically. "Anyway, it doesn't matter if I miss a session or two - I pick things up quickly. See you tomorrow?"

"Just a moment, all of you." The Narvellan had alighted from the flitter. "I wish to inspect that food. You seem to have more than your ration."

"If you think we stole it, Laughing Boy, why not say so?" challenged Ailsi, glaring up at him. "I have

109

grain cakes, yesterday's and today's, and some home-made spreads."

"I have some wildflower wine," added another girl. "Try it. It's very potent."

"And here is resnay," said one of the boys, "which isn't on ration."

"Try the two together," suggested Ailsi. "Live a little."

"Insolence is unbecoming in a woman," said the Narvellan coldly, and re-entered his craft. The group, with much tittering, wandered off in the direction of the monorail. Laura wondered where Lake Holpen was, but didn't dare ask in case it was common knowledge. Having opted to remain silent, she dutifully boarded the flitter with Idenion.

With the factories not in operation a feeling of normality had returned to the city, as evidenced by the lively activities she witnessed on the short flight to the akron. Students were out in force, lounging in the bright sunlight. The bakeries had many customers and some of the cottage industries had re-opened.

She reflected, too, on the banter between Ailsi and their humourless escort. It had begun to dawn on her that the nature of the occupation wasn't quite as bleak as she'd imagined. The Celestrians still conducted their lives without inhibition or guilt. They were enthusiastic or extrovert or exuberant, or sometimes all three. They were irrepressible, and in this lay their strength.

"There's one thing you didn't notice," Idenion said when he and Laura had been deposited on the akron plaza.

"What?"

"The students are all in groups of four or less. Larger gatherings are instantly broken up by the Moderators."

"Lydion said there had been riots."

"Yes, several. Tralvar tries to discourage it. It doesn't get us anywhere. But people don't always see sense."

The bland bulk of the akron loomed in front of them. Laura had always thought its architecture dull, and she therefore assumed the Narvellans would feel thoroughly at home in it. She was right. Once through the main doors, she saw some blatant changes to the slightly faded grandeur of the entrance hall. Every level, gallery, door and corridor bristled with notices in both languages, and several sections had been roped off. Immediately beyond the portal was a reception area, a five-sided desk containing five computer terminals. Idenion, understandably subdued, stated his business to an operator and was given a card with the number of an interview room. Laura was given another.

"Are we supposed to split up?" she asked as they climbed the stairs.

"Yes, but we're not going to," Idenion replied grimly. "When facing an irate member of the elite it's useful to have some moral support!"

"What will you say about the sphere?"

"Sorry, or words to that effect. Let's hope an apology suffices. If it doesn't I'll be in for a pile of extra work."

Laura followed him down a corridor on the first floor. "Who are we seeing? Anyone you know?"

"This card doesn't say, but I imagine the door will have a name plate. It's just round this corner; we'll soon know who....oh, chaos, it's Narad!"

"I take it he's trouble?"

"He's the one who blacked my eye. In fact, he knocked me unconscious. And then Tralvar let him give me healing!" Idenion repressed a shudder, and Laura looked puzzled.

"Was that so bad? He must have regretted what he'd done."

"I'll explain later." Idenion resolutely pushed the heavy door open and they tiptoed inside.

Narad's desk was at the far end of the room, next to a window. There was another Narvellan with him, obviously a subordinate. Idenion couldn't follow all of their low, rapid speech, but gathered that one of the Directresses was giving them cause for concern.

"What are we to do, Lord Narad?" the assistant was asking. "Salvi insists on being allowed to prospect alone, without retinue. It's most unorthodox."

"Does she produce good results?"

"Sometimes, Lord Narad. I'm told her work is erratic."

"So it's possible she may be untrue to her vocation," Narad mused. "Where is she now?"

The other man reeled off co-ordinates.

"She won't find anyone to consort with in that wilderness," said Narad, seeming to lose interest. "Install a tracker in her sphere and note where she goes. Report your findings to me in five days." Then he waved his visitor away and turned to Idenion with a genuine if somewhat patronising smile.

"First Poet! When I heard you'd be reporting here, I decided I had to make myself available. Some of our assistant Governors wouldn't look too kindly on your misdemeanour." He spared Laura a perfunctory glance. "And is this your partner in unity?"

"I am Lisset," Laura said frostily.

"I thank you, Lord Narad, for hearing my case," Idenion added formally.

"It was the least I could do, after my rough handling of you the other day." Narad smiled again, as if the memory gave him pleasure. "Hardly an ideal way of

112

introducing myself. I'm a devoted admirer of your work."

"I try to please," Idenion said. Laura, seeing him grow ever more tense, moved forward and linked an arm through his. It was only a small gesture of support, but she felt happier once she'd made it. Deep down, she was more than a little intimidated by Narad. He was powerfully built, even by Earthly standards, and had the easy confidence of a man who was used to getting what he wanted. He continued to focus exclusively on Idenion.

"I've not been on Celestra long, but long enough to know that accommodating someone of your passionate nature necessitates a little easing of our laws from time to time. Why did you not approach *me* with your romantic problem? I'm sure I could have found a less draconian solution."

"For all I knew, you would have injured me again," Idenion retorted. "I have never sought preferential treatment, nor do I seek it now. Name my punishment and let me go."

"You misjudge me, First Poet." Narad's voice had a slight edge. "In my opinion, you have no case to answer. You returned the sphere undamaged, according to this report from Treva." He indicated some papers on his desk. "I therefore discharge you from this hearing - with one proviso."

"Which is?"

"Control your woman. She has obviously been running around the planet avoiding her work duty, and chaos only knows what she was doing on Myrma. Such behaviour is unseemly and will not be tolerated."

"Lisset will - " Idenion began.

"Let me speak for myself," Laura interrupted gently. "Unless Lord Narad thinks that is unseemly too?"

113

"You may speak," said Narad coolly.

"I regret my recent past," Laura stated carefully. "Idenion has persuaded me to settle down and support the work effort."

"Chisrin has requested her assistance," Idenion added.

"The impudence of Chisrin ap Tuin is well known to us," Narad remarked. He strode round the desk and tweaked the appointment card from Laura's hand. "According to this, you will be seeing Administrator Myrig tyl Plessit. You will accept whatever duties *he* assigns you."

"As you wish, Lord Narad."

Narad returned the card and, as he did so, noticed the telltale chain about her neck. "Let me see that."

Reluctantly she drew the medallion from inside her dress.

"You wear the scieshanar." Narad sounded faintly contemptuous. "Do you enjoy flaunting your promiscuity?"

Laura was expecting this question. "As First Poet, Idenion attracts many female followers. I wear the scieshanar to show that he's mine." She held Narad's gaze steadily.

"Yours for the moment," he conceded, and returned to his chair. "You may go. I will notify Myrig that you will be with him shortly."

Back in the corridor, Laura hastily tucked the scieshanar out of sight and leant on the door for a moment. She was trembling with nerves.

"Now do you understand why I want to stay out of his way?" Idenion asked softly.

"He desires you," she said disbelievingly.

"It's not as straightforward as that, but basically yes, he does." Idenion steered Laura back to the staircase and up one more flight.

"You said you'd explain."

"Not here. Outside."

They traversed the public gallery, twice being stopped and asked to show their cards.

"You'll find Myrig less autocratic," Idenion informed her. "I've had dealings with him - he arranged my transfer from clerical. It's his job to re-allocate workers to wherever the need is greatest."

"Anywhere on the planet?"

"That's right. He could, in theory, transfer you to another city-state; but don't worry, he won't. He's not a hardliner. One word of warning - watch your accent. Narad's a comparative newcomer, so he isn't familiar with all the regional variants. Myrig is!" Idenion paused outside another door. "Here we are. Ready?"

"Is my prill all right?"

"It's fine. It's reflecting your nervousness most convincingly."

"Then here I go." Laura drew a deep breath and walked in, halting in confusion when she found herself in a very small office with Myrig's desk close at hand. When he looked up, however, she felt somewhat reassured. His green eyes were frank and friendly, with laughter lines at the corners.

"So you're the stateless one?" he inquired pleasantly. "Sit down, don't be shy. Stop hovering in the background, Idenion. Come in and shut the door."

They seated themselves warily.

"Now, Lisset." Myrig folded his arms. "I gather that Chisrin ap Tuin has made a bid for your services."

"As an outworker," Idenion put in swiftly. "Lisset is of the scolia."

"I see." Myrig ignored his idling datascreen and instead consulted a vast ledger in front of him. "Yes, Chisrin has twice requested more outworkers. I'm afraid he does have a tendency to be presumptuous. I can't allow Lisset to work exclusively for him; that would be an uneconomic use of her labour." He turned back to Laura. "Can you use a sewing machine?"

"Er...yes," she replied, slightly taken aback. She hoped the machine he had in mind didn't differ too radically from its Earth counterpart.

"Good. We need someone to repair overalls. You'll be working for Chisrin and two other overseers in the area. The damaged garments will be brought to you but you'll be expected to return them yourself. I'll have a machine delivered this evening. Any questions?"

"Do I get a supply of ylur?" asked Laura.

"We will provide offcuts, and you'll have to make them last," Myrig answered. "What instrument do you play, Lisset?"

The sudden change of subject startled her. "The...the zirid," she stammered.

"I enjoy music. Perhaps I will hear you play one day." Myrig jotted something on Laura's card and closed the ledger, concluding the interview. "Try to keep her out of trouble, Idenion," he added. "She's now classified as a textile operative. Take her down to the suppliers, get some sleeve badges and make sure she displays one at all times."

"Yes, Administrator." Idenion took Laura's hand and drew her out of the office, a little too hastily.

The supply depot - for new overalls, protective clothing and other accessories - was in the basement, near the room where Tralvar had once lived. After waiting for nearly two astallan and having their cards inspected several times more, they received a pack of five cloth badges and were able to depart.

"I quite expected to see the detention suite back again," Laura said as they regained the fresh air.

116

"What? Do you think they'd let any of us sit around doing nothing?" Idenion responded in an attempt at cheerfulness.

Laura didn't speak again until they were well away from the akron. Then she said: "He was laughing at us."

"Myrig? It's just his way. He thought it was highly comical when I was downgraded."

"It's frightening, Idenion. More than the Ten, in a sense. The elite are so complacent, so in control."

"Not for much longer," he declared. "Now, we're going to stroll into the new Narvellan archive - next to our old one - and ask them to find Floren. Agreed?"

"It seems a bit cheeky," she said dubiously.

"It's a public facility," Idenion pointed out. "Since when did 'public' mean 'for Narvellans only'?"

She smiled at his boyish enthusiasm. "All right, let's do it."

It was a level walk to the archive, past the white-walled dwellings of Lateral Two. A succession of young people cut across the narrow intersections, obviously heading for the Lyricon. Several greeted Idenion and politely included Laura in the greeting. No one recognised her. Apart from the lack of acclaim, it was almost possible for her to believe she'd stepped back into the past. This quadrant of the city was exactly as she remembered it from her teens. But then she saw the gardens gone to seed and glimpsed a Moderator in the distance, and the illusion was broken.

"You haven't told me why Narad's so interested in you," she prompted.

"Narad would like me to be his neph-khet, his favoured one," Idenion said slowly. "It's an accepted practice for one of the elite to select a youth from a less privileged background, to sponsor and nurture him."

"Like the Greek eronemos?"

"Similar, although the Narvellan youth is adopted, not just befriended. He takes on his new family's line and title, but with the suffix neph-khet."

"And what's the sexual element?"

"There isn't supposed to be one - at least, not in the physical sense. But telepathic unity is permissible, even encouraged."

Laura gave a sarcastic laugh. "Oh, so it's your mind Narad's after!" The only level I can't compete on, her thoughts continued in spite of herself. Fortunately Idenion wasn't reading her.

"It's not funny, Laura. All the time he was healing me I could hear his vile whispering in my head: Be my neph-khet, I can protect you. No more factory work! Plenty of time to write."

"A tempting offer."

"Indeed. But it wouldn't have ended there, would it?"

Laura decided to be annoyed. "As if things aren't complicated enough! Well, if he makes another move he'll have *me* to contend with."

"You've already told him I'm yours," Idenion pointed out.

"Then he'd better remember it," Laura said darkly.

Between the original archive and the central registry stood a white rectangular building that had once been a school. Here the Narvellans had set up their census office. The information contained in the registry had been used as a basis for an exhaustive survey: every Celestrian on the planet, with the exception of a few "stateless ones", had been listed along with their work category and character profile.

"They keep a record of known troublemakers," Idenion explained.

"What sort of trouble?"

"Shirking, stealing food, seditious remarks. It's to ensure that dissidents don't get together. They can't stage a mass uprising if they're scattered across the planet."

"*Real* dissidents would have destroyed that information."

"How could they? It's in every city-state and discord only knows where else. Narvella Prime, most likely."

Laura halted outside the schoolhouse. "Idenion, do we *have* to go in here? Surely the registry will have Floren's details?"

"It's dedicated to ancestry," Idenion reminded her. "Addresses are incidental."

The old archive, dilapidated and creeper-covered, huddled in its corner plot. Somewhere in its recesses, thought Laura, there would almost certainly be documents and commentaries on her last visit, hidden only by the shambles within. She sincerely hoped there would be no more attempts to tidy it up.

Idenion breezed defiantly into the records office, and Laura followed more cautiously. It was immediately evident that the staff had no concerns about security. There were no reception committees, no passes, no formalities; just a brightly lit room with a vaulted ceiling, rows of data files and one solitary attendant.

"Welcome!" he greeted them politely. "We don't often see Celestrians in here - they never seem to make use of this excellent service. How may I help you?"

"I wish to trace a friend," Idenion replied. "She went to Kassi about seven years ago, and then we lost touch."

"And the name of your friend?"

"Floren."

The Narvellan consulted his database, scrolling pages swiftly and expertly. After a time he frowned and began to search more slowly. Finally he turned back to Idenion with the air of someone suspecting a prank.

"There's no such person."

"Of course there is," Idenion insisted.

"She used to be custodian of the Lyricon," Laura put in.

"She isn't listed. See for yourself." The clerk swivelled the screen to face them, and Idenion scrutinised the contents in growing bewilderment.

"I don't understand. I thought you had everyone's name on this system."

"Just a moment." The Narvellan began to examine a different list; Idenion and Laura waited impatiently. "Ah, I have it. Floren, deceased. She was living in Kest, on a fruit farm, and is survived by one adopted daughter, Nefyrra."

"Floren's *dead*?" echoed Laura, dismayed.

Idenion nudged her with his foot to warn her against over-reaction. "This is unfortunate news," he said, contriving to sound mildly irritated. "When did she die?"

"A little over a year ago."

"Then may we have details of her daughter? She will be able to apprise us of our friend's last days."

The Narvellan accessed the relevant file.

"Nefyrra. Biological mother, Elanir of Kassi. Father..." He paused in surprise. "...First Citizen Tralvar. At present, Nefyrra is an inventory assistant at a warehouse in Tivenne. She also studies with the scolia masterclass there."

Idenion murmured a conventional phrase of thanks, resisting the urge to leave the building at a run. To Laura, the walk to the exit seemed interminable. She'd suddenly begun to feel tired - doubtless due to stress, exertion and Celestra's thin air. A long hike home was out of the question. Aware of her discomfort, Idenion steered her toward the redundant archive and its garden, where she subsided thankfully onto an ancient bench.

"It never occurred to me that Floren might be dead," she said dispiritedly. "Why? From what? She wasn't old!"

"When she gave up the Lyricon, it did seem to me that she was giving up on life," Idenion reflected.

"No, no, Idenion, it wasn't like that at all! Do you remember my concert tour? Floren went missing for two days when we were in Kassi and wouldn't tell anyone where she'd been. I think she went to see Elanir. She left the Lyricon because she'd already decided to adopt Tralvar's child and raise her."

"But why didn't she tell Tralvar what she was doing? And why didn't she bring Nefyrra back to Alda Mexa?"

"Maybe Elanir didn't want that," Laura suggested. "Well, I think our task just got a little harder. I'd hoped Floren might have been able to placate Tralvar, stop him being so spiky. Now it looks as though we're stuck with his bad moods."

"He's going to be upset about Floren," Idenion predicted. "So's Dena. You'd think someone could have let the Lyricon staff know, at least."

"I feel I should do something in memory of her," Laura said quietly. "But that isn't the Celestrian way, is it?"

Idenion gazed across the overgrown garden toward a young couple lying semi-naked in the grass. "It's said that when we hear about a death, we should celebrate life."

"As *they* are?" Laura inquired.

"Yes, my Clemoridys. But not here. Any moment now, a Moderator will spot those two and treat us all to a lecture on public morality."

"Then we'd better move," Laura said wearily.

"We don't have to walk far," Idenion reassured her. "We could spend the afternoon at the Lyricon and go home when Dena does. She's never been stranded yet!"

They took a leisurely stroll up the nearest of many paths to the theatre, Laura still a little dubious about returning to her old haunt.

"Are you *sure* I won't be recognised?" she fretted. "What if Cyphos the stonemason's there, or Melor...?"

"Cyphos and many other able-bodied men are in Treva, doing heavy assembly work. And Melor hardly ever leaves Tivenne these days. He still directs the masterclass, but his eyesight is failing. Telsa looks after him."

At last they emerged onto Lateral One - a modest square dominated by the Lyricon's magnificent portico. Eight elegant pillars, which Tyvian had so recently praised, concealed a huge amphitheatre set into the far side of the hill.

"I'd forgotten how beautiful this was," Laura said wistfully.

"You'll sing here again one day," Idenion promised.

They found Dena and several of her dance troupe in the canteen. They'd finished rehearsing for the day and given the scolia full use of the stage. Lunch had just been served - the ubiquitous grain cakes and a fish salad. The dancers nibbled daintily at their portions. Laura tried not to bolt hers.

Dena's unhappiness at Floren's death was far outweighed by her amazement over Nefyrra's parentage and upbringing. "But she's *here*!" she exclaimed. "It's her second visit. Melor sent three of his pupils to perform with the Lyricon scolia - it's good experience for them. If we hurry, we'll hear them play."

"Who's living in the apartments?" asked Laura as they passed the elevators. "The elite, I suppose."

"Tralvar saved *all* of the Lyricon for the people. I'm allowing the scolia to use the rooms. They keep an eye on things for me."

"Where's the custodian's key? I thought you'd be wearing it while you were here."

"It's on a hook by the campanile door," Dena replied. "No one will remove it - they know its symbolism. It will remain there until I'm able to take up residence again."

"Whenever that is," Laura muttered as they crossed the auditorium. Thereafter she was obliged to concentrate as she negotiated seated figures, cushions and pitchers of wine dotted about on the terraces. She had no trouble identifying Nefyrra amongst the eight players onstage. She was lanky and dark-haired, with Tralvar's aquiline features. She was playing the bass strelsis, which surprised Laura somewhat. The two smaller strelsi resembled harps, with many strings over a lozenge-shaped frame. The bass strelsis was heavy and unwieldy, with only eight strings which could be bowed or plucked.

"She likes a challenge," Dena explained.

Laura could hear nothing wrong in the music, a typically light piece with short delicate phrases; but Idenion had begun to frown.

"I may be tone-deaf but I can read a lattice," he said to Dena. "Nefyrra's just a little out, isn't she? Just now and again?"

"Yes," said Dena, "and now I know whose daughter she is, her difficulty makes more sense. It's his legacy. But she'll overcome it - she's determined to."

When the piece was over, Nefyrra exchanged the bulky strelsis for a classic one and began to play a solo. Suddenly she was transformed. Her hands drew rippling arpeggios from the clustered strings - a beautiful cascading melody representing a waterfall. As she

123

performed she swayed like a tall meadow-flower, completely at one with her instrument and oblivious to her audience. She finished to scattered applause.

Dena stepped forward. "You're truly your father's daughter," she said warmly. "I must let him know you're here."

Nefyrra's reaction was startling. "Oh, please!" she cried shrilly. "Please don't tell him. I don't want to see him!"

"You mustn't be scared of Tralvar's reputation," Dena said reassuringly. "He loves music, and I'm sure he'll be very proud of you."

"You don't understand." Nefyrra's thin intense face burned with suppressed anger. "I don't want to meet him, ever. Not after what he did to Floren."

"What do you mean?" asked Idenion in bewilderment; but just then a relayist's communication swept over the whole gathering, and Nefyrra took the opportunity to run off. The relayist was Kyrin - his mental autograph was unmistakable.

+Attention all citizens. Please make your way to the nearest radio receiver as quickly as you can. An important announcement from Governor Axmiol will follow in three astallen+

Idenion swiftly passed the message on to Laura.

"It was Kyrin? All the way from the akron?"

"It certainly was," Idenion confirmed. "He's quite amazing."

"Nobody seems to be taking much notice," said Laura, looking around.

"Why should they?" Dena sounded bored. "It'll only be more propaganda. Or maybe they're cutting our rations again."

"I'm not so sure," said Idenion thoughtfully. "There was an odd overtone in that relay. Kyrin may have been under pressure. I think we'd better go over to the kitchens and listen from there."

They went, Dena still puzzling over Nefyrra's behaviour. "I suppose she thinks Tralvar jilted Floren, and not the other way about. I'll have a word with her. Oh, I nearly forgot - Lydion was here earlier. He says Tyvian's got the new crystals."

"Good. Now I can have my songs retraced," smiled Laura.

About thirty people, mostly students, crowded round the radio to hear what Axmiol had to say. Significantly, there was no flurry of introduction.

"Attend, Celestrians. This is your Governor speaking."

Someone made a rude noise and was hushed by the other listeners.

"It is with the utmost regret that I deliver this news. In my last broadcast, I expressed concern that various acts of disobedience and disruption in the workplace were endangering our survival project. Events which took place this morning have confirmed my belief that a far more disciplined approach is needed to curb these trends.

"Today, a construction works at Treva declared an all-out strike. This factory has previously shown a tendency toward militant action, despite the attempts of my staff and your First Citizen to allay the problem."

"Why weren't they on holiday, like us?" whispered Laura.

"A good question," Idenion whispered back.

"Such action," continued Axmiol, "is a betrayal of the Narvellan Protectorate, and the participants will be dealt with accordingly. Every individual who took part in the strike will be deported to Narvella Four, where they will continue to serve the Protectorate under the strictest supervision. The culprits are already under arrest and the deportation will take place when the next consignment of spheres is ready, one octal from today." Axmiol paused, then went on inexorably:

"While the arrests were being made, the ringleader Cyphos attacked my officers. With great reluctance, it was decided to make an example of this man; and at noon today, Cyphos was executed."

The sudden outcry in the room convinced Laura that she'd heard aright. Idenion's fingers bit painfully into her arm.

Axmiol uttered one final warning about sedition before the radio launched into the Narvellan national anthem. It was swiftly turned off, and everyone began talking at once.

"What now?" Laura asked breathlessly.

"More uprisings, if we're not careful," Idenion said. "Tralvar will have to calm everybody down. He needs relative peace if he's to achieve anything at all." He looked round the room at the collection of youthful, angry faces. "Let's hope it isn't too late."

Chapter Five

Tralvar was furious. "Fools! Idiots!" he raged. "I told them, over and over, that they mustn't go on strike. Why does no-one ever listen to me?"

Jarras waited for the outburst to subside.

"I went straight up to the akron to protest," Tralvar continued, "and do you know what that walking glacier Axmiol said? Come to dinner. That'll look well, won't it? Cyphos dead, forty people arrested, and the First Citizen being wined and dined by the enemy."

"They don't have any more food than we do," Jarras offered.

"Figure of speech," Tralvar said sourly. "All right, tell me all about this debacle. That's why you came here, isn't it?"

"I thought you'd want to know."

Tralvar sighed and forced himself to stop pacing. "Yes, yes, of course I do. I can't present a case to Axmiol until I have the full story."

"I saw it all from my upstairs window," began Jarras. "When they heard they were going to lose their rest day yet again, Cyphos and about twelve others formed a barricade outside the factory and stopped the other workers from entering. They told them to go home and report for work at the usual time the following day. The trouble was, hardly any of them went. Some wanted to show solidarity with the men, and the rest just stood around waiting to see what would happen. Cyphos kept telling them to disperse, but they wouldn't.

"Then half a dozen Moderators arrived with a stun-cannon. They couldn't fire at the protestors because the crowd was in the way, so they fired into the crowd. Several of them fell and the rest panicked. The Moderators had begun to advance, lashing out indiscriminately as usual. Cyphos saw one beating up a woman and ran across to help her. He grabbed the Moderator and threw him against a wall, then overturned the stun-cannon. That was all he had time to do before he was overpowered and dragged off. His friends gave themselves up.

"After that, the mass arrests started. Everyone thought Cyphos would be reduced, and we were puzzled - and a bit hopeful - when it didn't happen. And then, long after all the workers had been marched off, some poor terrified relayist told us to close off our perception."

"The Ten," murmured Tralvar bleakly.

"We couldn't believe it," Jarras went on. "They wouldn't do that, people kept saying. Not to one of us. And then two of the Moderators brought Cyphos' body and dumped it outside the factory. It was two ilden before anyone dared claim it."

Tralvar perceived, through the burning-glass of Jarras' helpless anger, images of the fateful confrontation: the controlled fury of the Moderators, the lightning-flash of the stun-cannon, and the agonised face of Cyphos' wife. And he knew that Jarras had been the first to approach the murdered man, unwilling to draw attention to himself but unable to leave his dead colleague lying in the street. Fearfully he had turned him over, expecting to see signs of pain or terror. There were none.

"I almost thought he'd wake up," Jarras concluded shakily. "So did Tatra. I had to drag her off him."

"This is Axmiol's new regime," Tralvar said bitterly. "He warned us all. Well, I'll try to intercede for the prisoners, but I think I'll be wasting my time. I'd be better occupied making a broadcast of my own and telling everyone there's to be no more industrial action. It solves nothing."

"Then what will?" Jarras inquired sharply.

"Discords, Jarras!" Tralvar ran agitated fingers through his unruly hair. "I know it looks as though I've caved in before the Narvellans, but believe me, I haven't. I wasn't going to confide in you yet, but I'm planning a resistance. Laura's going to co-ordinate it. As you've just seen, nobody does what I tell them - so she'll be my spokeswoman. They'll obey *her*. She's already got Tyvian and Lydion eating out of her hand."

"Laura's *here*? How?" Jarras paused, realising. "The stolen sphere. Of course."

"So what I want you to do," Tralvar pursued, "is instruct all your militant pals to keep their heads down and keep working. You're not to tell them anything, naturally - just say you're convinced I'm up to something. Say it's intuition, based on long association with me. Can you persuade them?"

"I'll try."

"You'll have to do more than try."

"I'll do it," Jarras replied more positively.

"Good. I knew I could count on your commonsense," Tralvar said briskly. "Now I'd better find that ridiculous uniform of mine, and go and dance attendance on Axmiol. While I'm up there I'll look in on Rinyi. This may be my only chance to see him - he's going to Tafret Academy for rehabilitation. Kyrin and Alcis have worked wonders, apparently, but he needs specialist care."

"At least he's alive," Jarras remarked.

"Indeed," said Tralvar reflectively. "Please forgive my bad temper, Jarras. I do appreciate your being here, believe it or not. How long are you going to be in Alda Mexa?"

"About five days. I'll be working at the spaceport."

"Then we'll have time for another talk later. Sorry to cut this short, but I daren't keep Axmiol waiting."

Jarras rose to leave, then turned back. "Tralvar...where *is* Laura?"

Tralvar paused to consider the question. "Keeping her head down," he said at last.

***

After the events in Treva, no one at the Lyricon wanted to go home. A ferocious debate ensued, halted only by an increasing chill in the air and a lack of power to run the weather-shield.

It was early evening when Dena, Idenion and Laura arrived back at their house to discover a mysterious crate outside. It was the sewing machine, which Laura had temporarily forgotten about. They dragged it indoors and assembled it, Laura exclaiming at the familiarity of its design. But perhaps she shouldn't have been surprised, as its appearance was dictated by its function. It was, of course, hand-operated, and its elegant lines and dainty accessories pronounced it Celestrian rather than Narvellan.

"Yes, it's one of ours," Dena confirmed. "An obsolete model. We had to get them out of storage when the power cuts started."

"I was looking forward to melting a few seams together," Laura said ruefully, unpacking several reels of ylur thread and a bag of buttons.

"That only works with firi," Dena reminded her.

Laura was still examining the machine. "Could you show me how to thread this?"

"What's your hurry? You don't have anything to sew."

"Not yet, but I noticed the factory lights were on. Do you think anyone would object if I went in and looked for some mending?"

"It's only Chisrin. He often works during our rest days," Idenion said.

130

"I don't suppose he'd mind being disturbed," Dena added. "But try not to get into conversation with him."

"My accent again?"

"Not only that. Chisrin isn't one of the elite, so he doesn't necessarily follow their protocols. If he can't understand you he may try to read you."

"I'll go with you and keep him occupied," Idenion volunteered. "Provided you've a good reason for picking up your quota ahead of schedule."

Laura wiped a smudge of machine oil from her finger. "As I'm an outworker, I don't have to follow the factory timetable - right? Just as long as I get the work done. I want to make a good start so I can have time off before the next rest day - firstly to be retraced and secondly to fit in some singing practice."

"You still need to get Tralvar's approval on both counts," said Dena.

"That's the difficult part." Laura gave a thin smile. "Especially after this morning."

"I'll speak to him," Idenion promised. "It's simply a case of choosing the right moment. He'll understand the need to sustain your voice, and as for the retrace, he's too fond of music to say no. Now let's go and fetch these overalls before Chisrin locks up."

They reached the factory to find the lights still on and the door jammed shut. Idenion threw his entire weight against it as before. It finally grated open, the noise echoing through the silent corridors.

"He must have heard that," Laura said.

"He isn't alone," Idenion replied. "There are more Narvellans with him."

Laura stopped in her tracks. "Maybe we shouldn't stay."

"It will only be a work-related matter," Idenion reassured her. "No-one's going to discuss state secrets with Chisrin. He's non-elite, remember?"

"Can you read what they're saying?"

"No, they're shielded. But if I can just get through one more door without bringing the house down I'll be able to *hear* them."

They peeped gingerly into the girls' workshop. It was dark and deserted, but at the far end light streamed in from Chisrin's office. His two visitors were facing him across a paper-strewn desk. Chisrin's peevish words were loud in the silence:

"How am I supposed to know why she goes off on her own? Try asking her."

"We don't feel that's appropriate," said one of the men.

"We thought you might have privileged knowledge," said the other, snidely.

"I may not have much regard for tradition," Chisrin retorted, "but I have the utmost reverence for Directresses and their order. I'm a geologist, remember? I too study the land. I haven't spoken with Salvi except in the company of her retinue."

"And you have no complaints about her work?"

"None so far."

Laura, unable to comprehend their exchange, took the opportunity to make a covert study of Chisrin. She'd seen him once already, but had been too intent on escape to spare him more than a glance. He certainly differed from the bland, chilly elite. Luxuriant dark hair worn long in a plait, a strong handsome face, and muscular arms that looked as if they were capable of much more than pushing pieces of paper about. He eyed his interrogators with a healthy belligerence.

"He seems so normal!" she whispered. "Is he like the others?"

"Of course he is!" Idenion whispered back. "Look at the time he spends here. He's got no life of his own."

132

"You there!" Chisrin had risen to his feet, and all three Narvellans were now staring in their direction. They could, of course, see every detail of the darkened room.

"It's only us," Idenion said unnecessarily.

"What in chaos are you doing here, Idenion?" demanded Chisrin irritably.

"I've brought Lisset to collect her sewing," Idenion replied. Adding, daringly: "You were supposed to deliver it today."

"Was I? I've been busy." Chisrin was distracted enough to believe him. "It's by the back wall. Help yourselves."

One of the overhead lights flicked on, illuminating a rush basket full of crumpled overalls. Taking a handle each, they manoeuvred it through the door.

"Thank you!" called Laura as they went out. Chisrin didn't reply. In fact, he'd taken no notice of her at all. She was slightly annoyed about that.

"So you've fallen for him?" Idenion teased.

"He's quite attractive," Laura admitted.

"Ailsi would agree with you. Well, sorry to throw cold water on your fantasy, but he's lifebonded. And Narvellans take their marriages very seriously."

"Shame," laughed Laura, pulling a face. "In that case, I'll just have to make do with you!"

***

"First Citizen! You're going the wrong way!"

Tralvar paused at the foot of the akron stair and turned to face the anxious desk clerk. "I know this place like the back of my hand," he said coldly, "and I can assure you I know exactly where I'm going."

"But," stammered the clerk, "my Lord Axmiol is awaiting you in his chambers, on *this* floor."

"Then he'll have to wait a little longer," returned Tralvar, already halfway up the stairs.

133

Rinyi had occupied a small apartment near Grevin's suite, but had been ejected from it when his affair with Isylla was discovered. Since the attack by the Five, only a day after he'd forfeited his lodging, he'd shared Kyrin's quarters on the top floor. It was cramped and uncomfortable for them both, but Kyrin had been convinced that the only way to restore Rinyi's faculties was to throw him straight back into the business of relaying. To some extent Kyrin had been right, but although Rinyi had made good progress there was little likelihood of a full recovery. Tralvar had been asking to see him for the past seven days, but Kyrin, fearful of a relapse, had denied his request. Only now, on the eve of Rinyi's departure, had he bowed to the inevitable and given permission for one short visit.

Tralvar wasn't surprised to find Kyrin waiting at the top of the stairs, looking fraught and anxious. "You're late," the relayist said accusingly.

"Sorry. I mislaid my uniform. Since Kevis retired it's difficult to keep track of things."

"A pity you managed to unearth it," remarked Kyrin, eyeing the gaudy tunic with distaste. "Rinyi won't take kindly to seeing it again. He'll associate it with his punishment."

"I'll try and put him at his ease," Tralvar promised. "Now listen, Kyrin - I know this will be difficult for you, but you *have* to let me talk to him alone. If you're there, he'll lose focus. He'll see you're worried and that'll worry *him*."

Kyrin hesitated.

"Believe me, if there was any way this could be avoided I wouldn't be asking at all. This meeting is very, very necessary. He may have vital information in that poor damaged head."

Kyrin paused at his apartment door. "One astal only," he warned.

Rinyi was sitting by the window. His eyes were fixed dreamily on something only he could see, and he rocked gently back and forth. When Tralvar called his name he leapt up in a panic.

"Tralvar! I - I mean, First Citizen. Have I done something I shouldn't?" Then he burst into tears.

Tralvar glanced guiltily at the closed door, expecting an irate Kyrin to come charging through it; but the senior relayist honoured his promise and remained outside, his perception closed off. With brisk efficiency Tralvar steered Rinyi back into the chair, ordered him to blow his nose and proffered a drink of resnay from a tiny flask. Obediently Rinyi swallowed some of the strong liquor, and after a moment or two began to calm down.

"That's better," said Tralvar, with what he hoped was an encouraging smile. "I'm not angry with you - I've come to see how you are. Kyrin tells me you're much improved."

"He lets me relay easy things," Rinyi confided, "but sometimes it goes a bit wrong. That's why I'm going to Tafret."

"Before you go, I have an important question for you," Tralvar continued carefully. "Do you think you can answer it? It's about Isylla."

"She's kind," Rinyi said wistfully. "She comes to see me."

"No, that's Alcis," Tralvar corrected him patiently. "She's a relayist too. Isylla is Narvellan, and you worked for her. I'm sure you remember."

"So sad."

"Try not to be. We're all fond of you and want you to get well."

"No, not me!" Rinyi laboured to explain. "Isylla. *She* was sad."

So he *does* remember, thought Tralvar. I wonder how much? "Keep thinking about Isylla," he instructed. "Think of your time in unity. Did you ever see anything strange in her mind - anything that shouldn't have been there?"

"I didn't see her mind. I wish I had."

"But you made love to her," Tralvar persisted.

"Not total unity." Rinyi, briefly lucid, spoke clearly and positively. "She wouldn't do it. Highborn women don't, you see. She thought it was a sin." He smiled apologetically. "But yes, we often made love. We used to sneak away when Grevin was bonding with his neph-khet."

"I don't follow." Tralvar was genuinely puzzled, allowing Rinyi to puff up with self-importance.

"Oh, First Citizen! Don't you know *anything*? The elite don't have total unity with their wives but with their favoured young men. Sijek was Grevin's lover. Now he's Axmiol's."

"Sijek?"

"They keep him in the background, but *you've* seen him. On the day of...of...*that* day. He gave something to Idenion."

Tralvar recollected the boy with the microphone. "And you believe he's Axmiol's lover?"

"He is. Axmiol adopted him, took him from Grevin. Otherwise, he'd have shared Grevin's disgrace. He is now called Sijek tyl Thuuvin neph-khet." Rinyi pronounced the name carefully, pleased at having got it right. "I told Isylla that her mind was as good as Sijek's, that our unity could be wonderful if she'd only try. Maybe she wouldn't have been as unhappy if..." His attention drifted. "I used to say things to make her laugh. I was quite good at that. But they've taken it all. If only I could remember just a little..." He stared into vacancy, wrinkling his brow and appearing to forget he

136

had company. Tralvar, his expression unreadable, left him to his contemplations and went to find Kyrin.

"You didn't get the answers you wanted," the relayist observed.

"I had to try," Tralvar answered wearily. "Does the Academy really hope to improve him?"

"If they can stabilise his concentration, yes," Kyrin replied. "I doubt if he'll ever he able to cope with the demands of Alda Mexa, but he might be able to handle a provincial post one day."

Tralvar deliberated a moment before speaking again. "There *will* be a reckoning," he said eventually. "Can I rely on your help?"

Kyrin's steady gaze didn't waver. "Of course."

Tralvar thanked him and left, heading back downstairs to confront Axmiol. The visit to Rinyi had been a disappointing waste of time. He'd been certain that the hapless young relayist would corroborate Lydion's story, even add to it; but he hadn't bargained on Isylla's inhibitions. Kyrin's steadfastness was the only bright spot in a day that had been riddled with disaster. Automatically his fingers closed around the flask of resnay, but he refrained from drinking any. He'd doubtless have greater need of it later.

Axmiol's stateroom had once been the audience hall - the same room where Tralvar, long ago, had awaited his recalcitrant public. Its unchanged appearance prompted some unwelcome memories of despondency.

"At long last, First Citizen!" Axmiol rose from a high-backed dining chair, a glass of wine in his hand. Another place setting, and another brimming glass, awaited further down the table. "So you've been visiting Rinyi? A regrettable case, but brought about by his own weakness. A dedicated relayist should always be able to resist the blandishments of a woman."

"You blame Isylla?"

"Absolutely. A bored, spoilt elite-wife toying with a youth in her employ. Always beware women, my friend - they were only put in the universe to cause trouble. But I don't have to convince *you* of that, do I? Your unmarried state is as exemplary as it is rare."

An underling, obsequiously silent, brought in their meal: fish soup, followed by vegetables baked in spices. Tralvar ignored the wine and requested water, which was also delivered in silence. Once or twice he thought he detected a hint of disdain in the prowling Narvellan's eyes, and surreptitiously tried to smooth out his crumpled uniform.

"You really should find another manservant, Tralvar," said Axmiol pleasantly. "Appearances matter. You are, after all, the representative of your people."

"I'm not here to socialise," Tralvar retorted. "Send your man away and let us address ourselves to the matter of Cyphos and his friends."

The temperature in the room seemed to drop a few notches, but Axmiol duly issued a brief order to the waiter, who deposited a bowl of fruit and left with a final disparaging glance at Tralvar.

"You now have my undivided attention," Axmiol said, his eyes palely luminous in the growing twilight.

"I appreciate it. Just before we begin..." Tralvar strolled to the side of the room and switched on the chandelier above the table. Axmiol shielded his eyes for a moment as it blazed into life.

"That's better," said Tralvar, resuming his seat. "I like to see who I'm arguing with."

Axmiol said nothing, but subjected him to a reptilian stare.

Tralvar was one of the few people on the planet who could meet that look. Axmiol possessed a daunting intellect but, unlike Alendis, he had no charisma. Alendis had studied his opponents and targeted their

138

individual weaknesses; Axmiol treated everyone with the same chilly remoteness. Therefore, although Tralvar disliked him, he was not in awe of him.

"My eyewitness in Treva," he began, "says that Cyphos did nothing more than give one of your men a push and topple a stun-cannon off its wheels. Since when did a minor scuffle become punishable by death?"

"Hitherto, all instances of civil unrest were dealt with by the Five," Axmiol replied in measured, almost disinterested tones. "This was a ruling instituted by Grevin, which has now been rescinded along with other penalties I considered too lenient. Henceforth, perpetrators of public disorder will find themselves facing execution."

"This is totally unjustifiable," Tralvar protested.

"Not at all. Whenever a citizen is reduced it takes at least one other citizen to look after him. That is inefficient in terms of the work effort."

"There's no need to impose *either* penalty," Tralvar declared. "If you must punish those with legitimate grievances, a withdrawal of privileges would be sufficient."

"And where would that get me?" Axmiol seemed slightly amused at the suggestion. "Your people would simply do as they pleased. I have schedules to be met, quotas to fulfil - and they are not *being* fulfilled. The situation in Treva concerns me greatly. If I take no remedial action I will be failing my homeworld."

"And I would be failing mine if I didn't demand the release of the Trevan workers."

"Your protest was noted this afternoon," said Axmiol, looking irritated. "You already know my attitude toward strikes."

"What did you expect them to do?" asked Tralvar heatedly. "They'd had their rest day cancelled three octals running and the working day extended by two ilden."

"Because three other factories were on short time, awaiting theridolyte shells," Axmiol reiterated.

"Which won't be forthcoming if you deport everyone," Tralvar pointed out.

"Other workers will be drafted in."

"Then at least don't expect them to follow such a punishing regime. Shorten the number of ilden and reinstate the rest day."

"I will consider it," Axmiol stated magnanimously. He fixed his gaze on the fruit bowl, and after a moment a single pilif floated into the air and drifted across to his hand.

Tralvar was not impressed. He had yet to see a useful demonstration of telekinesis and was well aware of the effort it took. Picking up a pilif stone, he flicked it at the chandelier. It rebounded, ricocheted off the wall, clipped a shelf and landed neatly in an ornamental urn by the door - a feat he'd perfected during the long afternoons when nobody had sought an audience with him.

Axmiol raised his eyebrows. "And how long did it take you to master that?"

"About as long as it took you to learn the trick with the fruit," Tralvar replied indifferently.

"Perhaps we should both be less concerned with trivia."

"Perhaps," Tralvar agreed. "May I appeal to you one last time not to exile the prisoners?"

"It's out of my hands now." Axmiol sounded truthful. "I don't have complete autonomy in the matter."

"They'll die out there!"

"That is not our intention. Their health will be supervised; and if - *if* their successors perform their

140

duties well and commit no nuisance, the Protectorate may waive the sentence."

Tralvar knew this was the best offer he'd get. It was also a double-edged one: any more disruption from Treva and things would go badly with the exiles. "I take it our business is concluded?"

"Not quite. I wish to talk with you about Scapirion."

Scapirion. Tralvar permitted himself a grim little smile. He could imagine how galling it was for the Narvellans to be defied by an entire city-state, and the Scapirians were doing just that. Located near the south pole and made habitable by hot springs, Scapirion had practised isolationism for many years. It was a strange inverse city, with streets extending down into caverns and a geodesic dome protecting the upper laterals from the climate. When the Narvellans had staged their coup, Scapirion had closed its dome, barricaded its doors and let the weather do the rest. It could not have withstood a determined invasion, but the Narvellans had neither the time nor the resources to mount one - so Grevin had always maintained.

"If Scapirion would only co-operate, we could meet our production targets easily," Axmiol was saying.

"Scapirion doesn't recognise my authority," Tralvar informed him. "I was never *their* First Citizen."

"Did you know they were capable of being self-sufficient?"

"Yes. Before they ceased trading, they were only importing luxury goods. They can obviously do without those."

"What were they exporting?"

"Nothing much," Tralvar said candidly. Not since I had the foresight to open a resnay distillery at Ninka, he added to himself.

"Are they in radio contact with anyone?" asked Axmiol; but before Tralvar could reply, a startling scream echoed through the outer halls, followed by rapid footfalls and raised voices. An instant later Axmiol's manservant burst into the stateroom, all decorum forgotten.

"Another madness victim, Lord. Here, in the akron!"

Axmiol thrust the man aside and hastened to the door. Tralvar followed, just in time to see a panic-stricken figure hurtle past and collide with Sijek, who had unwisely left his rooms and walked straight into the fugitive's path. Immediately Axmiol was at the boy's side, helping him to his feet.

"Sijek! Sret enhar, neph-khet?" he asked anxiously. "Are you hurt, beloved?"

So Rinyi was right, thought Tralvar, still not quite believing it.

Recovering, the hunted man picked himself up. Zig-zagging wildly, he evaded his pursuers and fled into the lower levels.

"Seal all the exits!" Axmiol ordered. "Alert the kitchen staff!"

"I'll try to head him off," Tralvar announced, and was halfway to the basement before anyone could stop him. With his intimate knowledge of the akron's byways, he stood a good chance of catching the madman before anyone else - which was precisely his intention. He skirted the supply depot, descended two more flights of ill-lit stairs, took a short cut through the janitor's quarters - and was suddenly face to face with the terrified Narvellan, who whirled and attempted to bolt. But Tralvar, who had waited years for such an opportunity, reacted even faster. He launched himself at the fugitive, brought him down, and held on despite several painful blows from the flailing limbs. The

142

Narvellan, unable to break free, set up a high keening wail.

"Keep quiet, you imbecile!" snarled Tralvar. Everyone's perception was closed off for fear of contagion, but that wouldn't buy any time if the idiot didn't stop his noise. He'd lead his pursuers straight to him.

The noise *didn't* stop. With calm precision Tralvar slapped the frightened man as hard as he could, and kept on slapping him until the wails and struggles ceased. As the Narvellan slumped dazed and defeated to the stone floor, Tralvar belatedly realised he'd been fighting the desk clerk from the main hall.

Footsteps sounded above.

"Listen to me!" Tralvar ordered, unceremoniously shaking his captive.

The clerk refused to look at him. "You cannot help me, First Citizen. The Ten will have been summoned."

"I know," agreed Tralvar sombrely. "So before they arrive, *you* must help *me*. Tell me what has taken possession of your people!"

"I...they..."

"Out with it! Hurry!"

A cold hand caught his wrist in a crushing grip. "The Synectics. It's the Synectics. They hid from us...then betrayed us..."

The door at the end of the corridor crashed open.

"On your feet, quickly!" hissed Tralvar. "Pretend to overpower me - and make it look good!"

With surprising alacrity the Narvellan obeyed, grabbing Tralvar and flinging him into a nearby stack of brooms and mops. Then he allowed Axmiol and the others to seize him. He even remembered to scream.

Axmiol sauntered across to Tralvar. "You're not injured, I trust?" he inquired casually, making no attempt to help him up. "You really shouldn't interfere in our disputes. I hope for your sake you didn't try to read him; you Celestrians are so foolhardy in these matters."

"I didn't read him," Tralvar answered truthfully. He had, of course, tried, as his quarry's shielding had failed at the moment of defeat. But he had sensed only paranoia, hysteria and an aching incompleteness. The liberated man had been unable to cope with his freedom, which probably explained why the Narvellans had detected his altered state so quickly.

"Come along, First Citizen," Axmiol said, almost gently. "Let the Ten do their work."

"Could you tell them to wait?" asked Tralvar. "Just until I've had a chance to speak with Kyrin? He starts his routine relays about now and I don't want him getting caught up in anything harmful."

"We've put out a warning," Axmiol pointed out.

"Kyrin may not have perceived it. He meditates, you know, just prior to his night's work."

Axmiol deliberated a moment. The madman had to be dealt with at once - but Kyrin was a valued commodity. "I'll allow you two astallen. You'll have to hurry. And, Tralvar - we will talk again soon. About Scapirion."

Kyrin was, as Tralvar well knew, fully aware of everything that had happened. He was doing his best to comfort Rinyi, who was petrified of aught concerning the Ten. Swiftly, Tralvar repeated what the condemned Narvellan had said to him.

"It doesn't sound much like Lydion's creature," he added, "but it's the only lead we've got. I want you to scour the akron for information - find out anything you can about these Synectics. I'll contact Rillan and Thala: they may know something, although it wasn't mentioned in their debriefing."

144

"I've heard that name," Kyrin said, furrowing his brow. "I just can't remember where."

Rinyi whimpered.

"Yes, I know, Rinyi - it's time. Just stay closed off, as I am, and the danger will pass us by."

It was the closest Tralvar had ever been to a Ten. At that range, it was difficult to shut out the deadening, dampening effect of the massed minds. He felt nauseated. And he was glad his little flask still had some resnay in it.

In the aftermath Rinyi's agitation faded, and he drifted into one of his withdrawn moods. Kyrin gave him a herbal drink to prepare him for sleep, then turned his attention back to Tralvar.

"I still can't recall who mentioned Synectics," he apologised. "In my line of work there are so many people, so many conversations. I must start my relays very soon, and that will occupy me for much of the night, but in the morning I'll see if meditation will jog my memory."

"And if that doesn't succeed, I'd better put you on retrace," Tralvar said, dabbing at a smear of floor polish on his sleeve. "It's a little drastic, I know, but we need that reference!"

"I remember who said it," Rinyi piped up drowsily.

Tralvar stared. "You *do*?"

"Yes. Kyrin was trying to persuade me to go outside. I didn't want to go into the plaza, not after..." He shivered a little and swigged his nightcap. "But I *did* go out, just as a flitter landed. Do you remember now, Kyrin? There was a Celestrian pilot and a young Narvellan with some luggage." He paused, head on one side, trying to focus.

"Go on," Tralvar said with barely concealed impatience. "This Narvellan - did *he* mention the Synectics?"

145

"Yes, he was the one." Rinyi's hazy thought processes centred on the moment, held it. He again saw the unsmiling young Narvellan and recalled his words in full: "How do you solve your civic problems? Do you have a Synectic group? I once had the honour of working for such a group." And then, fervently but silently: "And I will again. I must!"

"You read him through his shields?" asked Tralvar sceptically.

"The newly reduced sometimes have that capability," Kyrin explained. "Their minds are raw, sensitised, drawn to suppressed emotion."

"The young man was very unhappy," Rinyi concluded.

Tralvar was profuse in his thanks. "I'm very grateful, Rinyi. I'm so glad I came to see you. You've just advanced our cause immeasurably."

Rinyi positively glowed with pleasure.

"Now, Kyrin," Tralvar continued briskly, "we need to identify this new arrival. Not just his name, but why he's here and where he'll be staying."

"Leave it to me," said Kyrin. "The Narvellans keep detailed records of their own people as well as us. I'll access their database."

"Will they allow you near the computers?"

"Of course. They trust me." Kyrin gave one of his calm smiles. "I can go anywhere in the akron. But finding an unattended terminal may prove more difficult."

"You'll be taking a serious risk, Kyrin."

"I said I'd help," Kyrin replied determinedly. "I owe it to my profession and to you. I'll bring you the information as soon as I have it."

Tralvar bade him goodbye for the present, wished Rinyi a speedy recovery at Tafret and went quietly down to the main hall. There was no-one on the front desk.

Outside in the night, a soft drizzle was falling - just sufficient to ensure he'd be thoroughly drenched by the time he'd reached his home. But although he was tired and bruised, his step was light. For the first time in five years, he'd begun to feel hopeful. That poor wretch of a clerk had provided the first real clue. Kyrin would identify Rinyi's young Narvellan, Tyvian would retrace him, and the enemy would finally be revealed. He didn't dwell on what might happen after that.

***

Idenion was quick to notice Tralvar's improved mood - although as yet he'd no idea what had caused it - and took the opportunity of presenting Laura's requests to him. Tralvar gave permission for the musical retrace, seemingly without much enthusiasm, and consented - grudgingly - to organise a suitable venue for her singing practice.

Laura wasted no time in going back to see Tyvian, and at his suggestion had arrived at first light, ferried by a sleepy Lydion. She'd expected Tyvian's health to be as uncertain as before, but to her surprise he seemed hale and fit. The high, pure resonance of the crystals had surrounded her as she'd taken her place on the couch, and such was her fondness for the memories in question that he'd called out "I've found the track!" while she was still fully conscious. She'd given the retrace in a waking dream, always aware of the crystal harmonies, and afterwards Tyvian had cooked her a delicious breakfast - grain cakes lightly grilled in plant oil and seasoned with herbs and tiny petals. It had sustained her for most of the day.

That evening, she went back to her machining.

"I'll soon be taking time off for singing," she explained, "and I haven't done as many repairs today as I intended. You wouldn't believe the state of some of these overalls. Look at this one!"

147

"I never expected you to be so good at sewing," Idenion said in admiration as she tackled the offending garment.

"All part of my expensive private education," Laura reminded him. "We were all taught to be good needlewomen. I'm glad Nathaniel's money wasn't entirely wasted!"

"I hope you haven't been at that machine all day," Dena chided her.

"No, I took a break and went for a walk. I saw a nursery school just where the road crosses into the older part of the city. Do you know the one? The children were outside, playing some incomprehensible game. They looked so adorable.... Idenion, why are you frowning?"

Because, he wanted to say, you long for a child and I know you won't conceive one. Instead, he chose an easier option. "You shouldn't linger in one place. The Moderators will challenge you."

"I know. I'm sorry." She searched through her ylur bag for a suitable scrap. "Speaking of challenges, there might be a bit of a problem with the other outworkers."

"In what way?"

"The girl who delivered this batch of mending told me they'd formed a little consortium, taking turns to work from one another's houses. She obviously expected me to join the rota."

"What did you tell her?"

"I said I'd consider it. But we both know I *can't* join them. I don't think my prill would stand up to such close inspection, do you?"

"Probably not."

"I could see the girl thought I was being stand-offish," Laura went on. "Ailsi did too, that day at the factory."

"I'm sure they haven't taken it to heart," said Dean soothingly.

"I hope you're right. I'm supposed to be blending in, not putting people's backs up."

"You wouldn't have much in common with the outworkers," Dena volunteered in an attempt at reassurance. "Most of them are nursing mothers."

"Oh," said Laura, suddenly despondent. "I didn't realise. In that case I suppose I'm better off by myself."

"You won't *be* by yourself, at least not tomorrow," Idenion promised. "I've arranged to help Malcor take crystals to the monorail, so I'll be able to dash in and see my favourite girl."

"For how long?" she queried.

"Long enough." Idenion gave a knowing grin, and despite her concerns she couldn't help smiling back.

"It all sounds wonderfully illicit."

"Doesn't it just? We have to keep the romance going, don't we, now that we're an old married couple?"

"*Are* we married?"

"The Narvellans say we are, so we must be." Idenion ruffled her hair affectionately. "Now leave that noisy machine and come here. It's time for your reading lesson!"

The following day Laura was in a much better frame of mind, in anticipation of Idenion's visit. As luck would have it a box of aldacite crystals had gone missing from a train, in the short distance between the Alda Mexa terminus and the goods yard to the north; therefore, despite another blistering row with Chisrin, the administrators had decided that the courier or couriers had to ride with the crystals to the goods yard and deliver them in person. The Narvellan recipients would then carry out an inventory before sending the packages on to Treva. Although the distances involved were not great, Chisrin estimated it would be one and a half ilden before his workers returned. The train only travelled at a crawl for most of the way as the gradient was against it.

Idenion and Malcor duly loaded the boxed crystals into large satchels and set off for the monorail - but only Malcor boarded the train. Idenion hastened back to Laura and their lovemaking was joyous and intense.

After he'd been retrieved by the amiable Malcor, Laura set up her trestle near the window and went stoically to work. She longed for something to listen to. She'd heard no music for days, and had begun to miss it keenly. After a while, to keep her spirits up, she began to hum to herself, the sound scarcely audible above the whirr of the sewing machine. When the heavens didn't fall, she dared to add words. Light, rhythmic songs to maintain the speed of her sewing; songs she'd known all her life, like the dance scene from Hansel and Gretel. She sang the simple words softly, bowing her head over her task.

"That's right, give us all away!" Tralvar's accusatory voice made her jump violently. He was leaning against the door jamb, regarding her with ill-concealed anger.

"I didn't hear you come in," she faltered.

"Obviously."

Her customary defiance soon returned. "I can see the whole street from here. No-one could have approached without my knowledge."

"I did."

"You sneaked in the back way."

"And what makes you think the Narvellans wouldn't?" inquired Tralvar. "I'm sure I don't have to explain, Laura, how foolish you've just been."

She faced him with quiet composure. "If you're looking for an apology, you have one. It won't happen again. Now may I ask what you're doing here?"

"Idenion said you needed a place to sing. I've come to escort you. And in the nick of time, it seems."

"You mean now? This instant?"

"I do. Just leave everything and come with me."

"I'll have to change out of my work clothes," Laura said uncertainly.

"No need for that. You don't have to impress an audience," Tralvar said brusquely. "A cloak might be a good idea, though."

She fetched one, and he swiftly ushered her to a flitter which waited discreetly behind a rockpile at the back of the dwellings.

"If anyone's noticed us leaving, tell them it was scolia business," he instructed as they lifted off.

Laura supposed it was, in a way.

Tralvar headed west, across the Lisir and the monorail track. To the east and south, Laura recalled, there were liman plantations; to the north, orchards and vineyards. But there was nothing to the west except scrubland.

"Where are we going?" she asked.

"Somewhere that will suit your needs," Tralvar answered unhelpfully. Realising from the set of his jaw that no more information would be forthcoming, Laura didn't ask again. She assumed he was still angry with her for singing around the house, and attempted to explain how the silence had unsettled her.

"Maybe, if I'd been able to turn on the radio and hear music, I wouldn't have had to make my own," she concluded. "What about broadcasting music to the workers? On Earth, it's been a recognised part of industry..."

Tralvar forced himself to pay attention to her words rather than her distracting presence. He was well aware that Idenion had made love with her earlier that day.

151

She radiated satiety, or rather, that infuriating little prill did.

"Yes, the Narvellans thought music would help productivity," he said, suddenly aware that she'd finished speaking. "They approached me about it and I arranged coverage of some concerts. The broadcasts went quite well, I thought."

"And?"

"And everyone stopped working to listen. End of experiment."

Laura would have laughed, but there was such tension in him that she forbore.

Shortly afterward, he brought the flitter to rest beside a disused quarry. Nearby was a shack, a series of markers stuck in the ground, and a sphere with a patch of colourful paintwork on its pristine white hull - a yellow stardrive symbol bisected by a heavy blue line. A frown crossed Laura's face. She'd seen that sphere once before in Tivenne, when Tralvar - then in thrall to Alendis - had attempted to bomb Melor's house.

"Where *is* this?" she asked suspiciously.

"It's my firing range," Tralvar replied with an ironic sweep of his arm. "I tested my therite launchers here, among other things."

"And this is where I'm to exercise my voice?"

"Oh, no, Laura! I didn't intend you to sing *here*. We've a little way to go yet." Tralvar strolled across to the sphere and opened the hatch.

"Do you expect me to ride in that?"

"It's perfectly safe," he assured her.

"It can't be, otherwise the Narvellans would have taken it."

Tralvar sighed irritably. "That painted motif simply means it isn't spaceworthy. The auxiliary systems are perfect. I argued long and hard to save it from the

Narvellan re-cycling teams, so don't turn your nose up at it."

Laura still wasn't convinced. "Are there any explosives on board?"

"None whatever. Now will you stop raising objections and get in?"

Reluctantly she entered the cabin and perched in the co-pilot's seat. When the hatch sealed itself and the control systems activated, she felt a wave of panic. Maybe this was all a trick. He hadn't wanted her on Celestra - he could easily take her back to Earth and throw her out. Then she saw the amusement in his eyes, and was furious at having her insecurities read.

After a very short time indeed, the sphere touched down. Laura, determined to be mistrustful, made Tralvar disembark first just in case he had any notion of leaving her stranded. Then she stepped onto the ramp - and came to a halt in astonishment.

Tralvar had landed on the stage of a ruined amphitheatre. The terraces rose in a mute semi-circle, cracked and festooned with weeds. To Laura's left was an unbroken view to distant hills; to the right a crumbling apartment block. The wall facing the terraces had collapsed, leaving the internal stonework exposed. In what had once been rooms, a few shreds of material fluttered in the persistent wind. The sky was iron-grey, the silence absolute. There was no dignity here, only desolation.

"Ilonna," Laura said suddenly, recalling the ghost town she'd once seen from the air. "You've brought me to Ilonna. Why?"

"You wanted to sing. Now sing!" Tralvar commanded, and went to sit in the front row. "Well, what are you waiting for? You didn't need encouragement earlier on!"

"Why are you being so hateful?" she shouted, discovering that the acoustics were still in working order. When he didn't reply, she stormed across and planted herself in front of him. "Answer me!"

"You have a complacent and unrealistic view of our mission," he said incisively. "Believe it or not, I didn't bring you all the way from Earth to mend overalls and keep Idenion's bed warm!"

"I know what we have to do," she retorted.

"Then you know more than I do. No need to enlighten me: in a couple of days I'll find out if you're prepared. I daresay you'll let me down. Everyone does, sooner or later." He stared morosely at the weed-infested ground, and after a moment Laura sat down beside him and touched his hand lightly.

"Something's happened, hasn't it, to make you this resentful? Something other than the Treva riot."

He stared at her in surprise. "If I didn't know better I'd say the prill was lending you perception."

She shook her head emphatically. "No chance. I just know you rather well."

"Now you sound like Alendis," he said despondently. "All right, I'll tell you why I'm angry. Every morning, the Narvellans send me reports of the previous day's offences - as if it's somehow my fault that they've occurred. Mostly it's just minor infringements of their protocols. But today, I read that a young couple in Ninka had been caught distributing anti-Narvellan pamphlets. The girl had only been involved for the sake of her lover - she hadn't even read the work. But *she* was the one they executed."

"And what happened to the young man?"

"They let him go. Do you see how cunning that was? People won't take risks if they think their loved ones will be singled out. There'll be no more protests in Ninka for a while."

Laura pulled her cloak more tightly about her. "Axmiol's new regime again," she said with a shiver. "Slap us down and keep us down. What about the boy - could we recruit him?"

"I thought about that," replied Tralvar. "No, I don't think we can. He'll be vengeful, impatient. We need to be as calculating as they are. And yes, I know that means I should keep the lid on my temper."

"Please, if you possibly can," Laura said gently.

"I'll try. Now, do you want to sing, or shall we go home?"

"Do you *want* me to sing?" she inquired.

"You know I do."

"Then I will." She stood up and moved further onto the stage, avoiding a patch of broken mosaic. "This is by way of a lament, for the dead girl and the lad who mourns her."

Alone, unaccompanied, she sang "The Wind that Shakes the Barley." She sang as if to a stadium full of people, projecting her voice to the far reaches of the deserted theatre. It was incredible, thought Tralvar, how she always found a song for every occasion. No, not incredible. Inevitable. Symerid Three had so many songs - and most of them seemed to be in Laura's memory. He'd hesitated to read her in depth until today, in case music no longer danced in her every thought; in case she'd lost her youthful intensity, become jaded. He now knew nothing could change her. That, too, had an inevitability about it.

Having challenged Ilonna's brooding silence, Laura felt happier about continuing. She ran through a series of vocal exercises, each more difficult than the last, until she considered her voice to be warmed up. She then uttered the first few phrases of the Bell Song from Lakme, but struggled with a high note and began to cough.

"Sorry, I shouldn't have attempted that," she apologised. "It's the most ambitious thing in my repertoire. I'll need a few days of solid practice before I can tackle it properly."

"There's some water in the sphere if you want a drink," Tralvar reminded her.

"It wouldn't go amiss," Laura admitted. "And then I think we should leave."

They stood just inside the open hatch, sipping their drinks and gazing out at the ruins of Ilonna.

"I can't promise to be free every time you want to rehearse," said Tralvar, "but Idenion can stand in for me sometimes."

"Are you going to let him fly your sphere?"

"I don't think so. It has too many idiosyncrasies," Tralvar replied with a brief smile. "But he doesn't have to bring you all this way. There's an area near my quarry with a natural bowl and a high cliff. The acoustics aren't brilliant, but they should suffice."

"Why *did* you bring me here, Tralvar? Was it simply to shake me up?"

"Absolutely," he replied blandly. "But also as a test of your confidence. Your younger self wouldn't have uttered a note here."

"All that emptiness is intimidating," Laura agreed. "I felt it was trying to shout me down."

"But you didn't let it," said Tralvar succinctly. "Remember that, won't you, when we run into opposition from our own side."

They returned the sphere to the quarry and transferred to the flitter. Before setting off for Alda Mexa, Tralvar made a short detour to show Laura the natural arena he had discovered.

"Do you want to try a sound check?" he asked. "I've only tested it by yelling."

Laura tried the Bell Song again. This time the top note didn't come out at all. She was annoyed, but laughed it off.

Crouched at the very top of the cliff, a lone Directress gazed in vague irritation toward the source of the noise. Then, as the flitter whirred away into the distance, she rearranged her veils and returned to her contemplations.

"While we're airborne," said Tralvar, "I want to discuss your zirid lessons."

"I told Dena not to ask you," Laura said awkwardly. "It was a silly idea on her part. You don't want to be bothered with that."

"And *you* don't want a crack across the knuckles every time you make a mistake," he returned. "Don't worry - I've never taught music and I don't intend to start now. I haven't the patience."

"But if the Narvellans think I'm lying about being in the scolia - " Laura began.

"You wouldn't be the first to do that," said Tralvar drily. "Now if you'd please let me finish: I appreciate your reasons for wanting to learn, and I've come up with a workable solution."

"Which is?"

"You have a modicum of keyboard training, do you not? I'll re-tune a zirid to your diatonic scale and make you a present of it. Then, if any Narvellans come calling, you can play them your little pieces. They won't have a clue what they're hearing." He executed one of his lightning swerves. "Are you happy with that?"

"Yes," said Laura, determined to sound positive for once. "Yes, I'm sure it'll work. Now, since you've been talking to Dena, I assume you know about Nefyrra?"

Tralvar's expression softened. "Floren was being so mysterious when she left. I never dreamt that she'd devote the rest of her life to bringing up my daughter. I'm looking forward to hearing her play."

"Did you ever send her a recorded greeting? You said you were going to."

"No, I...didn't get round to it. But I'm anxious to meet her now. She's the one thing I can be proud of in this sorry mess."

"She didn't seem too keen on meeting you," ventured Laura.

"So I gather. But Dena's going to convince her that I didn't abandon Floren." Tralvar brought the flitter to land with only a slight jolt. "Here we are. Back to your sewing - and no more music while you work!"

Laura grinned, made ready to disembark, then paused. "By the way, I've given my retrace. The lost songs, remember? Do go and see it."

"Very well," he said, slightly hesitant. "I could go there now, I suppose. Thank you for taking the trouble."

Laura slid out of the cabin, but didn't move aside. "Tralvar - you don't *really* think I'll let you down, do you?"

"Not intentionally," he answered with obvious sincerity. "But intentions sometimes have a habit of falling short - like your missing top note." Then, seeing her frown: "Forget what I said earlier. I was upset. We're going to be a good team, you and I." Then he closed the canopy, causing her to dart aside.

He didn't want to expose himself to Laura's retrace. At least, not today. He'd had a surfeit of her mind already. But if he didn't show willing, he'd risk more damage to their fragile relationship. So he turned up at the lab unannounced, hoping that Tyvian would be busy with a patient. But he was only pruning the hrilffa, and was quite happy to stop and set up the playback.

The songs were banal, as he suspected they would be, but laced with a youthful enthusiasm that was touching. He detected his own influence in the compositions. It didn't improve them. More intriguing was the sensation of actually being Laura, though he tried to ignore that.

One sequence was more recent than the rest; *very* recent, according to Tyvian. Laura was on a small stage at one end of a darkened roomful of people. They crowded the tiny dance floor or sat at circular tables where little lamps gleamed through a haze of smoke. Laura, her voice deliberately powered down, breathed words into a microphone. There were two musicians accompanying her, playing instruments which her memory identified as "guitar" and "double bass". The guitarist was a small pudgy man seated on a stool, his gnarled fingers producing beautiful chord sequences from the six strings at his disposal. The thin lugubrious bass player stared myopically into the middle distance and occasionally stole a sidelong glance down Laura's cleavage. Her song, sophisticated and full of regrets, was "The Night we Called it a Day". And throughout her performance, one mood predominated: her profound longing for Idenion.

Tralvar was still trying to shake himself free of these distracting images when he arrived back at his villa and let himself in. He went straight to the study, poured himself a double measure of resnay and drank it gratefully. Only then did he realise he had a visitor, patiently waiting in the gathering dusk.

"I've found him," said Kyrin.

Chapter Six

Lively strains of music and the animated chatter of guests issued from Tralvar's villa. It was just past sunset, and extra lighting had been placed at either side of the portal to guide latecomers. Tralvar, drink in hand, leant on a pillar and gazed out at the city. Any moment now, he thought, this little gathering is going to attract some unwelcome attention. In this he was correct, but it was not a Moderator who spoke to him.

"Walk in harmony, First Citizen. What means this celebration?"

"Greetings, Administrator Narad," Tralvar returned calmly. "There is no celebration, just a musical evening with friends. I *am* of the scolia, in case you didn't know."

"I didn't."

"Then consider yourself enlightened. I haven't time to visit the Lyricon as often as I'd like, so I invited some performers here."

"I hope they don't intend to form a lattice." Narad's eyes narrowed warningly.

"There are only three musicians present. Four, if you include me. The lattice requires eight."

"I'm aware of that."

"I've only the one means of enjoying music since your people confiscated my recording system," Tralvar added.

"You were offered the use of *our* system. You refused."

Tralvar affected disdain. "Those little baubles that play for less than an astal? What use are they?"

"Their duration has been carefully calculated," Narad informed him solemnly. "It is self-indulgent to imbibe too much music."

"Then you'd better not stand around listening to mine," said Tralvar ungraciously.

Narad bowed his head in formal acquiescence. "Please ensure your guests behave decorously when they leave," he advised. "It would be a pity to antagonise the Moderators." Then he strode majestically away, his cloak billowing about him.

Idenion peeped furtively out of the open door. "Has he gone?"

Tralvar stared thoughtfully in the direction Narad had taken. "You should have told me he was attracted to you."

"Why? I can handle it."

"Narad has influence. His misplaced interest could one day be used to benefit our whole group, or at least keep *you* out of trouble."

"But I couldn't - "

"Oh yes you could. And if lives depend on it, you *will*. Now wipe that scowl off your face - we're going back inside."

They returned to the dining hall where the scolia was performing. The room was austerely furnished in accordance with the First Citizen's taste, but with a cheerful frieze depicting a banquet. There was scant food on offer today, but several pitchers of wine were in the process of being consumed - mostly by Dena's dance troupe.

"Good; they're all nicely mellow," Tralvar observed. "Soon they won't notice whether we're here or not, and then we can hold our conference. Throwing this party was one of your better ideas. Eight key personnel, arriving at night from different directions, would have looked very suspicious indeed."

"The party was Laura's idea, not mine," Idenion pointed out. A burst of laughter almost drowned his words, allowing Tralvar to pretend he hadn't heard.

"I hope those friends of Lydion's don't get too rowdy. We need cover for our operation, not complaints from the Moderators."

"Here's Kyrin," said Idenion, spotting the tall, slightly bemused relayist hovering in the doorway.

"Punctual as ever," remarked Tralvar. "I'll round up the others."

He circulated casually about the room, pausing to speak briefly with Lydion, Rillan and Jarras, and subsequently with Laura, Dena and Thala. To each of them in turn, he said: "My study. Now."

They obeyed, trying not to leave in unison. When they were all assembled, Tralvar closed the heavy door against the noise.

"I'll come straight to the point, as Kyrin can't be away from his post for long," he began. "All of you, at one time or another, have expressed a wish to help me against the Narvellans. Now, at last, we have a chance to do something constructive." Briefly, he outlined what had happened at the akron four nights previously. "These Synectics, then, appear to be the key to our current problems. I don't suppose the term is familiar to any of you?" He looked none too hopefully at Rillan and Thala.

"Not to me," said Rillan.

"Thala? You were with the Narvellans longer than anybody."

"Yes, telling them about *us*," she replied morosely.

These were the answers Tralvar had expected. "Then you'll be pleased to hear," he went on, "that we've traced someone who was in the Synectics' employ. Kyrin, would you tell us about him?"

"His name is Quetri zyl Nyris," Kyrin began. "As Narvellans reckon age, he is twenty, still two years away from attaining adult citizenship. He arrived here just a few days ago; this datasheet contains his address, his likeness and other personal details." He smoothed out the crumpled paper on a corner of the cluttered table. "I understand very little of this, but I believe he was appointed neph-khet to Navarian, one of the tyl Pellon family. Navarian has since died, so Quetri may be seeking another guardian. There is a Hysek tyl Pellon among the administrators, but Quetri has not checked into the akron since the day Rinyi saw him."

"May I see the data?" asked Thala. "I can read Narvellan." Kyrin handed it to her and she began to study it closely.

"If he doesn't have anyone to keep an eye on his movements, so much the better," said Tralvar. "Some of you already know what I intend to do: Quetri must be retraced, so we can see for ourselves what the Synectics are."

"Can we depend on Tyvian?" asked Jarras.

"He will co-operate," Tralvar stated. "I saw no reason to invite him here tonight because he already knows what he has to do. And because our initial problems don't really concern him."

"What problems?" inquired Lydion, looking up from his contemplation of an empty wine glass.

"Logistical ones," Tralvar replied irritably. "If you were paying attention you wouldn't need to ask. For instance, how do we isolate Quetri? We can't kidnap him from his home, so we'll somehow have to lure him to the retracer lab at night. Can anyone suggest how we might do that? And secondly, how do we overpower him?"

"Knock him out," suggested Laura.

"Not possible," Tralvar informed her loftily. "The prill won't bond with an injured retracee; they'd see him as detrimental to their survival. The same goes for a sedated subject. It would be ideal if we could overwhelm him with a lattice and hook him up to the retracer before he recovers, but the moment we formed a lattice we'd have Moderators galore homing in on us."

"Not if they were busy elsewhere," said Idenion. "Not if they had an outbreak of sciesha to contend with."

"Agreed, but sciesha won't manifest itself to order."

"Yes it will!" Idenion spoke excitedly. "There's a girl at my factory, Ailsi, who says it's possible to induce sciesha. She says she's already done it."

Tralvar raised an eyebrow. "Do you think she'd honour us with a repeat performance?"

"Knowing Ailsi, yes," Idenion said with a light laugh.

"I can verify that," Dena put in.

"We wouldn't tell her why we needed it, of course," Idenion said hastily.

"We could say we wanted to form a lattice for music," Dena suggested. "She'd believe that."

"Good thinking!" Tralvar said approvingly. "Well, it looks as if we have our sciesha. But we still don't have a way of enticing Quetri to the right location."

"Maybe we do," Thala said, looking up from the document she'd been examining. "This says his family is indebted to the house of tyl Pellon - one of these obscure matters of protocol the Narvellans are so fond of. Anyway: Quetri wasn't, strictly speaking, a neph-khet; he was *given* to the tyl Pellons as part of a settlement. If he hadn't been fortunate enough to find a sponsor in Navarian, he would have been a servant or even a slave. Now that Navarian is dead, Quetri will have reverted to his menial status. I suspect he came here to win or buy his freedom - and judging by what you said, Kyrin, he isn't having much success."

"This is all very fascinating," said Rillan, "but how does it help us?"

164

"Don't you see? If Quetri gets a message purporting to come from Hysek tyl Pellon, he'll have to obey, however odd it may seem."

"So if we told him to go somewhere in the middle of the night - "

"He'd do it."

"That's excellent, Thala." Tralvar leant forward intently. "Does that paper have anything else we can use?"

"Only that Navarian was project leader to the Pahl-drehinor. That, I believe, translates as Synectics. A problem-solving body or advisory group."

"*Now* I remember!" exclaimed Rillan. "If you'd used the Narvellan term, Tralvar, I'd have known what you meant. The Pahl-drehinor's principal aim was to create a stardrive. I understood the project was abandoned when we signed our treaty."

"That poor clerk," Dena mused. "He was moments away from death but he still translated everything into Celestrian."

"They always do that," remarked Jarras. "It's inculcated into them."

"Synectics sounds so English," Laura murmured to Idenion.

"It's Greek. Synektikos," he replied. "Common roots, like so many of our words."

"Idenion, you'd sit and discuss etymology if the stars were falling," declared Lydion. "This think tank doesn't bear any resemblance to the being that nearly absorbed me - and you can put that into any language you like. This whole thing's getting more and more incomprehensible."

"Then the sooner we organise the retrace, the better," said Tralvar. "Idenion, get Ailsi lined up; Kyrin, stand by to deliver the false summons to Quetri. You're to take it to him personally, you understand. He won't doubt your word." He scanned Quetri's file briefly to confirm the address. "Tell him he's to meet Hysek tyl Pellon here."

"Here?" repeated Kyrin.

"That's what I said. He won't be familiar with the city yet, but he'll know where to find *me*. Not that he'll actually get here, of course; the route will take him past Tyvian's lab. I'll speak to Tyvian myself. The rest of you, hold yourselves in readiness to form the lattice. It should be quite an experience for you."

"How do you know we can do it?" asked Lydion.

"*Anyone* can," Tralvar assured him. "We're not talking about scolia precision. The most inept lattice, directed against an individual, will disorient him. On a certain day in Tivenne, I and my spacecraft were forced out of the sky by eight young girls who were terrified of me."

"But they *were* of the scolia."

"Indeed they were - which made it all the more difficult for them. They were betraying their calling."

Lydion looked only half convinced.

"Why do you think the Narvellans barred us from using the lattice in their presence?" persisted Tralvar. "They know what it can do. Believe me, we'll cope."

"There will be nine of us," Kyrin pointed out. "Ten if we count Laura."

"There will be eight conversants," Tralvar stated, catching Laura's eye and daring her to object. "You won't be there, Kyrin. You'd be missed."

A short silence followed as the participants assessed their various roles.

"And you do realise," added Tralvar, his tone suddenly ominous, "that we won't be able to release Quetri afterwards? He'd incriminate us all. As in the past, it falls to me to take on the role of executioner."

Cries of protest greeted this remark. Tralvar's gaze met Laura's a second time, and she realised he was expecting her to back him up. This, after all, was why she'd been brought here.

"I don't see any alternative," she said. "We can't let him go."

Tralvar didn't appear grateful. "We can't even allow him to regain consciousness," he elaborated.

"But," began Idenion helplessly, "he'll have no memory of the retrace. He won't even know we've taken it if we move him before he wakes up."

"He'll know we used the lattice on him. What do you think he'll have to say about that?"

"Then take him to a remote spot and release him," suggested Thala. Tralvar looked exasperated.

"He'd either be found or he'd starve. Is starvation preferable to a merciful death at my hands?"

"Assuming we agree, how would you do it?" asked Jarras.

"With the retracer, of course," Tralvar said coolly.

"You've got it all worked out, haven't you?" said Lydion reproachfully, and would possibly have ventured more criticism if Tralvar hadn't stopped him with a glare.

"I hope you don't think I've made this decision lightly. Take a good look at this picture, all of you." He held up the datasheet. Quetri's earnest young face gazed out at the conspirators. "I spent most of last night trying not to see him as an individual. He's simply a means to an end - and we're duty bound to end this occupation. We may never have another chance."

There were no more protests.

"Then are we all in accord? Dena, you've been very quiet."

"In matters like these, you know best," she said simply.

This, coming from the gentlest of those present, served to reinforce the collective decision.

"Then our business is over for tonight," said Tralvar thankfully, pouring himself a half-measure of resnay. "Just one thing more, before you go - "

Suddenly the door flew open and two very inebriated girl dancers tumbled in.

"*There* you are, Tralvar!" exclaimed one. "Is this a private party?"

"What's everyone doing in here?" asked the other.

"Resnay tasting," Tralvar replied, holding up his glass. "Would you like some?"

"Ugh!" they cried, wrinkling their dainty noses. "Put that nasty stuff down and come and play for us. The scolia's getting tired."

"Tell them I'll be out in a moment," he said genially, and they disappeared with whoops and shrieks.

"What were you about to say?" asked Laura.

Tralvar downed his drink in a single gulp. "Only that, party or no party, this is the only time we dare assemble at my house. If further meetings are necessary, they'll be held elsewhere. I'll keep you informed. And before that, of course, you'll receive instructions on how and when to approach the retrace lab. You'll have to arrive early, and singly. Now disperse, and try to look happy."

He wound the party up just before nadir, ensuring there was a small fleet of flitters to take the revellers home. Long after everyone had departed he remained at the zirid, trying out some of the intriguing chord progressions he'd heard on Laura's retrace. He resolved, as he'd done many times previously, to devote more time to his music - or at least try. It always focused his mind wonderfully. He could start by finding out from Dena when Melor's masterplayers were due back at the

Lyricon - as the very next time Nefyrra was in attendance, he intended to be there to meet her.

***

The plan ran into difficulties from the outset. The day after the conference, an anxious Jarras reported that Quetri had left Alda Mexa.

"I thought I recognised him," he told Tralvar amidst the wreckage of the party, "so I checked the spaceport manifest. He's gone to Corayn. *Now* what do we do?"

"Did he have any possessions with him?"

"No, but -"

"Then he hasn't left for good. We'll just have to wait till he turns up again."

"I can't stay in Alda Mexa much longer," Jarras warned. "I've nearly finished my maintenance work. They'll want me back on the assembly line."

"Treva isn't the opposite side of the planet, is it? I'll make sure you - *and* Rillan - are here when it matters."

"You're very calm," Jarras observed.

"Calm? More like comatose," Tralvar replied, yawning. "If anyone other than you had arrived this early I'd have thrown them out. Just try not to get in a twitch, will you? I imagine there's another of the tyl Pellon clan based at Corayn, and that's why Quetri's gone there. I might wander along to the registry later and check it out."

"Of course. That's what it'll be." Jarras looked less agitated. "Sorry to wake you up."

"Stay to breakfast?"

Jarras grinned. "I've had mine already, but I wouldn't mind another."

"Coming up. I think I've got some of the dressing that Tyvian puts on his grain cakes. Laura told me to try it."

"I hope Laura didn't think I was staring at her yesterday," Jarras ventured while Tralvar searched the

169

larder. "Discord's dreams, she's attractive. When she was here last, she was just a child in a woman's body; but now..." He paused appreciatively. "And you've heard her sing. I envy you."

"She's given a retrace if you want to hear her," Tralvar said, busy with the food.

"A retrace? Why?"

"To keep me apprised of her musical activities," Tralvar answered drily. "Her idea, not mine."

"But surely you told Tyvian to destroy it once it had been played?" queried Jarras.

"No," Tralvar said absently. "No, I didn't."

Elsewhere in the city, Laura knew nothing of Quetri's departure. She and Idenion were walking toward the factory, carrying the newly-repaired overalls in their basket. The day was unseasonably warm; little Alda blazed fiercely from a cloudless sky. Idenion was late by about two astallen, but didn't hurry as he was waiting for Dena to catch up.

"I've been meaning to ask," Laura began, "about this business of the lattice. Last night you all seemed very sure you could form one - but how many of you have actually tried?"

"All of us," said Idenion, to her surprise. "Children are taught to form an elementary lattice - it teaches them mental dexterity and co-operation. And then, at puberty, everyone's tested for the scolia in case anyone's been overlooked. We're all examined by the relayists' guild, too. Did I tell you I almost became a relayist?"

"Dena told me. That would've been awful," Laura said with a shudder. "You'd never have become First Poet, never have come looking for a singer..."

"Fortunately," Idenion put in swiftly, "I failed the tests. Hush now; no more talk of singers."

170

Dena, hot and flustered, joined them as they reached the entrance. "What excuse do we use today?" she asked breathlessly.

But there was no need for excuses. As they reached the inner door they could hear Chisrin in full rant, with Ailsi's shrill objections forming a counterpoint. The other girls were gleefully silent.

"What will you think of next, you destructive little brat?" the overseer yelled. "That was a perfect crystal and you've drilled a hole right through it. Sheer wanton vandalism!"

"Oh, lighten up, Chisrin!" Ailsi said plaintively. "I thought it was pretty. Look - it's kind of pink when it catches the light. I thought it would make a nice pendant."

"You've just destroyed a valuable gem," Chisrin reiterated. "That's sabotage, you minx. I could have you arrested!"

"Oh, Chisrin, don't be cross!" Ailsi wheedled. "One little crystal out of so many. And what's valuable about it? The other factories churn them out by the bucketful!"

"Not these." Chisrin spoke more quietly. "These are real."

Ailsi looked uncertain. "You're just saying that."

"Do you think I can't tell?" he countered. "You've been cutting real gems for the past two octals. Why do you think there was such a fuss when that box went missing?"

"You should've told us," she said sullenly.

"You didn't need to know," he declared. "Now get back to work, all of you. Ailsi, if you can complete your quota by midday I'll say no more about this."

She gave him a mutinous look and flounced back to her place. With the confrontation over, Laura and Idenion tried to sidle out - but not quickly enough.

171

"Lisset, don't leave those overalls back there," Chisrin called wearily from his office. "Bring them to me. I have to inspect them, and you have to sign a delivery sheet."

Trapped, she walked obediently toward the front of the room. She was glad Idenion was with her. Chisrin accepted the basket and took a perfunctory look through the contents. Then he looked again, more thoroughly.

"This is excellent work, Lisset. Very neat."

"Thank you."

"I could do with someone like you on my team. Diligence is what's needed, and diligence is something I seldom find."

"Lisset is exempt from factory work," Idenion reminded him.

"She can always choose not to exercise that prerogative," Chisrin replied smoothly. "So, First Poet, why don't you take yourself off to the packing line and allow Lisset to speak for herself?"

Idenion hesitated.

"Go on, *go*!"

Reluctantly he retreated from the office.

"Now, Lisset." Chisrin's smile was open and friendly. "Why not consider my proposal? These girls are only part of my operation. I employ grading assistants, despatch clerks, caterers..."

"I'm happy with my present assignment," Laura faltered, sure that he was about to read her and unmask her deception. He remained affable.

"Well, I'll be here when you tire of working on your own. Unless, of course, it's Idenion who's keeping you shut away? Not that I blame him...discord take us! He's still out there, gabbing to Ailsi." His voice rose to a roar. "Idenion! Get your backside through that door *now* or you'll be on overtime for the rest of the..."

172

Then his voice faded and his jaw went slack. In the workshop, the girls' chatter was silenced for the second time that morning. Four burly Narvellans marched into the room in single file, escorting a diminutive, veiled figure.

"Make way for Directress Passik!" boomed the leading official.

Laura seized the opportunity to slip out of the office and rejoin Idenion. Then she watched with undisguised curiosity as the little procession swept by. She'd never seen a Directress before, and neither apparently had the other girls.

"How does she see where she's going?" whispered one.

"They perceive things differently to us," another explained wisely.

"I've heard they're very beautiful," murmured Ailsi's neighbour.

"All lies, they're old hags!" said Ailsi cheerfully. "Chaos, will you look at Chisrin! I never thought I'd see him acting like that!"

The overseer was performing a deep bow before the mysterious Passik. His long hair trailed in the dust. Then he rose and, after a brief hushed conversation with her retinue, left the office and addressed the waiting workforce.

"Some flawed crystals have been found at Treva," he announced, his expression grave and serious. "All exports have been temporarily halted, and every factory working with natural crystal is having its supplies checked. Directress Passik will now examine the crystals you have in front of you. Do not obstruct her nor speak to her." He nodded to the men, who escorted Passik to a bench just beside Laura. An exquisite little hand, pale gold, emerged from beneath the finely woven veils; the watching girls breathed a sigh of wonder.

173

Passik took a crystal from the nearest pile, closed her hand around it and held it for several moments. Then she replaced it and moved on. It took her over two astallen to circle the room. Finally she uttered several words in a clear high voice.

"She says all the crystals are impure," Idenion murmured to Laura. Several people heard him.

After another few words with Chisrin, the four Narvellans departed with Passik in their midst. As soon as the outer door had grated shut, everyone began talking at once.

"All right, settle down!" Chisrin was understandably subdued, but could still command obedience. "As Idenion so helpfully explained, there's a problem with the crystals. We'll need to know where they were mined and who dowsed for them, to ensure there aren't any more in the system. Since I'll have to examine my paperwork, and since there's nothing for you to do until the next batch arrives..." He paused, surveying their expectant faces. "...you might as well have the day off."

A delighted cheer went up; but surprisingly, no one seemed in a hurry to leave. Instead, they grouped together and started to plan how to use their unexpected leisure. Chisrin watched them for a moment with just the faintest trace of envy. Then, suddenly irritable, he grabbed a handful of the useless crystals and slammed them down in front of Ailsi.

"Here," he growled. "Make yourself a necklace."

Laura's first impulse was to head for the Lyricon, but Idenion gently dissuaded her.

"There won't be anyone there," he pointed out. "Ailsi wants us to go to Lake Holpen, which seems like a good idea as it's so hot. Besides, I want Dena to have a proper break. If she ends up at the Lyricon she'll be substituting one type of work for another."

Lake Holpen was a wide expanse of silvery water fringed by shingle and surrounded by tall trees in their autumn colours - red, orange and purple. An assortment of coracles bobbed beside a wooden pier, and further out a floating platform awaited determined swimmers. Adjacent to the lake was the reservoir which supplied Alda Mexa - hence the proximity of the monorail.

"If there's all this water, why do we have so many stoppages?" asked Laura.

"Not because of drought," Idenion replied. "Either the pumps break down or there isn't enough electricity to run them."

Ailsi and her friends where already splashing happily in the shallows. Idenion, who couldn't swim, immersed one foot and pronounced the lake too cold. Laura could swim a little, but forbore as she wasn't sure whether the prill pendant was waterproof.

"Cowards!" taunted Ailsi. "Idenion, your sister's showing you up!"

Dena was an excellent swimmer. Clad only in two tiny wisps of cloth, she struck out for the platform. On reaching it she hauled herself out, squeezed her wet hair and stood shading her eyes from the sun, oblivious to the appreciative stares she was attracting.

"Look!" said Laura, giving Idenion a nudge. "The entire packing department's lusting after her and she hasn't even noticed."

Idenion sighed. That was so typical of Dena. +Don't be cruel to your admirers, little sister+ he sent teasingly.

Dena turned in the direction of the young men and gave them a vague wave before diving off the platform.

"I really do wish she'd find herself a partner," Idenion fretted. "It's just an added worry on top of everything else."

"There's certainly no lack of contenders," Laura observed, spreading out a rug in the shade.

"Not sunbathing?" inquired Ailsi, sauntering past.

"Er...no," replied Laura, caught off guard. Ailsi shrugged and moved on.

"You handled that badly," said Idenion reprovingly.

"Dammit, Idenion, how *can* I sunbathe?" she hissed. "I scarcely match the Celestrian pallor as it is. How would I hide a suntan from the Narvellans? You're lucky I spent the summer of '77 stuck in a shop or in the dark at the jazz club!"

"Shh. No English!"

"I'm sorry. I just don't know how to deal with Ailsi - she's so nosy!"

"She wonders why you're always closed off," Idenion admitted. "Especially here, with no Narvellans around."

"Great."

"Don't agitate; I've an idea. I'll get so close to the prill that it starts to reflect us both, and then I'll amplify the result. I think it'll work well enough to satisfy Ailsi's curiosity."

When Ailsi and Malcor wandered back along the shoreline they found Laura sitting beneath a tree with Idenion's head in her lap. Though not in unity, their minds radiated such affection that Ailsi was quite moved.

"You know, I've been quite wrong about that girl," she confided. "I thought she was too haughty for her own good. But see how she loves him! I don't think I could ever love anyone that much."

"Not even me?" asked Malcor, pretending to be hurt.

"Well, I might make an exception - if you behave!" replied Ailsi with her ready smile. "Oh, I nearly forgot in all the excitement over the crystals - Idenion has a proposition for me. Or should I say for us?"

"Oh?"

"Tralvar's hosting a full scolia event - you know, all lattices and nodes and cosmic resonances. Idenion wants me to induce sciesha in another part of the city, to draw the Moderators away!"

Malcor gave an anticipatory grin. "And when does all this happen?"

"I don't know. We get the word, we do it. It'll be at night." Ailsi's eyes sparkled with mischief. "I hope it's soon! I want to show those sexless Moderators what we're made of!"

By mid-day, after a picnic lunch consisting mainly of a huge fruit pie that Ailsi had filched from the caterers, Laura wanted to move on. "You could take me to Tralvar's quarry," she suggested. "My voice needs some serious exercise. I wasn't at all happy with it at Ilonna."

"Then we'd better go home and look for some transport," said Idenion, none too hopefully; but as they were walking back to the monorail halt he spied a trio of flitters parked near the pumping station. "Now there's a happy coincidence. Follow me!"

Laura hesitated. "The Narvellans left them there, surely? We can't go helping ourselves!"

"Flitters are still communal property," Idenion declared. "And we won't be leaving anyone stranded, will we?"

"I suppose not," she admitted. "Well, let's not dither around if we're going to take one."

They climbed into the nearest craft, seemingly without being observed. Idenion then sat poring over the controls, much to Laura's consternation.

"What are you doing? Get a move on before someone comes out!"

Idenion finally coaxed the machine into the air. "Sorry about that. I had to programme the locator as per Tralvar's instructions."

"Locator?"

"We use it outside the city on pre-determined routes. It follows magnetic beacons set in the ground. Very handy if you don't know the terrain."

"I always wondered why people didn't get lost out here," said Laura, watching the featureless plain speed by.

"The quarry's beyond the beacon perimeter, but Tralvar says the escarpment's visible long before you get there," Idenion added. "Do you realise that this will be the first time we've been alone since the spaceflight? I mean, *really* alone?"

"It had occurred to me," she replied with a coquettish smile. "But I'm still going to sing. For part of the time, anyway!"

"Do you still sing Nuit d'Etoiles?"

"No, not for years. It's too bound up with the past. But I discovered another French song called L'Invitation au Voyage, which is really beautiful. I'm glad I'll have a chance to polish it before I rehearse with Tralvar again. I know he'll love it."

"You seem more kindly disposed to him of late," Idenion observed.

"We had a frank talk the other day. I think we cleared the air," Laura said. "And he's such an appreciative audience. The next time he's with me I'll try to show *my* appreciation a little more!"

Dena remained at the lakeside for another two ilden. She'd intended staying all afternoon, but hadn't bargained on the curiosity of Idenion's young female following. As soon as he'd left, the questions started: How long had he known Lisset? Was she older than him? Where had she sprung from? How long did she,

Dena, think the relationship would last? Not surprisingly, she'd felt obliged to extricate herself and go back to Alda Mexa. From the station she went to the nearest street market in search of food, eventually returning home with a bagful of undersized vegetables and blemished fruit. While she was assessing what could be saved, someone tapped lightly on the front door; and opening it, she beheld Chisrin with a bundle of tattered overalls under his arm.

"Lisset forgot to take these this morning," he said. "Where would you like them?"

"Just put them by the machine, thank you," Dena replied, absently drying her hands on her smock.

Chisrin complied, his head almost touching the ceiling of the little room. "Your brother's been up to his pranks again," he remarked as he turned to leave. "Made off with a flitter from outside the waterworks."

"There's no law against that," Dena returned coolly.

"Maybe not, but the owner - correction, the previous occupant - was annoyed enough to contact my office and ask why Idenion wasn't at work. Naturally, I had to explain. It didn't reflect very well on me."

"It wasn't *your* fault about the crystals," Dena offered.

"Indeed not. Do you happen to know where Idenion went?"

Dena fidgeted, suddenly uneasy. "Sorry, I've no idea."

Chisrin appeared to accept her answer. "I'll see you tomorrow," he said affably. "Don't be late!"

Dena sighed and went back to the vegetables. Chisrin was always looking for excuses to pick on Idenion, and today was no exception. Soon afterward she heard a flitter land and went outside, expecting to see Idenion and Laura. Instead it was Tralvar, manhandling a zirid onto the street.

"For Lisset, as promised," he announced for the benefit of a few spectators, and wheeled the instrument across the threshold. "Find a corner for it, will you? I'll need to check the tuning again." Then, once the door was closed: "I heard about the crystals. Axmiol would have loved to call it sabotage, but he knew very well it wasn't. And where, may I ask, are the First Poet and his muse?"

"They flew out to the quarry."

"Chaos! Didn't I say everyone was to hold themselves in readiness? Well, at least *you* had the sense to stay put." Tralvar attempted to smooth his hair in the nervous gesture Dena knew well. "The retrace operation is tonight."

Dena looked stricken. "So soon?"

"We can't afford to wait. Quetri flew out to Corayn this morning and I thought we'd have a breathing space, but he must have turned straight round and come back. Jarras spotted him at the spaceport about an ild ago, looking thoroughly miserable and asking about flights to Narvella. Obviously his attempts to get sponsorship have failed - and if he goes offworld, we've lost him."

"I see," said Dena expressionlessly.

"I want you and the others at Tyvian's no later than one ild to nadir," Tralvar continued. "You still have plenty of time, so relax and have a decent meal. Hunger can ruin a lattice."

"Yes, I know."

"Just get them there, Dena. I'm sorry to give you this responsibility but it will take me the rest of the evening to round up everyone else."

"We'll be there," she promised. "Do you want me to speak to Ailsi?"

"That would be a great help. She'll need to start her diversion at, let's see, half an ild to nadir at the latest.

The location isn't important as long as it's well away from the laboratory."

"I'll give her the message. And, Tralvar..."

"Yes?"

"Make sure *you* don't go hungry." And make sure you don't drink, she added silently, not daring to let him see the thought. She suspected he'd understood.

She prepared a stew for dinner and braced herself to impart the news to her twin. It would doubtless ruin his day. But when the lovers returned at dusk, their mood was neither euphoric nor passionate. Instead it bordered on the forensic, as they continued to discuss the difficulties of translating French poetry into Celestrian. When Dena finally said her piece, their reaction was one of near-relief.

Later, while they ate, a lone figure stole into the street's communal backyard. Although darkness had fallen, the intruder avoided every obstacle with consummate ease. Occasionally his eyes glinted green, reflecting distant lights. Approaching the flitter which Idenion had arrived in, he soundlessly opened the canopy and slid on board. Activating a section of the controls and shielding the panel lights with his hand, he studied the locator settings with great interest. Then, returning everything to its previous state, he left the craft and hurried back the way he had come. A stray beam of light from someone's kitchen briefly illuminated his lithe muscular frame and plaited hair.

***

They waited, all nine of them, in the dimly lit retracer lab. Nearby, a monitor screen idled. Crystals adorned the sconces at each corner of the large tank, and an array of prill waited within it. The sliding panels at the back of the lab were open slightly, admitting the cool night air and a profound silence.

"Where in chaos *are* they?" muttered Jarras.

"They'll be here," said Tralvar with a confidence he didn't feel. "Kyrin won't fail us."

They listened to the silence again. Everyone save Laura was aware of sciesha raging in the northeast, and true to form, all the Moderators were hastening to contain it. Ailsi had excelled herself. Tralvar hoped her efforts wouldn't be wasted. Then, at last, the listeners heard faint footfalls and Kyrin's voice:

"This way. We're almost here."

"This is all very strange, Relayist Kyrin," said a second voice. "Why would Hysek tyl Pellon insist on such secrecy?"

"I believe he's under a certain amount of peer pressure," Kyrin replied. "I'm afraid I can accompany you no further, as I have to start work: but that is Tralvar's house in the distance, with the lit portico."

Laura peeped surreptitiously out of the lab doors. Kyrin, his duty discharged, was already hastening back up the path toward the akron. Quetri was standing uncertainly on the corner of the deserted street.

"Everyone form up," Tralvar ordered.

"Keep away from the prill!" Tyvian added hastily.

The lattice sprang into life, wavered, then steadied. Tralvar wanted to give his friends - and himself - longer to prepare, but there was no time. +Now!+ he commanded, and the eight minds reached out to enfold and overpower the lone Narvellan.

To the departing Kyrin, the lattice seemed as bright as a searchlight - so different from the insidious darkness of the Ten. It didn't have the finesse of the scolia, but it was strong and integrated. He was sure it would suffice, provided there were no interruptions.

Laura perceived none of this. The battle had been joined, but on a level she could have no part in. Her eight companions were ranged in a rough circle; they looked remote, strange and suddenly very alien. But she noticed that Idenion and Dena had clasped hands, a small but reassuring glimpse of their everyday selves.

The soundless conflict went on and on. Laura, in mounting apprehension, peered outside again. She caught one brief glimpse of Quetri on his knees, hands wrenching at the collar of his tunic - and suddenly the street lights were extinguished for the night. Now she had absolutely no idea what was happening.

Finally, just as she was about to give way to panic, a despairing cry came out of the darkness and the tableau was broken. Dena sobbed, Rillan and Thala embraced and Lydion wiped beads of sweat from his forehead.

"Discord's dreams, I hope I never have to do that again!" declared Jarras.

"Right, let's bring him in," Tralvar said briskly. "Got that torch, Lydion? Tyvian, get the equipment running - we don't know how long he'll stay under." He and Lydion disappeared outside, returning in a few moments with Quetri's slight form supported between them. With a notable lack of gentleness, they deposited him on the couch. Tralvar slid the door shut and secured it.

Laura, instinctively sympathetic, went to Quetri's side. The lattice had done him little harm; he was on the edge of consciousness, eyelids fluttering.

"He's so young," she murmured unhappily.

On the rim of the tank, the crystals began to emit their silvery cadences. Showers of static scampered across the monitor. Tralvar moved to strap Quetri to the couch.

"Oh, no, Tralvar!" Laura protested. "Don't tie him down. Have you any idea how frightening that is? I'll stay here and watch him."

"Is that allowed, Tyvian?" Tralvar inquired.

"She wears the seed; this is what it was designed for. The prill will ignore her."

"But she'll be standing in the energy field," Idenion objected.

"Not under normal operating conditions," Tyvian said, busy at the console. "The prill are in symbiosis with the retracee *and* with the aldacite; the energy will be contained in a feedback loop between Quetri, the prill...and me." He adjusted the diagnostic sensor on his forehead. "Now, I need the assistance of someone who can speak Narvellan."

"I think I qualify," Idenion said.

"Very well. I want you to take Quetri through the initial stages. Tell him to think of something familiar to him."

"Won't the prill detect me?"

"Not immediately. Speak, then move away."

The crystal resonance stabilised. The monitor fell dark, waiting. Quetri's drawn features relaxed into something approaching tranquillity.

"What if there's a power cut?" asked Jarras apprehensively.

"I'm running the experiment from storage batteries," Tyvian assured him.

Idenion leant over Quetri and uttered a few soft phrases in Narvellan. "I asked him to think of his home," he clarified.

Everyone watched as the screen lit. A red sky mottled with turquoise, a cluster of buildings on a barren hillside and a weird egg-shaped spacecraft drifting to land in the nearest valley. A discreet voice murmured:

"Quetri. It's time."

There was no sound on the monitor, so only Tyvian knew what was being said. The others, forbidden to use perception during the retrace, were left to deduce what they could. The child Quetri left the window he'd been gazing from and turned to face a gaunt, weary Narvellan in late middle-age.

"Why, Father? Why are you sending me away? Have I done something wrong?"

"No, Quetri," his father answered sadly. "The wrongdoing is mine."

Someone unseen grasped the child's arm and he struggled.

"There's trauma here," Tyvian called out. "Transfer him to something else!"

"Is all this necessary?" asked Rillan anxiously. "We're wasting time."

"I know that's what it looks like," said Lydion, "but I've given enough retraces to know what works best. Just leave them to it."

They continued to watch. Idenion had asked to be shown a recent memory, and was rewarded with a sequence in which a bored official was preparing Quetri's exit permit and asking if he'd completed the language induction course. There followed a doleful little interval with Quetri packing a few permitted belongings and reminiscing over a small telescope which his protector Navarian had given him years before.

Tyvian channelled this data with a growing sense of unease. Everyone had exhorted him to be on guard for anything unusual, but he'd found nothing. The prill seemed contented, and all aspects of the retracer were functioning normally. There was no reason not to go on. Aware of his companions' mounting impatience, he finally signalled Idenion to speak the key phrase.

"Show us the Synectics," the poet commanded.

With a vertiginous lurch back through time, Tyvian found himself accompanying Quetri the child as he walked nervously toward a set of automatic doors. Again, the unseen hand of an adult was propelling him forward. He felt, rather than heard, the throb of distant machinery. The doors opened onto a long narrow room, awash with soft white light which had no obvious source. Down the length of one wall stood ten cylinders of white metal, twice the height of a man, each fronted by a control panel on a small column. Quetri's companion moved between these columns, his slender able fingers making adjustments to the panel settings. On all ten cylinders the metal carapaces suddenly sprang apart, rotating noiselessly aside to reveal transparent inner chambers filled with pale green liquid. Floating in this liquid, along with tangles of tubes and catheters, were several people - or what had once been people. Their faces were wizened and shrunken, their limbs atrophied and useless. One, a woman, still had a few strands of black hair attached to her bald scalp.

"Are they dead, Navarian?" Quetri whispered.

"Far from it," replied his mentor. "You're looking at ten of the most daunting intellects on our twin planets. Over twenty years ago they sacrificed themselves to form a group mind, and ever since then they've been working continuously to solve the problem of the solar flares. I, as project leader, maintain their stasis units and monitor their environment for optimum efficiency. When you're older you will help me in this vital work."

Navarian proceeded to lecture Quetri on the importance of regulating the nutrient flow and maintaining the elimination of waste, as neglecting either could cause the group's concentration to become sluggish. Tyvian gingerly withdrew from the projection and rested a moment, knowing the recording would proceed for a while without him.

"Are *those* the Synectics?" quavered Laura.

He repeated Navarian's words, prompting various exclamations of dismay and disgust.

"How could the Narvellans do that to their own people?" cried Dena.

"They volunteered, apparently," said Jarras.

"It's obscene," declared Thala.

"So it was a group mind I encountered," breathed Lydion. "Incredible!"

"Well, at least we know what we're taking on," said Tralvar grimly. "Tyvian, are you ready to continue?"

"I think so." Tyvian readjusted the sensor and hunched down in his chair.

"We need to know their current location," Tralvar reminded Idenion, who accordingly instructed Quetri:

"That was the first time you saw the Synectics. Now show us the last."

A cascade of images followed, and Tralvar uttered a few choice words on the linear nature of Narvellan thinking.

"He's going through his whole career. Tyvian will never be able to channel it at that speed."

"We'll have to sort it out later," Lydion said.

Suddenly the picture stabilised. In place of the white light and pristine laboratory walls, there were dull red lamps in what appeared to be a cavern. But the cylinders, and what lay within, hadn't altered. Workers, intent and silent, continuously checked and re-checked the systems.

"Tell us the name of this place," Idenion intoned. "Tell us where -"

Quetri sat bolt upright, shrieked, then collapsed. The aldacite crystals flared blindingly bright, like miniature suns, then shattered one by one. The prill burst into flames. White heat stabbed deep into Tyvian's brain, and within that deadly radiance an indubitably female voice uttered one word:

+Spy!+

And then the Synectics took his mind and divested it of everything he knew - his distant childhood, his love of plants, his bizarre space explorations - and left him drained and dying, as burnt out as the prill. When the onlookers' dazzled vision had cleared they saw their stricken colleague sprawled limply across his desk. The blackened remains of the prill sputtered fitfully. There was no other movement.

Laura recovered first and rushed to Tyvian's side, Tralvar and Idenion at her heels. As they raised him up the sensor fluttered unnoticed from his forehead. He was ashen and still, the left side of his face drooping unnaturally.

"I think he's had a stroke," Laura whispered.

"We'd better take him to his sleeping quarters," said Idenion. "Help me with him, Laura."

"Shouldn't he be in hospital?" asked Dena.

"I can't permit that," Tralvar said regretfully but firmly. "It would draw attention to the retracer and thence to us. I'm sorry, but he has to stay here."

Laura and Idenion carried Tyvian to the tiny rest area and laid him on a pallet, where Laura tried to make him comfortable.

"Do you think anyone heard those crystals smash?" asked Rillan.

"If they did, they probably thought it was sciesha-related," began Tralvar. But as if on cue, someone hammered frantically at the rear doors.

+Let me in! Let me in!+

"It's Drusa," said Lydion, and unbarred one of the sliding panels to admit her and a clammy blast of night air.

Drusa's broad, pleasant features were taut with anxiety. "Where is he?" she demanded. "Where's Tyvian?"

Tralvar pointed silently; she hurtled into the rest room, elbowing Laura out of the way. Idenion forestalled an angry protest by seizing Laura's arm and steering her aside.

188

"She'll take better care of him than we can. Let's leave her to do her work."

Laura capitulated with bad grace. "Oh, no," she heard Drusa exclaim brokenly as they went back to the others. "He always said the retracer would kill him one day."

"Can she be trusted?" inquired Jarras.

"I'll deal with her," Tralvar promised. "But first, I want all non-essential persons to make themselves scarce. The longer we're together the more vulnerable we become. Rillan, Thala - take the torch and go to my house as arranged. Dena, go with them. Jarras, take the flitter back to the spaceport."

They departed obediently but reluctantly.

"Lydion," Tralvar went on, "I still need you here. Check the logic systems for damage and see if any of the retrace is intact. Laura - "

"I'm staying," she said firmly. "I won't run out on Tyvian."

"In that case I'm staying too," Idenion declared.

"The data's in a secure file," Lydion announced wonderingly. "Tyvian must have transferred it when the crystals shattered. He stayed in the loop and caught the full force of that backlash."

"But what use is the retrace if we don't know where the Synectics are?" asked Laura.

"I can tell you where they are," said a new voice. Startled, they realised they'd left Quetri unguarded. He was sitting on the edge of the couch, shaking his head groggily. Tralvar fought down his momentary dismay and addressed the young Narvellan in cold, precise tones.

"I am First Citizen Tralvar, and you are my prisoner. Any attempt to summon help will fail, as your Moderators are busy elsewhere - " He glanced at Idenion, who signalled confirmation. " - and the rest of your people have closed off their perception to avoid the effects of our revels."

"I don't want to summon help," Quetri said waveringly. "I want to offer *my* help against the Synectics. Your experiment has freed me."

+What a clever ploy!+ Lydion remarked cynically. +I bet you weren't expecting *that* one, eh, Tralvar?+

+Be quiet+ Tralvar shot back at him. Then, returning his attention to Quetri:

"If you're free, why aren't you running around like a maniac?"

"Because," said Quetri with great dignity, "I'm going to be sick."

Laura dashed forward with a bucket and he vomited into it with intriguing daintiness. When he'd finished she rinsed away the contents and brought him some water, holding the glass for him and encouraging him to drink.

"You are not Celestrian," he remarked suddenly.

"Chaos," muttered Lydion.

"Is my prill all right?" Laura demanded of Tralvar.

"Perfectly. It wasn't attuned to the aldacite."

"Then how did he know?"

"Your odour," said Quetri with devastating honesty.

She hid her embarrassment well, giving a nervous laugh. "I suppose I've been sweating."

"Not that I've noticed," Idenion reassured her. "Bear in mind this is the first time you've been so close to a Narvellan. They say we all smell of liman. You obviously don't."

"Something else to watch out for in future," she commented.

"I apologise. I meant no insult," Quetri said formally.

"You do realise," said Tralvar, fixing him with a glare, "that if our experiment had gone to plan, we wouldn't be having this conversation?"

"Because I would be dead," Quetri answered quietly, glancing in the direction of the rest room. "Instead, your friend has been struck down. I feel responsible for that."

"Indeed," Tralvar remarked. "These fine sentiments are all very well, but the fact remains that your behaviour is not typical of a newly-liberated Narvellan."

"You have to believe me!" cried Quetri.

"Fortunately," Tralvar went on magnanimously, "there's a way to verify your claim. Lydion, didn't you say you could perceive the Synectic presence in Eluthia's mind, like a veil or pattern?"

"Only when I attempted unity with her," he replied, slightly puzzled. Then, as realisation dawned: "No. *Oh* no. I'm not doing that!"

"You're the only one who can settle this," Tralvar pointed out.

"Forget it."

"I suppose you'd rather I killed him?" Tralvar's voice grew louder as the dispute gained momentum. "Do you think I'm going to let him walk free if there's the slightest possibility that he's lying?"

"Please, Lydion," Laura put in.

Idenion, uncomfortably reminded of Tralvar's stance on Narad, said nothing.

"Quetri deserves his chance to live," Laura was continuing. "It won't be *that* unpleasant for you, surely? Not after running into the Synectics themselves?"

Lydion sighed. "All right, all right. As you say, I've survived worse things. What did you do with that bucket? I might need it." Then, to Quetri: "Well, young man, you know what's at stake here. I have to unite with you. You've done this before, I imagine, in your time as a neph-khet, so it shouldn't be too onerous. But you're not to respond, do you understand? If I get just one hint of reciprocity you'll find yourself upside-down in that rain barrel over there."

"I will be compliant," Quetri said tremulously.

Lydion sat down next to him, placing a friendly but authoritative hand on his shoulder. In the silence that followed, Drusa's sobbing could be distinctly heard. Idenion quietly went to investigate.

Laura expected Lydion to fulfil his duty in double-quick time, but surprisingly this didn't happen. He maintained his pose, frowning a little. It was Quetri who eventually drew away, looking shaken and reproachful. Lydion merely looked apologetic; a lesser surprise.

"Listen, young one, I'm sorry about that. It wasn't very kind of me. But I had to be sure." Then he turned to Tralvar. "He wasn't lying. There was no hint of a pattern. At the moment, he's not best pleased with me as he thinks I've trivialised his memories of Navarian. But he'll get over it."

"Is there anything else I should know?"

"I didn't try to extract information," said Lydion testily. "I'll leave that to you. You shouldn't have any trouble - he seems to like you, in spite of the death threats. And now, with your permission, I think I'd better have another look at that retrace and get it into a more coherent form. Then we can ask him to explain the parts we don't understand."

"Do you know how to configure a retrace?"

"I've watched Tyvian often enough. I'll manage. But if I can't make sense of it visually I'll need one intact crystal and one prill." He went over to the workstation, leaving Tralvar to address Quetri's unresponsive back.

"Now that's over, supposing you tell me where I might find the Synectics?"

"Oh, Tralvar, leave him alone!" Laura protested. "He's been kidnapped, retraced, forced into unity - to say nothing of discovering he's been a pawn of the Synectics

192

for five years. You haven't even given him credit for not freaking out!"

"Very well - my questions can wait," Tralvar said reluctantly. "But here's one for *you*. What in chaos are we going to do with him?"

Laura was momentarily stumped. Behind her, Quetri anxiously raised his head.

"Then I am still your prisoner, First Citizen?"

"Let's say you're my guest," Tralvar replied, and would have added more had it not been for the reappearance of Idenion and a pale, composed Drusa. Laura confronted the healer accusingly.

"Tyvian's dead, isn't he?"

Drusa inclined her head silently.

"Why did you throw me out?" Laura went on angrily. "I wanted to be with him!"

"He didn't know Drusa was there," Idenion said to pacify her. "He was beyond all help before she even arrived."

"Which she did remarkably quickly," Tralvar commented. "Where were you, Drusa? Hiding up a tree?"

"I live in the attic of the frame-maker's shop, just opposite," Drusa explained. "Tyvian said that if I saw or heard anything tonight, I was to stay away. I'd never seen him look so fatalistic."

"So you kept watch."

"Exactly." Drusa peered past him at Quetri. "I can't imagine what's been going on here, but I might have known Tyvian was using the retracer at your instigation."

"You can't lay this at *my* door," Tralvar objected. "He had ample opportunity to train someone in the retracer's use, and he never would. This is as much his fault as anyone's."

"You still don't know, do you?" said Drusa, so bitterly that Lydion turned round in curiosity. "The prill emanations, in their charged state, are habit-forming. Almost from the outset, Tyvian was hopelessly addicted to that machine. It ruined his life."

"How long have you known about this?" asked Laura, startled.

"Only latterly, when he started going into withdrawal every time he ran out of crystals. That was why he'd never let anyone else conduct a retrace, not even counsellors from the Tafret Academy."

"If he'd told me, I'd have made fewer demands on him," Tralvar said defensively.

"No you wouldn't. You wanted results, First Citizen, just like all the rest. Well, I hope you're satisfied. He died believing he was still linked to the retracer. Eight crystals, always eight, eight is the key, over and over with his last scrap of consciousness. I couldn't break through it to ease his final moments."

"Eight is the key," Laura repeated. "He was talking about that the other day. All about the lattice and universal resonance and infinity. Why should he remember that on his deathbed?"

Quetri suddenly spoke up, agitated. "I knew it. The Synectics killed your friend."

Drusa regarded him coldly. "Tyvian died of a cerebral haemorrhage, triggered by the aldacite backlash. Who are the Synectics?"

"Show her, Lydion," said Tralvar wearily. "Like it or not, Drusa, you're in this now. I don't think you'll be so argumentative once you've seen the face of the enemy. Now, Quetri, what's this all about?"

"I've no proof, but I'm convinced retracing me left Tyvian open to attack. Your theory of the universe, your rule of eight, is the type of information the Synectics would kill for. It could conceivably bring them closer to their goal."

"Which is?"

"They want to become incorporeal." The youth's words hovered in the silence as if time had momentarily slowed. His audience was stunned, amazed, yet no-one attempted to read him. They believed.

"Do you think they can do it?" whispered Laura.

"Given what they've done so far, yes. Eventually."

"And what will happen to your people then?"

"Oh - please..." Quetri buried his head in his hands for a moment, then looked up at Tralvar through tear-reddened eyes. "I'm so tired. You can tie me up, lock me in, do whatever you feel is essential to keep me here - but you *have* to let me sleep!"

"We're *all* tired," Tralvar declared. "You'd better come with me, Quetri, and we'll make decisions in the morning. Lydion, how are you getting on with that retrace?"

"Not too well. I'll work on it for a bit."

"Did Tyvian know your plans, Tralvar?" asked Idenion. "If so, it might be wise to change them. "

"That won't be necessary," answered Tralvar with the merest hint of a smile. "I hadn't planned anything beyond tonight."

It was very late, and cold enough to make Quetri shiver violently. Laura found a piece of sacking and put it round his shoulders in lieu of a cloak. Idenion checked for Moderators; there were still none, but the sciesha had almost dissipated.

"We'll have to hurry," he said. "Quickly, Laura. Bring a rushlight."

She hesitated, gazing after Drusa, who had gone back to where Tyvian lay.

"She doesn't want our help," Idenion said gently.

"Because she blames us."

"She won't. Not when she's had a chance to think about it."

Along the street, Tralvar's house lights still burned comfortingly. In silence they stumbled toward this welcome oasis, too fatigued to dwell further on their eerie discovery.

Chapter Seven

Lydion worked on until morning, exhibiting a stamina he'd hitherto only applied to his love life. If he took away Quetri's retrace before it was fully processed, there might never be a chance to complete it. He had no idea what would happen to the retracer, or indeed the laboratory itself, once Tyvian's death was announced. Losing Tyvian had saddened him far more than he'd admitted to Tralvar and the others. The old man should have had a long and peaceful retirement, instead of ending his days in thrall to the machine he'd hated.

Lydion had wasted nearly an ild searching for the rest of the crystals, choosing a suitable prill and flushing the smoke fumes out of the tank. While turning out cabinets and drawers he'd come across dozens of programme chips - every retrace for the past five years, placed in small bags and labelled neatly as if they'd been packets of seeds. On an impulse he'd removed the recording of himself and Eluthia. It was too sensitive an item to leave for strangers to pick up. He'd also looked for Laura's music retrace, but it was not to be found.

It had taken a certain degree of courage to put on the diagnostic sensor and start up the retracer, even though Drusa had assured him that the playback, with its minimal use of prill and aldacite, carried no risk. He forced himself not to believe that Tyvian had been murdered. It was either that or head out of the door and keep running. The crystals' cascade failure had been un-nerving, but there had been instances of multiple backlash before. And as for the prill's spontaneous combustion, one spark could have caused a fire in the oxygen-rich atmosphere of the tank.

At first light Drusa returned with two stolid young men from the mortuary. While they went about their business she drifted over to see how Lydion was faring.

"I'm sorry I can't help you with that," she said, indicating the screen. "My concern was always with the retracees."

"I think I've got the measure of it now. Quetri's mindset is a little odd." To say nothing of that oh-so-familiar pattern surrounding everything, his thoughts wandered on. I have to keep telling myself it's only a recording, it won't recognise me...

"You're exhausted," Drusa said, her soft grey eyes full of concern.

"Try scared."

"*You're* scared?" she whispered fiercely. "How do you think I felt, walking into all this? How did you find out about - *them*? And how did you locate that boy?"

"I'll explain later," Lydion promised, noting that she hadn't said a word about Laura. That could only mean she hadn't recognised her; something else that would need explaining.

"I don't have to be at the hospital until this afternoon," she was saying. "When you've finished here, can I offer you some breakfast and a chance to catch up on your sleep?" Clearly she didn't want to be alone. At any other time Lydion would have accepted, in the easy way he accepted all such invitations. But for once, he forbore.

"Tralvar's waiting for this. I really should take it to him," he said apologetically. The two mortuary assistants reappeared, and he watched them in sober silence. It was a surprisingly small bundle they carried.

"Shall we notify the registry, Healer Drusa?" asked one.

"Thank you; I'd appreciate it," she replied, quietly professional. "I'll supply the paperwork tomorrow."

They disappeared outside with their burden, leaving the door ajar. Drusa left by the front entrance, checking the water levels in the hrilffa troughs as she went. Lydion resumed his work, soon realising he was closer to completing it than he'd thought. The further into the retrace he progressed, the less time the computer took to reorganise the data. *Now* I know why you're so keen on helping us, Quetri my lad, he thought idly as a tense drama was enacted before him. Almost before he knew it he was at the end, with Idenion's voice - distant, dreamlike - asking for the Synectics' location. He tore off the sensor just in time; the screen flashed white, then went blank. Thankfully, Lydion closed his tired eyes and leant back in his chair - only to jolt upright in alarm as a Narvellan voice said:

"Supposing you tell me what's been going on here?"

A Moderator stood at his elbow.

Startled, snatched back from sleep, Lydion could think of nothing to say.

"We had reports of a disturbance," continued the Moderator, then paused and peered more closely at him. "I know you! Lydion of Atris. Offences against public morality."

"*Your* morality, not mine," Lydion retorted; and, suddenly, was inspired. His salvation lay in his own hands - or rather, in his pocket. The Moderator had noticed the prill and crystal debris which Lydion had simply thrown on the floor after clearing the tank. While his attention was momentarily distracted Lydion palmed the Quetri retrace chip and substituted the one of himself and Eluthia. Now all he had to do was keep the Moderator talking while it loaded.

"I'm just a hopeless case, I'm afraid," he said with his most charming smile. "What is it you people say - moderation in all things? Does that include love?"

199

"You would be wise not to mock our tenets," the Moderator warned. "Now kindly explain why several honest citizens heard noise and screams coming from this building."

"Oh, you know. Sciesha." Lydion waved an arm vaguely.

"There was no sciesha in this area." The green-eyed gaze was implacable.

"Why must you people split hairs?" Lydion inquired wearily. "My friends and I had a bit of a wild night, and then they left to join the sciesha. I stayed here to clear up."

"A wild night," repeated the Moderator. "Here, in a scientific facility."

"Why not?" returned Lydion blandly. Behind his interrogator, the system signalled its readiness.

"You," pronounced the Narvellan, "are up to something. Shielding won't do you any good - we Moderators are trained to seek out guilt, and in your case it's almost palpable. Will you confess here, or at the akron? It's all the same to me."

Lydion appeared to give in. "I suppose I'll have to be frank with you. Please don't arrest me. Oh, discords, this is so embarrassing."

"Proceed with your statement."

"I...I..." Lydion hung his head. "I think it's best if I show you. Do you know how the retracer works? All you need do is sit here and put this sensor on your forehead."

The Moderator hesitated.

"It won't harm you," Lydion persisted. "Would I risk that? I'm in enough trouble already. That's right, make sure the sensor's properly adhered...and off we go."

The single crystal sang softly, the prill slowly unfurled its leaves, and the Moderator froze - either in shock at what he was perceiving or in resistance to it.

200

"Isn't she delicious?" Lydion whispered in his ear. "I bet you've never had a woman like *her*. Relax and enjoy being me!"

The Moderator scrabbled at the sensor with his gloved fingers, frantically peeled off his gloves and finally managed to remove the tiny disc. Then he stood up, trembling. "You are a corrupt and wicked creature, Lydion of Atris!" he spluttered. "How dare you expose me to your carnal excesses with that piece of theatrical trash!"

"You wanted to know what was going on," Lydion pointed out mildly. "I was entertaining my friends with this retrace."

"You're all depraved!" The Moderator drew several deep breaths and brushed furiously at his uniform as if depravity lurked in every dust particle. "I shall see what my superiors have to say about this!"

"You're not really going to report it, are you?" asked Lydion. "What we do behind closed doors is outside your jurisdiction. You could, I suppose, claim that I was misusing the retracer, but since it isn't Narvellan property I doubt if anyone would take much notice. Good morning!" He forced himself to turn his back on the Moderator. When he eventually looked round, the man was gone. On the screen, Eluthia laughed silently but delightedly at something the younger Lydion had said. The present-day Lydion gave her an ironic salute as he cancelled the playback. He didn't care to view the ending, with its descent into fear and chaos; and he'd gambled on the probability that the Moderator wouldn't be around to see it either.

"Too frivolous by half, eh, Tyvian?" he murmured as he took a last look round the still laboratory. "You didn't think I'd heard that, did you? Well, I daresay it's true - but I think my frivolity's just saved us. You won't have died in vain, old friend. I promise you that."

Stepping outside into a dazzling sunrise, he experienced a mind-numbing wash of tiredness. The confrontation with the Moderator had sapped even his reserves. He glanced down the road at Tralvar's house, hesitated, then turned aside.

"To chaos with it," he muttered. "They're probably all asleep anyway." A moment later he was tapping lightly on Drusa's door.

"Is it all right if I change my mind?" he asked when she opened it. Her face broke into a grateful smile.

"Come in," she said. "I'm so glad you're here."

***

That morning, Alda Mexa was full of people trying to get to their homes or employment after being stranded the night before. Chisrin surveyed his depleted workforce resignedly, uttering some disparaging remarks about sciesha. Latecomers who expected a verbal lashing were surprised to find him in such a reflective mood. He'd been perusing the report on the flawed crystals, and it had come as no surprise to him that Salvi had directed the mining.

Idenion and Dena arrived mid-morning, followed by Malcor and some other youths, but there was still no sign of Ailsi.

"Don't ask *me* where she is," Malcor replied with uncustomary ill humour when Chisrin questioned him. "She does as she pleases."

"That sounds as if she's run out on you," Chisrin remarked.

"She took sciesha with someone else," Malcor admitted sulkily.

"Oh, look, he's gone all possessive," giggled Ailsi's neighbour. "Never mind, Malcor - we'll look after you!"

"Settle down, everyone," Chisrin advised. "Boys, get to your posts."

They sloped off, Malcor falling aggressively into step beside Idenion.

"It's *your* fault she went to find sciesha," he accused.

"How can it be my fault? I wasn't even there," Idenion objected.

"You put her up to it. You probably wanted her for yourself."

Chisrin gazed after them with a trace of amusement. "Well, what a surprise. He really cares about the little so and so." Picking up a sack of crystals, he measured a careful amount onto each girl's bench. "These are only industrial, in case you're wondering, but that doesn't give you licence to hack them about. Dena, my sweet, I know it's hot in here but could you please button your neckline? You're ruining my concentration. Now I'm sure you're all aware that the day after tomorrow is a holiday. I don't intend to deprive you of it, despite what happened yesterday, so I want everyone to knuckle under and meet today's target. Get to it!"

Dena set to work mechanically. She was desperately tired, having been unable to sleep the night before. The image of the Synectics haunted her, as did the fear of discovery. Her only consolation was the certainty that her active participation was over. She'd been needed for the lattice, nothing more.

The mid-day break came and went. In the early afternoon Chisrin collected all the polished crystals, inspected them and despatched them to the monorail in the care of Idenion and Malcor. With her brother's departure, Dena's misery increased. She'd completed less than half her quota, her hands were hot and sticky and she was growing clumsier by the moment. Finally, when her vision started to blur over, she was obliged to put down her work and close her eyes. Just one astal, she told herself. I'll sit here quietly for one astal, and

203

then I'll feel better. As she rested she experienced a dreamlike sensation, as if she were slowly sinking through the floor. The noise of the workshop became muffled and inconsequential...and she suddenly realised she'd fallen sideways in her chair, and that a gentle but persistent hand was shaking her arm.

"Now, Dena, this won't do," Chisrin admonished.

She struggled up. "Oh, discords, I'm sorry. I'm awake now. I'll carry on."

"No you won't, my girl. You're in no fit state to handle sharp instruments. I've an exemplary safety record at this factory and I'm not about to let you spoil it. Come with me."

She stood up, stumbling a little, and followed him to a room near the latrines at the far end of the building. Although it had been designated a sick room she'd never known anyone use it. It contained no first aid supplies, only a washbasin and a narrow bed stripped to its mattress.

"I want you to rest for at least an ild," Chisrin instructed. "There aren't any blankets but I think you'll be warm enough." He disappeared briefly and returned with some water in a chipped cup, which he set down on the windowsill.

"Thank you for being so understanding," Dena ventured.

"Just safeguarding my interests," he said laconically, and was gone.

Dena kicked off her sandals, lay down on the unyielding mattress and fell asleep instantly.

At the same time, Idenion and Malcor were wandering around the goods yard trying to find someone to endorse their worksheet. They'd detected a large contingent of Narvellans in the station house, obviously in a meeting of some kind, which showed no sign of coming to an end. Idenion was beginning to feel weary and footsore. Unlike Dena, he'd had *some* sleep, but evidently not enough.

"I don't know why we both had to make this trip," he complained. "There's only the one box."

"I suppose Chisrin's being ultra-cautious since that other lot went missing," Malcor replied.

"The day I stole the sphere, I went to great lengths to avoid this place," Idenion continued. "If today's anything to go by, I could have saved myself the trouble. No one would've noticed if I'd walked straight in and caught a train to Treva."

"Today isn't typical," Malcor informed him. "I've been here dozens of times, remember. This must be post-sciesha disruption. No goods on the move, so no workers and no security men." Then, pointedly: "I'm surprised you didn't borrow Ailsi for your trip to Myrma. She'd have cleared the way for you."

Idenion was about to make an irritable reply when the station house door opened and a Narvellan peered out suspiciously.

"What is your errand, Celestrians?"

Idenion handed over the worksheet. The Narvellan scrutinised it, and them, at some length.

"Why has Chisrin ap Tuin sent two of you with such a small consignment?"

"That's just what we were wondering," Malcor said with what he hoped was a friendly smile.

"It would appear that Chisrin has been allocated too many workers," remarked the Narvellan, signing the docket and taking possession of the box. "Now be on your way. You should not remain here unsupervised."

"Ingrate," muttered Malcor as the door thudded shut. "Come on, Idenion, let's hurry. The driver's just re-boarded the train."

Idenion followed him unquestioningly to the rear compartment, noting that they were the only passengers.

Malcor, suddenly tense, sprawled on a seat near one of the doors. He appeared to be listening for something. Then, suddenly, he heard it - a tiny click from the automatic locking system. As the doors began to roll shut he bounded to his feet and leapt outside. The train began to move, but only as far as the nearest siding. Then the motor cut, the carriage lights went out and the driver walked off without a backward glance. The doors remained closed. Idenion, initially puzzled, suddenly realised he'd been duped.

+What are you playing at, Malcor?+

Malcor waved at him from the adjacent platform. +That'll teach you to exploit my best girl. You can cool your heels in there for a bit+

+Let me out, you imbecile!+

+Not a chance+

Another train, the correct one, pulled out of the sidings and hid Malcor from view. Idenion switched his perception to the Narvellan in the driver's cab - who was shielded - and then to the station house, which was just out of his range.

+I can see why you never made it to the relayists' guild+ observed Malcor, smirking at him from a window of the other train. +I can throw a thought twice that distance+

+Then tell them to open these doors!+ pleaded Idenion.

+If I do, you won't have learnt your lesson+ Malcor pointed out reasonably. +Don't worry, I'll make sure you don't have to spend the night in there+

Fuming, Idenion watched the rear of the last carriage dwindle southward. Then, resignedly, he made himself comfortable and waited for the Narvellans' meeting to break up. Long before it did, he'd dozed off - unaware that across town, his twin also slept.

***

At Tralvar's request, Laura had remained at the villa.

"I have to find Lydion," he explained, "and someone has to keep an eye on Quetri. He can't stay here on his own."

"You still don't trust him?"

"No, as it happens - but it isn't just that. He has information we need and we shouldn't let him out of our sight until we have it. He's awake now. Why don't you make him some breakfast, or should I say lunch, while I run over to the lab?"

"I hope Lydion isn't in any trouble," Laura said anxiously.

"If he were, I'm sure we'd have heard about it by now," Tralvar replied. "I think I know where he's gone."

Laura found Quetri leafing through some of Tralvar's books. He obediently followed her to the kitchen and sat sipping liman while she toasted some grain cakes. She was quite happy to supervise him, although she guessed that given the choice, Tralvar wouldn't have asked her. It was simply a question of expediency - everyone else had somewhere to be, and she didn't. But, she reminded herself, this was the second day she hadn't done any sewing. She'd probably have to work non-stop the day after.

She drizzled some syrup onto the toasted cakes and set them before Quetri, who rewarded her with a diffident smile. His table manners were a delight to watch: he cut each cake into four and held each portion lightly between thumb and forefinger while he took small, neat bites. When he drank, his grip on the cup handle was a study in elegance. Laura supposed this was all part of being a neph-khet.

"Navarian did not teach me how to behave at table," Quetri answered in response to her polite question. "I was trained by Tarysk tyl Pellon, his closest relative on

Narvella Prime. She took possession of me shortly after Navarian died."

"And you're not content with this arrangement?" asked Laura carefully.

"I despise Tarysk," Quetri replied candidly. "She sees me only as something to ill-treat. My hope was that Hysek would adopt me - he is Navarian's cousin and next of kin. Also, there is a younger cousin in Corayn. But all my attempts to meet with them have come to nothing."

"Will Tarysk force you to go back?"

"She doesn't need to. I was only granted temporary leave, and my time is already up." Quetri looked up at her searchingly. "And you too are here illegally?"

"Yes," Laura said quietly. There seemed little point in denying it.

"I heard the stories. Your home is on Myrma, is it not?"

Laura was about to foster this misapprehension when the door opened and Lydion catapulted in, pushed by Tralvar.

"I found him," the latter said grimly. "And do you know where he was? In Drusa's bed!"

"Oh, Lydion," Laura said reproachfully. "Don't you ever stop chasing women?"

"I do not *chase* women!" he replied, affronted. "I don't need to. Would it help if I said I only slept there? Drusa and I go back a long way; she saw I was exhausted and said she'd put me up."

They regarded him sceptically.

"All right, so I went there with the intention of having unity with her," Lydion admitted. "And if I hadn't been so tired, I might have. What am I supposed to do for a partner while all this is going on? I can't stray outside the group."

"I'm glad you're taking your commitment so seriously," Tralvar replied with less ire. "Where's that retrace?"

"Here." Lydion solemnly held up a Moderator's black glove.

Tralvar raised his eyebrows.

"I - er - had a visitor," Lydion confided, trying to keep a straight face. "He left in rather a hurry. The memory chip just fits nicely inside the index finger."

"You obviously can't wait to share the joke, so we'd better hear it," Tralvar said resignedly.

Grinning, Lydion recounted the story of the Moderator. Laura and Tralvar both saw the funny side, but Quetri frowned.

"You shouldn't make enemies of these people," he warned. "They always bear grudges."

"Goes with the job, I suppose," Lydion said airily. "Don't worry - I'll behave myself from now on. No more sciesha in the communal gardens. So, Tralvar, I'll just install this masterpiece in your logic system and then I must be away." He breezed into the study; Tralvar followed more slowly.

"Will it be compatible with other systems?"

"It should be, but I'm not promising anything."

"It has to work, Lydion. We need it to convince people to help us."

Lydion considered. "Well, put it this way: if it works here it'll work anywhere. These circuits are pretty fried."

"The equipment's old," Tralvar reminded him.

"So's most of the hardware in this city. It's worn out because you've thrashed it. No patience with machinery, that's your trouble."

"Just get it running," Tralvar said wearily.

"Kyrin's here!" called Laura from the kitchen.

"Ah. I thought he might turn up. Bring him through, would you, and Quetri as well?"

Kyrin put his head round the door anxiously. "I know about Tyvian," he said in reply to Tralvar's unspoken question. "I relayed Drusa's message to the hospital. What happened last night? Did you get your evidence?"

"Come and see."

The monitor was displaying an interesting chevron pattern; Tralvar whacked it with the flat of his hand and the picture settled down. Quetri gave a choked cry as he came face to face with the image of his father.

"Yes, your memories, Quetri." Tralvar was suddenly as autocratic as he'd been the previous night. "This is the recording Tyvian gave his life for. It's visual only, since I don't have the resources of the lab, but that's all we need for the present. Watch carefully. I'm going to want some definitive answers from you, such as the location of the Synectics' base."

Lydion was just disappearing out of the back door when Laura caught up with him.

"I just wanted to thank you for all you did yesterday," she said. "You've been brilliant. Tralvar never shows his gratitude but I know he'd want me to add his thanks."

"Your appreciation makes it all worthwhile, First Singer," he replied in his usual facile way, trying to avoid looking disarmed. "I'll be around if you need me - but I'm not sure what I could do after this. It's in the hands of the scientists now."

"We're bound to need a courier sometimes."

"No problem. My work takes me all over the city."

"And Lydion - Drusa's really going to miss Tyvian. Be kind to her."

"I'll do that. In return, keep in mind what I said about Tralvar. He's on a permanent knife-edge, so try not to make it worse by squabbling. Oh, I nearly forgot with all that's been going on: Melor's students, including Nefyrra, are performing at the Lyricon in two days' time. We've had a dispensation to run the weathershield."

"I'll let Tralvar know," Laura promised. "And I'll almost certainly be there myself." Then she hurried back to the study.

"The Pahl-drehinor Institute was based in Rhul, Narvella Prime's capital," Quetri was saying. "That's where Navarian took me as a child. When your people gave us the stardrive there were moves to close the Synectics down, but they persuaded the authorities not to act - at least, not straight away.

"It was at about this time that Navarian adopted me. I remember that first trip to the Institute so well. He was so proud of the project and totally dedicated to its furtherance."

"So we have *him* to blame for all this?" inquired Tralvar.

Quetri didn't reply. He looked away for a moment and Laura caught the glint of tears on his eyelashes.

"What are we seeing now?" asked Kyrin, intent on the screen. "Some kind of civil unrest?"

"Yes; things grew very unpleasant in Rhul," said Quetri, recovering. "Before the arrival of the Celestrians there had been very little trouble. Everyone was resigned to their fate, knowing that rich and poor would perish together. But once people knew there was a means of escape, they started accusing the elite of commandeering it. A lottery was set up to allocate places, but it was widely believed to be rigged. We needed law enforcers - and so the Moderators were born. The Synectics devised their creed, showed us how to recruit them with personality tests, and gave us the schematic for the stun-cannon.

211

"Here you see Navarian in communication with the Synectic loop. They have no way of speaking aloud, so he had to open his mind to them. The woman was normally the conduit; I hated the way she kept him pinned in front of her until she'd finished. It was at a session like this - perhaps this very one - that she declared the group felt vulnerable and wished to be relocated in secret. They chose Ipsa, a moon of Narvella Five, and supervised the building of an underground base.

"Everyone was told the Synectics had perished. Even the construction workers didn't know what they were building - they thought it was a bunker. The only people who knew the truth were the base personnel and the government. As soon as the relocation was complete the Synectics were asked for ways to speed up the space programme. They responded by creating synthetic aldacite."

There was a gap in the retrace chronology at this point. "I was separated from Navarian while I finished my education," Quetri explained. "On my fourteenth birthday I took up a junior post on the base, and Navarian officially named me his neph-khet. But as I was still a bondservant I was not allowed to use the tyl Pellon title."

Laura noticed that he was becoming more and more unsettled. He frequently paused in his narrative, once due to a spasm of coughing. Tralvar offered him some resnay well diluted with fruit juice, and poured a stronger measure for himself. Kyrin, as usual, abstained.

The screen showed the row of stasis units in their dimly lit cavern. Here, unlike the Institute, there had been no concession to aesthetics. Wires and hoses snaked out from beneath each cylinder and met in a plethora of joints and splices. The main feed artery disappeared into the pumping chamber overhead.

"After the success of the crystals," Quetri continued, fidgeting with his glass, "the government expected more innovations - but the Synectics offered no more sops to keep them happy. In fact they were scarcely communicating at all, save with themselves. They detested having the outer shells of their units opened and they had cut their nutrient intake several times, saying it blunted their concentration. We simply couldn't get through to them. Finally, the edict which we had been dreading arrived: funding had been suspended and the project was over. Navarian was bitterly disappointed. He delayed telling the Synectics, not knowing if he even should. But they knew.

"That night - the simulated night which was all we had on the base - I woke with the conviction that something was wrong. The air seemed fetid and I felt off-balance. I got dressed and went to check the life support, but it was functioning normally. So was the artificial gravity. I don't know what made me go into the Synectics' chamber, but - oh, chaos, why are you making me look at this? Surely you've seen it before?"

"Not in any coherent way," Tralvar said in less aggressive tones than he'd used of late. "An unedited retrace is seldom easy to follow. Lydion arranged these sequences in what he hoped was chronological order. I need you to confirm his accuracy and add your own interpretation."

"And then what will you do?"

"Show it to potential recruits. I haven't selected anyone yet, and I won't until I've seen all of this. So, with your permission, we'll go on."

"You will despise me," Quetri said unexpectedly. "You too, Kyrin - and you, Laura."

"Try to remember it's Lisset," she said anxiously.

"You will hate me," Quetri went on, unheeding. "You will all hate me for what I've done."

On the screen, the stasis units glowed greenly; their shells had been retracted. The rest of the chamber was deserted. Quetri's viewpoint wheeled about uncertainly.

"What's happening now?" Tralvar asked impatiently.

"I became even more nervous," Quetri recalled. "We never left the chamber unattended. Ever. Everything looked perfectly normal, but it didn't *feel* normal. As no one seemed to be in range of my perception I decided to check on the Synectics first and then find out who should have been on watch."

The absolute silence of the retrace only added to its sinister content. In the green-tinged light, Quetri made his way toward the column-mounted systems which displayed the Synectics' life signs - and what he saw made him step back in alarm. On each panel, the neural activity was off the scale. As he retreated he stumbled over something on the floor - a technician, lying half-hidden beneath one of the displays. He wasn't breathing. Quetri was poised to run for help when he froze, his gaze arrested by a movement within one of the cylinders. The Synectic woman had opened her rheumy yellow eyes and was staring in his direction.

"She couldn't see me, of course; she's blind," Quetri told his audience. "But she was aware of me - they all were - and for one brief instant I knew what they intended to do. When it began it was as if a tidal wave had hit me. I was carried along, terrified yet exhilarated. All around I could sense minds burning out, unable to ride the storm - but I knew I'd live through it. I could perceive the stars through the bedrock; I could sense the twin homeworlds thundering in their orbits. And I knew my future would be taken care of in the same inexorable way. Then, like a shutter slamming down, everything stopped. The vision, and my memory of it, was gone - until a day ago."

214

Quetri's viewpoint, which had remained fixed on the yellow gaze of the hag, shifted at last. The chamber lights began to strobe; someone had thrown an emergency switch. Laura suspected there was an ear-splitting siren in operation and was glad she couldn't hear it. In the flickering glare, Quetri coolly re-examined the dead man he'd tripped over. It was the duty technician, a newcomer to Ipsa, and - judging by where he lay - the one who'd had the temerity to look inside the stasis units. Slowly and deliberately Quetri extended his slippered foot and shoved the corpse off the control dais.

Beside Laura, the older Quetri cringed. "I'm so ashamed of that," he murmured.

"Did the Synectics really murder him just for looking at them?" she asked.

"Partly. I imagine he saw the abnormal readings and looked to see if they were in distress. His next move would have been to fetch Navarian, who would probably have sedated them until he found out what was wrong."

"And the others you perceived? The burnt-out minds?"

"Sacrifices," Quetri whispered. "To the Synectics' terrible ambition. Watch."

The young Quetri reverently closed the shells and left the chamber. On the way out he met Navarian, who had come to find him. Showing no alarm nor haste they fell into step and stoically explored the caverns, looking for survivors. There weren't many - perhaps a third of the base personnel. The dead were everywhere; in work areas, recreation rooms and their own beds. There wasn't a mark on any of them.

"And once you'd lost free will, you genuinely couldn't remember what had killed those people?" inquired Tralvar.

"Of course not. Navarian said it must have been some kind of mass hysteria," Quetri said sombrely. "The project was reprieved, of course, but help wasn't immediately forthcoming. We discovered via the radio that there had been a smattering of similar deaths throughout the Protectorate. The authorities called it brain fever and warned everyone to be on their guard against cases of aberrant behaviour. And we were instructed in the use of the Ten."

"What was it like, being controlled?" asked Laura.

"Like having no conscience. I could see how wrong everything had become, but I just didn't care."

The screen was displaying Navarian in close-up, addressing Quetri earnestly and at some length. The speech was accompanied by much emotion - hugs, tears, sudden caresses.

Tralvar hastily tried to skip part of the replay. "I'm sorry, Quetri. I told Lydion not to retain any personal interludes."

"He kept it for a reason," Quetri said, his voice low and sorrowful. "After about half a year, Navarian managed to break his conditioning. He planned to get rid of the Synectics by poisoning the main feed line. He made the preparations and then...then he told *me*." He was weeping freely now. "I don't know why he did that. He knew I was still under their control. I suppose he thought he could get through to me somehow - and I pretended he had."

The stasis units were on the screen again, their blank metal shells hiding the corruption within.

"Then I went and stood where Navarian had always stood," Quetri went on in a rush. "I called upon the woman with all my mental strength. And when she eventually answered, I denounced Navarian. Do you realise what I'm saying? I destroyed him just as surely as if I'd killed him myself. And the worst thing was, I didn't regret it. I believed he was a traitor. Yesterday when I woke in the laboratory I also woke to my guilt. I was so remorseful that my first instinct was to say nothing and let you do away with me - and then I realised that by helping you I could be avenged." He gazed tearfully at the monitor. "While you doubted my integrity I still couldn't allow myself to mourn Navarian. Now, I must. And I have to try and live with my crime - although I don't think I shall ever be able to."

He sobbed afresh, and Laura made a tentative move to comfort him. Kyrin, however, restrained her.

"The guilt may not subside but the grief may, if we allow him to express it," he murmured. But Tralvar, blatantly ignoring this advice, grasped Quetri's chin and tilted his head up.

"Don't consider yourself unique," he snapped. "You're not the only one to carry such a burden. I too was forced to kill someone I loved."

His words had the desired effect: Quetri's sobs diminished. "*You*?"

"Anyone will tell you the story of Tralvar and Tristell. My people forgave me, but I still haven't forgiven myself. We have much in common, Quetri, and it seems only fitting that we should have been thrown together in this way. I hope you'll continue to assist me."

The retrace ended, its final moments containing no revelations. Lydion had edited out the attack on Tyvian.

"Well, Quetri?" Tralvar persisted. "Do you think we can work together?"

"I would be honoured," Quetri responded, dabbing at his eyes. "But there's still the matter of my bond. Tarysk tyl Pellon will soon discover that I never met with Hysek, and she will demand my return."

"Let's assume for the moment that I can deal with her," said Tralvar. "What I *cannot* do is shelter you in my house. And once you leave, you'll have an exacting role to play. You'll have to live among the possessed and convince them you're the same as they are."

"Supposing he gets re-absorbed?" asked Laura before Quetri could reply.

"There's no risk of that," Tralvar assured her. "Consider how paranoid the Narvellans are about the free, and how ruthlessly they hunt them down."

"That's the Synectics' fear, not ours!" Quetri put in.

"Exactly! Whatever the Synectics did to all of you, I believe it can't be repeated."

"I agree," said Kyrin. "Imagine a vast net thrown to catch a myriad small fish. If a few escape they cannot be recaptured. The only alternative would be to gather up the net and try to cast it again, losing the rest of the catch."

"That's an intriguing analogy," said Quetri.

"Kyrin was born in a fishing village," Laura explained. "So, Quetri, how good an actor are you? Do you think you can fool your people?"

"I shall!" he vowed.

"There's something I'm still curious about," she went on. "If we're right - if this control net was a one-off - what about the children born on the Narvellan homeworlds since the enslavement began? Are we to assume they're free?"

"That never occurred to me," mused Quetri, wrinkling his brow. "I suppose they must be. But still too young to notice anything's amiss, and too young for the Synectics to consider them a threat. Long before that happens, the experiment will have ended - one way or another."

"There's one more thing that doesn't add up," said Tralvar. "Naturally the Synectics want to escape from the solar flares, and they'll need some devoted followers to look after them until they move on to a higher plane.

218

If they do! But why are they intent on saving so many of you? Not altruism, surely?"

"Have I not yet made it clear?" Quetri returned with weary patience. "Those so-called brain fever victims, thousands of them all over the Protectorate: I said they were sacrifices, but I didn't mean they were failed attempts at control. *They* are the reason the control succeeded! The Synectics drained them, absorbed their life energy. And if thousands were needed to establish their net, how many more will they need when they launch into a disembodied state? Possibly every single one of us. That's why we're being kept alive, and that's the knowledge which assails every Narvellan who becomes free."

"Then you believe," said Kyrin, vastly intrigued, "that everyone knew - too late - what the Synectics were doing?"

"Perception differs from individual to individual. But yes, I think everyone had a similar experience to mine."

Tralvar stood up and poured himself another drink. "Well, Quetri, you've certainly opened my eyes to a few things. I thought I'd be fighting the Narvellans, not trying to save them!"

"Then I have repaid you in kind," said Quetri, "as yesterday you opened *my* eyes to more than a little. The irony is, I only came to Celestra because I wanted to work for the Synectics again. Tarysk took me from the base; I thought Hysek might be willing to send me back. And now, I should return to my lodgings. I'm supposed to report to the akron shortly."

"Then you'd better keep the appointment," Tralvar conceded. "I'll see you out. And don't worry about Tarysk - I'll make sure you she doesn't reclaim you. I need you here!"

Quetri rose to leave. "I somehow don't believe I'm the only free Narvellan on your world," he said softly. "There must be others, keeping quiet, simply staying alive. The pity of it is, I shall never know."

All four of them crossed the hall to the door, but before they reached it several young Celestrians entered without announcing themselves. Their sleeve badges identified them as sphere assembly workers.

"There, you see?" said one. "I knew he'd forgotten."

"Forgotten what?" asked Tralvar.

"We've just come from Treva," said the spokesman in aggressive tones. "The forty prisoners were shipped out today. You were supposed to be there, to give them support if nothing else. Instead we find you junketing with Narvellans!"

"I regret it isn't possible for me to be everywhere at once," Tralvar replied levelly. "A delicate diplomatic situation kept me here."

"He's a bit young for a diplomat, isn't he?" remarked another of the group, looking Quetri up and down. "He's no older than we are."

"Never mind that," said a third. "Get on with the declaration."

"Didn't Jarras pass on my message to you?" Tralvar asked, suddenly appearing very tired. "These confrontations waste time and solve nothing."

Kyrin took Quetri's arm and steered him outside as unobtrusively as possible.

"Jarras!" scoffed the leader of the militants. "Of course he'd take your side when you're grooming him to be First Scientist. Yes, he told us to behave because you'd got everything in hand. Well, we don't believe you have."

"This is a vote of no confidence," said his crony. "We're here as representatives of the Trevan theridolyte

220

industry. We intend to ask the administration to remove you and appoint a First Citizen who'll stand up for our rights."

"Instead of one who spends his time drinking and strumming the zirid," said the fourth worker, taking cover behind the others as soon as he'd spoken.

Laura, who had been hanging back cautiously, took some angry steps forward. Tralvar put out an arm to restrain her.

"I assume you're calling on *our* administration, or what's left of it?" he inquired. "Go ahead, register your plaint. Who will you nominate in my place?"

"What?" The quartet's resolve seemed to waver.

"Surely you've acquainted yourself with the rules? If you move to dismiss a First Citizen you must propose a candidate in his stead. Who have you chosen? Which one of you thinks he can make the Narvellans respect him? You can't even look *me* in the eye - how long do you think you'd last with Axmiol? You'd be laughed out of the akron!"

"We didn't come here to be sneered at," the leader muttered.

"That's a pity, because it's all you deserve," Tralvar rejoined. "The next time you put in an appearance get your campaign properly organised and stop trying to hide behind one another. Do that and I might take you seriously. Until then I suggest you keep quiet, get on with your job and allow me to do mine."

They departed with some angry backward looks. Tralvar watched to see which way they went. They were still headed for the akron. Without a word to Laura he stalked back into the study and seized the resnay bottle. This time he didn't bother with a glass.

"You certainly saw them off," Laura said tentatively from the study doorway.

"Not really." He put down the bottle and leant wearily on the table. "You shouldn't be taken in by all that bluster. *They* weren't. You see, I did forget about the deportations. I promised I'd attend. I've done nothing for the prisoners' partners and I haven't even been to see Cyphos' widow."

"If you *had* remembered you couldn't have gone to Treva," Laura pointed out. "All this is very unfortunate, but we have to stay focused on the Synectics and what to do about them."

"You're right of course." Tralvar took one more swig of resnay, then put the bottle away. "Before I start planning countermeasures, I have to sort out this business of the tyl Pellon woman and Quetri's bond. I think I have a solution."

"You promised him," Laura said somewhat tactlessly.

"I did, and this is one promise I intend to keep. It will mean visiting the akron myself, so I'll give our militant friends time to be on their way."

"And I'd better be on mine. Any chance of a flitter ride?"

"Certainly." Tralvar made an effort to smile.

"Thanks. There'll still be time for some sewing if I go now. Oh, I've just remembered - Lydion said that Nefyrra's going to be at the Lyricon the day after tomorrow. Why don't we all make a day of it?"

"And what would my critics have to say about that?" he countered.

"You *need* a day off!" Laura argued.

Tralvar's smile became broader. "Don't worry, I'll be there. There's been too little music in my life of late. And besides - Nefyrra and I have a lot of catching up to do."

***

222

Dena awoke to an unnatural hush. The multitudinous noises of the factory had ceased, as had the mind-chatter of the workers. The place was all but deserted.

I must have slept for three ilden or more, she thought guiltily, sitting up and rubbing her eyes. The drinking water, lukewarm and brackish, was where it had been left. She drained the glass thirstily, then hunted in vain for her shoes.

"Looking for these?" inquired a masculine voice. She whirled to behold Chisrin leaning on the door and dangling her sandals by their straps. "I was just making sure you stayed put until I'd had a word with you, young lady."

"I'm sorry I slept so long," she said contritely. "You should have woken me."

"On the contrary. You needed to sleep, and the loss to the work effort was minimal. It's your brother I wish to discuss."

"Idenion?" Dena was genuinely puzzled. "Why?"

"Because his behaviour seems, shall we say, erratic - starting from the time he so spectacularly retrieved Lisset. There's something very odd going on, and I believe you know what it is."

Dena was thrown into a panic. She closed off her perception completely, realising too late that her reaction would make him even more suspicious. "I...I don't understand you," she stammered, trying frantically to think of something plausible. "Nothing's going on. Idenion and Lisset are very happy."

"All Celestrians are bad liars," declared Chisrin, "and *you* must be the worst ever. Let me tell you what's really been happening. Sit down, if it will make you less nervous."

Fearfully, Dena obeyed.

223

"They're happy, you say," he continued with studied nonchalance. "So why does she spend so much time with the First Citizen? What are these strange flitter trips into the middle of nowhere? And why, Dena, are you slowly going to pieces? It's my contention —" he leant closer - "that Idenion has a secret lover. Someone who isn't Celestrian."

Dena blanched, then recovered. But not quickly enough.

"In other words," Chisrin stated, "she's Narvellan. A Directress, sworn to chastity. Don't try to deny it - I checked the locator readings on Idenion's flitter, and they match the known whereabouts of Directress Salvi. Your brother has committed a serious crime against the Protectorate, and should be punished."

Dena felt trapped and confused. He was nowhere near the truth, but that would make no difference if he took his accusations further. The authorities would soon uncover the real plot. "Please," she said ineffectually, "don't make trouble for Idenion."

Chisrin's reply was a long, calculating stare. She shrank from his gaze, wondering how she had ever thought him kind. "If it's my silence you want, you must earn it," he said. "Could you manage that, little Dena? I somehow think you could."

It was a measure of her naivety that she didn't realise what he meant until he grasped both her wrists and pinned her to the bed.

"If I'm wrong about Idenion," he whispered conspiratorially, "you can summon help or scream the place down, starting now. But I'm *not* wrong, am I?"

Dena, trembling violently, averted her face.

Thus assured of co-operation, Chisrin released her and loosened his tunic. "Undress," he ordered. "And don't pretend to be modest - you bared all at the lakeside, so the lads were saying."

With shaking fingers, she undid a couple of buttons.

"Oh, for discord's sake stop wasting time, you little tease. I can see I'll have to do this myself." Swiftly and efficiently, he stripped off her overall and the thin shift which was all she wore beneath it.

Dena still refused to look at him. "I hate you," she managed.

He chuckled. "A reaction at last! Not quite the one I wanted, but it'll serve. Why so tense, my sweet? Just relax. That's right. That's right...."

Dena lay rigid and unresisting. She felt little pain, just a profound sorrow. She couldn't believe that her dream of perfect unity had been so cynically destroyed. She stared past his left shoulder at the grey ceiling, centred her thoughts on it, tried to distance herself from the harsh breathing, the reek of alien sweat and the invasion of her body. And presently, as if in sympathy, the greyness drifted softly down and settled around her.

Struggling back toward consciousness, she became aware of being drawn into a sitting position. Chisrin was supporting her with one arm and offering a tiny cup of resnay with his free hand.

"Drink this, ice maiden," he said, not ungently. She obeyed, although she detested the taste, and presently her strength returned enough for her to push his arm away.

"You gave me quite a scare, you silly girl," he went on. "You should have told me it was your first time."

"Would it have made any difference?" she asked miserably.

He considered. "Well...perhaps. But it's a little late to wonder about that, isn't it? Let's just concentrate on improving your pleasure."

She stared in dismay. In the name of harmony, was he not going to leave her alone?

"Dena," he said patiently, "go and clean yourself up. Then go home and smile at everyone, especially your brother, whose secret is safe for now. You might even get home ahead of him if you hurry."

"You sent him away," she accused. "To prevent him looking for me."

"In a manner of speaking," he admitted. "Malcor shut him in a stationary train as a prank, and I'm afraid I capitalised on the event. I agreed to radio the depot and alert them, and so I did - eventually."

"You're contemptible!" she declared, fighting back tears.

"That's my girl. Now run along. In a few days I shall require your presence after work, so make sure you have a plausible excuse ready for your nearest and dearest. And, Dena - " he paused for emphasis - "if you can't show some enthusiasm next time, we don't have an agreement."

***

At the end of the working day, Tralvar was admitted to Narad's office by a slightly aggrieved male secretary.

"My lord Narad was about to leave. I trust your business can be transacted speedily?"

"My business is not your concern," Tralvar replied coldly. "You may go."

The man seized an armful of folders and scurried out. At the other end of the room, Narad half rose from his desk.

"Greetings, Tralvar! I must admit, you handle my subordinates better than I do myself. How may I assist you?"

"I'd like a private word, Lord Narad, on a matter of some sensitivity."

"You can dispense with the formality," Narad said amiably. "We're persons of equal standing, are we not? And if your visit has ought to do with those disgruntled fellows who were here this afternoon, I can assure you there's no need to worry. We sent them packing."

"And what did *my* administrators say?"

"They say what we tell them to say. Forget about those ungrateful Trevans; you're an excellent First Citizen. Hardworking, an aesthete - "

"A murderer," Tralvar put in.

"To maintain one's position, it's sometimes necessary to be ruthless," Narad said noncommittally. "Now, I have some matters to attend to at home. If you'd care to walk with me, we can have our talk on the way."

Once they had left the akron, Tralvar fell into step beside the burly Narvellan and began - in a suitably circumspect manner - to explain what he wanted.

"After the shaming of Isylla, you said I could approach you if I ever required a favour. I'm taking you at your word. An acquaintance of mine, a young man, is in need of your expertise."

"This wouldn't have anything to do with Idenion, would it?" asked Narad hopefully.

"Sorry, no. The youth is Narvellan."

"Interesting," murmured Narad. "Do go on."

Briefly, Tralvar outlined Quetri's situation. "So," he concluded, "unless you can persuade Hysek to become his sponsor he'll be sent back to Narvella Prime, where Tarysk is waiting to punish him."

"Ah, the redoubtable Tarysk tyl Pellon," remarked Narad. "I met her once: a mean-spirited dowager. I'm not surprised to hear she mistreats her servants. And we all knew Navarian would come to a bad end. The tyl Pellons were outraged when he took up science, and I'm sure this is why Hysek will not consent to see the boy."

"Can you help?" persisted Tralvar. Narad smiled indulgently.

"Now let's get this clear. You want me to rake up some dirt on Hysek and compel him to adopt the zyl Nyris lad. That doesn't sound too difficult."

"I understand Hysek need only meet with him to sign the papers," said Tralvar. "In fact, I'd prefer it if that were so."

"May I ask why you're taking this trouble?" inquired Narad. "Not that I need to ask. Obviously you desire Quetri for yourself."

Tralvar had hoped he'd make that assumption. "Do you object?"

"On the contrary. I'm delighted that you're taking such a liberated view of our customs. Quetri seems personable enough; a little over-anxious perhaps, but I'm sure he'll prove a comfort to you. Of course, he's past the optimum age for a neph-khet. Ideally they should be fifteen Narvellan years old, such as Axmiol's Sijek, when sponsorship begins...."

"There's another minor point," said Tralvar, cutting short the lecture. "Assuming for the moment that Hysek will co-operate, it wouldn't be prudent for me to have Quetri as my house guest. The citizens wouldn't approve. And I, in turn, wouldn't approve if he moved in with Hysek. I suggest he stays where he is, and visits me when he can. Perhaps you could find him some sedentary employment?"

"I think that can be arranged," said Narad. "We're short of a desk clerk."

Tralvar returned to the villa on foot, as was his custom after visiting the akron. The walk always cleared his head. The retracer lab showed signs of occupation; he peeped in and found Drusa tidying up. She gave him a sour stare and he retreated without speaking to her. He'd just reached the villa entrance when his calm was rudely shattered. A clod of earth struck him on the shoulder, and another spattered against the pillar in front of him.

"Resign!" The yell echoed through the gathering dusk. He turned, and two more missiles smacked into his chest, muddying his freshly-laundered uniform. He dodged behind the pillar and squinted back the way he'd come; his assailants were, of course, the young Trevans. Only two of them, by the look of it - the others probably having decided that discretion was a better course of action.

+You morons! Get off the streets+ he ordered, hoping his thoughts would show true concern when words would not. The safety of the deportees was incumbent on the good behaviour of the remaining workers. Surely Jarras had made that clear?

+Resign!+ the youths repeated, and a hail of gravel flew in his direction. He ducked inside before they could graduate to stones.

He'd scarcely had time to throw on a clean tunic when there was a shriek from outside and someone beat a peremptory tattoo on the front door. He opened it reluctantly, knowing precisely what would confront him.

Two Moderators stood there. Between them, held fast, was one of the Trevans.

"His friend eluded us but this is the instigator," said one of the Moderators. "What would you like done with him, First Citizen?"

"Let him go," said Tralvar wearily.

They looked at him in surprise. "He was causing an affray," said the other Moderator. "If you won't charge him, then *we* must."

"These people have a legitimate grievance against me," Tralvar said calmly, "and one which I'm prepared to answer if they make their complaint through the proper channels."

"We already did that," said the captive sullenly.

"But you didn't wait to see if I'd respond. I have every intention of doing so."

"They also left their factory during the working day," the first Moderator pointed out.

"That is a matter for the overseer, not you," Tralvar replied in the same reasonable tone. "I shall expect tonight's incident to remain off the record. Perhaps you would also see that this petitioner is returned safely to Treva."

For a moment he thought they weren't going to obey him. Then the senior Moderator said: "As you wish, First Citizen," before he and his partner politely escorted the young man away.

Tralvar closed the door and stood gazing for a moment into the empty recesses of the hall. He switched on more lights; the villa was as empty as before. At any other time he might have been happy to be completely alone, but not after such a challenge to his authority. He hadn't been called upon to resign since the dark days following Alendis' death, and at that time there might have been some justification. But not now - not when he was trying so desperately to hold everything together. It wasn't fair. It just wasn't fair.

He sat down at the zirid, played a few desultory phrases and stood up. Not even the prospect of meeting Nefyrra could lighten his despondency and inspire him to make music. Wandering into the study he opened a drawer and took out a memory chip wrapped in lightproof cloth: the retrace of Laura's songs. He gazed at it a long time, then closed the drawer noisily and returned to his desk.

Presently he reached for the resnay bottle.

Chapter Eight

"I am master of all I survey," said Alendis, "but still I am not content. Listen while I tell you - all of you - of Celestra, as she once was." A matchless orator, he paused with one slender hand upraised until he had everyone's attention. "A mighty empire spanning every continent," he commenced at last. "Cities of adamantine beauty! Strong, energetic people whose colonies graced the planets of our system. And ultimately these explorers, these clear-eyed ancestors of mine, ventured outward to the stars!"

The flawless blue of the weathershield kept a cold, rainy afternoon at bay. The Lyricon audience festooned the terraces, their rest-day garments a motley splash of colour. They'd seen and enjoyed this play so many times they could quote it by heart - and some of them were doing precisely that. Silence was not mandatory during a performance. The actor continued his wickedly accurate portrayal of Alendis, his descriptions becoming more and more extravagant as the speech progressed. At the front of the auditorium, Laura turned to Idenion.

"He's very good - a bit *too* good! He's giving me the shivers!"

"Watch what happens next," Idenion replied. "You're about to see why your return had to be a closely guarded secret."

"One man alone cannot rebuild an empire," the fake Alendis continued. "Not even me. Not with an array of simpering pacifists at my heels!" He traded insults with the audience for a time, then went on: "I thought my dreams of conquest would be no more than dreams - but now there is someone who can remedy that if I can only persuade her. Behold! It is Laura, the singer!"

Laura watched curiously to see how her namesake would perform, but when the girl introduced herself it became obvious that she'd been chosen for her sturdy physique rather than her acting ability.

"I bring you my music," she concluded woodenly. "The music of Symerid Three."

Then she moved aside. The scolia assembled discreetly at the back of the stage, and to Laura's amazement began to play Coleridge-Taylor's "Demande et reponse" - or something very like it.

"Tralvar transcribed it from one of those old discs you gave him," Idenion explained.

A diminutive girl in white firi took the stage and danced exquisitely to the music. Laura had an even bigger surprise when the dancer came close enough to be recognised.

"It's Ailsi! I'd no idea she could dance like that!"

"Neither had I," Idenion replied. "Dena says she never turns up for rehearsals."

"On this evidence," said Laura, "she doesn't need to."

Ailsi finished her dance to a chorus of whoops and shouts.

"The audience is a lot noisier than it used to be," Laura observed.

"The Lyricon's the only place where everyone can be themselves," Idenion reminded her. "But they still maintain silence for the lattice."

"Didn't the scolia form a lattice just then?"

"No - it isn't customary during a play. It would shift people's focus away from the action."

"The music of Symerid Three!" reiterated the stage Laura as Ailsi flitted out of sight. "But where there is great beauty there is great peril. Symerid Three makes war on itself. We have deadly weapons - deadly beyond your imagining!"

"What has imagination to do with it?" asked the dictator, addressing the audience once more. "I know her mind. And now I must possess her and her knowledge!"

More dancers arrived to entertain him, performing a series of erotic moves to a tune Laura didn't recognise.

"Are *you* in this?" she asked Idenion.

"Thankfully, no; there are only the two players. I'm not sure if I'd want somebody pretending to be me."

"It takes some getting used to," Laura admitted. "I'd be happier if my counterpart was a better actress!"

Alendis was busy extolling Laura's virtues to the crowd. "Is she not magnificent?" he inquired. "Tall and strong, like my distant ancestors. Broad hips, perfect for childbearing..."

"Hold on - this is getting personal!" Laura muttered.

The spectators were making various ribald suggestions as to how he should proceed. Finally Alendis seized hold of the girl, who had been slowly gravitating toward him as he spoke. Laura wondered if the next line would be "Unhand me, villain!" Celestrians always liked their plays simple and overstated, but this one was pure melodrama.

"You presume too much, Alendis," said the stage Laura, too timidly.

"Laura!" he cried, his voice ragged with desire, "be my consort! Together we will go to Symerid Three and seize their weapons, and with them we will rule the stars!"

"She ought to say no, no, a thousand times no!" Laura remarked.

"Should she?" responded Idenion, taking her seriously. "I'll suggest it for next time."

In the event, the line was: "I'll never condone your evil schemes!" delivered with slightly more conviction than before.

"This is our destiny! Why do you resist it?" pleaded her suitor.

"It is not *my* destiny," she retorted, finally entering into the spirit of the piece. "I have a different purpose. It is - to destroy you!" With a flourish, she held up a large pasteboard gem. Its many facets caught the light convincingly. "With this crystal," she explained to the audience, "I will lure him to his doom. He thinks this will take him to Symerid Three, but his journey will end in a meteor swarm!"

"It was a dust cloud," Laura objected.

"Never mind the details. This is art!" declared Idenion loftily.

"Oh, does that mean I don't have broad hips after all?"

"I wish you two would shut up," said Tralvar, leaning forward from the row above. "You've done nothing but drivel on since the play started!"

Laura turned round in surprise. "Only because everyone else is. Does it matter?"

"It *would* do if someone overheard you," he answered drily. "Yes, I know they're all making more noise than you are, but just keep it down a little. Besides, I rather like this next bit."

"I fly," cried the stage Laura with her newfound enthusiasm, "across interstellar vastness, seeking my warlike home. Dare you follow, Alendis? If you would be my consort, you must first catch me!"

"I will not be denied," he warned.

"I am already far away," she called from the edge of the stage. "You must hurry! If you hesitate you will lose me!"

The troupe of dancers returned, tiptoeing forward in a cluster. They wore sharply angled costumes of rust and black, representing the debris field. The scolia began sounding one high keening note, building the tension.

"To chaos with pretty speeches!" the dictator snarled, and those who remembered the real Alendis' rages flinched a little. "Did no-one tell you, Laura, that I always get what I want?"

"This time," she trilled, "you'll get what you deserve!"

The dancers encircled Alendis and began to close in on him.

"Laura, what have you done?" he wailed from their midst. "I would have given you the galaxy!"

"Die, usurper! Die, detested one!" she rejoined fiercely.

He gave an eldritch shriek as the dancers whirled him off the stage. Just before they disappeared there came one last despairing cry:

"Lost! Betrayed! And I never heard you sing!"

There was a moment's silence before the audience began to stamp and applaud.

"That's absolutely right, you know," Laura remarked thoughtfully. "He *didn't* hear me sing."

"Wait," said Idenion. "There's more."

The actress, out of character, moved centre stage to deliver an epilogue. "Thus ends Vanity O'erthrown. After Laura had dispatched the tyrant, Symerid Three was pronounced too dangerous for further contact. The flight programmes were destroyed and the galactic co-ordinates suppressed. Yet I hope, as do we all, that a way can be found to bring Laura back - to lead us through these troubled times and banish our oppressors. It is a tradition of her planet to give its heroes three cheers: let us, therefore, honour Laura in a way she would know and understand."

Laura glanced about in consternation - but of course, no one was looking at *her*. The audience responded, not with the hoorays she was expecting, but with the salutation she'd first heard at her debut long ago:

"Lau-ra! Lau-ra! Lau-ra!"

"How does it feel to be an icon?" Idenion whispered as the noise died away.

"Terrifying," said Laura, and meant it. That ridiculous play had shown her all too vividly what would have happened if she'd revealed her presence. It could *still* happen. If she were discovered, the Narvellans would in all probability dispose of her straight away; alternatively, if they didn't, the people would rally to her and there would be a revolution. This, of course, would fail, leading to many more deaths.

The girl hadn't left the stage. She announced a short recess, after which Forlane - the actor who had captured Alendis so unerringly - would recite sections from Clemoridys.

"Pah!" said Tralvar. "I'm going to lunch." And suiting action to words, he swung to his feet and elbowed his way up the terrace.

"We should go too," Idenion said.

Laura gave a reluctant sigh. "The canteen will be inundated. I don't know if I can face that."

"No need! Dena's borrowed back the custodian's quarters for a couple of ilden, so we can eat there. Come on, let's collect her and go upstairs."

They descended to the basement area beneath the stage, encountering Forlane, who greeted them cheerfully. Without his wig and make-up, and with a sweat-stained towel slung about his shoulders, he looked nothing like Alendis. Moreover, he was significantly older than Alendis had been when he died. Laura was relieved on both counts.

"My dear young lady," he said when she'd congratulated him on his accurate portrayal, "I taught Alendis all he knew about oratory. So when I impersonate him, I'm simply emphasising an aspect of myself. Though today, of course, I tried to give it a little extra, It isn't often that the First Citizen requests a performance."

"Have you seen Dena?" Idenion asked. "I can't read her in this crowd."

"She's in one of the instrument repairshops, trying to persuade Nefyrra to come out of hiding," answered Forlane. "The silly child learnt that Tralvar was here, and she's refusing to take the stage."

"He'll be so disappointed if she doesn't play," said Laura, dismayed. "I hope Dena can talk her round."

"Try to keep Tralvar away from her," advised Forlane. "She's a very unhappy girl."

They thanked him for the information and set off for the custodian's suite, located above the colonnaded front portal. The basement route took them past the costume and props department, which was in its usual chaotic state. As they walked, Laura stumbled over something cylindrical which had fallen across the aisle. It rattled protestingly. Looking along its gaudy length, she recognised the looped metal frame and hinged jaw of the zarf - a puppet carried by seven young men during the Peisistrata street festival. She had tripped over its tail.

"Poor old zarf," she remarked sadly. "He's going rusty."

"We haven't held a Peisistrata for five years," Idenion told her.

"Banned, I suppose."

"Not exactly, although I'm sure the Narvellans would take a dim view of a mating ritual like the Zarf Dance. We simply couldn't do justice to a festival at the moment; there's no food for the feast day and there wouldn't be room for all the visitors."

As they passed the repair shops, Idenion signalled for silence. From somewhere amid the racks of strelsi, they could hear Dena speaking: "...and it just isn't professional to let your friends down. Had you thought of that?"

"All right, I'll take part for the sake of the lattice," Nefyrra's voice replied. "As you say, the others wouldn't interact well with a substitute. But I don't want that murderer anywhere near me!"

"You loved Floren very much, didn't you?" Dena continued, wearily determined. "Couldn't you try, for her sake, to be a little more charitable toward Tralvar?"

The girl's reply went unheard as Idenion drew Laura away. He'd made no attempt to communicate with his sister, not wishing to distract her.

"We'd better find Tralvar and tell him there's a problem," Laura said resignedly; but although they searched the bustling canteen and its environs, there was no sign of him. Above, a section of the blue sky began to oscillate.

"There's our answer," Idenion declared. "Tonor's running the weathershield and Tralvar's off somewhere with Lydion."

"Then we'll just have to hope that Dena can intercept him later," said Laura dourly. "Otherwise we can all look forward to some teenage histrionics." She paused, her hand on the elevator control. "Idenion, you heard Forlane. Why did Tralvar commission the performance? Was he trying to warn me against being careless?"

Idenion waited until they were in the elevator before replying. "It was to give you confidence, believe it or not. Hitherto, you've only had dealings with old friends - people who've already made up their minds to resist the Narvellans. Very soon now, you'll have to deal with strangers. You'll have to recruit them and bring them into our group - a tall order, you might have said. But not, I suspect, after seeing how many followers you have."

They emerged into the custodian's apartment, vastly changed since Laura had last visited it. The ascetic furnishings reflected its current use as an overnight lodging for the scolia. Near the door leading to the campanile, Dena's little key gleamed on its hook. Outside on the balcony overlooking the stage, someone had placed three reclining chairs - possibly at Dena's instruction, since there were no other concessions to comfort. There was also a covered basket left by the caterers, containing a basic lunch and a bottle of wine.

"Shall we eat now, or wait for Dena?" Laura asked.

"I'm not sure she'll turn up. She may have decided to stay with Nefyrra." Above Idenion's head, the weathershield gave a sudden spat. "We can wait a bit if you like. Forlane won't start while that's going on."

Laura wandered to the other end of the apartment and, braving the cold, went out onto the walkway overlooking the square. She should have had a panoramic view of the city, but the low cloud obscured everything but her immediate surroundings. It had stopped raining, however, so she stayed outside and watched the passers-by. She remembered, nostalgically, the very first time she'd stood there: one beautiful morning when she was scarcely sixteen. The evening before, she'd met Alendis for the first time, and she realised with hindsight how sexually charged that meeting had been. When he'd taken her hand she'd experienced an odd frisson which at the time she hadn't identified. Later she knew it had been desire. He would have known, of course, and been amused.

"Don't feel ashamed of it," said Idenion, coming to stand beside her. "Many women desired him. He'd have been annoyed if you hadn't."

"He treated me like a child. I was so clueless then," she reflected. "The play brought it all back to me. And now I've the oddest feeling about those days, as if they're about to spring a few last surprises."

"Alendis casts a long shadow," Idenion agreed.

Laura's attention was suddenly caught by a movement in the square. "Is that a bunch of Directresses over there?" she asked.

"Directresses always go about singly, with an army of guards," said Idenion. "Those are elite-wives. They're wearing dark grey, not black, and they haven't covered their faces."

"I thought they'd all been sent home!"

"Most of them were, in the interests of efficiency. It was too much trouble to watch them *and* us! But a few remain, shut away in the akron for the most part."

Laura looked more closely at the women. They wore ankle-length cloaks, buttoned to the hem, which effectively concealed every aspect of the wearer's figure. They were escorted by a Moderator and one uniformed attendant.

"It's very rare to see elite-wives in the street, and even rarer to see them up here," Idenion commented. "I think I know what they're doing, but I'm amazed they got permission so soon after the Isylla scandal."

"What *are* they doing?"

"They've come to hear Clemoridys. If the portal's open - which it is - you can easily hear the performance from the square. Especially when it's Forlane doing the performing. Now will you please come back inside? It's draughty out here!"

Laura obeyed. "Do the Directresses live in the akron too?" she asked.

"No, they live where they choose. They've a surprising amount of freedom. They don't marry, so they're no-one's property."

"I think I'd rather be a Directress than an elite-wife," remarked Laura.

"No you wouldn't," Idenion answered with sudden seriousness. "That talent of theirs is a form of synaesthesia involving their perception. Imagine trying to contend with such a welter of sensations! They need more counselling than the relayists do."

They seated themselves in the recliners with a glass of wine each. The temperature was comfortably warm under the correctly-functioning weathershield, and Laura waited eagerly for the poetry recital to begin.

"I'd rather *you* were reading this," she confessed.

"Forlane reads it better than I do," Idenion said modestly. "I'm not much good at declaiming - I prefer small gatherings. I'll read to you later."

"I'll hold you to that," she replied.

Forlane's voice ebbed and flowed, soared and whispered. He exulted, he wept, he celebrated, he agonised. Laura didn't understand all the nuances, but very quickly became aware that there was little of herself in this poem. It was purely Idenion, baring his soul to the world. A tear slid down her cheek and she caught his hand.

"How I love you," she whispered. "Oh, chaos, all those wasted years! I could have been *with* you. We could have had children by now."

"But Clemoridys would never have been written," he said sombrely.

Laura listened to the remainder in silence. Forlane finished on a note of hope, bowed quietly and left the stage. The applause was restrained and respectful. No encores were demanded, although there were a few calls for Idenion to put in an appearance.

"Are you going to?" inquired Laura.

"Not today," he declared. "You're all the audience I need."

Impulsively she embraced him; then, hearing footfalls inside the apartment, turned round expectantly. "Dena?"

"I'm afraid not," said a cold, measured voice. A tall imperious Narvellan stepped into view, followed by a beautiful youth with skin of the palest gold. Laura, not recognising either of them, glared her hostility. Idenion was more forthright.

"You're trespassing, Axmiol."

"Axmiol?" echoed Laura apprehensively.

"Why must you always be so belligerent, First Poet?" Axmiol's tone of quiet reproof didn't match the calculating look in his eyes. "Sijek and I came specifically to hear your great work. I was under the impression that you would be reading it yourself, but no matter: the actor acquitted himself well."

"You brought the elite-wives!" blurted Laura. He turned his shrewd gaze upon her.

"When they learnt of my errand, they begged to be included. I hope they were as impressed as I was."

"You shouldn't have entered the Lyricon, Lord Governor," repeated Idenion, belatedly giving Axmiol his title.

"Should I not?" Axmiol seemed amused. "Who makes the laws, First Poet? You? The Lyricon concession exists only as long as I permit it to. I also reserve the right to enter the theatre if I have good cause. Have no fear - my visit will be brief. I've no wish to be

242

on the premises when a lattice is formed. In fact, I should not have entered here but for Sijek, who espied you on the balcony and suggested that a quick word might be in order. He thought it would save me the trouble of summoning you to the akron."

"Then you *didn't* come here just to enjoy my poetry. How disappointing!"

"I do indeed have another purpose. But first let me congratulate Lisset on her remarkable forbearance!" He turned to Laura. "Does it not worry you, my dear, that your partner composed such exquisite verse for another woman?"

Laura had expected to be asked this, albeit not by the Lord Governor. "Poets love to dream," she replied. "Clemoridys is part of Idenion's dream. I am another."

"Well said," Axmiol remarked with a thin-lipped smile. "And well-rehearsed."

"Just tell me what you want, Axmiol," Idenion said irritably.

"Always so abrasive," Axmiol sighed. "So unlike your work. Basically, I'm here to offer you a commission."

"I don't accept commissions."

"This time, you will." Axmiol's smile turned to ice. "I've been authorised to use every means at my disposal to bring the renegade state of Scapirion under our aegis. I want you to prepare a broadcast in which you will urge them to join us. You will muster all the eloquence you're capable of."

Idenion was incensed. "Do you honestly think I'm going to write your propaganda for you?"

"I *know* you will. After your little adventure at the goods yard, it became obvious that Chisrin ap Tuin's factory was overstaffed. Even with two of you missing he was able to maintain his quota. Who leaves and who stays will largely depend on you: so unless you want to be sent to an aldacite mine I suggest you fulfil your task as instructed."

"I'm surprised you want me to do another broadcast after the Isylla fiasco," Idenion remarked.

"I agree that the aftermath was a little unfortunate, but the actual commentary worked well. You'll have a totally free hand this time, so you should do even better."

Sijek, who had been watching the distant stage, touched his master's arm and murmured something. The scolia were setting up their instruments. Swiftly Axmiol gathered his cloak about him and prepared to leave by the outside stair. Sijek followed obediently.

"Assuming I can rise to the occasion, how long do I have?" Idenion called after him.

"Bring me a preliminary draft in eight days. You need not report for your other duties during that time."

"And may I ask one favour?" Idenion added. Axmiol paused impatiently at the threshold.

"What?"

"I'd like unrestricted access to the akron library. Can you provide me with the relevant piece of paper?"

"Very well, you shall have it." Axmiol propelled Sijek through the casement door and disappeared, leaving Idenion staring after him in perplexity.

"What a creep!" declared Laura after making sure he'd gone. "Do you really have to become his tame diplomat?"

"You don't say no to Axmiol," Idenion replied grimly. "Yes, I'll give him what he wants, although it will be a complete waste of time. If Alendis couldn't cajole the Scapirians out of their dome, what chance do I stand?"

"Do you think the Synectics want Scapirion over-run?"

"If they did, I'm sure they'd have provided a means of getting in. No, this is Protectorate business. Now come back here and sit down - the concert's about to start."

Laura poured him some more wine and settled back into her chair. "You never said the library was off-limits."

"Strictly speaking, it isn't. But it's wearisome having to produce identification about twenty times before you even get to the right floor - and several more times while you're reading. I want to do my research in peace."

"You'll want to check on Scapirion's history, of course."

"Yes," Idenion said with an unexpectedly sad smile. "And some other things."

Melor's masterclass played to perfection. Nefyrra was among them, her brow furrowed in concentration. There was no applause or chatting between items, demonstrating to Laura that the lattice had been formed. Then the other musicians, all young, stood back to let Nefyrra perform her solo. She'd obviously put aside her concerns and become as immersed in the music as when Laura had last seen her. This time there *was* applause - a lot of it.

"Any sign of Tralvar?" Laura asked.

"Difficult to see from here," Idenion replied. "No-one's charging onto the stage, though, so let's hope he's decided to keep his distance."

The scolia started to play again, but halfway through their piece the blue sky suddenly fell apart and vanished. A universal groan went up. Everyone waited, beginning to fidget and shiver in the autumnal chill, but the weathershield remained inert. Presently Lydion appeared at the side of the stage.

"Sorry, people!" he called. "One of the projectors is down and I can't fix it till it cools. That could be a couple of ilden altogether."

Then Dena took over. She thanked everyone for attending and pointed out that as the scolia had almost finished their performance, there was little point in resuming later. The spectators, good-humoured for the most part, gathered their effects and departed. A few heavy drops of rain sped them on their way.

Nefyrra was still onstage, manoeuvring her strelsis into its carrying case, when a sinewy hand reached over her shoulder and positioned the instrument correctly. Turning abruptly, she found herself face to face with Tralvar.

"Nefyrra, I'm your father," he said gently.

Her face twisted in anger. "I know who you are. Now go away and leave me alone."

Tralvar remained where he was. "Won't you tell me why you're so hostile? If you think my relationship with Floren ended badly, let me assure you that it was *she* who left *me*."

"And you don't know why," Nefyrra said contemptuously. "You really don't. But then, why should you? All you did was take a good woman and damage her beyond her powers of recovery. And for all I know you've done it again since!"

"Why...what do you mean, Nefyrra?" Tralvar faltered.

"You killed her!" Nefyrra cried, her voice carrying to every part of the auditorium. The last few members of the audience paused curiously at the top of the terrace. Laura and Idenion, on their way down, halted in dismay. Dena and some of the scolia hovered irresolutely in the background.

"Yes, you killed her," Nefyrra repeated. "Poisoned her. Isn't that what you're good at? You confessed to murdering Tristell and straightaway had unity with Floren, ensuring that she took all your guilt and shame to herself. And after you'd killed Strephin - the very same

246

day! - you blighted her consciousness even more by taking sciesha with her. I saw her waste away, Tralvar. She only lived another five years. And do you know the worst thing of all? She never spoke of you except with love and compassion, urging me to forgive you. Well, I can't forgive. And I want nothing to do with you or your tainted mind. Now get out of my way, and stay out of my life!"

Tralvar, thunderstruck, stumbled backwards. Nefyrra seized her strelsis case and fled. No-one tried to stop her. Laura, Idenion and Dena all converged on Tralvar, who stood motionless at the centre of the stage. His arms were limply at his sides, and he was white as a sheet. Surprisingly, Dena spoke first.

"Don't listen to her! This is Elanir's doing - she turned Nefyrra against you long before Floren came on the scene."

"She was talking nonsense!" Idenion added.

"Was she?" asked Tralvar, very quietly.

Laura, though it pained her to see him so devastated, said nothing. She didn't feel qualified to.

"Spiteful little baggage," remarked Lydion, joining the group. "No-one ever died of unity. Take my word for it - I'm the expert!"

"Let me be, all of you!" Tralvar said raggedly. "No-one is to follow me. Is that understood?" Then he trailed off toward the basement exit. There was an alarming air of defeat about him.

Lydion dragged the others off the stage and away from the treacherous acoustics. "Someone has to talk to that girl!" he declared. "She doesn't realise the harm she could do."

"What can we tell her?" asked Laura helplessly.

"Oh, chaos, I don't know. Try saying that Tralvar needs a clear head to do his job, and that she has to be a bit more public-spirited. I wish Jarras had been here today. He's the only one Tralvar listens to."

"I vote we do nothing till tomorrow," said Idenion. "Everyone will be more objective in the morning. Then, if we still think it's necessary, we can get a message to Jarras."

"And maybe Dena could have a word with Melor," Laura suggested.

"What good would that do?" Dena returned sharply. "You know what *he* thinks of Tralvar!"

Perturbed at her tone, Laura scrutinised her closely. She was pale and tense, and looked as if she hadn't been sleeping. She'd probably had no lunch either, thanks to Nefyrra. Lydion followed Laura's gaze.

"Idenion's right, of course," he amended. "Nefyrra needs time to reflect. Now, shouldn't the three of you track down a flitter before the next cloudburst? Look at that sky!"

"It's a pity about the rain," said Idenion. "We could have ended the day at our rehearsal spot."

"I need to speak with you about that," Dena informed him hesitantly. "But not here."

Laura stared pensively in the direction Tralvar had taken. She hoped Nefyrra's bombshell wouldn't sour his love of music or put him off performing, for in her opinion music was the only thing that sustained him. She resolved there and then to ask if he'd accompany her singing, however difficult that might be to organise. No, she wouldn't ask; she'd insist. It would force him to play, and he'd be all the better for it.

***

A day went by, then another. Laura sewed overalls furiously, Idenion worked on his address to the Scapirians, Dena went to the factory and came back late. Jarras, summoned by Lydion, called on Tralvar and subsequently delivered a worried report to the others.

"He just stares at the wall. He answers when I speak to him but it's as if he's only vaguely aware of me."

"Has he been drinking?" Idenion asked.

"A little, perhaps, but he isn't drunk. In his present mood, I think even that would be too much trouble. I certainly can't get any sense out of him about the Synectics or what we should do next."

"We'll give him one more day," declared Laura, "and if there's no improvement we'll *all* go and see him."

"That would be drawing attention to ourselves. He warned us about that."

"I know, Jarras, but this is an emergency! Do *you* know who he was intending to recruit? No, neither do I. This business with Nefyrra has really knocked him sideways, and I'd love to give him time to get over it by himself, but we can't afford to wait."

"Why don't *you* try talking to him?" asked Jarras.

"That wouldn't help - he'd only yell at me. But I did think a trip to the quarry might improve his outlook. He enjoys hearing me sing."

"You can't do that," Dena said unexpectedly. Then, flustered, she carried on: "I've been meaning to tell you about that site. It might not be safe. I heard some factory gossip - I believe one of the Directresses is prospecting near there."

"I think I'd have noticed a bunch of Narvellan heavies," Laura said sarcastically.

"This Directress works alone," Dena persisted. "Her name is Salvi."

Idenion remembered the name. "Dena may be right," he told Laura. "Salvi's a non-conformist. I heard Narad discussing her the day we visited his office."

"I could fly you to the quarry now if you want to investigate," Jarras volunteered.

"That wouldn't be a bad idea," agreed Laura. "If the area's been compromised I'd like to know as soon as possible." And she hastened to get ready, aware that the daylight wouldn't last much longer.

"Do you want to come with us, Dena?" asked Idenion. "Laura might get a chance to sing, and as you haven't heard her for six and a half years - "

"I can't go," she said flatly. "I've things to do."

Laura shrugged, pulled on her boots and hunted out warm cloaks for herself and Idenion. Then, with Jarras, they piled into the flitter and pursued the greenish-yellow sunset into the west. Overflying the quarry, they could at first see nothing untoward; then, a little further on, Idenion spotted Salvi's clifftop encampment. They landed and disembarked, but not before both he and Jarras had trained their perception on the desolate scene and found it to be as deserted as it looked. Then Jarras, being of a forensic turn of mind, sifted the remains of a campfire and pronounced them over a day old. Salvi had gone, and it didn't take him to long to find out why. Although the sandy soil had been washed almost smooth by the rain, it was still possible to see the indentations made by another flitter's landing gear and several pairs of heavily booted feet.

"She *was* up here alone, till they came for her," he said grimly.

"Why would they do that?" asked Laura faintly.

"Someone let those flawed crystals into the system. I imagine she was responsible."

Laura didn't ask what would happen to the woman. She presumed there would be some sort of inquisition. Idenion quietly put an arm about her in the dying light, and together they re-entered the flitter.

Jarras ferried them to the far side of the chasm where the natural amplification was best. Laura had promised the young scientist that she'd sing for him, and for the sake of her voice she knew she should, but she simply didn't feel like it. She managed to perform Greensleeves, hoping he wouldn't realise how poor her rendition was. The coarse ylur cloak itched, the chilly air threatened to make her cough, and the wind moaned dissonances around the rockface. After the one song, she gave up.

"I'm sorry, but it's getting too cold to sing here," she apologised. "Tralvar will have to find me somewhere else."

"That should be the least of his problems," Jarras remarked.

Tralvar, meanwhile, was still immured in his villa. He sat in his study and brooded, at last realising he could no longer see what was on the table in front of him - a crystal globe, rough and unpolished, with a hollowed-out centre. Sighing, he went to switch on some lights, and while he was fumbling about in the near-darkness he heard a surreptitious knock at the back door. He ignored it.

+First Citizen, it's me, Quetri!+

He started. What in chaos had happened to his shields? Was he really that unfocused?

The call was repeated.

"Oh, discords, I suppose I'll have to let you in," he muttered. "If it isn't Jarras it's you. Never a moment's peace." He flung open the door: Quetri's jubilant expression took him by surprise, and he didn't immediately grasp the import of his words.

"Tralvar, I can stay! I don't know what you did, but Hysek sent for me this afternoon and said he was purchasing my bond. You should have seen his face! He obviously didn't *want* to do it. He said I'd only have one duty, and that would be to keep out of his way!" Quetri's first rush of enthusiasm faded as he noticed

251

Tralvar's bleak unsmiling expression. "Your pardon, First Citizen. This is obviously not a good time."

"Don't go." The words were out of Tralvar's mouth before he realised it. He felt wretchedly pleased that he'd apparently done something right.

Quetri followed him back to the study, which showed distinct signs of continuous occupation. "What has happened?" he asked politely.

"You mean you don't know?" Tralvar inquired. "I thought the whole planet knew." He felt sure there was no need to say anything else. He couldn't seem to restore his shields, and Nefyrra's words were still reverberating round his aching head.

"I see," Quetri said after a pause. "And in the four days since I last saw you, you have done nothing to advance our plans?"

"Nothing."

"I'm disappointed in you, First Citizen. Your friends are counting on you for leadership, as do I. This self-indulgence has to stop."

Tralvar gazed at the stern young face in vague astonishment. "It does, does it?"

"Yes," pursued Quetri. "You have a duty - a mission - and you must not let personal difficulties gain the upper hand."

"Don't lecture me, you little..." began Tralvar, then stopped. "No. No, I'm not going to fall out with you as well. I *have* been self-indulgent. What should I do about it?"

"During our last meeting," Quetri proceeded, "you said we had much in common and that it was appropriate that our paths should have crossed. I concur with those sentiments, and believe it is *my* duty to support you whenever your strength wavers. I will begin by helping you to disregard Nefyrra's accusations."

"And how will you do that?"

252

"By proving she is in error," said Quetri simply. "Your ex-partner may well have absorbed some aspect of your criminal activity, but it would not have killed her. A flawed psyche is only a problem if one's partner objects. Nefyrra cannot be right, or half the people who have ever served in a Ten would have destroyed their wives or lovers by now."

"That's something I hadn't thought of," Tralvar admitted. "But maybe your species is more resilient."

"Then what of your previous ruler - the one featured in that play everyone keeps talking about?"

"Alendis," Tralvar supplied uneasily.

"Didn't he murder his brother?"

"Yes, among others."

"Then you need look no further for proof. I presume he had unity with a great many women, in the manner of your world?"

"Some, certainly. He was always bemoaning the fact that he'd never sired any children," Tralvar recalled. "He used to be so jealous because I had. Ironic, isn't it?"

"Tomorrow, go to the registry," Quetri urged. "Or I can do it for you. We'll verify that his partners still live. Then you can stop blaming yourself for Floren's death."

"I'm halfway to believing you're right. But how do I convince Nefyrra?"

"Nefyrra has lost the foster-mother she loved and respected, and has not recovered from that loss. At the moment it's convenient for her to hate you. Given time, she should listen to your reasoning; but not yet."

"You have a wise head on your young shoulders, Quetri."

"Not really. Such situations are common within families, particularly the dynasties of Narvella."

"I know little about such relationships," Tralvar confessed. "Which isn't surprising, since I have no family." And then, to his own amazement, he found himself telling the youth about his mysterious origins and the parents who had never registered his birth. "So I've no idea where I came from," he concluded. "One day, for Nefyrra's sake, I hope I shall find out."

"One day," Quetri echoed softly, "I hope you will allow me to investigate with you. And now I must go. I have duties at the akron."

"I apologise for being such a poor host," Tralvar said, rising to show him out. "But as there's no food in the house I couldn't have offered you any. Thank you again for your help. I know I shall sleep well tonight."

"One final question." Quetri paused on his way to the door. "That globe on the table - what is its significance? Why does it cause you sorrow?"

"It's a failed experiment," Tralvar informed him, "and it shouldn't be on display. Etched into that crystal is my only surviving attempt at recording Tristell."

"Ah," said Quetri. "The singer you executed."

"I daren't try to play this," Tralvar went on, reverently touching the uneven surface of the globe. "My other recordings all shattered when I tried. Vain, vexatious Tristell, reduced to this. Soon there'll be nothing left of her except her name."

"Perhaps you didn't entirely fail," Quetri ventured. "Will you permit me to take the crystal? Our scanning techniques may be able to read it. Of course, it would have to be sent to Narvella Prime."

Tralvar looked sceptical. "I can't see that happening. You'd never get permission."

The youth gave him a broad smile. "Quetri zyl Nyris wouldn't," he agreed. "But the request will come from Hysek tyl Pellon!"

After Quetri had gone, Tralvar realised there was still one matter to resolve. If *he* hadn't caused Floren's death, who or what had? Was it the double blow of losing her lifepartner and her daughter - the same tragedy that had made her quit the custodianship of the Lyricon and disappear into obscurity? Or was there something in addition to that? He carefully poured himself a small glass of resnay, just enough to stimulate his mind rather than muddle it. He then set about compiling a shortlist of the scientists he thought could help him overthrow the Synectics. When he'd finished it, he sat down at the zirid and practised for two ilden. He played exceptionally well.

After he'd retired to bed, his mind returned to the question of Floren. And when sleep overcame him before he had reached a conclusion, his subconscious took over. He dreamt about his inauguration, which had been dramatic and unorthodox. He was about to walk onto his balcony and confront a crowd whom he believed would call for his banishment, while Kyrin was relaying the news of his latest misdeed:

+Attend, citizens! Strephin is dead, despatched by Tralvar at Floren's behest. She placed the box of poison in Tralvar's hand. So if you condemn him for this act you must condemn her also.+

He woke briefly, the echoes of that speech ringing in his head, and realised he had his answer. He and Floren had committed murder together. She had been the instigator. And that - even though their victim had been a serial killer - was the thing she couldn't live with. Soon, not immediately, he'd ask a neutral third party to tell Nefyrra. It might not make any difference to the way she felt, but at least he would have tried.

***

The following afternoon, Idenion made the first of several visits to the akron library. Laura travelled with him as far as Tralvar's villa.

"This will be my only attempt at getting some sense out of him," she warned. "I still think we'd be better off with a deputation, but I promised Jarras I'd try the individual approach. I'm not looking forward to it."

But to her surprise, she found Tralvar in genial spirits. "Ah! Just the person I wanted to see!" he exclaimed, hustling her into the kitchen. "Sorry, the study's off limits until I can make it habitable."

"How...how did you - " she began uncertainly.

"How did I pull myself together?" he concluded for her. "Let's just say you weren't the only one who thought I needed a talking to. And now, if you've the rest of the day to spare, I'd like to take you on a little trip."

"If you mean the quarry, I'm afraid there isn't much point. We went there just after -" Laura paused awkwardly - "just the other day, and it was suddenly too cold. And too windy."

"You don't have to explain how bad it gets. I worked there on and off for years, remember? I was hoping the weather would hold out a little longer, but it seems it hasn't."

"Then have you found me another venue?"

He smiled mysteriously. "I'm working on it, but that isn't where we're going today. I'm taking you to the observatory."

"I didn't know there *was* one."

"That's because it isn't in the city, or anywhere near it. Too much light pollution."

"What, here? Everything switches off at midnight!"

"The street lights do. But there's the spaceport and the power station and the hospital...need I go on? The observatory's due east, on a range of hills beyond the liman fields."

"And why are we going there?" Laura inquired.

"On a recruitment drive," Tralvar stated. "That's what you wanted, isn't it - some action? There are only a handful of ways to eradicate the Synectics and only a handful of people who can help us do it. For security's sake, I don't propose to contact all of them at once when we only require the services of one. If you fail to recruit the person at the top of my list, we'll move on to the next. But I sincerely hope you'll be successful today."

"Who's your first choice?" asked Laura quietly.

"An astronomer named Corython. His specialty is astro-dynamics, and we need him if we're going to get within striking distance of that base. The trouble is, he's a retiring sort of character. His partner's expecting their first child and he'll be determined to stay out of trouble. Do you think you can persuade him otherwise?"

"Not on an empty stomach." Laura opened one of the cupboards, then another and another. "Tralvar, you've got no food! Only a few grain cakes, and they're like bricks. When did you last eat?"

"I'm not sure," he confessed.

"Are any of the bakeries open?"

"Some, I think."

"Right. I'm going to find one. *You* find a flitter and we'll eat on the way. I presume Corython knows you're coming?"

"Yes, but he thinks it's just routine."

"Then we'll have to disillusion him. Have you got the retrace?"

"Of course."

"Then let's go." Laura hurried along to the intersection where the bakeries were to be found, and returned with a bagful of fresh grain cakes and some pilif jam. She wondered if she'd ever get used to walking out of shops without paying. As she rounded the corner into Lateral Three, she saw a flitter had appeared outside the villa. Tralvar was nearby, in conversation with Drusa.

"Some tutors from Tafret Academy came to visit," Laura heard her saying. "They're convinced they could conduct retraces with weaker crystals and less power, thus making it safe for the operator. They want to take the equipment and run some tests."

"Nothing's going anywhere," replied Tralvar with some asperity. "They can run all the tests they like, but the retracer stays in Alda Mexa."

"But why?" asked Drusa, puzzled.

"Because I say so." Tralvar turned his back on her and climbed into the flitter, giving Laura a dark look which said "follow!"

Once they were airborne, Tralvar apologised for his sudden show of temper. "That woman always irritates me," he muttered. "Who told her she could offer the retracer to her pals? We might still need it."

"Tell me more about Corython," Laura suggested, trying to spread the jam while the flitter lurched and swerved.

"Nothing much to tell really. He was working at Alcine, where our largest reflector is, but came back to Alda Mexa because his wife needed good medical facilities. Astronomers, by the way, are still allowed to follow their own occupation. The Narvellans value their skill."

"Will the place be crawling with Narvellans?"

"I doubt if there'll be more than one or two. You're more likely to run into a gang of children on a school trip."

The observatory's circular white buildings looked - as Laura remarked - like the liman mill minus the river. The hill on which the complex stood was bare and cheerless. The landing strip was covered in coarse gravel that shifted under her feet as she stepped down from the flitter cabin.

She'd been hoping for a visit to the dome, but instead Tralvar led the way to a single-storey block of workshops and offices. Inside, several people paused to converse with him, treating him as a fellow scientist rather than the First Citizen. In their eagerness to discuss their researches they overlooked Laura – somewhat to her relief.

Corython, when they found him, was pinning some reference material on the wall of his work area. He was younger than Laura had expected, with a mop of blond hair and a slightly harassed expression. He greeted her with polite non-recognition.

Tralvar examined the bulletins which had just been posted, each containing abstruse formulae. "You've lost me here," he commented. "What are you working on?"

"What am I *always* working on?" Corython responded with a tired smile. "A means of accelerating transposal. I can understand why the Narvellans want to do that, but I'm not making much headway."

"Transposal's built around universal constants. How can it be speeded up?"

"That's just it - they think we've misunderstood its nature, that a better mode of utilisation can be achieved."

"Sheer conceit," declared Tralvar. "They've had transposal for all of six years and suddenly they're experts. The only way to shorten an interstellar trip is to spend less time accelerating and decelerating. In other words, improve the Drive - which is a matter for engineers, not physicists."

"I'm inclined to agree, but the Narvellans won't be told. Well, I've taken the problem as far as I can. As soon as Pannyra's had her baby I'm going back to the Alcine array and some real work!"

"I might be able to help with the work aspect," said Tralvar casually. Laura, who had been examining some pictures of nebulae, hastily returned to his side.

"Exactly what is it you want, Tralvar?" asked Corython, his expression still one of mild curiosity.

"Before I answer that, I want to ensure we won't be interrupted," Tralvar replied. "Are there are any Narvellans here today?"

"No."

"I thought not. Are any expected?"

"No," repeated Corython with just the faintest trace of unease. "What *is* this?"

"Find me somewhere with a logic system and a lock on the door," said Tralvar briskly.

"But surely my colleagues needn't be excluded?"

"Just *do* it, Corython!" Tralvar snapped.

"We don't lock our doors. We trust one another," said Corython huffily. "I'll take you to the study suite. There won't be any students here until evening."

He led them to a row of interconnected rooms, each with basic library facilities including a computer. Tralvar chose a terminal at random, loaded the retrace, then helped Laura drag chart tables across both doors.

"This reminds me of the first time I encountered sciesha," she commented. "You made me barricade myself in my room."

"I'm still surprised you did as you were told," Tralvar remarked.

Corython looked from one to the other in growing bewilderment.

"Well, I thought I'd behave myself for a change," Laura replied. "After all, you'd just welcomed me back on bended knee."

"I did a lot of stupid things in those days," Tralvar said flippantly. "Ah. I think you're just about to be recognised."

Corython was staring intently at Laura. "On bended knee," he repeated slowly. "Is it possible...?"

"Do you know me now?" Laura asked quietly.

"Discord's dreams, *now* I do. I was outside the akron when you made your triumphal return."

"You were in a demo, Corython?" queried Tralvar. "You do surprise me!"

This is *all* I need, thought Laura in exasperation. I wish Tralvar had warned me they didn't get on. And I wish he'd shut up and stop making my job harder!

"Not a demonstration - a vigil," Corython corrected him irritably. "We carried lanterns to light the First Singer's way back to us."

"How poetic," said Tralvar drily.

Corython glared, but let the jibe pass. "Esteemed Laura," he continued formally, "I still don't understand. You were a non-conversant."

"I still am," said Laura ruefully.

"Read her again," Tralvar suggested. "And this time don't be so deferential."

Corython's eyes widened as he uncovered the deception, and he began to exhibit real nervousness. "You've obviously taken great pains to conceal her, Tralvar. What are you up to, and why have you come to me?"

"Explain," Tralvar instructed Laura, and went to sit on the other side of the room.

Laura did her best, wishing he hadn't stayed within earshot. He hadn't mentioned her accent for days, but she was sure he was studying it now. She told Corython of Lydion's bizarre experience, of the ill-fated clerk who had first named the Synectics, and of Quetri's capture and retrace. Then she asked him to view the transcription and waited while he did so. He sat riveted to the screen, his knuckles white as he gripped the desk.

"We still have the full retrace if you want more evidence," she said when the playback had ended. "But it should already be obvious why we approached you. We have to get rid of the Synectics and that means destroying the base on Ipsa. Tralvar says you're the best mathematician for the job."

"Couldn't we..." Corython swallowed hard. "Couldn't we just wait until the Narvellans leave?"

"They won't leave in the way you mean," Laura answered. "They'll all be dead, or they'll all be here. And at any time, if the Synectics decide we're a threat or we're in the way, they could initiate genocide. I have faith in Tralvar's judgement and I believe we must act now, in self-defence. Please help us."

"You could come out of hiding," Corython said almost pleadingly. "Everyone would pledge their loyalty. Then you wouldn't need me."

"Proclaiming my presence would only bring about more deaths," said Laura adamantly. "We don't want any more riots. We want a clear, precise, workable plan."

Corython rubbed his eyes as if to banish unwanted images. "Are you ordering me to do this?"

"I don't have any such authority," Laura said gently. "I'm just asking you."

"You wouldn't be working alone," Tralvar said, perceiving the need for back-up. "We have good engineers - Jarras and Rillan - to implement your findings."

The young astronomer took one final look at the retrace - the Synectics floating grotesquely in their stasis tubes, the litter of dead bodies scattered throughout the complex - and reluctantly made his decision. "I shall need detailed maps of the Narvellan solar system, especially the Ipsa region," he said. "Fortunately, extensive studies were undertaken during the first year of the alliance. They're presently lodged at Alcine." He paused a moment, his diligent mind already busy with the problem.

"From this distance, we have only one effective weapon," he continued. "That, of course, is the transposal drive itself. I believe it would be possible to make use of a process called spalling, where the crust of a planetoid is peeled off like the skin of a fruit. An impact at near-light speed should achieve this. You would, of course, have to over-ride all the usual protocols when programming the spacecraft."

"That could be arranged," said Tralvar.

"In that case I'll do some preliminary calculations and let you have them as soon as possible," Corython promised.

"Don't show anyone your work and be careful what you say over the radio," Tralvar warned. "It would be best if you came to see me in person. We could risk that once or twice."

"Very well."

"And Corython - however difficult it may be, you have to keep this from Pannyra."

"Pannyra is unwell and fearful for the safety of our unborn child. She won't want unity."

"I do hope you're right," said Tralvar with a cold smile. "It'll save you having to refuse."

When they were airborne again, Laura rounded on Tralvar angrily. "Just what was all that about? Did you have to be quite so overbearing? If that's the way you're going to treat potential allies I'd be better off seeing them on my own!"

"Corython asks for it," he retorted. "He's such a pain. To be honest, I never thought you'd sway him. Expect a crisis of conscience when he realises how many ordinary Narvellans are on Ipsa."

"I still think your attitude needs adjustment."

Tralvar didn't reply immediately. "There was something else on my mind - something that wasn't Corython's fault," he said at last. "Until today, I'd always had a vague hope that I could keep Jarras in the background. I taught him everything he knows about the stardrive and I've always felt responsible for him. But now, I've just volunteered him for the most dangerous part of the operation."

"He's best suited to it, isn't he?" queried Laura.

"No, I am. But with so many Narvellan eyes on me, I can't lift a finger to help." Tralvar fell silent, squinting into the late afternoon sun. When it became apparent that he was taking her straight back to the slum quarter, Laura ventured:

"Now might not be the best time to remind you, but I really do need somewhere else to sing. You said you were working on it."

"Since I can't lend my engineering skills to the resistance, it's a perfect time to ask me," he countered. "And yes, I've been working on it. Do you remember my recording studio in the akron? I couldn't go on monopolising the radio room, so I re-located to the old textile factory where I had my record press. The factory's been re-converted to ylur production, but the studio's still there."

"How can that benefit me, in the middle of town?"

"Think, Laura! It's completely soundproof. You could sing your head off in there and no-one would hear you. I could install a zirid and play for you. That's what you wanted, isn't it?"

"Someone might see me going in. Correction: someone might see *us* going in. Some of the aldacite workers already think we're having a relationship."

Tralvar gave an odd little smile. "It's a good cover story, wouldn't you say? But I've a better one. I was offered the use of the Narvellan recording system when they confiscated mine, but I declined due to its restricted playback time. I could always say I'd changed my mind. We could get the scolia in, make it look convincing."

"Tralvar," began Laura, intrigued but perplexed, "if this facility existed all along, why have we been making these expeditions into the wild?"

"There are several problems associated with the studio," Tralvar replied. "Dead acoustics, for one thing. You won't like the way you sound. And secondly, we could only rehearse at night or on rest days. To play for you I have to read you, and I can't compete with shop floor babble. Soundproof doesn't mean thoughtproof, unfortunately. Thirdly, if we're there at unsocial times there's always a chance that someone will read *us* - a Moderator, for instance, checking for the presence of a lattice."

"Put that way, it does sound a bit fraught," Laura conceded. "Couldn't we post Idenion as a look-out?"

"When we tried that before, his attention kept wandering - and at the time, we were only talking. How vigilant do you think he's going to be when you're singing?"

Laura admitted defeat. "All right, using Idenion was a bad idea. But there must be some other way to guard our backs."

"Don't worry, I'll sort something out." Tralvar made a remarkably gentle touchdown close to Laura's house. "I'll have that studio up and running by the next scheduled factory break - five days, unless I've lost track of time completely. By then, Corython should have delivered his work."

"It's also Idenion's deadline for the Scapirion address."

Tralvar made a derisive noise. "I can't believe Axmiol's going ahead with it. He'll get nowhere."

"If he fails, he'd better not try and blame it on Idenion," Laura said darkly.

As she walked to the door she was aware of some critical stares from a group of loitering girls. Vaguely, she wondered why they weren't at their workplace. Doubtless they'd now spread the word about her latest assignation with the First Citizen.

Idenion wasn't home yet. Laura poured herself some liman from their meagre store and sipped it gratefully, suddenly feeling very tired. She'd put in a lot of effort into recruiting the nervous Corython. She carried her drink into the main room - and halted, dismayed. She'd repaired a batch of overalls that morning and left them neatly folded in a basket: they were now scattered all over the floor. When she began to collect them up she found to her disbelief that her work had been unpicked - or in some cases, ripped undone. The sewing machine had been unthreaded, the yarn removed from its spool and thrown down in a coiled heap.

Laura's first impulse was to utter some choice English expletives, but wariness made her refrain. "Who's done this?" she murmured, baffled.

"We did," came an unexpected reply. Two of the girls had followed her in and were now hovering in the kitchen doorway. One was conspicuously pregnant. The second, Laura realised, was the young mother who ran the consortium of outworkers - the group she had from necessity declined to join.

"I don't understand," she said, hurt and puzzled rather than angry. "Are you punishing me for turning down your invitation?"

"We did it to stop you showing us up," said the pregnant girl sullenly.

Her friend took up the story. "Ever since you arrived we've had nothing but criticism from the overseers. They've even started giving our work back to us to do again. And all we hear is Lisset's so quick, Lisset's so neat, if she can do it why can't you? Well, we can't. I have two small children to look after, and Alkesta here can hardly sit at her machine any more."

"I'd no idea this was happening," Laura protested. "Why didn't you speak to me first instead of ruining my work?"

"We intended to, but you weren't here. And when Alkesta saw that pile of mending all complete and ready to go, she knew it would mean yet more complaints. So she started taking it to bits, and I helped."

"In future," said Alkesta, "we want you to slow down and make a few mistakes. Or we might have to do this again."

"How very unfriendly," said a Narvellan voice behind her.

Of the three of them, Laura was probably the most startled. "Administrator Myrig!" she gasped.

"Perhaps you'd care to explain that last remark," said Myrig casually, addressing the two interlopers. "Sabotaging the work effort is a serious offence."

"It's my fault," Laura said quickly. "I didn't explain to Chisrin and the others that I'm a trained seamstress. Someone's been making unfair comparisons."

"I shall speak to the overseers myself," Myrig promised. "In the meantime, you two, consider yourselves lucky that Lisset had spoken up for you. And I hope for your sake that there's no repetition of this."

Shamefaced, they shuffled away.

"A trained seamstress," Myrig repeated. "What other training do you have, Lisset?"

"I'm educated in arts and crafts," Laura replied with complete honesty. "Sewing, cookery, painting - and, of course, music."

"Interesting," remarked Myrig. Once again, Laura had the distinct impression that he was laughing up his sleeve. "As I recall," he continued, "you style yourself Lisset of Treva. Yet an education consisting purely of the arts must be very rare in Treva."

"I've lived in many places," Laura replied coolly. But inwardly she was far from calm, wondering what in chaos he wanted. "You haven't yet told me the purpose of your visit, Administrator."

"Purely social," he smiled. "I came to see Chisrin about the re-allocation of two workers, and thought I'd pay you a call at the same time. Do you remember - I'm sure you do - that I expressed a wish to hear you play? I shall help you gather up these rags and tatters and then perhaps you'll oblige me by playing a tune. Something lively, I think."

"I'm not exactly in the mood," Laura ventured, beginning to rewind the ylur yarn.

"I shall make allowances," Myrig assured her. He still had the knowing twinkle in his eye.

A little later, Laura took her place at the zirid. She fervently hoped that Tralvar's tuning hadn't gone askew, and that her memory wouldn't suddenly go blank in the middle of her chosen piece. She played Rondo alla Turca, amazed when she made only a couple of minor mistakes. Myrig, she noted with satisfaction, looked surprised. He thanked her gravely and left, leaving her sitting exhausted on the stool.

When Idenion came in he found her curled in a chair, almost asleep.

"Difficult day?" he asked.

"It ended badly."

"So did mine," he said grimly. "Axmiol came to see me when I was working on the speech. Apparently, it's only the first step of the softening-up process. After that, he wants me to be chief negotiator on the expedition."

She peered up at him sleepily. "What?"

"Don't you understand, Laura? When Axmiol and his cohorts invade Scapirion, they're taking me with them. To the south pole!"

Chapter Nine

"As I was saying before we were so rudely interrupted," droned Axmiol, "tell me about Scapirion."

"There isn't a lot to tell," replied Tralvar, fidgeting in the high-backed chair. Now that he'd made up his mind to resurrect the recording studio he wanted to be at work on it, not answering the Lord Governor's interminable questions in the audience hall. "The Scapirians claim a more direct lineage from our ancestors, the ones who gave us starflight. No one has studied their society for many years. They used to favour arranged marriages to ensure an even genetic spread, but I've no idea if that's still the case. They speak the same language but with strong regional variants, and their name for Celestra is Nevri - 'mother'."

"When was the last time your people had anything to do with them? I believe you mentioned trade."

"Yes, until about seven years ago they supplied resnay and an assortment of medicines. Their medical science is reputedly superior to ours."

"It could hardly be worse. Have you visited the city itself?"

"No, that wasn't the way things were done," Tralvar explained. "There was a trading post about four silmi from the dome, and we weren't allowed beyond it. We brought our goods and we waited; to do anything else would have nullified the trade agreement. Presently a representative would appear with an exchange of merchandise. Sometimes they kept us waiting for days."

"In freezing conditions?"

"It wasn't too bad. There was heat, light, a place to sleep and a radio relay."

Axmiol cogitated a few moments. "And I gather they are subject to the same low birthrate as the rest of the planet?"

"Of course."

"Good. Idenion has used a cogent argument against inbreeding in his address to them. I wanted to make sure that it was in fact a problem."

"It must be by now," Tralvar conceded, trying not to fuel Axmiol's enthusiasm for the project. "But that won't induce them to surrender. I wish I could convince you, and whoever authorised this venture, that you'll be wasting time and resources."

"We shall see," said Axmiol calmly. "Now, what is the composition of the dome? Is it theridolyte based?"

"Discords, no. One thing I do know, because I've seen it happen, is that the surface of the dome can be heated to counteract heavy snowfall or icing up. Theridolyte does not conduct heat."

"And you're the leading expert on theridolyte, aren't you? Or should I say, the expert on its raw therite state? Oh yes, I heard about your experiments. Such a pity we can't blast or bomb our way in, but compromising the Scapirians' environment is not an option."

"Then why not forget the whole thing?" Tralvar suggested.

"My dear First Citizen," said Axmiol patiently, "try and put yourself in my position. I have a quota that isn't being met, and a city full of people doing nothing toward the work effort. Moreover, a rich vein of aldacite has been detected very close to the aforesaid city."

"I know about the aldacite. Drusa treated Passik for frostbite. If it's just the crystals you want, take them and leave the Scapirians alone."

Axmiol was still determined to be urbane. "I surely don't need to remind you that Narvella Prime is much warmer than Celestra. We're incapable of carrying out a mining operation under such extreme conditions, and all Celestrian miners are currently occupied elsewhere. I didn't intend telling you this, but Directress Passik traced the aldacite to the very edge of the dome. The vein obviously extends into the Scapirian caverns."

Tralvar gave an unpleasant laugh. "So your little campaign's all about avarice. I might have known."

"Not avarice. Necessity." Axmiol abandoned his show of politeness as he spat out the last word.

"Oh. I stand corrected," said Tralvar carelessly. "But nevertheless, let me assure you that no amount of necessity will persuade the Scapirians to mine their own crystals and obediently hand them over. Preaching at them won't work, and neither will trying to get at them through mistreating *us*. They have no regard for us whatever."

Axmiol, furious at having his intentions if not his thoughts read, concluded the interview. Tralvar was free to return to his studio in the textile factory. He felt no pleasure at having bested Axmiol in conversation, merely irritated with his intransigence. Although Tralvar had always decried the Scapirians' isolationist policy he had no particular wish to see them become slaves to the Protectorate, and he only hoped the climate and other factors would suffice to keep Axmiol at bay. Outside the dome the Narvellans could do little, but once inside they would have the advantage of superior mental and physical strength - not to mention the stun-cannon. Whatever move Axmiol intended to make, Tralvar knew it would be soon. The region's brief summer, when the temperatures were only just below freezing, would arrive very shortly.

At the textile factory, the Narvellan recording apparatus was being installed by two technicians whom Tralvar had daringly filched from Communications. Because the system was alien to them, things were not going smoothly. Their ineptitude gave Tralvar the opportunity to shout - not because he wanted to, but because it was expected of him. Since he wouldn't be able to record Laura, the sound quality seemed of little importance.

The ylur weavers looked on curiously, much to the wrath of their overseer. Tralvar explained - painstakingly and none too politely - that once the studio was equipped, it would only be in use when the factory was closed.

"So this is where you've hidden yourself, Tralvar!" said a familiar voice. "When you invited me to inspect your new facility, you might have been more accurate with the address. I went to the wrong intersection."

"On your feet in the presence of Lord Narad!" bawled the overseer. About half the girls obeyed. Narad absently waved them back to their places and strode regally into the studio. The technicians, at a look from Tralvar, sidled away.

"I sincerely apologise for the mistake," said Tralvar, and meant it. "I've a lot on my mind at the moment."

"Such as Axmiol's little foray into the frozen wastes," responded Narad with the hint of a sneer. "I share your opinion, my friend: it has all the makings of an expensive disaster. So, does the new equipment meet with your requirements?"

"We had a little trouble converting it to our power source, but it will suffice," said Tralvar noncommittally. "Now as I'm sure you're busy, I'll come straight to the point. I hate to presume on your good nature yet again, Lord Narad, but if this studio is to function properly I must have freedom to work without interruption. As you can see, space is very limited. There will be no more than four musicians here at any given time, so there will be no temptation to form a lattice. We do, however, need to read one another, and we'll doubtless be working into the night. Could you instruct the Moderators to let us perform in peace? You know how temperamental musicians are. An extraneous thought at the wrong moment could ruin a session."

"You must have a very close relationship with your scolia partners," remarked Narad after a short silence.

"Naturally."

"And that, of course, includes the girl Lisset."

"Of course," Tralvar confirmed unflinchingly.

"Doesn't the First Poet object to all the time you spend with her?"

"Idenion has no aptitude for anything musical," Tralvar replied with a lofty smirk. "Lisset has chosen not to involve him in her studies. I'm sure he understands."

"Let us hope so," said Narad impassively. "Very well, Tralvar, I shall instruct our patrols to steer clear of these premises. Only a foolhardy Moderator would seek to interpose himself between you and your music."

"Once again I'm obliged to you," responded Tralvar with just the right amount of deference. Then he escorted Narad back through the noisy workshop to the street door, where an underling stood guard by a flitter.

"By the way," said Narad as he boarded it, "how is young Quetri shaping up? Will he be part of this select group?"

"I - hadn't considered it," faltered Tralvar, caught unawares.

"Then maybe you should. I believe he has a pleasant singing voice - and that is what you Celestrians prize, is it not?"

"What a gossip that man is!" Tralvar muttered to himself as the flitter departed.

"Don't be such a grouch!" someone admonished from very close quarters. "I think he actually likes you.

273

Hey, don't step back - you'll tread on my fingers!" It was Lydion, peering out of a nearby manhole.

"What are you doing down there?" Tralvar asked in some bewilderment.

"Checking the cables, ostensibly. I dodged down here when I saw Narad." Lydion accepted Tralvar's outstretched hand and hauled himself out. "Drusa sent me to find you. She said Corython's been hanging round your villa half the afternoon."

"Chaos!" began Tralvar automatically. Then, suspiciously: "How does she know Corython?"

"She's seen him at the hospital with his wife."

"Oh. Of course." Tralvar ran a hand through his hair distractedly. "This sounds ominous - he can't have finished his calculations yet. Is the rest of your team close by?"

"They've gone home," Lydion said in surprise.

"Is it recreation time already?"

"It certainly is." Lydion glanced at the workshop chronometer through the window. "And in precisely half an astal, there's going to be a stampede out of that door. So I shouldn't stand just there."

Tralvar moved over. "I want to ask a favour, Lydion. I know how busy your people are, but is there any chance of running a genuine check on those cables tomorrow? I don't want any blow-outs while I'm in the studio."

"I can't do anything about the routine power cuts," Lydion pointed out.

"Of course not, but....I just want to minimise the chances of being left in the dark. I don't like *any* situation where the Narvellans can see and I can't."

"I'll get it done," Lydion promised. "I'll lend you a couple of torches, too."

The clattering of the looms ceased and the girls streamed outside, jostling and giggling. Lydion eyed them shrewdly.

"If you wait while I have a word with my assistants - " began Tralvar.

"Hey, didn't you see that?" Lydion interrupted. "Those two stragglers looked quite smitten."

"You know the rules. No new partners."

"With *you*, idiot! Smitten with *you*. And I don't think full unity was what they had in mind. I know lust when I see it."

Tralvar looked startled, then irritated. "Discords, Lydion, they're younger than Nefyrra. Stop being so absurd."

"I thought you'd be flattered."

"Under different circumstances, perhaps; but not now. As I was saying, if you don't mind cooling your heels an astal or two I'll give you a lift back to Drusa's. And then I'd better see what new species of trouble Corython's brought me. I didn't expect anything to go wrong this early."

**

"It won't work," said Corython.

"What won't?"

"The spalling - we'll never do it. I'm sorry, Tralvar - until I looked at it in more depth I honestly thought it was the best solution. I hope you didn't mind my waiting in your hall? Drusa said it would be all right."

"It's better than pacing up and down in the street," Tralvar answered pointedly. "Come into the study - we might as well be comfortable while you tell me the bad news. Now, exactly why can't we achieve the spalling effect?"

"Because our spheres aren't big enough." Corython waved away the wine Tralvar offered him. "In order to inflict that amount of damage, even at near-light velocity, we'd need an impactor many times the mass of a sphere."

"How many times?"

"Er - about two thousand."

Tralvar was taken aback. "It isn't like you to make such a bad mistake!"

Corython looked acutely embarrassed. "I know, and I'm sorry. For a start, I didn't realise Ipsa was the size of a minor planet. I hadn't studied the Alcine data to any great extent and I was envisaging something a lot smaller."

"That doesn't explain such a vast discrepancy."

Corython sighed. "I'm not trying to shift the blame, but much of the error lies with the existing reports - which I admit I hadn't seen for a while."

"Go on," said Tralvar impatiently.

"They were all drama and no accuracy. The observations weren't made until after the spalling had occurred - well after - and there was very little mathematical evidence to back them up."

"I'm surprised you forgot that minor detail."

Corython turned faintly pink. "With respect, Tralvar, I wasn't trying to create a weapon at the time. Anyway: I went on looking for an event someone had actually witnessed - something to base my calculations on - and at last I found this." He smoothed out a crumpled piece of paper. "This planetoid lost only half its crust, and that was in collision with an object one hundred silmi in diameter travelling at thirty silmi per isk."

"Our hypothetical sphere will be travelling many times faster than that."

"It's still no use." Corython turned the paper over. "Here - " he pointed - "is the rest mass of a sphere, and here is its effective mass on the brink of transposal. Do you understand my conclusion?"

276

"Just about. You're saying the damage to a body the size of Ipsa would be quite localised."

"We can still put a considerable dent in it," said Corython. "An impact crater approximately two hundred silmi across. But that won't achieve our purpose unless I know the exact location of the base and how far underground it is."

"I'll speak to Quetri," Tralvar promised.

"I'm sorry to be so negative," Corython concluded. "My major fear is that the impact event will be too superficial. We won't get any second chances, as you were so quick to point out when you enlisted me. I suppose there's no hope of a practice run somewhere else?"

"It's not viable," Tralvar said after a pause. "You'd have to squander time doing two sets of calculations, Jarras would have to risk his neck modifying two spheres..."

"All right, I only asked." Corython's frown had become a permanent fixture.

"We can still make something of this," Tralvar assured him. "Go home, sit tight, and wait for me to contact you - which will be after I've spoken to Quetri and Jarras." He handed back the sheet of calculations. "I hope I don't need to remind you not to leave any of this on a database?"

"You don't. This is the only copy."

"You're catching on," Tralvar said approvingly. "Would you like a meal before you go? I've just had the larder re-stocked." He didn't particularly want to exchange small talk with Corython over dinner, but thought it was his duty to offer. He was relieved, therefore, when Corython said:

"Thank you, but I mustn't neglect Pannyra any longer."

"I thought she was in hospital?"

"They let her out, with strict orders to rest. If she doesn't, she'll lose the baby. I've been so preoccupied recently - first with my work on transposal, and now this. The least I can do is spend the evening with her."

Tralvar framed a warning about the encroachment of family ties, but failed to deliver it. He was on shaky ground where such advice was concerned. Silently he watched Corython head off in the direction of Lateral Four. The astronomer's house wasn't far away; his protected occupation had guaranteed him a residence in the old part of the city. But, like everyone else in Alda Mexa, his standard of living was poor. He had no scientific materials at home, not even a logic system. He'd have to use the observatory's facilities for his vital work. Tralvar sincerely hoped that wouldn't prove a hazard.

Quetri, at the akron, was about to go on desk duty when Tralvar appeared. It was late evening and the reception hall was empty. Nevertheless, Quetri was a little dismayed to see him.

"Is this wise?" he asked, glancing about. Tralvar seized his arm and marched him into a small ante-room.

"Given the relationship we're supposed to have, it would look odd if I *didn't* show up sometimes. Anyone watching will think we've had a falling out. Remember that when we leave here." He paused for breath, then continued in an urgent whisper. "I'm sorry about the high drama, but this couldn't wait. I'm going to Treva tomorrow and I need an answer from you first. Do you know the planetary co-ordinates for the Synectic base?"

"N-no," Quetri faltered. "If I did, I'd have told you earlier."

"You must have some idea, surely! You travelled there!"

"I was taken there," Quetri corrected him. "I can't pilot a sphere. The flight data wasn't displayed and the viewscreen was off."

"Isn't it nice to be trusted," Tralvar commented.

"All I know is what Navarian told me," Quetri went on. "He said we were beneath the great northern plain of Liapa. He took me to the surface several times, and I can confirm it was the northern hemisphere due to the position of the stars."

"This plain - is it broader than two hundred silmi?"

"Much broader. Six or seven hundred at least."

"This gets worse," Tralvar muttered. "How far beneath the surface were you, do you think?"

"Not far; about half a silmos. The base had to be hidden from view, but there was no need to make it blastproof. Ipsa is a long way from the sun."

Tralvar exhaled slowly. So it wasn't *all* bad news. "Now, Quetri, think carefully. Obviously a visual scan would be a waste of time, but what about variations in temperature? Is there anything that would give off a discernable heat signature?"

"There's the machinery in the complex," Quetri said slowly. "The gravity enhancers, life support for the crew, and the Synectics' environments."

"Which amounts to an oasis of heat in a dead world," Tralvar concluded for him. "Heat produced on a continuous basis for seven years."

"Well...yes."

"Then that's our best hope. By now, the surrounding rock should be slightly warmer. I'll get my team onto it."

"Is there anything I can do, First Citizen? You promised I could help."

"Later, Quetri. Later. Now you'd best get to your post before someone comes looking for you. We'll say goodbye at the main doors - and remember, we've just made up after a quarrel."

Quetri played his part to perfection. When they reached the doors he murmured "Tralvar!" in a voice which trembled, and at the same time brushed his companion's hand with his fingertips. Two passing Narvellans exchanged knowing smiles.

"Oh by the way, Quetri," Tralvar said as he was leaving, "can you sing?"

***

The next day, as scheduled, Tralvar paid a belated but high-profile visit to the sphere assembly plant in Treva. He was pleased to find that shorter working rotas had been established, following his request to Axmiol; but he was not so pleased to encounter silent hostility wherever he went. Disconcertingly, Tatra - Cyphos' widow - now seemed thoroughly dismissive of her husband's sacrifice.

"I told him not to get mixed up in that strike and he wouldn't listen," she said dully.

"Who have *you* been listening to?" Tralvar asked.

"My own commonsense," she replied. And, imprisoning her golden hair in a cap, went back to monitoring the viscosity levels of the latest theridolyte batch.

Tralvar continued his tour, becoming more and more despondent as he went. Even another spat with the four young demonstrators would have been a welcome relief, but they were nowhere to be seen. He suspected they were keeping out of his way. One or two workers seemed grateful to see him and thanked him for restoring their days off. In return, he promised to keep up pressure on Axmiol to recall the deportees. At last his duty was over, and he thankfully accompanied Jarras to his house for dinner. Rillan was there, but not Thala. Tralvar wasn't surprised to hear that the relationship,

280

founded on past idealism, was in difficulties. Her loyalty to the cause was not in question, however, and she'd prevailed upon Rillan to say so.

"Why do you *think* everyone's so resentful?" Jarras replied testily when asked about conditions at the factory. "You wanted them to put up and shut up, and that's what they're doing. But they don't have to like it."

"You won't win them over," declared Rillan. "They're bearing the brunt of this forced labour. The work's exhausting, dirty and dangerous. It's not so bad in quality control, where I work when I'm not delivering spheres, but every so often it gets to me."

"Then here's something to divert you." Tralvar briefly outlined his conversations with Corython and Quetri.

"Discord's dreams!" exclaimed Jarras. "You never told me the Synectics were on Ipsa!"

"Is that a problem?"

"No, quite the reverse." Jarras leant forward intently. "Let me explain. When a fleet of spheres leaves Treva for Narvella, most of them are unmanned. On average, we send only three navigators per consignment - Rillan's usually one of them - plus a few civilians. The unoccupied spheres are programmed to drop out of transposal, define their quadrant and go into a parking orbit, all without anyone's intervention."

"Did *you* write this programme?"

"I did. And so far it's performed without a hitch." Jarras gave a sudden grin. "Maybe it's about to develop one!"

Tralvar dug a spoon into something inedible. "Chaos, Jarras, what *is* this?"

"A bit of a disaster. Thala usually did the cooking."

"If you think this is bad," Rillan put in, "spare a thought for a friend of mine who tried to eat kyffu."

Tralvar grimaced. "I hope he lived to tell the tale! Didn't the fact that they're so plentiful suggest anything to him?"

"He knows now," Rillan said darkly. "Tough as baked theridolyte!"

"Sorry, Jarras." Tralvar turned back to his friend. "I interrupted you. What were you saying about Ipsa?"

"When the spheres define their quadrant, Ipsa's one of the things they triangulate on," Jarras explained. "I chose it because of its unusual appearance - two contrasting hemispheres, smooth in the north and pockmarked in the south. To obtain our data, I suggest we have a sphere go off course and overfly the north. Rillan can chase after it and download its readings under the pretext of trying to stop it. After that we'll have to crash it on Narvella Five, to hide what we've done. Corython will get his figures and, hopefully, we'll then be ready to stage the impact event."

"A pity the spalling idea had to be dropped," said Rillan. "The Narvellans think that's how those mis-matched hemispheres came about."

"So Ipsa's no stranger to rough treatment," mused Jarras. "I wonder what hit it?"

"What matters now," said Tralvar, "is what's *going* to hit it. I like your impromptu scheme, Jarras. How long do you need to set it up?"

"I'll start modifying the programme immediately," Jarras promised with enthusiasm. "I won't be able to put it into effect for another three octals, though. There won't be another consignment till then."

"That's soon enough," Tralvar declared. "We've waited years for this. We can survive a little longer."

Later, when he set out for the monorail, he asked Jarras to walk with him for a final briefing. It had become stuffy in the little house and he hoped the cool evening air would clear their heads.

"I think I'll give the Lyricon a miss tomorrow," Jarras said hesitantly. "So don't look for me."

"You worked through the last rest day," Tralvar accused.

"I've a good reason this time."

"I suppose," Tralvar conceded. "As it happens, I won't be at the Lyricon myself. I'm going to try out my recording studio."

"With Laura?"

"Of course. Is there something wrong with that?"

"She..." Jarras paused, reluctant to continue. "She could be a dangerous distraction."

Tralvar stopped walking. "I have a planet I don't rule, a resistance I can't take part in and a daughter who won't speak to me. What is there to be distracted from?"

"I only meant - "

"I need my music, Jarras. And since you're being so solicitous of my welfare, I'll give *you* a warning. Be vigilant when you're working on the new programme. I can't emphasise enough how careful you'll have to be. Watch your back, maintain your shields, don't drop your guard for an instant."

"Rillan will be taking more risks than me."

"Rillan will be in deep space, on his own, with time to cover his tracks. You'll be working right under the Narvellans' noses."

"Don't agitate. They seldom check my work."

"But they *will* do, after the fly-by. They'll think you've started making mistakes."

"Then I'll accept a reprimand and keep working," Jarras said testily. "They won't suspect anything. Ipsa doesn't hold any significance for them, and the people on the base won't detect what we're doing."

"We hope."

"Discords, Tralvar! Retraces don't lie. The base has no surveillance equipment and the Synectics even ration the use of the radio!"

"Quetri's not been there for years."

"Then they'll be even more isolationist now. You saw the way things were going."

"I'm missing something," Tralvar muttered. "I know I am."

Later that night he dreamt of Quetri, his face alight with wonder, re-living the moment when the Synectics cast their net: "I could perceive the stars through the bedrock. I could hear the planets thundering in their orbits..."

And then Lydion entered his dream, uncharacteristically sombre, describing the same moment: "Patterns, Tralvar. Endless patterns instead of stars. That's how they see things. I didn't fit so I was cast aside..."

"I was part of the pattern," said Quetri.

"I was not," said Lydion.

And the aldacite crystals blazed like miniature novae, exploding him into wakefulness.

Unlike the time he'd dreamt of Floren, no insight followed. He blearily assumed he was more scared than he wanted to admit. To divert himself he began to compile a mental checklist of everything that would need his attention at the studio - beginning with the airconditioning. Before he reached item three, he was asleep again.

The airconditioning was, of course, sphere technology. Nothing else at his disposal could be guaranteed to run lastingly and silently. The overseer, who - like many of his race - had an overabundance of curiosity, turned up to inspect Tralvar's project and had the temerity to suggest that it was against the work effort to power it from the city grid. Tralvar told him to take it up with Lord Narad, and ordered him off the premises. It was not a good start to the day.

Four scolia players arrived next, young and eager, pointing out that he only had their company for the morning. In the afternoon they'd be performing at the Lyricon. He made a few test recordings of them, mainly for Narad's benefit.

Then Laura was standing in the doorway, alone. She'd removed her cloak to reveal a classically simple dress of pale green ytil. Tralvar tried not to stare, and failed.

"Oh, do you like it?" Laura asked ingenuously. "I thought it was about time I made myself something. It wasn't easy, but I managed."

"It's cut on the cross," Tralvar observed. "The Narvellans will say it's a waste of material."

"It's only an old curtain!" Laura peered through a reinforced window at the demi-scolia, playing merrily but silently in their soundproof chamber. "Isn't Quetri with you? You said you'd invited him."

"He had to work. And where's Idenion?"

"I didn't think you wanted him here."

"I still thought he'd show up. Or is he already tired of hearing you sing?"

"As it happens," Laura said coldly, "he has to present his dissertation to Axmiol today. And then he has to attend a pre-mission seminar."

The inner door opened, saving Tralvar from having to apologise. One of the scolia girls looked out and addressed Laura.

"You're Lisset, aren't you? The one who played for Myrig? We thought you'd like to join us for our final session."

Laura thought furiously. "I've a better idea," she replied after only a brief hesitation. "Tralvar was just saying how much he'd like to sit in with you, so why don't you give him the opportunity while I monitor the recording levels?"

This suggestion met with instant acclaim, and Tralvar had no choice but to go along with it. Despite his reluctance he soon began to enjoy himself, and his playing - relayed to Laura via a headset - was lively and accomplished. She looked on almost benevolently as a smile transformed his face.

And then the music was over. The young performers bundled up their instruments and rushed out of the door. Laura carefully returned all the panel settings to zero and relinquished her temporary role of sound engineer.

"How did they know about Myrig?" she muttered.

"I expect your outworker friends put the word around," Tralvar said drily. "Welcome to the scolia."

"Be serious," Laura said irritably. "I wanted the scolia to think I'd lied about myself to avoid factory work. What do I say the next time they ask me to play?"

"I'm sure you'll think of something." Tralvar slid open a section of panelling and removed a small white globe on a spindle. Taking care not to touch the surface of the globe, he placed it in a protective case.

"Was the recording cut directly onto that thing?" Laura inquired.

"None of your Symerid Three superiority!" Tralvar admonished lightly. "I'm well aware that the system has shortcomings - as did my own."

"Aren't you going to play it back?"

"I could, but it might spoil. It has to go through a laminating process along with the others I decided to keep. Narad's going to see to it." He latched the case and set it to one side. "Well, First Singer, are you going to stand there asking questions all day or shall we do what we came here to do?"

Laura gave him a haughty look and stalked past him into the performance area. Tralvar followed her in and secured the partition carefully.

"Now you can stop being Lisset for a while. No one can sneak up on us. If anyone came through the outer door we'd see them at once."

"That's nice to know." Laura uttered some experimental phrases to warm up her voice and test the acoustics. "Hmm, I see what you mean about this place. The walls swallow the echo."

"You'd sound perfect on a recording," Tralvar said impulsively.

"Perhaps," Laura said in a gentler tone than she'd used of late. "Let's pretend we're making one, shall we? And while we're about it, let's pretend we never quarrel. Can you do that?"

"I will if you will."

"Good. Then how about choosing the first song?"

Tralvar didn't hesitate. To Laura's surprise he requested "The Night we Called it a Day" from her Firelight Club retrace.

"Can you play jazz?" she asked dubiously.

"I'll play whatever the occasion demands," he answered.

So she sat next to him at the zirid and sang torch songs to his assured accompaniment. After a while it didn't seem strange. She was loath to stop him when he was playing so well, but - as she pointed out after the third song - her voice was not being stretched.

"Then we'd better move on," he said reluctantly. "I believe you have something new for me."

Laura's eyes sparkled. "I do, and you're in for a treat! This is called L'Invitation au Voyage, and the music's by Henri Duparc - someone you might just identify with. He was a perfectionist who destroyed most of his own work."

"I didn't write mine down in the first place," Tralvar said laconically. "What key are we in?"

Laura sang a note. "Ready?"

"Ready."

"Then here I go. This'll blow your mind!"

Stupid expression, thought Tralvar. He assumed it was a warning of sorts, and tried not to be taken unawares, but the languid eroticism of the song was dazzling. He had to read her fully now, at the conscious level - reach past the strange duality of the prill for the harmonies she needed. "Like little waves lapping round a boat," she'd suggested. During her Firelight Club reprise he'd hardly used his perception. He'd heard her sing there - had *become* her as she'd sung there. He scarcely needed fresh input after that.

He tried harder to focus on the new song. Not English, but the same seductive syllables she'd used to good effect in Nuit d'Etoiles. Laura threw her head back; her voice soared as if it would burst the confines of the tiny room. Then she delivered the chorus in a soft monotone, unconsciously leaning towards Tralvar as she did so.

"Là, tout n'est qu'ordre et beauté,

Luxe, calme et volupté."

The differing melody line of the second verse was already crystallising in her head. He tried to anticipate her, but she stopped him peremptorily.

"No, no, Tralvar! You didn't pause long enough. Let the last note of the chorus die away, then it's one, two, *and*."

"I pause for two isk?"

Laura looked puzzled. "What's an isk? A second?"

"Approximately."

"I didn't know you measured seconds. None of your clocks do."

"Because an isk is no use except in music and stellar navigation. Now can we go on?"

"Sorry. I didn't mean to break your mood," Laura apologised. "Before we start again, do you think I could have some water?"

"Go ahead. I'm at your disposal."

She went to the carafe he'd provided, then turned round rather suddenly and caught him regarding her with an unhappy expression. "Are you tired?" she asked. "Do you want a rest?"

"Tell me what the words mean," he said, not answering her. "You learnt the song phonetically. It's difficult to accompany an abstraction."

"It's about an exotic land," she replied slowly. "I don't know all of it but the chorus says, 'There, all is harmony and beauty: luxury, peace and pleasure'."

"Sensual pleasure?"

"I think that's the general idea."

"Good. Now I can play it." He turned back to the keyboard. "You shall have your pauses and your arpeggios and your little lapping waves. And one day, perhaps, I'll be able to give you peace, contentment and the rest. That's if Corython does as he's told and Jarras doesn't get caught."

"Tralvar - "

"Just sing, will you?"

She capitulated, and this time it was better. Much better. It was amazing how Tralvar could cope with Earth harmonies without re-tuning the zirid. She asked if she might play, and they spent almost an ild comparing the two musical systems.

When Idenion came into the studio he found them with their heads together, engrossed in their studies and, so it appeared, sharing a rare moment of companionship. He would have waited, but Tralvar sensed his arrival and sprang away from Laura as if he'd been caught in a compromising act.

Laura hastened to open the soundproof door. "What news?" she asked anxiously.

"Not good. The expedition leaves tomorrow."

"So soon?"

"We're not going straight to Scapirion. We'll go to Ninka first and get kitted out: weatherproof clothes, ear muffs, boots and so on. There's a piece of special equipment on its way from Narvella Prime, and we'll have to wait at Ninka till it arrives."

"Oh, Idenion!" She clung to him, suddenly very emotional. Tralvar folded his arms and looked bored.

Idenion extricated himself goodnaturedly. "Hey, what's all this?"

"I don't want you to go!"

"I can't get out of it, Laura. It's crazy and a nuisance, and they'd no business involving me, but it isn't particularly dangerous. I can handle the cold far better than they can."

Tralvar cleared his throat. "I think you two should be alone. Do you need a flitter?"

"I have one outside in the yard," said Idenion.

"Then beat it, both of you. I was about to call a halt anyway - all that concentrating wears me out."

"He *wasn't* tired, you know," remarked Laura as they headed for home. "And I don't think he was being tactful either. All of a sudden he couldn't wait to get rid of me."

"He had a good reason," Idenion said evasively.

"What reason? Did you say something to him?"

"No, nothing. I didn't need to." Idenion made a less than perfect touchdown on the piece of wasteland. "Maybe you'd better look in a mirror."

Laura rushed indoors and peered into their one tarnished looking-glass. On her face and neck, very faint but growing more distinct every moment, was the bloom. She turned to Idenion with a delighted smile. Surprisingly, he didn't smile back.

"Laura, I've something to tell you."

"Well it can wait, whatever it is. Come on, you dope - don't just stand there! We have to make love - now!"

"Would you please listen?"

"Oh, do hurry up. Dena will be back soon." She dashed into the bedroom and began pulling off her dress.

"Wait, Laura. *Wait!*"

The sheer unhappiness in his voice finally made her pause. "What's the matter?"

"Oh, chaos, I've been dreading this. I was trying to put it off until things were more settled, but you've been so intent on having a child, and..." He hesitated one last time, then hurried on: "The truth is, there won't *be* any child. Ever. Your race and mine can't interbreed. It's mentioned in the Hellas scrolls several times."

She stared at him blankly.

"Nathaniel knew," he went on. "He was worried I might get you into trouble, as he called it. I thought he'd told you. I was so dismayed when I realised he hadn't."

"Nathaniel and I never talked about anything like that!" She gave an odd little laugh, staring at her reflection. The red whorls of the bloom were all over her shoulders and breasts. "There has to be some mistake. Look how well your protections have adopted me! That wouldn't have happened if our species weren't the same."

"Similar," Idenion corrected her. "For harmony's sake, Laura, don't make this more difficult that it need be. Do you think I'd be telling you this if I wasn't sure? Even when those scrolls were written our population was in decline. We considered introducing new blood, but it was never done because it *couldn't* be done. Don't take my word for it, read it for yourself!"

"Tralvar knows, doesn't he?" Laura said slowly. "That's why he was so keen to pack us off home." She switched to English in mid-phrase. "He didn't want to get mixed up in a godalmighty row!"

"Keep your voice down!"

"No I will not. You should have told me years ago instead of leaving it to Uncle Nat. Or at the very least you should have said something when I first came back, instead of letting me plan and dream. But you took the line of least resistance, as usual."

"If that were the case I'd *never* have told you, and you'd have gone on believing the protections were working against you."

"Then why didn't you let me think that? You *are* able to lie to me, you know. We don't have total unity, or had you forgotten?"

"So we're back to that again." Idenion was quietly furious. "If you really want to know, Laura, I didn't tell you because I knew you'd behave exactly as you *are* doing. Listen to yourself! There are many, many women in your situation, albeit for a different reason. They learn to live with it. So must you."

"I got rid of Paul's baby, back on Earth," she said, suddenly very quiet and still. "It was conceived on tour. I'll never forget his embarrassment when I told him I was pregnant. I thought of you at the time, and how different it could have been - how special you'd have made me feel - " She dissolved into tears, and Idenion made a fruitless attempt to comfort her. She didn't push him away, but simply acted as if he weren't there. She was still crying when Dena came in, an astal or two later; and she cried herself to sleep that night.

Dena, in her tiny room, covered her ears and turned a desolate face to the wall.

***

After seeing Laura and Idenion off the premises, Tralvar went back to the zirid and made a careful transcription of L'Invitation au Voyage, incorporating the vocal line into the arrangement and taking care to include the pause he'd had trouble with. When the piece was firmly fixed in his mind, he vacated the studio and headed home - reluctantly, because it had been so peaceful all afternoon. Someone was always pestering him at the villa.

Once there, he gave way to an unwise impulse and went straight out again. He found Drusa and ordered her to run Laura's retrace for him, losing his temper when she reneged a little. Three times, under the pretext of studying the Earth musicians, he absorbed the smoky intimacy of the Firelight Club. And thereafter, returned to the villa in a state of sensory overload, trying to ignore the dissatisfaction that still gnawed at the edges of his mind.

"I've been waiting for you, First Citizen," said a sweetly lilting voice. A young girl was sitting on the front step, an unopened bottle of wine next to her. Before Tralvar quite knew what was going on, she'd skipped indoors ahead of him and was bouncing cheerfully on his favourite settee. She was quite pretty, he noticed vaguely, with softly curling hair and mischievous eyes.

"I'm sure you remember me," she continued, "but here's a hint. I work at the ylur factory."

"What do you want?" he asked stupidly.

"You," she answered with devastating candour.

"Have you been at that wine?"

She laughed. "Not yet! It's like this, you see: my friends and I decided you needing saving, so here I am."

"Saving from what?"

"From Narvellan boys. Believe me, it's much better with a girl."

Normally, Tralvar would have chased her off. But he was in a far from normal mood. "What's your name?" he inquired.

"Ninfi."

"Well, my bold Ninfi, I hope you're not looking for total unity. If so, you're in the wrong place."

"What I'm looking for," she replied, "is fun. Unity makes everything so complicated, doesn't it?"

"You could say that."

"Then we understand eachother." Ninfi smiled up at him through her eyelashes. "Should I be afraid of you, First Citizen? Are you as dangerous as everyone tells me? Say something dangerous!"

"Boo."

Ninfi laughed again. "Do you know what I think? You would, if you'd just lower your shields a bit. Oh, all right then, don't! I think you haven't had any fun in a very long time - and that means you're ready for it now. This - " she held up the bottle - "will help us relax. It's wildflower wine. Distilled." She found a nearby glass which contained a little resnay, and carefully poured some of the brew into it.

Tralvar scarcely noticed what she was doing. Her prattle faded into the background; he again felt Laura's warm breath on his neck and heard the alluring phrases of her song:

"Là, tout n'est qu'ordre et beauté,

Luxe, calme et volupté."

Ninfi held out the glass, supremely at ease in her role as seductress. "Drink, First Citizen. Then we can start to enjoy ourselves."

And why not? thought Tralvar. Why in chaos shouldn't I take what's offered?

He accepted the glass and drained it to the dregs.

294

Laura awoke from a torpid sleep to become aware of three things: one, the chime to summon the workers - which she normally managed to sleep through - was sounding relentlessly; two, Idenion was not beside her; and three, an anxious Dena was shaking her by the shoulder.

"What is it?" she mumbled.

"Idenion had to leave. I have to go to work in a moment, and I didn't want you waking up to an empty house."

Laura gazed, puffy-eyed, at the empty half of the bed. "He left without saying goodbye."

"They came for him at first light. We decided to let you sleep on, as you were exhausted. He'll try to radio us from Ninka before he..." Dena's voice trailed off and her frown deepened.

"I know I'm a mess," Laura said defensively. "Do you have to stare?"

"Something's wrong," said Dena ominously. "I can't read your prill. I think it's dead." She concentrated again. "We knew this might happen. I'll have to send for another as soon as possible."

"I must have killed it," Laura said bitterly. "Tyvian told me to avoid strong negative emotion. So much for my latest attempt at nurture. I couldn't even keep *that* alive!"

"Laura, I don't have time for this." Dena spoke briskly. "Let's just concentrate on what we have to do. We know Drusa has more seeds at the ready, but without Idenion we can't collect one."

Laura, with an effort, pulled herself together. "Should I try to get to the lab?"

"No! Absolutely not. You must stay here until a replacement's brought to you. I'll have a message relayed now." She fell silent. Laura, while awaiting the outcome, took off the scieshanar-locket and sat staring at it. She felt exposed and strange without its slight weight about her neck. The only other time she'd taken it off was during her retrace, when wearing it would have confused the result.

"It's no good," Dena said at length. "The local relayist says most of the chain is asleep. I'll have to use the factory radio to contact the hospital, and they'll tell Drusa."

"Isn't that a bit public?"

The chime increased its tempo.

"I must go." Dena took a few hasty sips of liman and pulled a comb through her hair. "I'll tell the hospital you need more medicine. Drusa will guess what's happened."

"But surely Chisrin won't let you use the radio?"

"Oh, he will." Dena gave a twisted little smile. "I'll ask nicely."

"I'm supposed to be collecting more overalls this morning!" Laura called after her.

"Leave them! Stay inside!"

Left alone, Laura decided that the best thing she could do was go back to sleep. It would, if nothing else, be temporary camouflage for a mind now open to anyone's inspection. She lay down on Idenion's side of the bed, trying to detect some faint scent of him, but Dena had been so zealous with her cleaning and laundering lately that even this comfort was denied.

She woke again at her usual time, about an ild after the start of the working day. There was no chronometer in the house, of course, but she was becoming quite good at knowing the time without one. Resolutely she began to make herself presentable. She dressed in bright colours, combed her tangled hair and bathed her eyes with a facecloth soaked in cold water. Someone - Drusa, Lydion or even Tralvar - would, she assumed, soon

296

arrive with a new prill, and there was no point in looking a wreck.

Presently Lydion appeared. She'd been hoping it would be him. If *he* couldn't cheer her up, then no-one could.

"Now what's all this, First Singer?" he inquired gently. "A lovers' tiff? You must have been in a fine fury to have slaughtered your little guardian."

"I'm not proud of it," Laura admitted, and briefly outlined the cause of the problem. "Use your perception if you want the details," she concluded wearily. "I don't want to talk about it any more."

Lydion ventured a brotherly hug. "I know all I need to. Let's get your new prill into position." From his pocket he drew a small, insulated cube, identical to the one which had housed the first prill. Then, picking up Laura's locket, he opened it deftly and unceremoniously tipped the dead seed into a wastebasket. Finally, using a tiny pair of pincers, he extracted the new seed from its case and placed it in the locket, together with its scrap of nutrient gel.

Laura bowed her head and permitted him to re-fasten the chain about her neck. "Thanks. Sorry to drag you away from your work yet again."

"Glad to help as always." He sat down opposite her, folding his arms. "I've had strict instructions from Drusa not to leave before the prill wakes up. We have to make sure it isn't defective. So, while we wait, I'll tell you a little story."

Laura raised an eyebrow.

"You wouldn't believe, would you, that I've had a disappointment similar to yours?"

"No, I wouldn't. I don't think you know what disappointment is."

"Ah, my public image. Never-a-care Lydion, lover of a thousand women - well, almost. Let's just say there

297

have been a great many. So doesn't it strike you as odd that I'm not a father?"

"I thought you probably had children in other towns."

"Of course you did, because statistically I should have. And for a time I thought oh, there'll be one or two. My ex-lovers haven't bothered to notify me. Until one day curiosity got the better of me and I went to the registry and checked. There wasn't a single one. And that hurt me, First Singer. I had to conclude I was infertile, and for a while that made my lifestyle seem meaningless. But eventually, after a lot of soulsearching, I decided I owed it to myself to be happy, enjoy life and leave the procreation to others."

Laura was about to speak, but he hushed her.

"By far the most touching thing," he continued, "was the number of women who said they didn't care - that they wanted to be with me anyway. You've heard Clemoridys - you know how much Idenion loves you. So when he says he's accepted your childless state, believe him. Learn to accept it too. Don't let him down."

Laura tried a smile. It was a little shaky, but she sustained it. "You're a good friend, Lydion. To me *and* Idenion."

"I try. And before you ask, there was no conspiracy of silence. I'd no idea the Hellas scrolls contained anything about a species divide."

"I'd like another look at those scrolls," mused Laura.

"Another?"

"Tralvar showed me some of them years ago, during the Peisistrata. I was due to sing later that day so I couldn't join in the feast. Then he was called away, and..." She paused, frowning. "While I was lying awake last night, I racked my brains trying to remember what we'd started to read. Something about the explorers and the Greek women. It's a crazy notion, but I think the truth was staring me in the face all along."

"In which case?" prompted Lydion.

"In which case Idenion will receive a prolonged, sincere and most loving apology." Laura's smile was less tentative this time. "What are the chances of getting into the akron library before he comes home?"

"Tralvar could get you in, I suppose," Lydion replied. "But you'd better not ask him this morning!"

"Why not?"

"Well," confided Lydion with a knowing grin, "he'll probably have the most terrible hangover. Before I came here I left two of my team at the recording studio, to finish some work Tralvar wanted done. The ylur girls were there, of course - and a delightful little creature called Ninfi was regaling her friends with stories of the First Citizen's inexhaustible virility. I caught her eyeing him the other day but he pretended he wasn't interested. I shall have to watch out - it sounds as though I might have a rival!"

"But," said Laura, concerned, "we aren't supposed to have unity with anyone outside the group."

"Who said anything about unity? That wasn't on the agenda. Anyway, he ended up roaring drunk and threw her out when she asked for a scieshanar. Bad mistake on her part."

"Quite. He gets so touchy about not knowing his ancestry," Laura reflected.

"And speaking of ancestry..." Lydion hesitated a moment. "About your problem. It may be too early to start thinking of such things, but if Idenion were to take sciesha with someone - and if there were a child of that sciesha - you as a couple could adopt it. It wouldn't be yours, but it would at least be his. Forget it if you like."

"You're right, it *is* too early," Laura said slowly. "But I won't forget." Equally slowly, as she spoke, the prill began its first faint emanations.

"Ah! Signs of life," Lydion said thankfully. "I was beginning to think Drusa had chosen an inactive one. Well, First Singer, that's my cue to leave. I'll have a word with Tralvar about the scrolls, but I doubt if I'll see him till tomorrow. I've a date with the refuse re-cycling system."

"And I've a date with some overalls." Laura put on her cloak and went with him to the door. "Strange as it may seem, I shall enjoy sitting here with my sewing. I'll have plenty to think about."

***

"First Citizen! Tralvar! Wake up!"

Tralvar groaned, trying to ignore the voice and the hammering in his head which accompanied it. Someone drew back a curtain and a shaft of light speared his fragile consciousness. He realised, then, who had disturbed him.

"Quetri? What in the name of chaos are you doing in my bedroom?"

"Your pardon, First Citizen," said Quetri, more reproachful than apologetic. "Kyrin and I were concerned for you."

"Why? Can't I even have a hangover in peace?"

Quetri pointedly threw open a couple of windows. "Kyrin's been trying to reach you. Idenion has radioed twice, expecting you to be at the akron to speak with him. And there are some other messages which I'm not privy to."

Tralvar shaded his eyes against the merciless daylight. "Why's Idenion calling in so soon? He only left this morning."

"*Yesterday* morning," Quetri informed him. "You've lost a day, Tralvar."

300

It took a moment to sink in. "What...time is it now?"

"Nearly noon. I was here earlier, and - "

Tralvar lurched upright and nearly fell out of bed. "Have you been in my study, you little sneak?"

"No!" Quetri protested, shocked.

"Oh, discords, I'm sorry, I'm sorry. There was this girl..." Tralvar tried to run a hand through his matted hair. "She doctored my drinks - resnay and wine together. I never could handle wine. Anyway, she went looking for a scieshanar. I caught her opening my desk."

"I was about to say," Quetri went on stiffly, "that I came to your door earlier and couldn't make you hear. Kyrin persuaded me to enter."

"You did right." Tralvar was vainly trying to remember what he should have been doing yesterday. Seeing Corython, that was it. It *would* have to be Corython. "Quetri, I want you to do something else for me. Go to the kitchen and see if there's any ice in the freezer cabinet. If there is, put all of it in a bowl and bring it to me in my dressing room."

Quetri went, still looking a little pained. When he returned with the ice - only partly frozen as the power had been off during the night - Tralvar was slouched in an easy chair. He'd sponged his face, put on trousers and sandals, and was looking a little more alive. He placed the bowl of half-melted ice on the floor and proceeded to sluice it liberally over his head. Then he towelled his hair, put on a tunic and, palely sober, took Quetri down to the kitchen and poured two tall glasses of liman.

"This is bad, Quetri," he said at length, leaning his elbows on the table. "You once offered to be my strength. Could you try and prevent me from being so self-indulgent?"

"I am to stop you ravishing young girls?"

301

"Now just a moment, my lad. Don't judge me by the precepts of your people. Ninfi was an experienced, sexually active young woman. In fact, she taught *me* a thing or two. No, I want you to help me stop drinking - for a few octals at least. Otherwise we could be looking at something much more catastrophic than a lost day."

Quetri, suddenly ill at ease, was slow to reply. "If I knew your mind, I'd be better able to help you," he said at last. "Since the day you freed me from Tarysk - the day I pledged you my loyalty - I've hoped..." He paused again and swallowed. "Many people think I'm your neph-khet. It's surely no secret that I care for you, Tralvar. In some ways you're so like Navarian - forthright, driven. I'd be happy to bond with you if you'd have me."

Tralvar wasn't entirely surprised; and though his head still throbbed from the effects of Ninfi's wildflower potion, his mind was quick enough to sense an opportunity. To complete his plans, he needed Quetri to put his life on the line. Now he'd learn how far he could push the boy.

"First Citizen?" Quetri's voice trembled as if he were on the verge of tears. With slow deliberation Tralvar moved round the table, lifted him to his feet and embraced him.

It was not unpleasant. Quetri's slender arms, when he responded, were warm and somehow comforting. He smelt of soap and hair oil. Tralvar stroked the nape of his neck with light, practised fingers, feeling him shiver, seeing his lustrous eyes half-close.

"Quetri," he said softly, "you'd be so good for me. But I cannot unite with you now. Every time I commit myself to total unity, it ends tragically. Tristell, dead; Floren, dead; Elanir, my estranged wife, consumed with bitterness. There's so much danger confronting us - I'd be terrified of making you more vulnerable."

302

Quetri began to voice a protest. Tralvar stifled it.

"When the Synectics are vanquished, if I still live, come to me again." He released Quetri and held him at arm's length. "Until then, let's work together toward our freedom."

"Very well. You're right, of course, First Citizen."

I'm a liar, thought Tralvar privately. And I'm not very proud of myself.

"Are you angry with me?" Quetri asked dolefully.

"No. No, not at all," Tralvar said with genuine sincerity. "Sit down, have some more liman, and listen to me for a moment."

Quetri obeyed.

"When I came to the akron - when we pretended to have the quarrel - you begged for an active role in the campaign. Do you still want it?"

"More than ever!"

"Then you shall have it. But it will be difficult and dangerous."

"I won't let you down," Quetri declared.

"I know you won't. Now, for security's sake, I don't propose to tell you what the rest of my team is doing. And conversely, they won't know what *you're* doing. In about six octals from now, I shall require you to go back to Narvella Prime and wait. You'll have certain devices with you and I'll have instructed you in their use. You're my second line of attack. If the initial plan succeeds, you need do nothing. But if it fails, everything will depend on you."

"How will I know if it has failed?"

"You'll know," Tralvar said grimly. "And then your real mission will begin. If we can't defeat the enemy from here, you'll make your move from closer at hand - inside the Synectic base itself!"

Chapter Ten

Idenion, muffled in an overcoat of synthetic fur, stood at the trading post's door and gazed at a hostile, beautiful landscape. The persistent wind made his eyes water; the droplets then froze on his eyelashes. Behind him, the Narvellans huddled in overheated rooms and planned their next action.

The Scapirians, of course, had been openly dismissive of his carefully crafted message. He had read it, very expressively, over the radio link in the cabin - and had read it again the next day. He'd expected no response, but the third time he requested an answer a peculiarly accented voice said:

"First Poet! We assume you made this broadcast under duress and thus absolve you of any unfriendly intent toward our city. Tell the Narvellans that Scapirion does not open its doors to raiders. You of the outer world have lost your way: it is no wonder you allowed yourselves to be invaded. We are the Scapirians, guardians of the truth. We will not communicate with you again."

Idenion surveyed the forbidding terrain before him and wondered what "guardians of the truth" meant. He didn't envy these taciturn people nor their bleak environment. There were no trees nor foliage, not one blade of grass - just barren earth with occasional pockets of snow. Ahead of him, Scapirion's geodesic dome rose silvery-white against the eggshell blue of the sky. The surface of the dome was criss-crossed with faint traceries, reminiscent of the weathershield's matrix - another remnant of science from a bygone age.

On the side of the structure which faced him was a circular metal door. A rough road led straight to it. To the left, rocky crags loomed. To the right was a frozen lake. On the far side of the lake was a towering wall of ice, the cliff edge of a glacier, sculpted into jagged shapes by the relentless wind.

Sijek came out to stand beside him. "The rocks on the lake bed are warm," he remarked. "The water flows freely about them."

Idenion was unsurprised by this utterance. "There are hot springs all around this region," he replied.

He had been in Sijek's company for three days now - initially at Ninka, then here - and by noon of the second day had realised there was something very special about the boy. Sijek was a male synaesthete, with the same enhanced perception as the Directresses. According to Axmiol, most male children who carried the gene died at birth, and the rest soon after. Sijek, therefore, was unique - but in a strange reversal of their usual gender bias, the Narvellans had refused to let him join the exclusively female Sisterhood of Directresses. Instead, he had become a plaything of the elite. No-one, not even Grevin, had treated him as anything other than a curiosity; it was not until Axmiol had adopted him that his fortune changed. But he was still not permitted to develop his talents. His extra senses, instead of being honed to perfection, were untrained and erratic.

Idenion had asked him if he minded.

"A neph-khet does not presume to know what is best for him," Sijek had replied in his docile way, adding: "I enjoy our conversations, First Poet. If you continue to ask leading questions I may not be allowed this privilege."

Since then, Idenion had steered clear of the subject. Sijek was often excluded from the Narvellans' debates, and he didn't wish to leave the boy with no-one to talk to.

From within came the sound of raised voices, Axmiol's among them. Sijek hunched his shoulders and pulled his hood tighter about his ears. He'd smeared grease on his face to avert windburn, and was contriving to look quite unattractive.

"You shouldn't stand outside," Idenion advised. "The cold could do you harm."

"So could Axmiol when he's in this mood," Sijek said dourly.

"What's the problem in there? I daren't try to read them."

"They're communicating with Narvella Prime via the transposer at Ninka," Sijek explained. "Unfortunately, radio contact with Ninka is not good. Tempers are becoming frayed."

"But what's going to happen next?" Idenion asked. "We can't wait here for ever. What's in that crate we brought with us?"

"A drill," Sijek informed him. "Our government requires its immediate use. Its two operators are about to unpack it and convey it to Scapirion's door."

"Do you believe they can break into the city?"

"It's possible," Sijek said with a degree of hesitation. "The drill bit has been specially calibrated from the strongest substance known to us. And yet...I'm not confident. I cannot divine the nature of that door: neither could Passik. It's not theridolyte, but seems to have some of theridolyte's characteristics. Thus, it's resistant to our scans." He hesitated again. "Axmiol is angry because his superiors won't not listen to his doubts. He hates the idea of failure."

"Don't we all?" Idenion said softly.

During the next two or three ilden the huge drill was assembled and trundled into position by means of a motorised sled. Flitters were not suited to the cold. The engineers fussed over the drill and kept it wrapped in layers of protective sheeting while awaiting the order to switch on. Before the attack commenced, Idenion was ordered to deliver one final warning over the radio. There was, of course, no reply; and with a dull grinding sound that reverberated down the valley and set everyone's teeth on edge, the siege of Scapirion began.

A day and a half later, little progress had been made. The groan of the drill permeated every activity at the trading post, a noise only made tolerable due to the frequent stops needed to clean the mechanism.

"Couldn't I go home now?" asked Idenion miserably.

"Certainly not," said Axmiol. "Your negotiating skills will be needed once we are inside. Sijek, beloved, would you accompany me to the drill site? I'd like you to study the door and tell me what damage has been sustained."

"As you wish, my lord."

Idenion, mildly interested, went with them. He suspected the weather was on the turn; the wind seemed more biting and there were stray snowflakes in the air. Axmiol was aware of this too, and was furious when Sijek informed him - very timidly - that the drill had penetrated less than a quarter of the total distance. At this rate the weather would break before the portal could be breached. There followed a lengthy altercation with the engineers. Axmiol wanted them to run the drill at full power. There was a risk that it would burn out, but a half-year's wait was not acceptable to Narvella Prime.

Idenion grew tired of their bickering and wandered down to the lakeside. With a vague sense of alarm, he saw that Sijek had ventured some way onto the frozen expanse and was gazing fixedly downward. He was about to issue a warning to the youth when several things happened at once. The drill started up with an eldritch shriek, causing him to cover his ears; the topmost pinnacle of the glacier, disturbed by the vibration, broke off and crashed down onto the ice; a deep crack appeared and zig-zagged unerringly toward Sijek. He turned as if to run, then flailed his arms and disappeared.

Idenion threw off his cumbersome coat and half ran, half slid toward the scene of the disaster. Sijek had not been swept away - yet. His terrified thoughts were proof of that. Eyes streaming in the raw wind, Idenion neared the schism and peered about. For a moment all he could see was whiteness and a pool of dark water; then he spied a small, gloved hand clinging feebly to the ice at the pool's edge. He flung himself flat and made a grab at the hand, nearly losing his grip on it when the glove came off. He then locked his free hand round the emerging forearm and pulled. Sijek's head broke the surface, and Idenion struggled to keep hold of his arm as he thrashed and spluttered. The eerie scream of the drill died away, leaving only Sijek's mental wail to challenge the sudden silence.

"Give me your other hand!" Idenion shouted. Sijek barely had the sense to comply. Idenion hauled him up until his shoulders were clear of the pool, then rapidly realised he hadn't the strength to do more. He was achingly cold, and wished he hadn't been so quick to discard his coat. He had on a padded overtunic from Ninka, but it was scant protection against a bed of ice. He tried to shift his position a little, and the fractured surface creaked under him.

+First Poet!+ Axmiol's agonised thought slammed into his mind so violently that he almost let go of Sijek.

+Stay back+ he warned. +The ice won't support you+

+Do not let him drown!+ There was a terrible entreaty in the Narvellan's mind. An implied threat also.

Idenion didn't know how much longer he could hold on. The lake had an undertow, and Sijek seemed to be getting heavier and heavier. +Throw me a rope+ he demanded. +Quickly+

Their only rope was still attached to the drill. Axmiol's subordinates laboured to free it.

Idenion was so numb with cold he scarcely knew whether he still had hold of Sijek. He felt as if he were sinking through the ice. Then, curiously, things seemed to improve. The cold was less intense and Sijek was no longer a dead weight. When the end of the rope thudded next to him he was able to seize it and loop it tightly round Sijek's waist. Then they were both dragged away from the pool in a tangle of sodden fur and ice shards.

Apart from the two engineers hauling on the rope, no one moved. Axmiol and the three others, in a silent row, were concluding a complex mental ritual - the winding down of an exercise they had just performed. And suddenly, Idenion understood.

Discord's dreams! he thought. They levitated him! Partly, anyway. Just long enough for me to get the rope round him. And - what did they do to *me*? Best not to wonder, I suppose.

Axmiol hurried forward, lifted Sijek tenderly in his arms and hugged him. "You're safe, beloved!"

"There's something under the lake," Sijek murmured hoarsely.

"Crystals?"

"No, an artifact. Something strange...ancient..."

"Hush, beloved. We'll talk later."

During these whispered endearments - as he presumed them to be - Idenion struggled to get up, furious that no-one was helping him. He'd only just regained his footing when Axmiol whirled about and, with easy confident steps, carried Sijek back to the shore. Idenion trailed after him, shivering.

"Thank you so much for saving my lover, First Poet," he muttered. "That's all right, Axmiol. Anytime."

Then, raising his voice: "Hey! That's mine, you ingrate!"

Axmiol had removed Sijek's ruined overcoat, picked up Idenion's from the lakeside and draped it adroitly about the youth in his arms. Then he and his cronies boarded the sled and set off for the trading post.

"I can't believe he *did* that," Idenion said aloud. He found his mittens, which Axmiol had overlooked; then, fuelled by his anger, stumped back to the road. At least he'd managed to keep his boots on and his feet dry.

The two technicians were inspecting the drill head, which seemed to have buckled. Idenion picked up some of the insulating material it had been transported in, wrapped it around himself and sat down by the roadside. Presently a delicious warmth began to steal over him - but he still hadn't forgiven Axmiol.

One of the technicians read his unshielded thoughts and came across to remonstrate. "Do you not realise," he said sternly, "that Lord Axmiol restored your strength - which he could ill afford to do whilst trying to elevate Sijek."

"He left me here without a word of thanks," Idenion pointed out.

"You're out of danger; *that* was his thanks," said the Narvellan stubbornly. "He has not abandoned you, nor us. Returning Sijek to the cabin had to take priority. He will need more than energy transference if he is to avoid hypothermia."

Idenion was too exhausted to argue further. He placed a wad of packaging at his back and leant on it, leaving the ever-industrious Narvellans to dissect the drill. Here, in the shelter of the great dome, the windchill was much less. And soon, as his body heat increased, he began to feel sleepy. He gazed idly in the direction of Scapirion's portal, the source of all their recent trials, and vaguely thought that his eyes must be playing tricks as the door appeared to be moving. It *was* moving! Suddenly wide awake, he watched it begin to pivot on its horizontal axis. Smooth and silent, up and over, until its reverse side was outermost. Then it shut again with a dull boom that sent echoes far across the valley. The two Narvellans looked up, startled, and could see nothing amiss.

Idenion, a little lightheaded, began to laugh. He wondered how long it would take them to notice that the door was whole again. The damaged area was now on the inside - where, presumably, it would be swiftly repaired.

"I fail to see anything amusing, First Poet," said the Narvellan who had previously criticised him; but Idenion simply laughed all the more. The siege of Scapirion was over before it had hardly begun.

When Idenion re-entered the trading post about an ild later, Axmiol was already screaming down the transposer link at his distant adversaries on Narvella Prime. His message was unequivocal: there would be no more attempts on Scapirion while *he* was in charge, and if anyone tried to dismiss him he would overthrow the government singlehanded. Evidently this was no empty threat as they eventually backed down.

Just as I always thought, Idenion observed. This expedition was an elite-driven whim, not the Synectics' will. *They* wouldn't have allowed him to give up. And since it isn't their will, they obviously don't care about the extra crystals. Their needs have been met.

Sijek was receiving healing from one of the elite prior to being transferred to Ninka, where the hospital routinely dealt with victims of the cold. Axmiol, surprisingly, didn't involve himself with the boy's care. Presumably his energies had been depleted during the rescue.

Idenion was relatively unscathed, except for some strained shoulder muscles. After a long hot bath he was virtually back to normal and ready to repel any offer of healing that came his way. None did. Presently Axmiol asked to see him in his quarters. He went, and found the Narvellan governor briskly writing out a report. But behind the cool efficiency was an air of world-weariness.

"I suppose," he said, "that I owe you some kind of reward for your prompt action."

"I'll leave that to your discretion, Lord Governor."

"Such uncustomary reticence!" Axmiol remarked with a brief return to his usual sarcasm. "I'd be failing in my duty to myself and to my neph-khet if I didn't acknowledge your good deed. I presume you'd like to be excused from the work effort? I'm afraid I can't authorise a complete exemption, but I can recommend an extended leave."

"In fairness to my people I can accept only a short leave of absence," Idenion responded. "Instead, might I select the nature of my work? I was about to be removed from Chisrin's factory when you hired me, and I have no idea where I would have been sent."

"What work did you have in mind?" inquired Axmiol.

"Since Tyvian's death," Idenion proceeded, "Healer Drusa has taken over the running of the retracer lab in addition to her hospital duties. I'd like to help her with the plants Tyvian had in his care."

Axmiol looked faintly surprised. "You're volunteering to tend the hrilffa? That's a most insalubrious task."

"It is my choice," Idenion said quietly.

"So noted," stated Axmiol, scribbling on the page in front of him. "We will soon be departing for Ninka, and as soon as Sijek is settled we can proceed to Alda Mexa. I shall inform Myrig of your wishes and he'll finalise the details of your transfer. You'll need different lodgings, no doubt."

"My sister and my partner in unity still work for Chisrin," Idenion reminded him. "As I don't wish to live apart from them, I shall need transport to the laboratory."

"That can be arranged." Axmiol was already losing interest. "Now go. I have several tasks to complete before we can abandon this place."

A day later, Idenion was back in Alda Mexa. Tralvar was waiting at the spaceport with a flitter.

"You seem to delight in being foolhardy," he commented as they flew westward toward Idenion's house. "But at least it's paid off this time. That was a good move, getting yourself transferred to the lab. I'll be able to liaise with you effortlessly. But before you go back to work, and while Axmiol's still in a conciliatory mood, I'd like to send you to Treva."

"What for?"

"To give some poetry readings in the factories. Improbable though it seems to me, people - especially the Narvellans - enjoy hearing you recite. The Trevans are always saying they feel marginalised by Alda Mexa, so it will be a good exercise in public relations; and more importantly, you'll divert the Narvellans' attention away from the assembly lines."

"How long is this exercise going to take?"

"Four, maybe five days."

"I can't leave Laura *again*!" Idenion expostulated.

"I'll bring her over a couple of times. I need this diversion, Idenion. Jarras has written the fly-by programme, and he now wants to install it and run a simulation. But the Narvellans won't stay out of the way long enough for him to do it."

"Thus is the first I've heard about a simulation. Is it necessary?"

"You know Jarras. Meticulous. He'd have preferred a real practice run if one were possible."

Idenion sighed. "All right, I'll do the readings. But Laura isn't going to be very happy about it. When I spoke to her from Ninka she was looking forward to having me to herself."

"You're a public figure," Tralvar reminded him. "She can never have you completely to herself."

"I suppose not. In that case would you do me a favour and keep her company while I'm away?"

"What do you think I've been doing?" Tralvar set the flitter down with a thud, opened the hatch and elbowed Idenion out. "Tomorrow's a rest day. Make the most of it. You'll be on your way to Treva the day after."

***

Dena brushed a strand of hair from her eyes and tried to concentrate on the crystal she was trying to cut. Almost three octals had passed since her ordeal in the empty factory. For two days afterward Chisrin had hardly spoken to her, and she'd begun to think he wouldn't carry out his threat. Then he'd accosted her as the others left, and thereafter had detained her many times.

The weather had turned mild again and the heat in the workshop was stifling. The other workers were at recreation, but as usual she hadn't met her quota and had decided to stay in. Chisrin had gone outside too, and that was another good reason to keep working.

"You look dreadful," said a voice in front of her. It was Ailsi, whose irrepressibly high spirits were both a comfort and an aggravation. Dena murmured a brief reply and tried to ignore her, but Ailsi was not to be put off. "Dena," she said without preamble, "has Chisrin been taking advantage of you?" Then, before Dena

314

could answer, she went on: "I just want to help. You're obviously finding him more of a problem than I did."

Dena looked up, amazed. "I thought I was the only one!"

Ailsi grinned. "That's what they *all* say. Oh, Chisrin's very discreet - has to be for his own sake. But *you're* not. If you want to keep this quiet, you'll have to stop looking petrified every time he speaks to you."

"I can't help it. He frightens me."

"That's really stupid," Ailsi declared. "Sometimes I think you scolia people don't live in the real world. He's not a wicked man, just a man." She paused. "Do you want my advice or not?"

"You're going to give it whatever I say," Dena answered resignedly.

"Right. Now the most important thing is, try not to show him you're nervous. It spurs him on."

"I've already found that out."

"Next, you have to understand him," Ailsi continued. "He's light years away from home and family. He's part of a weird society that allows only one partner for life, but she isn't allowed to be here. What would *you* do in his position?"

"Find someone who was willing," Dena said promptly. "As you obviously were."

Ailsi flushed. "It isn't that simple," she said. "Chisrin doesn't want an eager partner - he seems to prefer some reluctance. He's very embittered. I couldn't get the reason out of him, but I think some woman hurt him badly. That's why he's so averse to mind games, as he calls them. Don't attempt unity with him, Dena - he'll be really angry if you do."

"I'm not likely to try it," said Dena sharply. "I detest him."

315

"He'll keep after you in that case," Ailsi pronounced. "Try a few smiles and stop being so dramatic. He might get bored then."

"But why does he do it, Ailsi? The Narvellans have such a strict morality. Why does he break their laws?"

"The elite made those laws," Ailsi said solemnly. "Chisrin isn't like them. He doesn't like boys, for a start. I take it there's some reason why you can't refuse him?"

Dena hung her head. "Idenion is...has...broken Narvellan law. Chisrin promised not to say anything if..." She brushed away an angry tear. "I wish I could be as casual as you."

"How many times has he sent for you?" asked Ailsi sympathetically.

"Several," said Dena evasively, still staring at the floor.

"In how many days?"

"Three octals...and, Ailsi, please keep this to yourself. Idenion mustn't know. He mustn't ever know."

Impulsively, Ailsi put a skinny arm round her. "I won't tell," she said earnestly. "And if it's any consolation, Chisrin always keeps his promises. So whatever Idenion's done, it shouldn't come to light."

"That's something, I suppose," said Dena miserably. Ailsi sat down beside her and took her hand confidentially.

"Now listen," she said. "You don't understand the way Chisrin operates. You're his woman of the moment, so you're entitled to some concessions. Ask favours and he'll grant them."

"I don't want any favours from him."

"Of course you do," said Ailsi patiently. "You want your quota halved for a start. And if you can't think of anything else, get our rations increased."

Just then the door opened and Chisrin himself sauntered in.

316

"What's this?" he inquired suspiciously. "Ailsi, get out." She dived past him, uttering some Narvellan epithet which Dena didn't understand. "Nature's pest," Chisrin growled. "What nonsense has she been filling your head with, Dena?"

"Only that.....you and she..."

"A bad choice," Chisrin commented. "As she doubtless explained."

"She also said," Dena went on steadily, "that I could ask a favour of you."

"Name it," said Chisrin calmly.

"I don't want to finish these." Dena pointed to the crystals on her table, wondering if she'd taken Ailsi too literally. But Chisrin merely smiled.

"I'll see to them myself," he said. "You will, of course, attend me this evening - but at my house this time. Make a suitable excuse for being out all night."

"Idenion and Lisset are in Treva."

"Good! No one to notice your absence." He paused, scrutinising her pained expression. "What's the matter? Didn't Ailsi tell you I made up the rules as I went along? *Be* there, ice maiden. It should prove...educational."

***

Laura, Tralvar at her side, sat in a gallery overlooking the sphere assembly bay. It was the midday recess; Idenion's voice drifted faintly up to them from below as he recited poetry to the workforce. They crowded as close to him as possible, perching on every available surface. The Narvellan overseers stood by indulgently. Tralvar looked on with a scowl, the Narvellans with benign smiles.

By this time Laura was no longer apprehensive in crowds, knowing that the confusion of perceived thoughts would mask her prill-enhanced consciousness. "Did you find Jarras?" she asked.

"He's running the simulation now. So far, so good; but he needs at least another astal to restore everything to normal."

Laura watched, slightly bemused, as a horde of girls mobbed her partner at the end of his performance. "I imagine it will take the foremen longer than an astal to settle *them* down."

"Don't worry, it's only vanity. They're hoping Idenion will write about them."

Laura continued to study the proceedings intently. "Any one of those girls would be proud to have his child," she murmured.

"I could kick Lydion for putting that idea in your head," Tralvar said savagely. "You wouldn't tolerate infidelity on that scale. Remember Tarit, and the girl from your village?"

"I was young then," Laura said defensively.

"You can't outgrow jealousy. No one can."

Idenion finally extricated himself from his following, and with a last goodnatured wave ascended the stairs. "Thank you for bringing her, Tralvar," he said warmly. "Have you been here long?"

"*Too* long," Tralvar declared.

"I asked for that, didn't I?" Idenion's grin didn't waver. "Remind me what's next on the itinerary."

"This afternoon you're at the theridolyte plant, and tomorrow morning at the logic systems lab. Jarras and Rillan are working at the spaceport till dawn, so it's confirmed that you and Laura can stay overnight at their house. Thala says she'll cook your dinner on condition you tell her all about Scapirion."

"Aren't *you* staying?"

"You don't need me." Tralvar glanced down at the shop floor. "They're about to resume production. As soon as I've checked on Jarras I'm going back to Alda

Mexa. I'll give you a lift to the theridolyte plant if you like."

"I'd like some lunch first," Laura said.

"And a long cool drink," added Idenion.

"Suit yourselves." Tralvar turned on his heel and quit the gallery, leaving them to exchange puzzled glances.

"Why's he in such a hurry to get home?" asked Laura. "He doesn't have anything scheduled."

"Maybe that's what's bothering him," mused Idenion. "It can't be easy, having to distance himself from his own plans."

"He's been so odd lately," Laura continued. "That business with the girl, for instance..."

"It's a normal Celestrian thing to do," Idenion said gently.

"It isn't normal for Tralvar," Laura began, but was interrupted by the Narvellan supervisor, who had come to thank Idenion for keeping the workforce happy. He too seemed surprised that the First Citizen had departed so swiftly.

For the rest of that day, true to Tralvar's prediction, Laura and Idenion were never alone. After joining the last sitting in the canteen, consisting of clerical staff and the caterers themselves, they were ferried to the theridolyte complex. The afternoon did not go well. What began as a civilised recitation in a pleasant indoor courtyard degenerated into a near-riot when the Narvellans, worried about production targets, called an early halt to the performance. The workers were incensed. Idenion spotted one of the more volatile youths about to throw a flowerpot, and much to Laura's surprise seized the young man and wrestled him to the ground. After that, a strategic departure seemed in order.

"That's left your image a bit dented," Laura remarked as they travelled to Jarras' house in a flitter crammed with shift workers.

"I had to do something. My presence caused that quarrel," Idenion replied. "If he'd lobbed that pot they would have reduced him - or worse. The trouble is, no one ever believes it will happen to *them*."

Ourselves included, Laura thought grimly.

Thala was waiting at their lodgings with a meal in preparation and numerous questions at the ready. Laura could understand her eagerness to talk - the split with Rillan had left her out on a limb with little or no contact with the conspirators, and she felt guilty that Rillan and Jarras were taking all the risks. But Idenion was tired, and she seemed determined not to notice. It was twilight before she finally said goodnight.

"I've a little something to show you," Laura said mysteriously as soon as the door had closed. "I've been carrying it around all day." She unclipped a small travel pouch from inside her cloak and drew out a folded paper. "Look. Tralvar copied it out for me."

"From the Hellas scrolls?"

"Yes. It's the piece I've been looking for, the one I was trying to decipher when I was sixteen."

Idenion unfolded the paper and read: "The people of the village at first hailed us as gods, and the maidens were very generous with their favours. Several romantic attachments developed, which we renewed on later visits. One day, however, we noticed the women had grown cool toward us; and when we asked what we had done to offend, the youngest reproached us in this manner: 'We believed you to be gods, for who else would know our thoughts? And when we lay in your embrace we rejoiced that the gods had desired us. But as no life has quickened within me nor the other maids, we know you are but men, as a god's seed is always fertile.'

Thus in her simplistic way the girl confirmed our suspicions: we could not interbreed with these people. To us and to our race in general, this was a sad disappointment. The natives of Symerid Three are a comely species, if somewhat ill-disciplined."

"I should have read to the end," Laura said ruefully.

"It might have saved you some misery," Idenion agreed. "That account shouldn't be taken too literally, of course. My ancestors loved to embellish the facts. But the central message is true. I traced the research when I was granted free access to the library."

"That was *why* you wanted access, wasn't it? Nothing to do with Scapirion."

"History and folklore so often become entangled," said Idenion softly. "Before I spoke out, I had to see proof. I so desperately wish there had been none."

How could I ever have believed he didn't care? Laura asked herself as she warmed some liman. I've been so selfcentred. He wants children just as much as I do.

They took their drinks to the window and sat gazing out at Treva's industrial heartland. "Won't you even consider Lydion's suggestion?" Laura ventured after a long pause. "There wouldn't be any shortage of volunteers."

"No, I won't consider it," Idenion answered quietly. "Tralvar's right: you'd be jealous."

"And what makes *him* so omniscient?"

"Don't disregard his advice, Laura. He does have an empathy with you - I've seen it when you work on music together. Sometimes I think he understands you better than I do."

"Oh, Idenion, what an absurd thing to say!" Laura exclaimed.

"I'm serious," he began, but she swiftly leant across and placed her finger on his lips. Then she kissed him.

"I'm not going to have another row with you - especially not about Tralvar. Now let's change the subject, shall we?"

***

Tralvar left his vehicle at a flitter park near his house and walked the remaining short distance to the villa. As was usual in the middle of a working day, the street was deserted. By disposing of his flitter correctly and not, as was his normal practice, abandoning it outside the front portico, he was hoping to give the impression that he was still in Treva.

Once safely home, he made his way to the kitchen and thence to the cellar door. Inside, a flight of neat stone steps led down to a series of racks containing his supply of wine and resnay. Approaching the far wall, he applied pressure to a specific building block; soundlessly, it and four others rippled aside to reveal a dark recess with a curved ceiling and a faintly unsavoury smell. He switched on a light, allowing the theridolyte fixture to ripple shut behind him.

Cyphos had helped him construct this portal into a disused sewage tunnel. He'd initially intended it as an escape route, if one should ever have been needed; now it housed bomb-making equipment. In one octal from today, Jarras' sphere would scan Ipsa. Three octals after that, another sphere would be launched to annihilate the Synectics. And in the time between, Quetri would be dispatched to Narvella Prime with an incendiary device. If the sphere failed to find its target, Quetri would convey the bomb to the Synectics' base.

Tralvar cast a critical eye over his small collection of timers, fuses and launchers. Then his gaze came to rest on a row of carboys, each containing a chunk of therite in neutralising fluid. It all seemed very primitive. In less than three octals he had to have a serviceable device ready. Never mind that it was only back-up and

322

probably wouldn't be used - he had to assume it *would* be.

He crossed to a small table and studied the calculations he'd made. The timer and detonator presented no real problems, but the bomb itself was a different matter. As it was to be planted, not launched, it didn't have to be aerodynamic; but it had to be small enough for Quetri to conceal in his hand luggage. And it had to remain stable until detonated - not easy where therite was concerned. His chief fear was that it would be confiscated before Quetri had even reached Narvella Prime. And then, quite suddenly, he knew how this could be avoided. Quetri's telescope, the one given to him by Navarian, went everywhere with him. Only it wouldn't, not this time. The scope would remain on Celestra, and the conveniently padded carrying case would have a very different cargo.

He made more calculations, based on a cylindrical design with an airtight shell to house the neutraliser, until Quetri's now-familiar call nudged gently at his perception.

+First Citizen!+

Thankfully Tralvar laid his work aside, secured the hidden door and ascended the cellar steps. He was glad Quetri was there. It was a little too easy to grab a resnay bottle on the way up from the tunnel, but the loyal young Narvellan would deal efficiently with any such lapse.

***

Dena picked her way carefully along the unmade road toward Chisrin's house, which lay in an adjacent street. As instructed she had gone home, bathed, washed her hair and put on a clean dress. Then in the late evening, just ahead of the Moderator patrols, she had set out.

She wondered, not for the first time that day, why Chisrin had summoned her to his home. She supposed he'd grown dissatisfied with hasty couplings in the rest room. Perhaps she no longer attracted him when she was hot, tired and dishevelled. Or perhaps, as Ailsi had suggested that afternoon, he was trying to raise their liaison above the level of sexual blackmail. She hoped that wasn't the case. Surely not even Chisrin would offer that kind of insult?

Predictably, Ailsi had listened at the door after Chisrin had ejected her from the workshop. "*All night,*" she'd sighed later in envy. "Oh, Dena, I wish I could take your place!"

"So do I."

"He's going to turn on the charm," Ailsi predicted. "And *you're* going to fall for it. You won't be able to maintain that ice maiden act."

"It isn't an act," exclaimed Dena, stung.

"Haven't I been right so far?" Ailsi continued remorselessly. "I'm telling you, he'll seduce you."

"He will not!" Dena declared.

"He will," said Ailsi sweetly. "I'll bet on it if you like. If you still hate him tomorrow I'll work half your quota. Otherwise you take half mine."

"Agreed," said Dena, supremely confident.

And now she had arrived. The house was a small, one-storey apartment, not much different to hers and Idenion's. The entrance was fronted by a tiny walled garden full of shrubs and fruit trees, which she thought incongruously pleasant. Transparent double doors led from the garden to the living area. She stepped inside cautiously.

A small table displayed two place settings and a simple meal: chilled soup, grain cakes, fruit and wine. Music - alien but acceptably melodic - issued from a slowly rotating globe. Chisrin was nowhere in sight. Dena removed her shawl and waited, knowing he was nearby.

Studying the room closely, she discerned a certain shabbiness everywhere. The furniture bore many scratches, and sections of the carpet were almost worn through. Some of the tableware was chipped. It seemed that his living standard was no better than her own. What were his people thinking of?

"So you've finally realised," Chisrin said, stepping out of the adjoining bedroom. Dena regarded his changed appearance with frank surprise. In place of his work attire he had on a short turquoise tunic, belted at the waist, and a floor-length cloak of the same iridescent material. His hair was unbound and his arms and legs were bare. The colour of his garments complemented the gold of his skin and the green of his eyes. As he moved closer to her, she realised he was wearing perfume - something Narvellan men normally considered effete. It enhanced, rather than detracted from, his powerful masculine presence - a presence which she acknowledged and feared. She looked up at him guardedly.

"Why have you done all this?"

"For you, of course," he replied. "Don't you like it?"

She shifted her gaze to the far wall. "I'm here because I have to be. It doesn't matter what I like or dislike."

"Of course it matters," Chisrin insisted. "You're a respectable girl - "

"I *was*," Dena said bitterly.

" - and as such, you're entitled to a few basic courtesies. If it weren't for those confounded Moderators, I'd have taken a lot more time and trouble from the start."

"Ailsi warned me what you're trying to do. It won't work."

"We'll see." He smiled complacently, poured a glass of wine and handed it to her. She sniffed it cautiously.

"It's not drugged," he informed her. Then, when she still hesitated, he poured another glass from the same bottle and drank it himself. "Satisfied?"

She drank then, and he watched her narrowly. "That's better. Your planet has some excellent wines and I doubt if you've learnt to appreciate them. And now, before we eat, I've a present for you."

He beckoned her toward the bedroom and she followed reluctantly, lingering in the doorway. Just inside the room was a small wardrobe with a full-length mirror, and inside the wardrobe was an exquisite dress. It was of palest gold, layer upon layer of material so soft that she thought it would melt at her touch. The skirt was ankle-length and straight, with tiny pleats; there was a narrow girdle at the hips, linked by a sunburst inlay. The high waist was designed to emphasise the wearer's slenderness. The bodice was delicately beaded, as was the scoop neckline and dainty short sleeves. She didn't bother asking where it had come from; there was nothing like it on Celestra. Nor did she ask how he'd managed to inveigle it past the spaceport authorities. She merely said:

"It's lovely, but I can't accept gifts from you. It wouldn't be ethical."

"You believe it might condone our relationship," Chisrin remarked. "Let me put it another way. I want to give you this because of the exemplary way you've behaved. So different from my other young ladies. No sooner had they secured my interest than they looked for ways to exploit it. Avaricious little beasts. You, on the other hand, asked for no concessions - at least not until Ailsi put the idea into your head." He paused. "You

326

can't take the dress with you - its origins are too apparent. But wear it here, as a favour to me."

Dena turned to re-examine the garment. "What did you trade in order to get it?" she asked.

"I *paid* for it, dear girl, with some of the credit I've amassed since I've been here. It cost about a year's worth, I think."

Dena relented. "All right, I'll wear it for you."

"And for yourself too, I hope," he replied, dismissively eying the plain white smock she had on. "Now let's get rid of *this* drab little item."

She flinched a little as he tweaked at the laces, and for a moment he grew irritable. "What's wrong with you, Dena? Do you realise how aggravating it is when you do that? Anyone would think I made a practice of hurting you. Do I? Well, do I?" His arms encircled her like twin iron bands, demonstrating an alien strength that was normal to him, forcing her to realise that he had in fact handled her with much restraint. He read her admission, and let her go.

"You don't hurt me, but you belittle me," she said when she had her breath back.

"Nonsense!" said Chisrin as he finished unlacing her. "You're the only girl of my acquaintance who can keep her dignity when her dress is round her ankles." To prove the point, he let go of the smock; blushing, she darted forward and grabbed the Narvellan creation from its peg. Quietly amused, he helped her with the fastenings, then watched her shyness evaporate as she twirled in front of the mirror.

"See, Dena, what a difference it makes? You're a woman, not an inhibited little girl."

Looking at her enticing reflection, Dena had to admit the dress had transformed her. "How did you know it would fit?" she asked.

327

"Your measurements are recorded on the factory computer," Chisrin reminded her. "But since the overalls tend to fit only where they touch, I simply used my eyes."

"I noticed," said Dena, sounding a little arch.

Smiling, Chisrin led her back to the table. "Just one final detail," he said, stepping into the garden. One bush was still in bloom: he picked one of the white blossoms and, returning, fixed it in her hair with a jewelled pin. "What's the name of this flower?"

"Eprys," she replied. "An archaic word meaning constancy."

For once he made no reply, sarcastic or otherwise. The music ended and he placed another globe on the spindle. Presently Dena began to relax a little. She ate sparingly and watched him covertly as he reclined in the chair opposite. She asked him about his impoverished lifestyle, and listened as he explained how a trained geologist like himself - and scientists in general - ranked poorly on Narvella Prime. Science was considered vocational in the hope of attracting the best minds. He spoke lazily, fluently, and her scolia training drew her to the timbre of his phrases as well as the gist of his words. His eloquence impressed her.

"Why shouldn't I be proficient in your language?" he asked quietly. "I seldom hear my own." He leant forward and refilled her wine glass. Dena drank without further prompting, thinking it might make the rest of the night more tolerable, as well as giving her the courage to speak freely.

"About these basic courtesies I'm entitled to," she began carefully. "I'm going to ask you some questions and I think I have a right to some honest answers."

"You look so very beautiful," said Chisrin irrelevantly.

328

Undeterred, she went on: "I accept that you need women, but I don't see why you have to choose unwilling ones. Ailsi desires you and I'm sure others do too."

"But not you," he commented, fixing her with one of his piercing stares. "Very well, then: it's like this. A good Narvellan wife is supposed to be modest, demure and reticent in all her dealings with her husband. The women of my race are socially conditioned to behave this way and most of them keep to it, apart from the theatricals - about whom the least said the better."

"I met them," Dena said. "The ones that came here initially. We thought they were so like us." Her voice trailed off unhappily.

"I never considered that before," Chisrin said, staring thoughtfully out of the window. "I suppose they *are* like Celestrians. What a misleading bunch of emissaries. Do you think we cheated you?"

"I think the rest of your women must lead a wretched existence," Dena stated, evading the question.

"We all lead wretched existences, ice maiden," he retorted, "only sometimes it isn't immediately apparent. So, there you have it - my renegade spirit still yearns for the ideal mate. If I could make do with the Ailsis of this world, everyone would doubtless be happier, but I'm afraid all that brazen sensuality has a disastrous effect on me."

He means impotence, Dena thought, then realised he was dismayed that she'd understood him.

"Passive shyness like yours," he continued, "superficially resembles the behaviour of a Narvellan bride. For a time anyway."

"What do you mean?"

"I mean it won't last. You'll soon lose your innocence. You've already begun."

Dena struggled to follow his logic. Why was he out to destroy the very thing he sought after? "It must be difficult to go against the tenets of your people," she said.

"At first it was," he admitted, "but it soon became easier. These things have a habit of growing easier, don't they?"

Dena looked down, biting her lip. He had again managed to trap her with words. She remembered, all too vividly, how her second visit to the rest room had proceeded. She'd become hopelessly, irrationally frightened, and he'd lost his temper with her. On her third visit, she'd been tearful but stoic. By the fourth, she'd learned not to care. Yes, it did get easier.

Night, clear and cloudless, settled over the city. In the garden the eprys flowers had closed their petals, and several bright stars peeped through the branches of the trees. Chisrin drew the curtains and moved quietly about the little house, lighting subdued lamps in every room. Even Ailsi had been unnerved by the way his eyes glowed in the dark, and he wasn't about to give Dena such an obvious excuse to resist him.

"And now, you want to know what set me on this path," he said, seating himself once more and taking one of her small pale hands in his. The music globe clicked to a standstill; this time he didn't replace it. "What makes you so sure there's a reason?"

"There has to be," said Dena wretchedly. "Tell me, I beg of you, if it will help me accept what you've done."

Chisrin was silent for a long moment. Then he pointed to a plain gold cuff, slightly darker than his skin, adorning his left wrist. "This, as you probably know, means I'm married. Look at it carefully."

Dena examined the cuff minutely. She'd always thought it to be removable, like a bracelet. Now she saw it was one unbroken circle.

330

"Narvellans marry for life," Chisrin said. "At the close of the Netsamet - our bonding ceremony - the cuff is welded on."

"Isn't that painful?"

"Momentarily. But the Mark of Netsamet has to be permanent, just as our marriages are." He stood up and paced restlessly across the room. "Perhaps you've wondered why I object to mind games. Suffice it to say that I, like you, believe that total unity is the truest expression of love. And no-one has ever known my mind nor shared it, save the woman I reverence above all others. Her name is Sarune." He returned to Dena's side, carrying a small transparent disc in his palm. "Soon after our marriage, she gave me this likeness of herself. The impress will only respond to my psychokinetic commands. It's a measure of my regard for you, Dena, that I allow you to see it."

Swirls of white-gold light moved across the surface of the disc, coalescing into a landscape: a grassy hillside, coniferous trees and a mountain beyond. A lithe young Narvellan woman ran up the slope, turning to wave at the unseen recordist. Dena, who had been expecting to see a static image, was fascinated. The picture then centred on Sarune's face. She had a haughty, imperious beauty. She smiled - a level, challenging smile which didn't quite reach her brilliant green eyes. A dauntless intellect dwelt behind those eyes. Unaccountably, Dena shivered. The picture blurred over. Chisrin, looking rather tired, put the disc down.

"Psychokinesis isn't one of my better accomplishments," he said ruefully. "But she - did you sense it, Dena? - she had a superlative mind."

"Had?" queried Dena.

Chisrin swore softly in Narvellan. "I vowed I'd never speak of her in the past tense," he said. "I haven't seen her for over twenty years, but I know she's still alive."

"Twenty years?" echoed Dena. "Why? Where is she?"

"Sarune has a unique mental talent," Chisrin replied. "I believe you know something about lattices and the like?"

"Yes, I've worked with the scolia," said Dena, trying not to be reminded of the attack on Quetri. But Chisrin was deep in his own reflections and no longer making any attempt to read her.

"Then you know how difficult these things are to sustain. Someone always loses the synchronicity. But with Sarune in control, there was no decoherence - she could link individual minds for days at a time, with hardly any effort. It was particularly useful to the Directresses when they were deep-probing for geological instabilities. That's how we met. I was scarcely more than a boy, but I knew we had a life-bond. I couldn't believe my good fortune when she agreed to marry me. And then, after only half a year - the happiest time of my life - the Governors took her away." He reached for the wine bottle: it was empty. Sighing, he went to look for another. "Have you ever heard of the Synectics?" he inquired over his shoulder.

Dena, horrified, could make no answer.

"There's no reason why you should have," Chisrin went on, misinterpreting her silence. "The Synectics were - are - a group of scientists who combined their mental resources to help the homeworlds. There were nine of them, I think. Old men, probably. Sarune was needed to stabilise the group mind." He'd set the wine on the table, but hadn't touched it. He sat motionless, head bent, remembering.

"If you'd rather not speak of it further..." Dena ventured.

332

"You asked, now you'll listen," he said tersely. "And stay away from that bottle - you've had enough. As you can imagine, I did everything in my power to keep Sarune off the project. The whole thing sounded obscene. But the Governors were adamant - there wasn't anyone else with her abilities. I argued, fought, petitioned - nothing could sway them. I should be honoured, they said, to have her serve the Protectorate in such a way."

"Did *she* want to do it?"

"She believed the propaganda and wanted to be useful," Chisrin said sombrely. "I railed at her, accused her of mental infidelity, told her she'd be prostituting herself. She just kept smiling sweetly and saying it wouldn't be for long. But once they had her, they told me in no uncertain terms that I'd lost all rights to her. Our environmental problems were paramount. And, because I was only young, I bowed to their wishes and kept quiet, while year succeeded year." He paused to take a long drink of the wine he had forbidden her. "I worked hard, thinking it would endear me to the authorities. I became a leader in my field. My youth fled away. And still my Sarune was a captive."

"And what happened next?" prompted Dena, trying not to look as though she already knew.

"Can't you guess? The Celestrians made contact and gave us interstellar travel. I was overjoyed. My race had a future again, and so did Sarune and me, for surely there was nothing more for the Synectics to do. Eventually I went to the project headquarters, expecting to be allowed in." His fingers clenched around the wine glass so tightly that Dena feared it would shatter. "Everything had gone - nobody knew where. I was frantic by then, and started pestering the authorities for an explanation. I didn't get one - at least, not an accurate one. They told me Sarune was dead." Abruptly he rose, flung off his cloak and threw open the casement. A cool breeze drifted in, billowing the faded curtains. He stood at the threshold for nearly an astal, breathing the night air, fighting his sorrow. "After that, I was ready to break every law I could," he said at last. "And it looked as though someone, somewhere, was determined I should do just that. Sending me here to get me out of the way, putting me in charge of a lot of young women...the result was inevitable."

A departing sphere blazed a bright trail across the indigo sky, the light smearing characteristically as the craft accelerated toward transposal. Chisrin watched it longingly.

"One day, I'll get leave to go home and continue my search. I'm convinced Sarune's alive - it's almost as if she's found a way to communicate. I intend to find her and set her free." He closed the doors with a defiant slam. "Well, get it over with. Tell me I'm crazy."

"I can't. You're not," Dena said. She was trembling. "It's a sad story. So very sad."

Chisrin was puzzled. He had foreseen indifference, scepticism, even polite sympathy, but Dena's response went way beyond that. He raised her to her feet. Normally she was as taut as a strelsis string, but tonight she was soft and pliant, leaning into his embrace without a hint of resistance. "What *is* all this?" he asked, with a tiny edge of suspicion in his voice.

It was too late to call the reaction back, so Dena did the only thing she could. Unhesitatingly she threw her arms around him.

"I swear I'll never understand you," Chisrin declared. With an air of triumph he swung her up and carried her into the bedroom, his fingers already at work on the hooks of her dress. Unnoticed, the flower tumbled from her hair. When he'd disrobed her she lay down on the cool sheets and waited for him, modestly averting her eyes when he put aside his tunic.

In her mind, unbeknown to him, all was becoming surreal. The image of the young vital girl in the impress disc alternated with Quetri's nightmare vision of the Synectics in stasis. Chisrin, who had once seemed such a threat, had suddenly become as exploited as she. Don't look for her, she wanted to cry. Forget about your evil wife. But of course, she could say nothing at all. She drew him close, hardly aware of what she did, trying to use his warmth and normality as a shield against her fears.

"At last," he whispered. "This will be just for you, ice maiden. Just for you."

The Mark of Netsamet was cold against her skin.

Now that she'd ceased to fight him, Chisrin knew he was within sight of his goal - to evoke passion in this strange inhibited young woman. He was patient and considerate, adapting his moves to suit her tiniest reaction, all trace of his innate cynicism well hidden. His perseverance was rewarded when, at last, he teased her into an unwilling climax. She cried his name almost in protest, turning her head away as if to deny her own traitorous response. In the stillness which followed he studied her resting profile, expecting to see some visible change, but she still had her usual look of injured innocence. He wondered how much longer she would retain it.

She stirred and turned toward him wordlessly.

"Tell me you enjoyed that," he murmured, stroking her hair.

"You know I did," she whispered. "Except..." And her mind - all of her mind - reached out to him beseechingly.

He denied her, just as he'd denied Ailsi, but held his anger in check. He merely gave her a little shake and said, "Now stop it. Remember what I told you." He expected tears or recriminations, perhaps both; but Dena only sighed, as if at the confirmation of an old belief. She curled up close to him, putting an arm about his waist. This he allowed, in the knowledge that it was only the third time she'd voluntarily touched him. Her eyelids drooped, and presently she slept.

Waking in the soft light of dawn, she reviewed the previous night's events with calm, dream-like quiescence. She remembered the last time she'd woken, how Chisrin had gently resumed his lovemaking. She had again tried to embrace his thoughts, and again he'd refused, but with less vehemence and more sadness. She stretched out a lethargic hand to him - and froze aghast, the gesture incomplete. She had offered him total unity twice...*twice*! The conspirators would have been betrayed, the Synectics alerted - all because of her lack of willpower. If Chisrin woke now and wanted her, she'd probably lose control again, and this time he might just forget his vow of abstinence. She didn't feel inclined to leave - a lesser shock, this - but she would have to, while he still slept. She could make it seem like caprice, something which wouldn't offend him. Carefully she slid out of bed, picked up the golden gown and placed it where she'd been lying. Then she found the crumpled eprys flower and laid it on the pillow. And that, she decided, would have to do. Hurriedly she donned the white smock she'd arrived in, retrieved her shawl and tiptoed outside.

The morning promised to be bright. Dena paused briefly to gaze at the mist rising from the direction of the river, and for the first time in many days felt at one with herself instead of aimlessly adrift. She took heed of the subtle, silent messages her body was sending her, knew herself changed, driven aside from any future she had once planned. But for the moment, she was virtually at

336

peace. The mist would soon vanish in the sunlight, and her way forward would become equally clear as time passed.

Chapter Eleven

"Good news!" Idenion announced as he arrived home from the retracer lab. "Rillan's back from Narvella Prime. The fly-by worked: we have the information."

"Did he get into trouble?" asked Laura anxiously.

"Not really. They gave him a bit of a roasting over losing the sphere, but they don't think the crash was deliberate. Tralvar's going to collect the data in person as soon as he decently can." He came up behind her as she worked at her sewing and imprisoned her arms. "Why the worried face? Everything's going well."

"That's what worries me," she replied. "And how were the horrible hrilffa today? How many new scratches?"

"Two."

"Only two? That's good going."

"Well, actually," Idenion confessed, "three of Tyvian's students turned up this afternoon and I didn't get much work done. We were having a debate."

"What about?"

He grinned. "What *wasn't* it about? They're a lively bunch. Time really flies when they're on form."

"And where was Drusa while this was going on?"

"Oh, she had some visitors of her own. From Tafret. She seemed more cheerful than of late."

"There, you see? Everyone's cheerful. You, Drusa - and Dena too, since we got back from Treva. I don't like it. Something's going to happen."

"Superstition!" Idenion declared, dabbing salve on his scratched hands. "Anyway, Tralvar isn't happy. Look how he spoilt your last music session by yelling at you. My fault, I suppose, for being there. He knows I can't appreciate your voice the way he does."

338

"It's just nerves," Laura said forgivingly. "He'll be more amiable once he's seen Rillan."

"I suppose," Idenion conceded. "He's probably trying to dream up a good excuse for going to Treva yet again. No visits for years, and then three in a row, might seem a little odd to some."

But Tralvar had found his excuse. In the bulletin of citizens' misdemeanours which was still regularly delivered to him - and which had grown much shorter lately as Axmiol's zero tolerance laws were grudgingly heeded - he saw that three more Trevans were marked for deportation. Their crime was stealing food. Myrig, when questioned, was strangely reticent on the subject.

"This was none of my doing," he maintained. "I suggest you take it up with the Governor of Treva. I agree it does seem an extreme penalty for such a minor matter, and I will personally recommend that it be commuted to overtime or something similar."

"There are rumours circulating," said Tralvar after a moment of deliberation, "that the previous deportees are dead. No-one seems to know where they are."

"And who, precisely, is 'no-one'?" Myrig queried with sudden asperity. "Industrial action is a politically sensitive issue. There are those who would free the strikers and there are some who advocate an even harsher punishment. It makes sense to keep their location secret." Then he lowered his voice and continued almost pleadingly: "For everyone's sake, Tralvar, do not pursue this line of questioning. There is a power struggle amongst the elite. Its subtleties will escape you, so I will only say that the lives of your workers depend on your discretion."

"Can you assure me they are alive?" persisted Tralvar.

"Yes," said Myrig unequivocally. "They are."

Tralvar had to be satisfied with that. It was late when he arrived in Treva, too late to see the local Governor, whom he detested in any case. A meeting with him would do no good; a direct communication from Myrig just might. He did, however, obtain permission to see the prisoners - all women - and apprise them of Myrig's comments.

Jarras and Rillan were at the spaceport, working on a faulty transposer under the watchful eye of the Narvellan operator. Tralvar, who had expected to find them at home, reacted with more irritation than the occasion demanded. Jarras in particular was aware of the long puzzled look the Narvellan gave them as they left.

"Discords, Tralvar, did you have to make such a fuss? He's going to remember that!"

"Good!" snapped Tralvar. Jarras could smell the resnay on his breath. "Well, Rillan, hand it over. I want that data crystal!"

"It's in my desk at the factory."

"*What*?"

Rillan bridled. "I couldn't risk keeping it. There were a couple of Directresses floating around the spaceport earlier, with the usual hangers on. You know how those girls react to aldacite - how could I justify carrying any? The only safe place for aldacite is with *more* aldacite."

"What were Directresses doing here?"

"Just passing through. One was that girl who was under suspicion - she's almost cleared her name, apparently. She and her friend were going to the place those flawed crystals came from."

They reached the sphere assembly works without encountering any Moderator patrols.

"Just in case anyone asks, what's our cover story?" inquired Tralvar. "I assume you do have one?"

"You prevailed on us to supply fresh crystals for your ailing logic system," Rillan answered smoothly. "A lie must contain at least part of the truth; isn't that the rule?"

"Yes," Tralvar admitted grudgingly. "I wasn't aware there was a second rule, though."

"And what's that?"

"Blame the First Citizen as often as possible," Tralvar replied with a cold smile.

The Narvellan in the gatehouse, recognising them, simply waved them through. Inside, the harsh overhead lighting had been turned off: isolated pools of radiance marked the areas where maintenance staff - including one or two Narvellans - worked on the machinery. The muted sounds of industry were a welcome change from the cacophony of the day shift. An overseer paced the semi-deserted shop floor, disappearing eerily into the darkened areas and gliding unconcernedly out of them.

"Tonight's shift will be having an easy time," whispered Jarras. "That's Quodos: he knows nothing about procedures here. As long as you look busy he'll leave you alone."

Entering the quality control section, Rillan switched on a lamp, opened his desk drawer and unhesitatingly removed a crystal - one of several. He handed it to Tralvar and pocketed the others.

"Are you sure that's the right one?" asked Tralvar dubiously.

"Of course."

"He can tell them apart," Jarras put in. "It goes with the job."

They retraced their steps along the main aisle, trying not to hurry. Presently they drew alongside a huge, encased drum, where the additives which kept theridolyte in its liquid state were spun off prior to casting. A solitary Celestrian, intent on his work, knelt beside the big machine. Jarras, ever observant, glanced at the man: and what he saw brought him to a halt, so suddenly that Rillan stumbled into him.

"Ibri? What are you doing?"

Startled, Ibri dropped the tool he was holding. It clanged against the side of the drum.

"Not now, Jarras," protested Rillan. "Let's go, while Quodos is at the other end of the assembly line."

Jarras ignored him. "I said, what are you doing, Ibri? You're not supposed to touch those inspection plates."

"The gimbals needed adjustment," Ibri replied sulkily.

"With a metal cutter?" Jarras took three quick steps, pushed Ibri aside and peered into the depths of the machine.

"Jarras!" repeated Rillan, agitated. The other workers were too far away to hear what was being said, but still close enough to recognise the beginnings of a row. An assortment of queries tweaked the edges of Rillan's shields. +It's personal+ he returned, hoping that would shut them up. It did, for a time.

Tralvar merely stood by and waited. He hadn't known Ibri by name, but had recognised him at once as the youth who had thrown mud at him and been arrested. If Jarras was suspicious it was probably with good reason.

"I thought so," said the engineer's muffled voice from halfway inside the inspection hatch. "Tralvar, Rillan - come and see this."

They approached resignedly.

"See that stanchion there? It's almost cut through at two stress points. It'll sheer off under pressure and look like metal fatigue." He turned back to the guilty but defiant Ibri. "Very efficient. The broken strut would

342

have gone flying into those gears. It would have taken days if not octals to repair the damage."

"Why have you done this?" asked Tralvar calmly.

"If no spheres are finished then nobody gets deported," Ibri said with a mutinous glare.

"Don't be so näive!" exclaimed Rillan. "The women would be transferred to another city or put on a scheduled transport."

"After a delay. There'd be time to plan a rescue."

"Do you realise," Tralvar said icily, "that this act of sabotage may have endangered the lives of your colleagues on Narvella Four?"

"They're dead already," retorted Ibri. "Everyone knows that."

"Quodos is coming!" announced Jarras. "What should we do?"

"Say nothing!" Ibri urged. "Whose side are you on?"

But there was only one thing they *could* do. After this very public quarrel, no one would believe the breakdown of the drum was an accident. If they tried to protect Ibri they would all be implicated. And nothing, but nothing, must be allowed to interfere with the production line and phase two of their plan.

A look passed between Tralvar and Jarras. Shielded though they both were, they understood one another.

Ibri intercepted the glance and tried to bolt. He made it through the exit but was marched back by the security guard. Quodos appeared from one direction, and three Moderators - always swift to pinpoint trouble - from the other.

"What is the meaning of this disruption?" demanded Quodos.

"Attempted sabotage," said Jarras.

Ibri aimed a blow at him; Rillan slapped his arm aside.

The guard frowned. "If you had intelligence of this, Jarras, you should have reported it to us."

"I wasn't sure. I didn't want to make false accusations," Jarras replied deferentially.

Quodos returned from inspecting the damage, which was obvious even to his untrained eye. "I must commend you on your vigilance," he said formally.

"Ibri of Treva," mused one of the Moderators. "Did he not perpetrate an assault on your person, First Citizen?"

"He did," replied Tralvar.

"Do you now see," said the Moderator condescendingly, "how pointless it is to show clemency? His type always re-offends."

"It would seem so."

"I take it you do not wish to intervene this time?"

Ibri, pinioned between the two remaining Moderators, gazed hopefully at Tralvar.

"How *can* we intervene?" This was Jarras. "The crime is against the Protectorate, not us."

"First Citizen?" persisted the Moderator.

Tralvar hesitated no longer. "He's had his warning. Do what you like with him."

Ibri gave him a long level stare - a mixture of contempt, reproach, and profound disillusionment. After a moment Tralvar turned aside.

"Prepare to summon the Ten," said the senior Moderator.

"Defer that order!" said Quodos, surprisingly authoritative. "There was a previous incident: one sphere in our last consignment went off course, and regrettably we accused Jarras of carelessness. It's now obvious that the programme was tampered with, either by this felon or an accomplice. I insist that you keep him alive for questioning."

344

"Very well," said the Moderator impassively. "He will remain in our custody until your superiors wish to examine him."

Without more ado they bundled Ibri out of sight. The guard exchanged a few words with Quodos and then went back to his post. Tralvar gave the overseer a quizzical glance. Was his intervention due to mercy or self-interest?

Quodos was aware of his scrutiny. "If I were to serve on a Ten, I'd have to absent myself for the rest of the night. There would be no-one to supervise these good-for-nothings." Then, raising his voice to an impressive bass-baritone bellow: "Back to work, all of you. Back, this instant. There's nothing more to see."

"Do you wish me to effect repairs on the drum?" asked Jarras.

"What? - No, no, don't sacrifice your night off." Quodos looked as though the notion of repairs had only just occurred to him. "The morning shift will take care of it. Thank you again for your timely intervention."

Tralvar gazed speculatively after him as he hurried off to berate two workers lingering by the drinking fountain. "I wonder..." he murmured to himself.

"What is it, Tralvar?" asked Rillan.

"Just something Quetri said to me once about the Free - that he thought there were others like him, just keeping quiet."

"An interesting notion," said Jarras. "But since we can't put it to the test, let's move."

The guard glanced at the gatehouse chronometer and noted their departure time in his log. Tralvar suddenly realised he'd missed the last monorail to Alda Mexa - and that meant he'd lost a whole night's work in his bomb factory. It also meant that Corython wouldn't get the data crystal until halfway through the next day at the earliest.

345

***

It was almost mid-day in the aldacite workshop, and Ailsi was discussing Chisrin with an unwilling Dena.

"And that was the end? He hasn't sent for you since that night?"

"No."

"I told you, didn't I?" said Ailsi triumphantly. "As soon as you showed a bit of appreciation he lost interest. You just made it worse for yourself, putting up barriers."

"Yes, Ailsi," Dena said wearily.

"Tell me again about the dress. I can't believe he traded all that - what does he call it - money for something you only wore once!"

"I don't think he was expecting such an easy victory," answered Dena with a rueful smile.

"I was right about that too, wasn't I?" cooed Ailsi, infuriatingly smug. "I'd love a peek at that dress. Do you think he's still got it?"

"I imagine he'll make it available to my successor," said Dena with a trace of cynicism.

"That's a point. Who do you think it will be?"

"No idea. I'm hardly the best person to ask."

Laura struggled by with her latest batch of mending. Chisrin, seeing her, bounded out of his office and took charge of the unwieldy basket.

"Lisset! Always a pleasure to welcome you." He carried the basket to his desk, set it down and commenced his usual inspection. He seemed to take an inordinately long time. Laura waited just inside the office door, anxious to sign the worksheet and be on her way.

"Will that be all?" she ventured at last.

"Ah, Lisset. Must you leave so soon?" Chisrin's smile was dangerously charming. "This is wonderful work, as usual - and once more I'm desolate because you don't want to join my team."

346

"At least you haven't bothered asking me again." Laura was outwardly poised, but she knew he wasn't fooled. The last few times she'd brought work in he'd shown an inclination to dally, and it troubled her. She tried to abscond without signing the docket, but he moved between her and the door.

"You're a mystery and no mistake. Always closed off! We're a friendly group here, you know: it concerns me that you're so uncommunicative."

"Your concern is misplaced." She tried to edge past him, but a brawny arm barred her way.

"Tell me at the conscious level that you'd rather work alone, and I'll have to believe you. Well, Lisset? Nothing difficult about that, is there?"

Dena had been following these proceedings from her place near the open door. Now she turned swiftly to Ailsi.

"Fight me," she suggested.

Ailsi sniggered. "Isn't Lisset big enough to look after herself?"

"Just *do* it!" Dena insisted, with such an edge of fear in her voice that Ailsi decided to co-operate.

"This'll cost you," she warned. Then, shrilly: "You idle little baggage! I saw that!"

"Saw what?"

"You sneaked some of your crystals onto my worktop."

"Liar!"

"Don't you call me a liar!" Ailsi's voice doubled in volume. "Here, take them back."

"Get those off my table!" Dena yelled, throwing the handful of crystals to the floor. Ailsi slapped her, Dena returned the slap, and in a trice the argument escalated into shrieking and hair-pulling. Then Chisrin was beside them, hauling them apart.

"What in chaos is going on? Ailsi, I've told you before that I won't tolerate fighting. Dena, I'm surprised at you."

"She started it."

"I don't care who started it. You'll work overtime for the next three days, one ild per day, starting this evening. Any more scrapping and I'll double it. Now behave." He stalked back to his office. Laura, of course, had gone.

When Dena eventually returned home that night, an apologetic Laura had dinner waiting for her.

"Thank you so much for distracting Chisrin. I feel such a fool - I should have been able to handle the situation. I'm sorry you were punished because of me."

"It doesn't matter. Ailsi kept me entertained." Dena managed a brief smile. "But we'll have to ensure there are no more incidents. Someone else must take him his overalls."

"If we weren't so close to our objective I'd suggest a new work placement," said Idenion. "But I think I can keep Laura out of harm's way for the next three octals!"

The smile froze on Dena's face and she busied herself in the washroom.

"Idenion has some news about tomorrow," said Laura when the three of them were sitting down to their meal.

Dena turned to him expectantly.

"No, not a rest day treat," he said gently. "It's the start of the final phase. Tralvar's meeting Corython at the recording studio to discuss the impact event. Corython's done some preliminary work but there are a couple of things he isn't happy with, apparently."

"In fact," Laura put in succinctly, "Corython isn't happy at all. Time for another of my pep talks. And how Tralvar hated to ask me!"

348

"We were hoping you'd come along, little sister," Idenion continued. "You could help me keep the peace!"

"I realise how important this is, but I have to put in an appearance at the Lyricon tomorrow," Dena apologised. "Before everyone forgets what their custodian looks like."

"You still can," Idenion said. "In fact, we *all* can. Corython can't leave the observatory until he's seen his Narvellan patrons - and he doesn't quite know when they'll turn up."

"What do they want?"

"What they always want. A way to accelerate transposal, or incontrovertible proof that it can't be done. I imagine they won't be easy to get rid of - so you, me and Laura can have a relaxing morning at our favourite theatre."

In fact, it was a dismal morning. It rained and rained, and a generator failure at the power station meant that there was insufficient current to run the weathershield. Huge raindrops plopped mercilessly onto every terrace and puddles started to form on the stage. The canteen had been commandeered by students wanting to free Ibri and end the oppressive regime in Treva. Idenion spent most of the morning convincing them it would be a bad idea to try. Dena shut herself in the custodian's apartment with some of the scolia; Laura, at a loose end, wandered down the basement corridors and ended up in the props department. There she found a group of dancers, tipsy on wildflower wine, trying to enact the Zarf Dance in the midst of the detritus from performances long forgotten. They welcomed her and gave her a generous measure of their brew, but before too long she excused herself and went sadly back to the apartment. Today, the Lyricon seemed very far removed from its glorious past.

349

"It's only the rain," she told herself fiercely. "When we can run the shield, everything will be back to normal and we can forget today ever happened. I hope Tralvar isn't in one of his moods. I don't think I could stand it at the moment."

They made their way to the studio in a far from hopeful frame of mind, but Tralvar - despite Corython's continued absence - seemed alert and focused. While they waited, Laura sang "L'Invitation au Voyage" for Dena at Tralvar's own suggestion. It was, Laura was a little slow to realise, the first time Dena had heard her in many years; and rather to her surprise, unconditional praise was not forthcoming.

"Your voice has matured, but you've not been using it to the full. Judging by what I've just heard, this neglect pre-dates the six octals you've been here."

"Yes, it does," Laura admitted. "I'd been doing my club appearances but not much else."

"She sounded perfect to me," Idenion ventured.

"Fortunately, Laura knows better than to believe you," said Dena with an indulgent smile. "Before she appears at the Lyricon again I shall insist that she resumes her training."

Tralvar raised an eyebrow but said nothing in the way of defence.

"Well, that's put *me* in my place!" said Laura cheerfully. "But you're right, Dena. When I was sixteen I practised every day."

"Tralvar, where can Corython have got to?" Idenion asked anxiously. "Do you think he's lost his nerve? Maybe he thought he'd look odd coming here."

"Whatever's delayed him, it isn't that," replied Tralvar with certainty. "He wouldn't feel out of place - he's quite an accomplished keyboard player. He never tried to join the scolia as astronomy was always too important to him, but he could have had a career there if he'd wanted."

Laura pounced on this information. "Then when he arrives, we'll get him to play. It'll settle him down."

"I'm all for that," Tralvar said wryly. "I might even record him. After all, that's what we're supposed to do here."

Finally Corython appeared, bringing his flitter to a bumpy halt outside the ylur factory. "Oh, discords, you're all waiting for me. I'm so sorry. Those lackwitted administrators just wouldn't accept my findings on transposal - I had to go over it about sixty-four times. And on top of that I've just had a row with Pannyra."

"What about?" asked Tralvar.

"I wouldn't tell her where I was going." Corython thought that was explanation enough. "Now, I've some figures here - "

"Put them away for the moment," Laura instructed. "We'll finish our recital before we start on the serious stuff. Tralvar tells me you play the zirid well: would you mind playing for us now?"

Corython looked taken aback. "Is this really the time and place? Besides, I'm not in practice."

"Neither am I, but I don't let it stop me singing. Why not play some exercises and see if you feel like going on? If you do, Tralvar would like to record you."

"It would make a wonderful present for Pannyra," Idenion put in. "And it would explain your secrecy tonight."

Corython found this idea tempting. "If I play, Laura, will you sing afterwards?"

"Of course," she promised.

"Why don't you and Tralvar play the same piece?" suggested Dena.

"As a duet or a competition?" Corython inquired.

"Neither; just for comparison. I'd like to see how your interpretations differ."

"They won't!" Idenion declared. "They're both scientists, aren't they?"

After a swift confab, the two musicians chose Hymorel's Dance. Laura monitored the recording and soon discovered that Idenion was quite wrong. Corython's rendition was gentle and lilting, in contrast to Tralvar's bright, incisive delivery.

The strategy worked. At the end of the session Corython was more relaxed then Laura had ever seen him. When at last he began to discuss Operation Ipsa (as Laura had nicknamed it) he remained positive and at ease.

"First, I'm assuming that Jarras can disable the safety protocols."

"Of course he can," Tralvar said impatiently.

"What protocols are these?" asked Laura.

"They prevent transposal-related manoeuvres near planetary bodies," Corython explained. "Let's assume for the moment that Jarras can override them - "

"Which he will have done," Tralvar interrupted again.

" - then there's another problem which isn't so easily solved. The convoy will lose transposal just outside the Narvellan system and continue decelerating. Even if our sphere starts its run immediately, the distance to Ipsa is simply too short for it to have regained sufficient impact speed. What I propose to do, therefore, is to send it around Narvella Five."

"A sling-shot effect?" asked Tralvar.

"No; the sphere will be moving too fast for the planet to have any influence on it. This is just a convenient route to give it the extra time it needs. I - "

"Shh!" Idenion held up a cautioning hand. "Someone's outside."

The same misapprehension flared in all their minds.

"No, not a Moderator," he hastened to add, "but someone who's extremely good at concealing their presence. They're almost undetectable."

Tralvar, who could sense nothing, slid open the studio partition and peered out. Rows of deserted looms stared back at him. Then, in the silence, he heard a surreptitious rattle at the front shutters.

"That two-faced Narad!" he growled. "He promised to keep everyone away. Stay put, all of you - I'll deal with this." And before anyone could urge caution he charged across the workshop, slammed back the shutters, grabbed a handful of tunic and pulled. A moment later, he released his captive in surprise.

"Kyrin!"

The relayist smoothed his crumpled garments. "Forgive me for not announcing myself. My mental autograph's a little too well known, I fear."

"What in the name of discord are you doing here, Kyrin? I gave you strict orders not to involve yourself any further."

"I'm already involved," Kyrin replied calmly. "Excluding me at this stage won't make me any less culpable."

"Then you'd better tell me what's wrong," Tralvar said resignedly.

"Jarras is at your house. He needs to see you urgently."

The others hurried up in time to hear this.

"It isn't like Jarras to relay our business all over town," Laura remarked in dismay.

"No-one relayed anything," Kyrin assured her. "I was on my way back to the akron when I saw his flitter touch down. He asked if I knew where you were. We both thought it would be less incriminating if he remained at the villa while I came to find you."

"Did you see any patrols on the way?"

"No, none."

"Then we'd better not push our luck. Laura, Idenion - I'll take you home first and then see what Jarras' news is. It's bound to be something about Ibri and the situation in Treva. Corython - the Narvella Five manoeuvre sounds feasible, so go ahead on that basis and I'll pick up the work in, say, three days from now. Will that be enough time?"

"It should be. But what if Jarras knows something that jeopardises our plan? Have you no idea what he wants, Kyrin?"

"He told me I didn't need to know," Kyrin answered.

"Absolutely!" said Tralvar. "Just concentrate on what *you* have to do, Corython. If the news affects you I'll see you that you're informed. Now let's go!"

After depositing Laura and Idenion outside their house - and promising to keep them informed too - Tralvar set a course for the villa; but he had only reached Lateral Four when the flitter engine suddenly died, its charge exhausted. Seething, he completed the steep ascent on foot.

When he arrived home an ild later he found Jarras asleep in the study - occupying the same chair that Idenion had slept in, six octals earlier. So sound was his sleep that Tralvar's far from subdued entry had failed to wake him. He slumbered on while Tralvar poured himself a drink and sat brooding. He remembered Idenion's look of joy on being told to fetch Laura - and remembered, too, how difficult it had been to admit he needed her help. Had she, in fact, sustained the conspiracy as he'd believed she would? Indubitably yes. Jarras would have supported him, and so would Kyrin, but not Tyvian - and definitely not Corython. And

354

without those two, he could have achieved nothing. If, indeed, he'd achieved anything now.

"Wake up, Jarras!" he said, more sternly than he had intended.

Jarras opened an eye.

"I'm glad your nerves are so strong," Tralvar remarked. "If that had been me I'd have hit the ceiling. Now, have some of this booze and tell me what's brought you over here. I suppose they've executed Ibri?"

"Far from it." Jarras sipped at the resnay, winced, and went in search of some liman. "Ibri's been very clever," he continued when he returned from the kitchen. "He knows who all the malcontents are, and has given out enough hints and snippets to make the Narvellans keep him alive. They've tried to deep-read him, with the same nebulous result."

"So he's either very resistant to their probing, or..."

"Or he doesn't know anything. That's my feeling. But the Narvellans are so paranoid about their fleet they're leaving nothing to chance." He drained his cup, then continued: "And that's why I'm here. All spheres off the production line are to be placed in a parking orbit, effective as of now. Or rather, as soon as they've been re-programmed, which will take a day at the most. Do you realise how impossible this makes things? There'll only be two or three spheres on the ground at any given time, and the Narvellans will be all over them. How am I to install Corython's data?"

Tralvar's only visible reaction was to pour himself another drink. Then he said: "If you're asking me to intervene, I can't. They'd say I was being obstructionist. What about the production centres in Alcine and Kest? Have they been co-opted into this scheme?"

"It's being talked about," Jarras answered. "They've had no major problems with the workforce, so no-one's falling over themselves to join in. But within the next few days, they'll have to comply."

"No they won't," said Tralvar softly. "This is one area where I can beat the Narvellans at their own game. There are safety issues involved here. We can't have three city-states launching dozens of spacecraft without consulting one another. Before anything like that takes place I'll require written evidence of the measures being taken to avoid collisions. I shall also need charts to show the position of the orbiting spheres, their proximity to the satellite array, and the existence of safe corridors for other space traffic. These reports will, of course, need to be endorsed by Celestrian astronavigators."

"I get the picture," Jarras grinned.

"We don't have to buy ourselves much time," Tralvar added. "Three octals at the most."

"And how are you going to re-locate me to Kest or Alcine?"

"Well," pondered Tralvar, "the Narvellans think you uncovered Ibri's plot, don't they? Supposing you hear of a similar plot in, let's say, Kest? They'd need advice on tightening their security - and who better to advise them than you?"

"That isn't bad for an impromptu solution," Jarras said, impressed.

Tralvar gave a lukewarm smile. "That's the good side of resnay. In moderation it sharpens the wits. In excess..." He spread his hands eloquently.

In the brief silence, the back door opened and shut. Jarras stood up apprehensively.

"It's only Quetri," Tralvar reassured him.

"I didn't know you'd given him the run of the place," Jarras remarked, slightly disconcerted.

Quetri hastened in, halting uneasily when he saw Tralvar was not alone.

"Oh, I forgot - you haven't been properly introduced," Tralvar said genially. "Quetri, this is Jarras. He hasn't seen you since the night of the retrace, and I believe you were unconscious at the time."

Quetri gave a barely perceptible nod of acknowledgement. "I realise you weren't expecting me tonight, First Citizen, but I have some news. Our technicians were successful in transcribing your recording of Tristell. They didn't quite get it all before the crystal broke, but it's almost complete. A globe of the transcript arrived this morning - only of course, it was sent to Hysek. I'm to collect it tomorrow while he's out."

Tralvar should have been overjoyed, but instead felt a curious apprehension.

"That's fantastic, Tralvar!" Jarras exclaimed. "All your research vindicated! Well, aren't you going to thank him?"

"You have my sincerest thanks, Quetri," said Tralvar, recovering. "I can't play it here as the villa doesn't have the facilities, but bring it with you tomorrow night and we'll visit my studio together. And while we're there, I might get you to record a song or two. Narad says you have a pleasant voice."

"My Lord Narad exaggerates," said Quetri modestly.

"Nevertheless, I wish to hear it."

"As you please, First Citizen." Quetri turned to leave.

"One thing more," said Tralvar. "I want you to bring your telescope."

"Again? But - " Quetri began, then checked himself. A neph-khet did not question his master's instructions. He bade a formal goodnight to each of the Celestrians, and went out.

"Why the telescope?" asked Jarras, who was under no obligation to keep his mouth shut.

"Sphere-spotting," Tralvar replied facetiously.

Jarras gazed thoughtfully in the direction of the closed door. "Tralvar....I know you must have your reasons for leading him on, but is it wise?"

"In my opinion, yes," said Tralvar quietly.

Jarras' frown deepened. "Be very sure. You must have noticed he was jealous of me. You can't let his unrequited love threaten all we've worked for."

Tralvar glared at him. "Sometimes, Jarras, you say the most aggravating things."

Precisely one day later, Quetri unwittingly compounded the aggravation. He'd handed over the recording of Tristell, and was unsurprised when Tralvar made no move to play it. Of course, the First Citizen would still be plagued with guilt over his role in the singer's death.

"I came to terms with that a long time ago," Tralvar informed him. "But not with my role in her *life*."

"There is nothing so painful as unrequited love," said Quetri with pedantic earnestness.

That phrase again! Tralvar swallowed his annoyance but not his cynicism. "So you believe I worshipped her from a distance? Let me tell you a few home truths about Tristell. She had scores of lovers, me among them. She'd grant me unity a couple of times, then pick a quarrel and not speak to me for octals. She enjoyed tormenting me, and like a fool I kept going back for more. This recording will be a telling reminder of all that."

Resignedly he set it spinning. Through a layer of white noise, a woman's voice said peevishly: "Tralvar, I'm getting sick of this. How much longer do I have to stand in this stupid booth? It isn't going to work!" Then, after an inaudible prompting: "All right, just once more. But after this, forget it."

She began to sing. It was excruciatingly bad. She struggled for notes and gasped for breath, the vocal quality shifting between a little-girl squeak and a throaty whisper.

Tralvar listened without comment to that poor inadequate voice. When the recording ended he stepped purposefully forward and, still without a word, picked up the globe and dashed it to the floor. When it didn't break, he ground it under his boot. "Her flamboyance, her stage presence, was everything; her voice was next to nothing," he explained, staring down at the pieces. "I can't let anyone hear it in retrospect. She's earned her place in history and I won't deprive her of it."

"You must have loved her very much," Quetri said wistfully.

Tralvar straightened his shoulders. "Well, my lad, now it's your turn to sing. What's it to be?"

"I've chosen a Narvellan setting of one of Idenion's ballads - Isylla's Eyes. Maybe you know it?"

"Yes, I do," Tralvar responded, heading for the mixing panel. "One of his better efforts. It's *short*!"

Quetri's voice was a pure unbroken alto. He sang the simple ballad very expressively, accompanying himself on the zirid with slow, careful chords. His high notes in particular were so perfectly pitched that Tralvar felt tears start to his eyes. Quetri happened to look up at that point and, when the song was completed, hurried out of the performance area.

"Why do you weep, First Citizen?"

Superficial sentiment, Tralvar wanted to say. Instead, with less honesty, he replied: "Because the time has come to send you away. Discord only knows I don't want to, but I must."

"I am prepared," Quetri announced steadily.

"Then come back to the villa and I'll brief you on what you have to do."

Someone had taken their flitter. Tralvar had forgotten to immobilise it. They hastened through the deserted laterals in sheeting rain, holding hands like lovers. By the time they reached their destination they were both soaked to the skin, and Tralvar, anxious to avoid an erotically charged situation, bundled Quetri into a guest room and threw a clean set of clothes in after him.

"Hang your wet things over the heating grid," he directed. "I'll be in the cellar."

He unsealed the entrance to his hideout and began assembling items on the table. Presently Quetri joined him, peering about in wonderment and more than a little apprehension.

"My secret life," Tralvar announced, less than enthusiastically. "I'll explain what you're looking at in a moment. First of all I want to give you your instructions for the next few days."

Quetri waited attentively.

"A sphere leaves for Narvella Prime at noon-plus-one tomorrow. It delivered some elite migrants yesterday and it's scheduled to go back with just the pilot on board. You're to be on it as well. You'd better clear it with Hysek first."

"He won't care. The further away I am, the better he'll like it."

"Just notify him," Tralvar repeated gently. "No one will think it strange that you're leaving. You only came here to petition Hysek, and now he's purchased your bond you're free to go once he permits it. As soon as you get to Rhul, inform the Synectic base that Tarysk no longer owns you and that you intend to resume your old career. Don't ask; demand. Your status has to be affirmed straight away."

"They won't refuse. They were sorry to lose me," Quetri stated. "I'm Navarian's heir. I know more about the Synectics than anyone."

"Make sure everyone's reminded of that. Once you're reinstated, say that you've some business to attend to in Rhul and you'll fly out to Ipsa when it's concluded. Do not, under any circumstances, go to the base too soon."

"Otherwise I could become a casualty of your attack?"

"Precisely. Now assuming for the moment that my first strategy hasn't worked, this is how you must proceed. When you leave here tonight you'll be carrying an incendiary device and a remote detonator. I've designed the bomb to fit inside your telescope case. On your return to the Synectics you're to plant the device in the stasis chamber and set it off. Sit down and I'll show you the mechanism in detail."

Quetri backed away as Tralvar casually picked up a transparent cylinder. "First Citizen, I - "

"It won't bite you," said his mentor with a hint of asperity. "This is just an empty shell. I'm going to assemble it in front of you so there's no mystery about it."

"But - isn't that glass?"

"A glass-based compound. Flitter canopies are made of this - it's quite resilient. I didn't have a lot of choice: theridolyte is *too* strong and would mask the explosion. And both therite and mythol - that's the neutralising agent - corrode every metal they touch. Now, the thing to remember about therite - " he lifted one of the carboys from a shelf - "is that it exists to explode. It can't help it. So that part of the operation's guaranteed.

"When the bomb's in position the mythol must be drained off, and to achieve this I've incorporated a tiny theridolyte seal at one end of the cylinder. It will respond only to this remote." He picked up a second object which resembled a tile, opened it by exerting pressure on the edges, and rippled the cylinder open and shut a few times.

"The detonator was the most tricky part. A sphere's remote usually consists of a short-range transposer linked to the aldacite on board. But if you carried aldacite, not only would you risk detection by sensitives, but it could interfere with your sphere's systems. Either way, you'd be discovered. So this is a radio beam, pure and simple - which does mean, of course, that you'll need a line of sight when you detonate the bomb. The signal can't travel through rock. But hopefully that won't be a problem. Mythol evaporates very quickly once the air hits it but you'll still have about half an astal to get clear."

"How..." Quetri swallowed nervously and started again. "How extensive will the damage be?"

"I'm not sure," Tralvar admitted. "Even after working with it for many years, therite can still surprise me. Hopefully the blast will be contained in the stasis chamber." He began to place the active components in the cylinder: first the therite, three misshapen lumps separated by a woven mesh. "Therite smoulders before it detonates. This mesh will burn away in the initial stages and the fragments will combine for a better result." Then came the mythol, forced in under pressure - speedily, as the therite was already slightly warm - and finally the theridolyte seal. Quetri, awed and silent, watched Tralvar's capable hands at work and fought down a disrespectful surge of desire. He'd felt the touch of those hands just once, and he longed to do so again before he left on his mission.

In a daze he accompanied Tralvar back to the kitchen, where they had supper. Neither of them spoke much. At last, with great reluctance, Quetri went to change back into his own clothes while Tralvar positioned the bomb in the telescope case. It didn't fit snugly in the lining; obviously his previous measurements had been slightly out. All due to haste, he supposed. At that time he hadn't wanted Quetri to know what he was doing. Wearily, he looked about for something to use as padding.

His workshop was littered with rags, all of them dirty. His much-missed manservant Kevis had carefully cut old tunics into squares, saying they'd doubtless be useful someday. The remainder were in a box under Tralvar's bed - a sensible precaution, since all discarded ytil should have been recycled. Well, Quetri, he thought as he retrieved the box and took two more rags from his dwindling collection, I hope you don't get caught on the way to Ipsa. With *these* as evidence, no one will be in any doubt where the bomb came from. I might as well write "a present from Tralvar" on it.

On his way downstairs he passed the guest room and paused by the open door. Quetri, naked from the waist up, was about to put on his heavy, high-collared tunic - a garment which did nothing to flatter his youthful slenderness. A frown creased Tralvar's brow.

"Quetri? What's that on your back?"

"It's nothing, First Citizen."

"Not from where I'm standing. Move closer to the light."

Unconcerned, Quetri obeyed. The smooth gold of his upper back was disfigured by a circular scar the size of a palmprint: two Narvellan letters interlinked. "It's the seal of the tyl Pellons," he explained.

"Who did this to you?" demanded Tralvar.

"Tarysk. She was entitled to brand me. I ran away."

Tralvar was genuinely distressed. "That despicable woman!" he breathed, and had to resist the urge to hug Quetri as if he were an injured child. "You intend visiting the tyl Pellon estate, don't you, while you're in Rhul? I forbid you to go."

"But I have possessions there," Quetri objected.

Tralvar seized him by the shoulders and shook him. "Do as you're told! If she's capable of maiming you she's more than capable of holding you against your will if you're fool enough to turn up. Now finish dressing and get down those stairs."

Quetri gave him an oddly coy look. "Are you jealous of my previous life?"

Tralvar wasn't, of course, but immediately saw that Quetri wanted him to be. He decided to play along, doing his best to sound resentful. "You bear the mark of the tyl Pellons. Tarysk may have put it there but it's just as much Navarian's as hers. You don't seem to mind carrying a brand - and it's because of him, isn't it? It reminds you of *him*."

Quetri looked almost happy. "Now I know I am loved," he declared. Still with the same half-smile, he accompanied Tralvar to his study and watched as he finished packing the deadly cylinder.

"There. All done." Tralvar tucked the remote into an accessories compartment, zipped the case and handed it over. "I'll keep your telescope safe till you return," he added.

"Don't make futile promises," Quetri admonished, suddenly very adult and calm. "If I have to use this device, your plot will have failed or been discovered. When I go to Ipsa it will be in the certain knowledge that you and your friends are dead, or under sentence of death."

Tralvar could say nothing to reassure him.

"This may be the last time we see one another, First Citizen," Quetri continued softly. "If anyone asks I'll say jealousy broke us up. I shall leave now, for if I stayed I should try to bond with you regardless of our pact." He opened the front door, strode confidently into the night, and was immediately lost to view. Beyond the circle of light around the portico Tralvar could see nothing. He extended a hand into the darkness; still nothing, not even the rain. It was as much as he could do not to call Quetri back. He'd already begun to realise how lonely the next few days would be.

He went back into the study and poured a triple measure of resnay.

He spent the next day, or what was left of it when he woke, removing all signs of recent experimentation from his workshop. If anyone discovered it they'd have a hard time proving it hadn't been derelict for years. After that he sat in his study and scribbled, page after frenetic page, adding to a bundle already in his desk. The task seemed to give him no pleasure.

Eventually he was interrupted by Kyrin. +Axmiol asked me to remind you about the reception tonight, in honour of Sijek's return from Ninka. You and Idenion are invited+

+You mean summoned+ Tralvar retorted. He knew what he was in for: an evening of fidgeting in his uncomfortable uniform, making guarded small talk with the elite, and in all probability having to listen to Idenion's poetry. In the event he drank too much wine, behaved boorishly and picked a quarrel with Narad when he made a snide remark about Quetri. Idenion and Kyrin helped him home.

At noon the next day he descended on the retracer lab, accompanied by the all too familiar pounding in his head.

"Ah, First Poet, First Poet!" he declaimed to a startled Idenion. "How are the hrilffa today? Be careful they don't scratch your tender skin - Narad wouldn't like that, now would he?"

"For harmony's sake!" Idenion said in exasperation. "You're not *still* drunk? Go home before you upset anyone else."

Tralvar ignored him. "Where's Drusa? I want Drusa. *Drusa*! - oh, there you are. Make yourself useful and run Laura's retrace for me."

"I can't," said Drusa unapologetically. "Look around you."

He looked, with mounting degrees of incredulity. There was no tank, no couch, no computer terminal and hardly any prill.

"As you can see, the retracer isn't here any more," Drusa concluded.

"What have you done, you imbecilic female?"

"I've given it to the Tafret Academy in response to repeated requests. What use has it been to us since Tyvian's death? None of us can operate it fully."

"When did this happen?" asked Tralvar, ominously quiet.

"Three days ago."

"And I suppose *you* knew in advance," Tralvar continued, rounding on Idenion.

"Of course not! I thought *you* did."

Tralvar switched his attention back to Drusa.

"Three octals ago, I forbade you to dispose of the retracer," he said in carefully enunciated tones. Idenion fixed his attention on the hrilffa and waited for the storm to break.

"I don't have to answer to you," Drusa retorted. "The retracer wasn't yours."

"Then whose was it?" roared Tralvar. "Yours, you deceitful little drab? You were terrified of it - and you couldn't bear to see it doing me good!"

"It *wasn't* doing you good!"

"So now we're an expert on music, are we? You know nothing! You've the brains of a kyffu and a personality to match!"

"That'll do, Tralvar." Lydion had appeared at the back entrance. "You've no right to insult Drusa. I supported her decision to give the retracer up. The Academy can educate people to run it safely and help relayists who burn out. A slightly worthier cause than keeping you entertained!"

"Laura made that retrace specifically for my use!" snapped Tralvar. "I was studying musical improvisation."

"And how many more times would you have run it?" inquired Lydion. "Till it wore out? Somehow I don't think music was the main attraction. It was more to do with getting inside Laura's head!"

"That's a lie!"

"Is it? I know you of old, remember."

"What do you mean, Lydion?" asked Idenion.

"Has he still not told you? It seems he - "

"Just shut it, Lydion!" Tralvar snarled, whitefaced. "One more word and - "

"This has gone far enough," Drusa interrupted. "Be quiet, all of you. The retracer's gone and it isn't coming back, so there's no point in trying to apportion blame. Tralvar, you'll have to make your own music from now on."

He stared belligerently at her for a long moment, then seemed to come to a decision. "All right, I will!" he declared. "By chaos, I will!" And he headed out of the laboratory at a stumbling run.

"Shouldn't someone go after him?" Idenion asked.

"When he's in this state he's best left alone," advised Lydion. "I'll go and see him later." But he was unable to perform this duty. Halfway into the afternoon a massive power failure crippled Alda Mexa, and every qualified technician was needed to patch up the ageing and overtaxed grid.

***

Corython was frantic with worry. He'd completed his calculations by the third day as arranged, and was waiting at home for Tralvar to collect them. It was now almost dark, and no Tralvar had appeared. Corython began to wonder if the arrangement had only been provisional - but if it *had* been, surely he would have had an update by now? With something as important as this, no one could afford to be vague. It was just possible that the power cut had been to blame for the delay, but he could think of nothing to link the events.

He waited a little longer, terrified of doing the wrong thing, but at last realising that inaction was equally wrong. He had but one choice - to go at once to Tralvar's house, alone, and find out what was happening.

Pannyra was fitfully asleep. He hated to leave her, imagining her distress if she woke to find him missing, but he had no choice there either. He had to ignore his conscience and stay focused on finding Tralvar. Taking his handwritten notes and a torch in case the electricity failed again, he commenced the uphill climb. It was a little early for Moderator patrols, but he kept a sharp look-out, nonetheless.

When he reached Lateral Three he found that there were indeed whole areas of the city still in blackness, including Tralvar's immediate neighbourhood. But the First Citizen's villa was ablaze with light, causing Corython to wonder if Tralvar had his own generator or some special arrangement with the power workers. As he drew closer he became aware of an odd sound: badly amplified singing, echoing tinnily through the dark silent street.

The front door was ajar. He pushed it cautiously and stared in astonishment at a blaze of candles, rushlights and oil lamps lined up in a row. He followed their trail back to the study - and there was Tralvar, lolling in an armchair with six empty bottles at his feet. The desk and the floor were littered with sheets of paper, and on the table in front of him was the source of the noise - a polished wooden box with a hinged lid. Inside the box a large disc rotated rapidly on a turntable. Corython had never seen the device before, but he'd heard about it. This was Laura's machine, and Laura's music.

Tralvar vaguely realised he wasn't alone and swivelled round in the chair. "Corython! Come in!"

"What are you doing?" asked Corython stupidly.

"Enjoying myself, Cory old pal. Got lights, got music - who needs electricity?" He managed to re-start the gramophone after two attempts, and the raucous song began afresh. Naturally, Corython didn't understand a word.

"All by yourself in the moonlight," Tralvar translated obligingly and loudly, every time the phrase was repeated. Which was often.

Corython recovered his wits. "Discord's dreams, Tralvar, have you lost your mind? Have you any idea how that sound carries? You'll bring all the Moderators here!"

"Good! We'll have a party. All by yourself...."

Corython looked in vain for a way to turn the volume down, then in desperation grabbed the pick-up and flipped it onto its side. The turntable slithered to a halt.

Tralvar gave a yell of protest and tried to start it up again, but Corython shoved him back in the chair.

"You drunken idiot! Do you want to ruin everything?"

Tralvar glared up at him in bleary self-righteousness. "You know what you are, Corython? Dull. Dull, dull, dull! Why'd you barge in here and spoil my evening?"

"You shouldn't be playing *that*!" Corython stabbed a finger at the offending gramophone.

"Why not? Moderators won't take *these* records. Not theridolyte. They're made of shell - Shelley - no, that's another blasted poet - shellac. That's it. Shellac. Break it as soon as look at – *put that down*!"

Corython had picked up a piece of paper from the floor.

"Give it back!" Tralvar made a lunge at him, missed, and fell flat on his face.

Corython continued to read. Then he picked up another sheet, and another. "So *that's* it," he breathed at last. "So that's what all this boozing's been about!" He slammed the pages down and, in a fury, half dragged and half carried Tralvar upstairs to the shower room. Then he hurled him fully clothed into the cubicle and turned on the cold tap. "Cool off, " he advised, and was gone.

Tralvar tried to get up, slipped, and struck his head on the wall. He lay dazed, blocking the outlet, while the water began to pool around him. Then someone at the pumping station cut the supply and the overhead torrent dwindled and ceased. Which was probably just as well.

Meanwhile, Corython gathered up all Tralvar's pages and studied them a few moments more. Tralvar was no poet, but his writing had a raw honesty which in its way was quite compelling. On his way out Corython glanced up the stairs, but was still too angry with Tralvar to bother with him any further. Besides, he still had his original problem - he had to hand over his calculations and get back to Pannyra. He didn't know many of the

370

conspirators, and those he *did* know were too far away - Jarras in Treva, Laura and Idenion across town. That left only one person he could turn to: Kyrin.

Still furious, braving the Moderators and the Narvellan elite in general, he made his way to the akron. Fortune was on his side. As he neared the building the city's lighting was restored in a sudden surge of incandescence, and every Narvellan using night vision was too dazzled to notice him. No one was manning the front desk, as Quetri had not yet been replaced.

Soon Corython had delivered his work into Kyrin's safekeeping. He also left Tralvar's written material, as for security's sake it had to be brought to the notice of the entire group. Tralvar had confided to those sheets of crumpled paper the secret he'd guarded for years: his unspoken, all-consuming love for Laura.

***

Early the following day, Laura learnt of Tralvar's confession and wasted no time in going to see him. The bottles and burnt-out candles were still in evidence, but Tralvar himself looked the picture of sobriety in his scolia robe. He'd even trimmed his unruly hair. Of course, he would have been expecting her.

"Why didn't you tell me?" she asked gently.

"I thought I could live with it," he responded, avoiding her gaze. "And I didn't want you feeling sorry for me."

"I don't - "

"Oh, you do. Even your prill feels sorry for me. But there I go again, trying to start an argument. Let's save it, shall we, until after I've told you the rest."

Laura stared. "There's *more*?"

"Much more. Those scribbles only dealt with the here and now. To get this off my chest once and for all, I have to go back six and a half years." He gave a tired smile at her incredulity. "Do you remember, when you were arrested in Tivenne and brought to the akron, how I separated you from the others and took you back to my apartment?"

"Of course I remember!" Laura removed a trio of empty bottles from an easy chair and sat down opposite him. "I discovered so much about you that night."

"Not as much as you might have done," he said with a mirthless chuckle. "But let's keep the story in sequence. Quite simply, I desired you - and of course, Alendis knew it. He was in one of his capricious moods after his success with Zenzie, and decided I needed a reward. Idenion and Dena were to be sent directly to him, he said, but as a favour to me he'd put off dealing with you till the next day. He told me I could keep you till morning and amuse myself."

Laura was silent for a moment. "And why didn't you....amuse yourself?" she asked eventually.

"I realised what a child you were," he answered candidly. "Nevertheless, you had a very narrow escape that night. You provoked me with your clinging and pleading. You even said you were scared to be alone."

"Which wasn't true," Laura said. "You were going to lock me up and I wanted to talk you into letting me escape. Oh, Tralvar, I'm sorry. I had no idea..."

"I was aware of that. Your innocence deterred me. Just consider yourself fortunate that Alendis didn't take a fancy to you. He had a singular disregard for the innocent."

Laura, abashed, allowed herself to be scolded. "But you don't have anything to reproach yourself for," she said in a vain attempt at reassurance. "Nothing happened."

"Not quite nothing." Tralvar's reply was so quiet that she had difficulty hearing it.

"What do you mean?"

372

"I'd spent all evening with you. I'd accompanied your singing and read you very closely at the conscious level. Can't you imagine what that did to me? All that music! I'd never known anything like your mind and I wanted more. I drank too much, became aggressive, and finally did a reprehensible thing. I attempted unity with you."

Laura's hands flew to her mouth. "Oh my God, Tralvar! That headache!"

"No English," he corrected her automatically. "Yes, the headache which you believed to be a punishment was the beginning of unity. But I never intended to hurt you, I swear. I stopped as soon as I realised you were in pain."

"I forgave you the very next day," Laura reminded him. "I don't intend reversing that decision."

"You still don't see, do you? I thought you wouldn't know! I thought I could rampage through your mind without any fear of discovery. No reciprocity either, of course, but I didn't care."

Laura recalled another detail of the night in question. "Rietta knew, didn't she?"

"Yes, moments later. I panicked and asked her to check you over."

"Did you tell anyone else?"

"Only Lydion. He was suitably scathing about my ignorance, as I recall, but since I'd never been offworld I couldn't be expected to know that nonconversants and unity didn't mix."

"Sounds a good enough excuse to me," said Laura, genuinely unconcerned. Then, when he didn't reply: "So you got carried away for a moment. I can live with that. Now let it go."

"If you insist," he said unhappily. "Well, that was the start of it. Later, when you and I began working together, I realised I was becoming much too fond of you - although of course, you were already fixated on Idenion. When you came to me in tears after you'd caught him with Tarit, I felt like thrashing him. At the very least I should have dissuaded you from leaving Celestra. But I didn't, because I thought it would solve a lot of problems all round." He paused to drink some liman. "And now to my final misdeed."

Laura was suddenly silent. She'd guessed what was coming.

"As soon as five Earth years were up - a little over three years here - Idenion wanted to keep his promise and look for you. I wouldn't let him. Without my help there was nothing he could do, as I'd hidden the flight programmes. I knew that if you came back it would all begin again - and so it did."

It was typical, thought Laura, that he should tag on - almost as an afterthought - an admission that was far more upsetting to her than unity and its obscure etiquette. But she'd previously made up her mind not to berate him, and she held to that. If Idenion had come for her when he was supposed to, she might not have been ready to abandon her former life. "Now I know why you kept playing my retrace," she said slowly. "Lydion was right. You wanted to be me."

"Absolutely," he agreed with an unexpected grin.

Laura returned the smile a little awkwardly. She wished he wasn't being so polite. It was weird when he didn't yell. "What's going to happen now?" she ventured. "Can we successfully put all this aside, do you think?"

"What will happen," he said decisively, "is that I'll finally admit the impossibility of my dream. Once we've dealt with the Synectics I'll look around for someone to share my life."

"Someone like that girl Ninfi?"

"Discord's dreams, no! A few more nights like that would kill me. That was more in the nature of a lone act of sciesha. But it was good to be desired so unconditionally." He smiled again at the memory. "Finding a companion won't be easy. As well as putting up with my temperament and accepting my murky past, she'll have to acknowledge that I'll always love *you*. That isn't going to change. I don't apologise for my feelings, only for coping with them so badly. That *will* change."

"Thank you," Laura said gravely. "You....will still play for me, won't you?"

"I'd be very hurt if you didn't want me to. Would tomorrow be suitable?"

"I'll look forward to it." Laura stood up to leave, but he held up a hand to restrain her.

"Would you take a message to Idenion? I wrote some insulting things about his tone-deafness, and that was gratuitous. Tell him I'm sorry. I still think it's ironic that he can never accurately perceive the music in you, but he's your lifebonded and there's no gainsaying that."

"I'll tell him," Laura said.

"Does Jarras have the calculations?"

"He should do by now. We sent Lydion to Treva this morning."

"It always surprises me that I have such loyal friends." Tralvar walked with her to the front door. "I'll try to be more deserving of them in future. We've only two and a half octals left to wait, and during that time I'll show you how responsible I can be. I won't touch a drop of resnay."

"Promise?"

"Promise," Tralvar replied; then, with only a hint of wistfulness, watched Laura hurry away in the direction of the lab and Idenion. Yes, he'd stay off the liquor, but for no reason other than to please her. She and the rest of the team had safely taken charge of Operation Ipsa. They wouldn't need his help any more.

Chapter Twelve

Two octals went by and everything settled into an uneasy calm. Laura carried on with her mending and kept out of Chisrin's way, Chisrin continued to ignore Dena, and Pannyra was re-admitted to hospital. Tralvar, true to his word, kept control of his drinking. Now that he no longer had anything to hide from Laura, their music sessions had become much less fraught and - from his point of view - more rewarding. Idenion tended the hrilffa and pondered the nature of love. He began to write a poem about Tralvar, then thought better of it.

The Treva spacefield stood empty, the Narvellans commenced a protracted study of parking orbit safety, and the departure date of Kest's sphere consignment drew ever closer. Jarras, his conversion of Corython's figures complete, obtained a temporary posting to Kest on the pretext of upgrading their security. Once in residence he installed his programme in one of the waiting spheres, ran a simulation, then hid the data in a subroutine to foil any technicians with checklists.

One octal remained before the final phase of Operation Ipsa. Each of the conspirators had begun to hope that nothing else would go wrong. For a time, nothing did; then, five days before the scheduled launch, Dena was summoned to Chisrin's office. Ailsi was having a voluble argument with her neighbour and the other girls were taking sides. Normally Chisrin would have shut them up, but for once he let them continue. The noise would mask what he had to say.

"I've just received the report on Salvi," he announced.

Dena was slow to recognise the name. "Who?"

"The Directress who approved that flawed aldacite - the one I believed Idenion to be involved with. Only he wasn't, was he? This -" He tapped the report for emphasis - "exonerates her completely. There were some unusual geological strata in the area the crystals came from, and her perception was obstructed. Her senses aren't defiled and she's still a virgin - or she was until the Inquirers got to work on her. So it seems my theory was a little wide of the mark."

"I never said it was correct."

"But you never said it wasn't." Chisrin's face was grim, weary. "So what in chaos have you been hiding, Dena? What was so worldshattering that you were willing to submit to me rather than disclose it?"

Dena said nothing.

"No matter; I'll soon have the truth." He gave an eloquent but hollow smile. "One more night in my embrace and you'll tell your secret."

"But you don't *want* the information, do you?" asked Dena feebly. Her hands fluttered like trapped birds.

"I didn't. But this thing's important, isn't it? Important enough, wouldn't you say, to buy me a trip back to Narvella if I disclosed it to our grateful Governors?"

Dena was silent, stricken.

"Doesn't the prospect of my absence please you?" Chisrin went on. "You'd be free of me then. I have to get home - I have to find Sarune!" His anguish was genuine and unmistakable.

He still doesn't want to unite with me, Dena thought bitterly. To him it will be a disagreeable necessity.

Chisrin read her at the conscious level and gave another of his sad smiles. "We all have to make compromises, ice maiden. Doubtless I'll be able to put up with it."

Dena suddenly felt ill. "May I take the rest of the day off?" she asked, never considering that he might refuse.

"No more favours," came the cold reply, much to her dismay. "You'll stay here under my supervision, and go home with me after dark. Now get on with your work."

Shaken by the change in him, Dena backed out of the room and nearly collided with the caterer who was distributing rations on a trolley - sticky little cakes, reeking of synthetic sweetener. Dena's stomach churned. Clamping one hand over her mouth she rushed off to the latrines, where she proceeded to be violently sick. But despite her physical distress, her mind was operating swiftly and sensibly. She had to escape and go to Tralvar with the whole sorry tale. No-one else could help her. To leave by the main entrance was out of the question, as Chisrin would see her instantly, but the attack of nausea had given her a possible alternative. There had been two girls dawdling in the washroom when she'd entered. They'd hastily left her alone, and it would probably be about an astal before anyone returned to inquire how she was. Within that time, she had to get out of the building. Chisrin was forbidden to leave his workforce unsupervised, so he couldn't pursue her. And there was too much at stake for him to report her missing.

Dena visually measured her slender build against the room's one circular window and decided she could just get through. Climbing onto the sill via a basket of dirty overalls, she opened the window to its fullest extent and swung her legs out. There was a drop of about twice her height to the rough ground beneath. She pushed herself forward, knowing a moment's panic when her shoulders jammed in the window's swivel mechanism. She twisted free, kicked herself clear of the wall and landed awkwardly on her right foot. Running, stumbling, she set off for the older part of the city. She crossed several streets before slackening her pace, though her right ankle had begun to swell. Thereafter she walked idly, as did all workers on errands.

Her safety was still far from assured. Tralvar's house was over eight silmi away, and she had to reach it unaided. If any Narvellan suspected her of being a runaway worker he could in theory arrest her, so she dared not draw attention to herself by contacting the relayist chain. And if she requested a flitter she could well find it had a Narvellan pilot.

Already she'd begun to tire. Her ankle ached abominably and she was feeling sick again. Darting flashes of light teased her vision and her steps grew laboured and erratic. She was in the landscaped part of the city now, with its gardens and seats and white terraced walls, but she didn't pause to rest. She still had three laterals to ascend, and if she stopped she knew she'd never be able to go on. When she was at last within a silmos of her goal, she risked sending her thoughts ahead to alert Tralvar to her presence, but her concentration was minimal and there was too much background buzz from other minds. She couldn't locate him. So she wandered on, slower, slower. "Please be there, Tralvar," she whispered. "And please be sober."

Afterwards she recalled seeing the house in the distance, but had no memory of having walked those final steps. Tralvar and Corython, in conversation within, saw the main door fly open; and just for an instant Dena's frail silhouette was outlined by cold winter sunlight. Then she fell forward like a windblown leaf and lay crumpled on the mosaic floor.

***

Returning suddenly to consciousness, Dena felt her overall being unbuttoned by a pair of capable hands. She shrieked in protest, and instantly Tralvar was beside her, stroking her forehead.

380

"Hush, Dena, no-one's going to hurt you. You came to my house, remember?"

"Did I get there?" she murmured, confused.

"You're in one of the guest rooms," Tralvar went on, trying to sound reassuring. "Corython and I brought you up here. And this," indicating the elderly woman who'd been trying to examine her, "is Mahra, Pannyra's midwife. Corython thought she should take a look at you."

"You have to help me," Dena began, agitated, but he put a warning finger to his lips and went quietly from the room. Corython was waiting outside.

"Why did she scream?" he inquired.

"Why indeed?" Tralvar said grimly. "And why did she drag herself over here in person instead of using a relayist? This looks very much like trouble - but what kind, I wonder?"

After a few moments, Mahra came out of the bedroom and shut the door firmly.

"That was astute of you, young man," she remarked to Corython. Then, to Tralvar: "She's about seven octals pregnant, tired out from traipsing the city, and very overwrought. I wanted to give her a sedative, but she wouldn't take it. She insists on speaking to you."

"I'll attend to her at once," Tralvar said blandly. "Thank you for your time."

Mahra regarded him critically. "You haven't been taking proper care of her," she accused.

"I'm not - " began Tralvar, then checked himself. "No, no, I haven't - but I will from now on."

"She's going to need plenty of rest," Mahra continued. "She isn't very strong. Rest and sleep, and no more industrial work. Come along, Corython - the First Citizen will want to be alone with his partner."

Reluctantly, Corython accompanied her downstairs. "You'll keep me informed?" he asked anxiously, looking back.

"At all times," Tralvar assured him. Then he returned to Dena's bedside.

Mahra had persuaded her to part with her day clothes, and she was now wearing a night-robe which was much too big for her. It made her look more vulnerable than ever.

"I'm sorry to be such a nuisance," she whispered.

Tralvar sat down next to her. "How may I help?"

"This is so difficult," Dena said, twisting the sheet in her fingers.

"Well, since Mahra thinks I sired your child, why not begin by telling me who did?"

She looked at him with agonised eyes. "Oh, Tralvar, he's...he's Narvellan...!" Then she collapsed in a torrent of tears. Tralvar, stunned, gathered her to him.

She told him everything then, in a scarcely coherent mixture of words and thoughts - sometimes both at once. She kept no chronological order. But Tralvar, with his ready understanding of dark deeds, found all the explanation he needed.

"And I knew that if I stayed with Chisrin tonight, I'd have betrayed us all," Dena concluded haltingly. "I suppose I'm just weak."

"My poor girl," said Tralvar, still holding her close, "that's the only part of the story that doesn't surprise me. Being cajoled into unity is neither weak nor abnormal. It happens all the time. Elanir, Nefyrra's mother, always took some persuading."

"Oh." Dena blushed a little. "I'm still very ignorant, aren't I?"

"Unworldly," corrected Tralvar, "but brave and resourceful. It will be to my everlasting shame that I didn't realise what was going on at that factory. The least I can do is put an end to Chisrin's depredations."

"How?"

"I'll just turn him over to the elite, of course. It'll be interesting to see what punishment they dream up for him."

Dena clutched his arm. "Tralvar, you can't do that! They'd punish *me*, just as they did Isylla."

"But, Dena, she was one of them. You aren't subject to their laws."

"Aren't I? If their moral codes are broken, they always look for some woman to blame. You can't tell anyone I'm pregnant."

"No sense in creating more trouble, I suppose," Tralvar conceded.

"And that applies to Laura and Idenion too - at least for the moment," Dena added.

"Why shouldn't they know?"

"Because Idenion's going to take this very badly. He was always so protective of me. If he hadn't been so preoccupied with Laura - "

"Don't talk about Laura," Tralvar said hastily.

Dena pressed his hand apologetically, remembering that he was as much in need of comfort as she was. For a while their conscious thoughts echoed a melancholy counterpoint as they shared their differing experiences. Almost too late, Tralvar realised that they were drifting into unity, and that Dena either didn't care or wanted it to happen. Her mind opened to his like a flower at sunrise: pellucid, alluring, and with the merest hint of the scolia which reminded him achingly of his youth. Incredibly, she was without taint. And for that reason he decided to caution her.

"Think what you're doing, Dena," he said reluctantly.

She flung away from him, hiding her tearstained face. "So I'm not good enough for Chisrin *or* you, is that it?"

"You're *too* good," Tralvar declared with the utmost sincerity. She didn't move, and he gently but firmly took her shoulders and turned her around. "He violated your body, not your spirit. And I...I have no right..."

"I want you," she said quietly.

"You want fulfilment. Don't you realise I'd hurt you? Far more than *he* ever could?"

"I don't believe that! Nefyrra was wrong!"

"Not entirely. I'm still carrying the stigma of those killings and you'd absorb that without a doubt. You're the Lyricon custodian and a scolia-sensitive; unite with me and you risk losing it all."

Dena was momentarily silent. Tralvar released her and stood up. "Think it over," he said. "I'm going to visit Chisrin now, and hopefully frighten him a little. My reputation should help for once. Since Corython's already a party to this, should I ask him to sit with you while I'm gone?"

"If he doesn't mind," Dena said. "What was he doing here anyway?"

"We were discussing how to study the impact event as it happens. Naturally he's keen to know how the sphere performs." He paused. "Will you try to sleep a little? I won't be leaving until Corython's back with a flitter. I don't intend walking, despite your good example."

"Tralvar," she ventured, "what will you say to Chisrin? You aren't planning to harm him, are you?"

A shadow crossed Tralvar's face. "Don't defend him, Dena. Don't ever defend him." Then, more reasonably: "Since you won't let me report him I have to do something for the sake of the other girls. I promise I

384

won't pick a fight, if that makes you feel any happier. I've got more sense and I'm sure Chisrin has too. He won't want to make things any worse for himself."

"I daresay you're right," she said with a wan little smile. "You're always right about these things. I shall sleep now - and thank you, Tralvar."

"Thank me later," he said enigmatically.

***

Corython, returning at Tralvar's behest, found the door barred against him. He rapped on it impatiently, even though Tralvar knew he'd arrived.

"What's all this about?" the astronomer demanded angrily when the door was opened.

"Quiet! Dena's asleep," admonished Tralvar. "I see you've brought a flitter as I asked. Good. Very good. Immobilise it, if you please, and come with me. I want you to stay with Dena while I perform an errand." He headed in the direction of his study, and Corython followed helplessly.

"Tralvar, do you realise how inconvenient this is? I missed a hospital visit because Dena turned up - I only managed to see Pannyra for an astal or so. And now you're keeping me off work!"

"Where does Pannyra think you've been?"

"She knows I was here, but she thinks I'm trying to keep you sober. I'm afraid I had to tell her about the shower incident. She said you were a self-indulgent, undisciplined... what are you *doing?*"

"I should think that was obvious," said Tralvar, busily assembling a therite gun. Before Corython's horrified eyes, he produced a jar of mythol solution and, wielding a pair of tongs, extracted an innocent-looking pebble from its depths.

"Discord take us, Tralvar, that stuff's lethal! Even under factory conditions - "

385

"Don't lecture me about safety. I was handling therite before you were born!" He put the finishing touches to the gun and laid it down carefully. "This tube is vacuum sealed. Stop panicking."

"There's no such thing as a perfect vacuum," objected Corython.

"I never said it was perfect."

"You're going to kill somebody," Corython accused. "Aren't you? *Aren't* you?"

"Now, Corython," Tralvar said soothingly, "don't be so presumptuous. I couldn't even hit the side of a house with this. I know - I've tried. But it *can* be used to intimidate."

"On Dena's behalf, I suppose?" said Corython. "Aren't you being a bit drastic?"

"No. Sit down." Tralvar found a chair for the younger man. Then, rapidly, he told the story of Dena and Chisrin. Corython paled when the Synectics were mentioned. His only other reaction was a slight frown which deepened as Tralvar proceeded.

"But she's several octals pregnant, according to Mahra," he said when Tralvar paused.

"So?"

"So why didn't she come to you at once instead of trying to make bargains with this man?"

"She was mortified. She didn't want anyone to know," Tralvar said, surprised at the question.

"So mortified that she wanted total unity with him?" Corython inquired sceptically. "That hardly seems - "

"She propositioned me this afternoon," Tralvar said, effectively silencing him. "I just thought you should know that. She'll probably do it again. And if I find you've been criticising her I'll send you home in little pieces."

"Save your threats for Chisrin," Corython retorted.

"I intended to," Tralvar said, a little regretfully. He hadn't expected such an unenlightened reaction. "Let's stick to the practicalities, shall we? Obviously we have to keep quiet about Dena's condition."

"I gathered that. It's very fortunate that Mahra jumped to the wrong conclusion. I warned her not to discuss your private life."

"Thank you, that was sensible. I only wish Idenion was less of a problem. Dena can't bring herself to tell him what happened."

"That's understandable at least," remarked Corython. "Do you think he might come looking for her?"

"Unlikely. He'll think she's at the Lyricon. But she'll need a better alibi than that."

"I'll give it some thought," Corython promised. "Now, if there are no further instructions, would you mind taking that incendiary device out of here? It's making me nervous."

Tralvar wrapped the gun snugly in a tablecloth and took the bundle out to the flitter. Corython maintained a safe distance.

"Are these yours?" Tralvar asked, emerging from the hatch with a couple of small bottles.

Corython looked uncomfortable. "Oh, I'd forgotten about those. They were Pannyra's - remedies for morning sickness. I thought they might help Dena."

Tralvar patted his shoulder. "That was thoughtful of you. I'm reassured. By the way, she doesn't remember being sick all over my hall. It might be better not to mention it."

Corython readily agreed, and Tralvar left him guarding the flitter and its dangerous contents while he hurried back to change his clothes. He returned wearing the tunic which bore the insignia of his rank. The garment no longer fitted well, and for the first time Corython realised how thin Tralvar had become.

"Resnay and nerves. My diet of late," the older man said with a tired smile. "Well, I'd better be on my way. I'll be gone for about two ilden. And if for any reason I don't come back..."

"Don't even *think* that," Corython protested.

"With therite, there are always risks - as you were so quick to point out. If anything goes wrong I nominate you my successor. I can rely on you to keep a clear head."

"Thanks," Corython said drily. "Try it yourself sometime." He stepped back, the hatch slammed shut, and the flitter whirled away.

***

Chisrin remained in his office that evening, compiling statistics. Ailsi had peeked in once, but had soon disappeared when he hefted a paperweight meaningfully. While he worked, he mused about Dena. Had she found the idea of unity with him so repulsive that she'd made herself ill? After their previous intimacy such a reaction seemed strange, but Dena was a strange girl. He wished she hadn't run off like that, because scarcely an ild had elapsed that morning before he'd had second thoughts about his plan. If he were to reveal Idenion's crime - whatever it was - the obvious delay in reporting it could lead to accusations of collusion. So Dena's panic flight had been for nothing, and all the careful nurturing he had put into the relationship had been wasted. She wouldn't be back tonight.

Sighing, he stood up and stretched, then quit the building. He looked up at the sky, as he always did at such times. A sprinkle of stars greeted him - alien stars, unfamiliar constellations whose names he still didn't know. He regarded them pensively, resignedly. Why had he ever imagined he'd be able to bribe his way home? The elite had never listened to him and they never would. Idenion's intrigue was best left to run its course.

"A wise decision," said a voice behind him. Chisrin turned, startled.

"You know me, I presume?" inquired Tralvar.

"Yes, First Citizen," said Chisrin respectfully. "Of course." He hoped his apprehension was not too obvious. Clearly, he'd underestimated Dena. He'd been expecting someone to intervene on her behalf, but thought it would merely be Idenion, not the highest authority on Celestra.

"I have removed Dena from your employ," Tralvar said. "And now there's something I wish to show you. Come with me." He gestured toward a nearby flitter, and Chisrin took an involuntary step backwards. The First Citizen, it was said, had murdered men, women and children to achieve his supremacy. Chisrin had given little credence to that, but now that he stood before the alleged perpetrator and perceived the unveiled menace in his thoughts, he was suddenly and alarmingly convinced that the rumours were true.

"I'm waiting," Tralvar reminded him.

"I...need a cloak," Chisrin stammered. He was dressed only for the workplace, in a short sleeveless tunic, and the night was already growing chill.

Tralvar surveyed him indifferently. "You'll come as you are," he stated, giving Chisrin a push in the direction of the flitter. And obediently, Chisrin went. The craft swung into the air and headed away from the city; Ailsi, wide-eyed, crept into the street and watched it depart.

***

A combination of hunger and dark dreams brought Dena to reluctant wakefulness. She cast about for Tralvar's presence and, not finding it, lay dreary and listless in the darkened room. When Corython came in

389

with a bowl of hot soup, however, she sat up gratefully, realising she was hungry.

"There's liman if you want it, and some stale cake," Corython said. "That's all I could find, other than resnay."

"I'll just have the liman, thank you," she replied.

"I brought some of Pannyra's medicines with me," Corython added hesitantly. "They should help you through the early stages. I'd better fetch your drink..."

He shouldn't have been embarrassed, not after the dedicated and diligent way he'd tended his pregnant wife. But awkwardness radiated from him, along with a certain amount of disapproval. Dena felt profoundly sad. This, then, was how it would be once her secret was revealed: sidelong glances, curiosity, conjecture. She'd envisaged it so, over the many nights she'd lain awake with her turbulent thoughts. And if Corython can't look me in the eye, what of the scolia? she asked herself. She suspected she knew the answer.

Corython came back with the liman. He silently handed over the glass, then turned on the overhead lamp and began closing the blinds.

"Tralvar's taking too long," Dena said, suddenly anxious. "It must be time for the patrols. He'll be stopped."

Corython gave her a quizzical look. "The Moderators never stop our First Citizen. Didn't you know that?"

"No, I didn't."

"They're afraid of him, Dena - too afraid to approach him alone at night. They know what he's capable of. *You* should bear it in mind, too." He came forward and took up the tray. Dena laid a hand lightly on his arm to detain him.

"So he's told you I wish to be his partner," she said quietly. "I wonder if he's told you why."

"I didn't ask," Corython said uncomfortably.

"Then *I'll* tell you," said Dena. Her face was pale and drawn, but her gaze was resolute. "Tralvar understands guilt and shame. He didn't censure me, and he knew more about my motives than I did. I value that. And now, I'd like to be left alone. I'm still tired."

Corython tried an apology, realised he was only making matters worse, and retreated. He extinguished the light at her request, relieved that she hadn't taken him to task over his attitude. He was sorry for her, but still found it hard to understand why she hadn't sought Tralvar's help sooner. And he couldn't begin to comprehend her improbable liaison with the Narvellan who had mistreated her. Tralvar apparently had more insight: not a reassuring thought at best. In Corython's opinion, the last thing Dena needed was another difficult man in her life.

***

"First Citizen, where are you taking me?" asked Chisrin, to no avail. For the duration of the journey, Tralvar had maintained a studied silence. His thoughts, too, were carefully obscured. The further into open country they travelled, the more unnerved Chisrin became. He'd always been prepared for retribution, but from his own kind. He could have handled that - he'd even rehearsed his answers. This situation was so unexpected, so wrong, that he could only sit numbly and wait for it to resolve.

At last the flitter lost height and jarred to a halt on uneven ground. "Out," ordered Tralvar peremptorily, and Chisrin obeyed without a word. Tralvar made no immediate move to follow him. The flitter's lights stabbed into opaque darkness, revealing little. But when Chisrin's eyes had adjusted, he realised that Tralvar had landed near the edge of a quarry. It looked disused: scarred granite, loose shale, the sullen gleam of water far below. On the other side, rocks loomed high and forbidding.

Chisrin suddenly realised where he must be. Salvi's encampment - Idenion's flitter trips - this was the very place which had prompted his erroneous guess. Like it or not, it looked as if he were about to witness the truth. Tentatively, he scanned for other minds. As he'd suspected, there was no-one save Tralvar within range. He shivered as the cold struck through his thin tunic and, trying to seem unconcerned, moved closer to the precipice and leant against a granite outcrop. The solid rock at his back was strangely comforting.

Behind him, Tralvar gingerly removed the therite launcher from the storage compartment. So far, so good. The elite knew of his work with explosives but he'd been willing to bet that Chisrin didn't. And it appeared he was right. Chisrin's bewilderment was genuine, although there something insolent about the way he hadn't bothered with shields. Sliding out of the flitter, Tralvar leant against the hull and brought the gun to his shoulder, bracing himself for the recoil.

"Well, First Citizen?" Chisrin's voice was measured, almost supercilious. "What's so interesting about this beauty spot?"

"Observe," said Tralvar. The flash and roar of the ignited therite was daunting, even to him. With a hissing snarl, the projectile hurtled across the quarry and exploded against the cliff face. As the green incandescence faded, Tralvar permitted himself a smile of satisfaction; then a low moan from Chisrin alarmed him. Seizing a handlamp he hastened forward guiltily, flinging the now-useless launcher from him as he went. He'd forgotten about the Narvellan's night vision.

For Chisrin, the scene had lit up in a blaze of agony, then darkened through green to blue to black. A host of afterimages danced mockingly against the darkness.

Certain that Tralvar intended to kill him, he clung to the granite mound as if it offered some kind of refuge. Perplexing world, so surprisingly young, and no time now to tell of his findings. Tralvar was scrambling over the pebbles toward him. Dazed, sightless, he waited for the grasp of the hands that would send him plummeting over the quarry's edge. He wondered if he'd still be conscious when he hit the water.

Under his breath, Tralvar uttered a choice variety of curses: Earth's, Narvella's and a few of his own devising. He hadn't meant this to happen - he'd only intended to let off a squib or two and give Chisrin a scare. Anything more permanent carried a risk. Now he'd have to feign indifference while he tried to assess the damage.

"Finish it," Chisrin muttered hoarsely.

"If you think that's what you deserve," said Tralvar, fleetingly amused in spite of himself. "Can you give me one good reason why I shouldn't push you in there?"

"Return me to my people," Chisrin ventured. "I'd prefer their justice to yours."

Tralvar held up the lamp, but Chisrin appeared not to see it. His eyes wept copious, helpless tears.

"I've just taught you a much needed lesson," Tralvar said coolly. "Now I shall take you home - unless you really want me to deliver you to Axmiol?"

Chisrin's terror evaporated. "You've blinded me, you madman!" he spat.

"Therite blindness is only temporary," Tralvar said mildly. "I'm sure you'll soon put it right."

"Don't count on it," Chisrin said sulkily.

"Oh? Pardon my ignorance, but I thought all Narvellans could heal themselves to some extent. Can't *you*?"

"Not with you breathing down my neck," said Chisrin ungraciously. "Psychokinetic regeneration is difficult and delicate."

"That's *your* problem." Tralvar prised him away from the rock and dragged him by one arm toward the flitter. He walked rapidly, pausing only briefly when Chisrin stumbled and fell, and again - irritably - when he asked permission to relieve himself.

Finally, having regained their transport, Tralvar hauled his morose, shivering passenger on board and closed the canopy. Then he took a bottle of resnay from under the pilot's seat, unstoppered it and placed it in Chisrin's hand. "Here. I thought I might be glad of this, but you need it more than I do." So saying, he started the engine and turned the craft about.

The little flitter hummed quietly, carrying its two occupants back toward civilization. Chisrin, warmed and drowsed by the resnay, finally relaxed enough to begin treating his damaged eyes. His psychokinetic senses tentatively explored each retina, banishing the afterimages. Then he moved back through the intricacies of the optic nerve, trying to soothe away the effects of the therite flare. As usual, the effort quickly tired him and he had to give up. But when he tested his sight he found to his infinite relief that he could perceive light and shadow. Despite his misgivings, he'd soon be able to effect a cure.

Tralvar was glad to see him come out of the odd meditative state. He wondered if Chisrin could remember that whilst trying to heal himself he'd had a tender but one-sided conversation with the absent Sarune.

It was Chisrin who again broke the silence.

"That...weapon," he said haltingly. "You've been testing it - out there?"

"Well done," Tralvar said lightly. "I was beginning to think you'd missed the point of our excursion. The next time you're home by yourself, or working late after everyone's gone, think seriously about my invention and what it can do. You've had your warning. Leave the girls alone, or I'll visit you again. And I won't even have to get close." Now he was on top of the situation again, he was quite enjoying his little speech. "And when the Governors ask me why I did it, I'll take great delight in telling them. I'm sure they'll forgive me. They might even thank me."

Chisrin glowered and moistened his lips. "You won't report me to Axmiol?"

"I've no intention of doing so. He'd probably blame the women."

"Surely not?" Chisrin said, taken aback. The thought had never occurred to him, and for once he had the grace to feel ashamed. "If that were to happen I'd take full responsibility," he added.

Tralvar's unspoken scepticism was still manifest when they landed near the factory. The demoralised Narvellan allowed himself to be raised from his seat and guided safely onto solid ground. And there, he found another helper. Running footsteps came toward him and a pair of warm little arms encircled his neck. "Oh, you poor thing!" Ailsi's voice said. "What's he done to you?"

"There's no permanent damage except to his pride," said Tralvar sarcastically.

Chisrin returned her embrace shakily. One hand tentatively touched her curls, and a tear - not her own - fell onto her upturned face. Amazed, Ailsi looked from her employer to Tralvar and back again. Chisrin was still unshielded; in a trice she knew all about the therite launcher and Tralvar's ultimatum, and couldn't help being vastly impressed by the First Citizen's handiwork.

"Ailsi, a word in private," Tralvar said, returning to the flitter cabin.

"Don't leave me!" Chisrin entreated her. "I can't see, Ailsi. I need you."

"I mustn't offend him," Ailsi said reasonably. "Just sit on this wall a moment while I see what he wants. That's right. Now give me my arm back."

"I'm in a hurry, Ailsi," Tralvar announced. She slid obediently into the cabin, positioning herself a little too close to him. Tralvar was unappreciative. "I take it *you're* in no need of rescue," he remarked.

"I can look after myself, First Citizen," she said pertly.

"Dena thanks you for your kindness," Tralvar continued.

"I only tried to explain what was what," Ailsi said with candour if not tact. "She was so näive. Chisrin called her the ice maiden."

"Indeed?" commented Tralvar with one of his rare smiles. "Then he didn't know her very well."

Just then a Moderator materialised out of the shadows and paused by the open hatch. "And what might *you* be up to?" he said to Ailsi. "Soliciting men? Explain yourself, or that's what goes on my report."

"On your way!" snapped Tralvar.

The Moderator, belatedly recognising him, stepped back hastily. "Your pardon, First Citizen," he mumbled, and was gone.

"As I was saying," Tralvar resumed, wishing Ailsi wouldn't gaze at him so admiringly, "you've been very helpful and you can possibly help me further. I believe you're acquainted with Chisrin's other victims. I want you to explain what happened here tonight, and let them know that if necessary I can arrange for them to leave the factory."

"I'll tell them," Ailsi promised, "but I don't think anyone will come forward. Unless I'm very much mistaken, they'll be able to keep their concessions without having to earn them. Anyway, who would protect eleven of us? We can't *all* take refuge in your arms!"

"You don't miss much, do you?" Tralvar said a little ruefully. He glanced out at Chisrin, who still sat dejectedly where Ailsi had left him. "You'd better get him into his house while I wait. I don't want that Moderator coming back."

"All right," Ailsi said brightly. "I shan't be coming out for a while, so don't linger on my account." Then she skipped back to Chisrin and began talking to him inanely. "Ailsi's here. Up you get! Put your arm round my shoulder, and off we go. Mind the potholes. I'm going to take such good care of you..."

To Chisrin her prattle was a minor indignity. Without direct light his impaired vision was useless, and he was suddenly very grateful for Ailsi's presence. Grateful, too, that she was following orders and guiding him toward his own home rather than hers. The welcome scent of eprys greeted him as Ailsi led him through the little garden and paused to unlatch the glass doors. At the same time the flitter took to the skies, describing a noisy arc before veering off toward the city centre. Ailsi gave a wistful sigh.

"Now there's a man I could fall for. I can see why Ninfi threw herself at him - he really is s-o-o-o dangerous. Did you know he poisoned our last singer because she didn't love him?"

"I can believe it," muttered Chisrin.

"Well," said Ailsi dismissively, "so much for your ice maiden. She won't be the same after tonight."

Chisrin paused halfway across the threshold. "And what's that supposed to mean?"

"He's got her at his house, and he's going home to exact his price for helping her. I caught a stray image of her in his thoughts." Ailsi placed him in a chair and then busied herself lighting lamps, pretending she hadn't noticed the effect her words were having. "Tralvar's not the type you can say no to," she continued mischievously, "and I know what he's after. Mind games, Chisrin!"

"She wouldn't," Chisrin said, dismayed. "Not with *him*." But even as he spoke, he read Ailsi's truthfulness. Dena had given herself to that madman, and he didn't dare wonder why.

"Out of our depth, are we?" Ailsi said patronisingly. "I warned you not to interfere with scolia people. It's common knowledge that Tralvar wanted to be a scolia master but couldn't integrate, and that all his partners have been ex-scolia. Or more specifically, ex-Lyricon. He probably wanted Dena all along." She returned to Chisrin's side, seeing for the first time how dirty and scratched he was. "Discords, you're a mess! What happened to your knees? I'll have to bathe these cuts." She laid a hand on his forehead: it was clammy. The green of his eyes was dulled over. "Maybe I should send for a healer."

"Little one," he said, "why do you concern yourself with me when I've never been kind to you?"

"You *were* kind, once," she said uncertainly.

"No, I exploited you - just as I exploited Dena. And now that murderer has her." His voice was full of bitterness.

"She really got to you, didn't she?" Ailsi said softly.

Chisrin didn't answer her question. "Stay with me, Ailsi," he said unexpectedly.

"Oh, you don't really want me here," she demurred. "Don't worry, I can outrun the Moderators."

"I want you to stay," he repeated. "I'll give you her dress. You'd like that, wouldn't you?"

Ailsi hugged him delightedly. "You didn't have to bribe me, silly. Haven't I always wanted to stay the night?"

His lips twisted in a parody of a smile. "Under rather different circumstances, I imagine. Now, in answer to your earlier suggestion, I can't summon a healer because questions would be asked. And for the same reason, I have to go to work tomorrow. To restore my sight quickly I'll need to use enhanced psychokinesis, and I shall probably look rather strange to you. Promise you won't get nervous and run off?"

"As if I would!" Ailsi said indignantly.

"Thank you," he said, to her added surprise. "It's a disorienting procedure. Your presence will lend stability." He was anxious to embark on his healing, and Ailsi, practical as always, did her best to make him comfortable. She coaxed him into the washroom, only to discover that the water supply had been cut to a mere trickle. Undaunted, she removed his sandals, cleaned his skinned knees as best she could, then confiscated his grimy tunic and threw it in a corner.

"You'll do," she remarked cheekily, giving him a shove towards the bedroom. "Now go ahead and fix your eyes."

Under her unwavering scrutiny, he fumbled open a cabinet near the bed and took out a tray of ampoules. There were only a few left. Breaking one open, he inhaled from it deeply until the contents had evaporated. Then, swaying a little, he repeated the dose. Ailsi caught a trace of the odour and recognised it as the Breath of Corayn, a distillation used by Celestrian healers to enhance their powers. She made no comment, but continued to watch gravely as Chisrin stretched himself full-length on the bed and closed his eyes. She guessed, from what Dena had told her octals ago, why he had a ready supply of the very drug he needed. He'd been using it to operate the imaging device left to him by his wife. And had doubtless been hallucinating about her.

He was soon in a trance-like state which only half resembled sleep. True to his earlier pronouncement, he looked very unlike his usual self. He trembled, twitched and murmured. Ailsi wished he'd stop it. She'd always been attracted to his laconic strength, and to see him brought so low was disconcerting. Presently she became aware of an additional light source in the room, and tiptoeing up to the half-open cabinet, found a tiny flat object which twinkled and sparkled. It was the impress disc, alive in abstract response to whatever psychokinetic impulses Chisrin was generating. She dropped it hastily.

The shivers and whispers went on and on. Ailsi became increasingly fretful, wishing she'd had the sense to ask how long the process was likely to take. She took one of his cloaks and tucked it round him. Then, when it wouldn't stay in place, lay alongside him and held him as tightly as she could. Since she didn't dare risk even a peep at his thoughts for fear of interrupting the cure, she had no way of telling if her closeness helped or if he was even aware of it. But at last he began to grow quieter, until finally he lay still. His face and limbs relaxed into something akin to normal sleep. Loyally, Ailsi remained beside him, keeping him warm, while he completed his journey back to consciousness.

***

Tralvar's flitter lifted clear of the ground, its landing lights briefly illuminating Chisrin and Ailsi before darkness returned to the shabby street.

"Well, First Citizen," Tralvar remarked to himself, "that wasn't a bad night's work." Then he threw the craft into a tight turn, ignoring a protesting whine from the stabilising unit.

As he skimmed rapidly toward Lateral Three, he reflected briefly on the ease with which his impromptu kidnap had been accomplished. There had been several instances on the outward flight when Chisrin could have overpowered him, or at least tried. Instead, he had simply acquiesced. Perhaps, mused Tralvar, a race of beings used to self-imposed restrictions found it second nature to accept other disciplines from without. Chisrin had submitted to Tralvar's authority in much the same way as he and the rest of his kind bowed to the Synectics' will. Was the Celestrian immunity to the Synectics merely a question of attitude? With that slightly oblique thought in mind, Tralvar brought the flitter to land and prepared to face Corython's wrath. The accident to Chisrin's eyes had caused a lengthy delay, and Corython had now missed a whole evening's duties.

Corython had indeed planned to say plenty, but his resolve deserted him when Tralvar strode into the study. He retreated a little, just as Chisrin had earlier, and Tralvar laughed.

"Not scared, are you? This is *me*, remember - the same Tralvar you nearly drowned a few days ago!"

"You're *not* the same," said Corython pedantically. "I think I preferred it when you were drunk." He scrutinised Tralvar's fevered expression at some length, while his own grew steadily more worried.

"How's Dena?" Tralvar inquired, and without waiting for an answer, bounded upstairs to find out. She was asleep again. Restive, she'd thrown off most of the bedclothes and now lay beneath a single sheet, one arm curved about her stomach as if to protect the tiny life within. Tralvar found this so unexpectedly erotic that he lingered in the doorway. But at last, nudged by Corython's impatience, he returned downstairs.

"She still wants you, never fear," the astronomer said dolefully. "Yes, we talked. I rather wish we hadn't. She disconcerts me."

401

"Because she learnt pleasure from a Narvellan?" Tralvar queried. "Perhaps you'd rather she'd been broken by the experience? Anyway, for what it's worth, Chisrin's conscience was beginning to trouble him. I read him in depth before he knew I was there. He'd grown quite fond of her."

Corython was nonplussed, trying to equate fondness with the exhausted and terrified creature who'd stumbled into the house that morning. "For harmony's sake be kind to her, if that's possible," he said finally.

"You're inferring that it isn't," Tralvar observed.

"I'm inferring that tonight isn't the time to begin a new relationship," Corython replied. "Not while you're in this mood."

"What mood?"

"Whatever it is that makes you enjoy frightening people," Corython elaborated carefully. "Yes, I know he deserved it; and yes, I'd probably do something similar to anyone who abused Pannyra. But I wouldn't think it was fun." He gazed in the general direction of Dena's room. "How many more of us are going to be hurt or killed before this nightmare ends?"

"Now don't start getting twitchy again," Tralvar said, picking up a resnay bottle he'd concealed behind a row of books. He poured a measure, sniffed it appreciatively and then shoved it across to Corython. "I've told you before, just concentrate on the project and your part in it. Shall I run through the operational sequence one last time?"

"If you would. It helps to have an overview." Corython took a swallow of the resnay and coughed as it burned his throat.

"Very well, here goes. At dawn, four days from now - a rest day, incidentally, so we can all move about more freely - Rillan will take off from Treva in the last sphere to leave the assembly line. One ild later the entire orbiting contingent will depart for Narvella. We should be able to see the trails. Two astallen after that, Jarras will launch his fleet from Kest, first ensuring no-one boards the Ipsa sphere."

"What about the Alcine consignment?"

"They're two days behind schedule so they won't be involved. That's to our advantage, I think - it makes for a less complicated strategy. Jarras instigated the two-astallen delay to give Rillan time to set up a tracking programme; otherwise he could miss the event as it will be over so fast. Once he has the data he'll immediately transpose it to you at the observatory."

"I'll be waiting."

"Nothing's going to happen till mid-evening, remember, due to the fourteen ilden it will take the spheres to reach Narvella. When the time comes, make sure you're alone. I've absolutely no idea how the Narvellans will act when they're freed, and we must all keep a low profile until we find out."

"That makes sense." Corython downed the rest of his drink, sighed and stood up. "I should go."

"The patrols will be out."

"I'm not staying," Corython said emphatically. "I'd be in the way. Did you leave your flitter outside?"

"Yes, but it won't have much charge left."

"Doesn't matter. If it gets me even halfway home, I can tell the Moderators I was on my way back from the observatory."

Tralvar saw him out. "Please give my sincere apologies to Pannyra when you see her. Tell her I'm still sober, if it will help."

"If she'll listen," rejoined Corython. "She thinks I've been seeing another woman."

"In four days' time you'll be able to tell her how wrong she was," Tralvar promised. "She'll be so proud of you!"

"Maybe. Frankly, I can't see that I've much future with her. There have been too many things unshared." Corython spoke sorrowfully but with quiet restraint; Tralvar, thinking of his own maudlin self-pity, felt suitably chastened. He began to realise why Corython had shown so little patience with his drinking.

"Oh, I nearly forgot," Corython added. "You wanted an excuse for keeping Dena here - something Idenion would believe. Why not make her your secretary? Laura was telling me that *she* would have assumed the role if she hadn't displayed her illiteracy to the first Narvellan she saw."

Tralvar liked this solution. It was simple, logical, and would keep everyone fooled for the next few days. He kept watch until Corython had boarded the flitter, then bolted the door and ascended to his suite. He bathed carefully, removing all traces of quarry grit and therite ash. Then he retired to bed and lay in wakeful anticipation, a nearby lamp burnishing his limbs and hair. He could have gone to Dena, but refrained. This time, she alone had to make the choice.

At last she appeared, walking hesitantly as her ankle was still paining her. "I've thought over what you said," she stated calmly, "and I've decided that my place is with you. I...think we need each other, Tralvar."

He drew her down to embrace him. "I'm so grateful you're here."

And suddenly she was caught in the torrent of his possession as it whirled through every level of her mind. Desire made him reckless: she was briefly aware of some aspect of herself that was precious and delicate and elusive - just before it was rent to shreds. His warning had been well justified.

She didn't falter. Unflinchingly she beat aside his momentary dismay and, with the innate knowledge that

404

had always been hers, completed and held the circle of unity.

She knew him now, in all his complexity. She was loved. She was no longer alone.

Presently, spiralling down from that dizzy duality, she was astonished to find herself lying chastely on top of the sheets. She was exhausted, as if after a night of sexual passion, and yet the only physical contact had been his arm about her shoulders. The little lamp burned steadily, casting his features into deep shadow as he gazed at her.

"That's the difficult part out of the way," he said softly. "Now for the rest."

***

It was immediately obvious to Corython that the flitter wouldn't carry him to Lateral Four, so he dumped it at the nearest intersection and continued on foot. But unlike the night of the power cuts, luck was not on his side. An imposing group of elite, presumably on their way back to the akron, came face to face with him as they rounded a corner.

"Stand aside for Directress Passik," someone ordered, even though Corython had already done so. The cloaked and booted Narvellans swept past him: three bodyguards, a senior Moderator, Passik in her veils, Narad, and two of his cronies. Corython was about to hurry on his way when a voice said:

"You are out late, Corython of Alcine."

Corython forced himself to pause and look back. He knew that querulous voice - it belonged to one of the administrators who continually plagued him at work. "I've just finished my shift, Lord Besu," he said with what he hoped was a confident smile. "My flitter didn't quite make it home."

They waved him on and fell into stride once again - all but the Moderator. "The Celestrian is lying," he remarked.

"Really, Hapka? What makes you say that?" asked Narad.

"The observatory is to the east; he approached us from the west. If you knew your flitter was short on power, would you overshoot your destination and have to walk back?"

"That *is* a little curious," conceded Narad. "This must be the flitter in question."

"Parked west of the intersection with its nose facing east," observed the Moderator, walking slowly around the craft. "The landing gear is very muddy."

"The observatory has a gravel parking strip," commented Besu.

"Does it now?" Narad remarked thoughtfully. "Passik, can you tell where this mud came from?"

Passik knelt in the street, extending her delicate hands toward the clods of earth. "Clay...granite traces...flint," she intoned. "The soil signature is consistent with that found to the west of the city."

"Are you sure?"

"Positive. I studied the area for Salvi's inquisitors."

"Corython has been researching ways to enhance transposal," the elderly administrator said. "He claimed it couldn't be done. Perhaps he lied about that too."

Narad reached into the flitter and tried to activate the control panel. It was completely dead. "He left it on discharge," he muttered. "Any locator settings will have been blanked. Well, there's certainly some irregularity here, although I'm not sure that it's worth our attention."

"I disagree," objected Besu. "We should investigate."

Narad sighed gustily. "If you insist. Hapka, have your men search Corython's home for anything unusual.

You'd better check his office as well. Discreetly, you understand; if he *is* up to something I don't want him alerted. Happy now, Besu?"

"I'm glad you recognise the need for vigilance, Narad."

"Bah," said Narad expressively. "This will be a complete waste of time. We'll probably find he's cheating on his wife."

***

"No," said Laura.

Idenion, who'd been contemplating the stars through the bedroom window, turned round quizzically. He could just see her, a pale form in the darkness, propped on one elbow.

"I may not be telepathic but I know exactly what you're thinking," she went on gently. "You think that if something goes wrong with Operation Ipsa you can spirit me back to Earth out of harm's way. I want you to forget all about that, because I won't go."

"Laura - "

"I'm staying no matter what," she insisted. "Dena knows it, Lydion knows it, and I'm sure Tralvar does too. Besides, I doubt if you'd get anywhere near another sphere. So don't let's talk about this, or even think about it, any more." She slid out of bed and curled herself lovingly against his slender back. "Nothing will ever separate us again."

Chapter Thirteen

"Convoy leader to Rillan."

"Rillan here."

"All Trevan spheres accounted for. Cutting transposal beam and switching to proximity comm-link."

"Why can't you just say radio?" inquired Rillan in the brief time before he activated it. There would be solar interference, of course, but traditional radio was necessary for information sharing within the convoy. Transposal, by its nature, was restricted to contact between two points.

"Concluding deceleration," the leader's voice crackled. "Entering Narvellan system in one astal from now."

Oh, shut up, thought Rillan. Typical bureaucrat, always stating the obvious. I've made this trip a dozen times more than you, and with twice as many unmanned spheres. Just let me get on with it.

"Prepare to disengage programme and initiate holding sequence on my mark."

"Acknowledged." Rillan already had Ipsa on the long-range scanners and omitted to notice that his flight programme had ended a fraction too soon.

"Holding sequence established," continued the Narvellan. "Kest contingent on course for our position. Rillan, hold formation; you're beginning to drift."

Startled, Rillan checked his readings and corrected the error. The sphere was handling very badly, which perturbed him. He'd used this craft on many escort runs precisely because it was so trouble-free. It *would* decide to start acting up now!

"Kest contingent will reach these co-ordinates in one astal," the Narvellan droned on.

"You're going to get such a surprise," Rillan muttered inaudibly."Three...two...one - "

"Alert!" called the Narvellan, on cue. "We have another runaway. Rillan, do not pursue. Maintain your position."

Rillan, of course, had no intention of chasing anything this time. He focused the viewscreen on distant Ipsa and waited breathlessly.

"Runaway's velocity increasing," said another Narvellan. "Stardrive emissions detected."

"Shut it down," ordered the leader.

"I've lost it! Where - "

A flash of white light, brief but brilliant, signalled the sphere's demise. Cries and complaints arose from various Narvellans in the flotilla, even though Rillan had been the only one looking directly at the blast. Then the leader spoke, icily calm.

"Rillan? What was that?"

"I - don't know," Rillan stammered, unprepared.

"I think you do."

Rillan hardly heard him. He was staring at Ipsa. There before him was the plain of Liapa, intact and unblemished. There was no crater, no sign of impact, nothing. It didn't work, Rillan thought disbelievingly. It didn't work! He could hear the Narvellan calling Rhul on the transposer. He was warning the people about the incandescence which would reach their skies in less than two astallen. Narvella Four was on the far side of the sun and would not be affected.

Numbly, Rillan forced himself to act. He shut off the radio, activated his transposer and contacted the observatory. He was not endangering Corython in so doing; the Narvellans would know the transposer was in use but would have no idea what was being said, nor to whom.

"Corython? I know you weren't expecting voice contact but I'd no choice. Are you alone? Good; now listen. It hasn't worked. I don't *know* why - I had a quick look at the data but I don't understand it well enough. I'm going to send it through anyway. You'll have to warn Tralvar."

"But what happened?" demanded Corython shrilly.

"There was a bright light, and that's all I know. Just listen, will you - I think my transposer's going to fold. Just before I called you I heard the convoy leader speaking to Rhul. He thinks the runaway sphere was a bomb, intended for Narvella Prime. I'll get this data to you and then I'm coming home. They may send word ahead but at least I can be arrested on my own world. If I surrender to them here I'll never get back. Stand by."

The information had only just been transferred when the link failed. Corython studied the figures, his expression growing ever more desolate. He had the satisfaction of knowing that his calculations had been flawless: the sphere had been heading unerringly for the heat source on the plain of Liapa. But then - Corython checked twice to make sure there was no mistake - something had risen from the surface of Ipsa and interposed itself between the missile and its target. Something smaller than a sphere; something no larger than a rock. No ordinary Narvellan could have reacted that fast. This had to be the Synectics' work.

Corython's habitual fatalism made him almost calm. He believed he was in no immediate danger and thus remained where he was, in the observatory's communications gallery overlooking the great reflector. What was he to do? Rillan had wanted him to warn Tralvar but there was no way he could accomplish that without incriminating him. He could, however, speak to Jarras, who - despite the encroaching night - would be waiting to hear from Rillan. He re-tuned the transposer

410

to the spacefield at Kest, opting for a visual link. That way he'd know if Jarras was by himself without wasting time asking.

The two young scientists exchanged wary looks for a moment. They were not well acquainted, and were taking no chances. Then Corython said:

"We're in trouble, Jarras. The Synectics vaporised the sphere prematurely and now the Narvellans are saying it was a bomb, aimed at them. It won't take them long to realise you were involved. Get out of there!"

"But how did - "

"Discords, Jarras, just *go*! Is the place as deserted as it looks?"

"No spheres, so no security," Jarras answered succinctly. "I can get out. But what about Tralvar? If the Narvellans think the sphere was armed he'll be their chief suspect. I can't run off and leave him!"

"He'd want you to," Corython answered steadily.

"Then what about *you*?" Jarras asked. "What will - "

Behind Corython, the door crashed open. Unhesitatingly the astronomer took the beam decoder off-line. Jarras could still see and hear what was happening, but his image was no longer on the observatory screen.

Administrator Myrig tyl Plessit strode in, accompanied by two Moderators. The newcomers did not approach Corython but remained just inside the door, blocking his escape. Two of his workmates hovered fearfully in the background.

"Corython of Alcine," said Myrig with quiet authority, "you are under arrest for crimes against the Narvellan Protectorate."

"I don't know what you're talking about," Corython declared.

411

"These." Myrig held up a sheaf of papers, some with scorched edges.

Corython stared in disbelief. "But - I burnt them!"

"You attempted to," smiled Myrig. "The incinerator flue was clogged. I imagine one of your colleagues fished them out and put them in the re-cycling bin - which was where we found them when we searched these premises several days ago." He ambled forward to inspect the logic terminal Corython had been using. "To be perfectly honest, we weren't sure *what* we'd found - or rather Narad wasn't, since his knowledge of mathematics is minuscule. We decided to pass it on to some experts, who had their own ideas but hitherto no proof. This data, I presume, came from your ally in the convoy. I'll take charge of it." He paused before ejecting the crystal. "Do you deny that this is your work?"

"How can I?" Corython's voice was a ragged whisper.

"He admits his guilt!" exclaimed one of the Moderators.

"Let me speak with your experts," Corython pleaded. "Let me explain what I was doing!"

"Corython," said Myrig, sounding almost fatherly, "you sent a weapon of war into Narvellan territory. No one's going to concern themselves with minor details. Now come with us."

The other Moderator suddenly threw a punch, a blow as vicious as it was unexpected. Corython doubled up and fell to his knees, trying not to vomit.

"Haven't you any sense?" roared Myrig, and cuffed the Moderator round the head. "Justice must be seen to be done. Lord Axmiol wants a public trial."

"This creature tried to murder our people," said the Moderator sullenly.

"He will be judged," Myrig promised. "Take him to the akron and restrain him - but do not injure him."

412

The Moderators dragged Corython out. Myrig, left alone, went quietly to the transposer and reactivated the beam decoder. It showed an empty control room. With a secret little smile, Myrig turned off the transposer and followed Corython's captors into the night.

The two disgruntled Moderators obeyed orders and refrained from harming their prisoner, although when they entered the akron he was slapped a couple of times to indicate where he should walk. The Narvellans' usual code of summary justice meant that there were few places to sequester wrongdoers, but they found an empty storeroom with a lockable door and threw him into it.

He was left alone for two ilden. He was cold and his stomach hurt, but his surroundings could have been worse. A standpipe in a corner provided drinking water and a drain in the centre of the room sufficed as a latrine. After attending to his needs he huddled disconsolately on the floor, wondering why he felt resigned rather than frightened. He allowed his perception to drift slowly round the building, taking care not to focus on anyone for too long. Narvellan minds, shielded for the most part, cool and businesslike. Axmiol was fulminating somewhere in the middle distance. It was scarcely amicable company, but it was better than being alone. And then, on the top floor, Kyrin commenced his nightly work. From further off, other relayists took up the rhythm. Corython was wretchedly grateful for this tenuous contact with his own people.

Presently Myrig came back. "I thought I'd allow you a little time to consider your situation," he said affably.

"What's going to happen to me?" Corython ventured.

"That depends on you," Myrig answered suavely. "Obviously, we need the names of your co-conspirators - and there are several methods we could employ to get

413

them. Let's consider three options, shall we? Firstly, there are two able young men outside who would enjoy beating the truth out of you. I don't believe that will be necessary, which is why I've warned them off. There's no doubting their enthusiasm but they have a tendency to overdo things, and if I let them loose on you we could well find ourselves with only half a confession. Secondly we could deep-read you, which would be thoroughly unpleasant for you *and* for us. Moreover, these things take time, and the homeworlds are already screaming for results."

"And thirdly?"

Myrig paced slowly across the stone floor. "This is a little distasteful, but I must be guided by necessity. Do you recall a political activist called Jedak, arrested in Ninka for distributing seditious pamphlets? We let him go, but executed his woman."

Corython, horrified, saw where this was heading. "Lord Myrig, no! Don't let them hurt Pannyra! She knows nothing!"

"Your wife will not be harmed as long as you're open with us," Myrig promised.

Corython covered his face and rocked back and forth in an agony of indecision.

"I'll try to lessen your dilemma," Myrig went on. "Let us suppose, for argument's sake, that the First Citizen recruited you. I say this because he is, in my opinion, the only one of your kind with sufficient aggression to perpetrate an act of war. Do you really think he'd rely exclusively on *your* efforts?"

Corython looked up uncomprehendingly.

"Have you ever heard the phrase 'need to know'?" Myrig pursued.

"Yes, several times. I was told to concentrate on my part of the work and ask no questions."

"Because Tralvar, if it was he, had contingency plans in the event of your capture. I don't believe you were attempting wholesale slaughter of my people; I rather think you had a specific target in mind. We need not discuss that now. But whatever you were trying to achieve, it was a spectacular failure, was it not? All Narvella knows about it and soon all Celestra will too. I surmise that even as we speak, other agents - having seen you fail - will have taken appropriate action. When you capitulate, you'll only be describing a defunct aspect of Tralvar's strategy."

"And betraying my friends," Corython said bitterly.

"They knew the risks," Myrig declared. "We're talking of damage limitation now. Give me the names and let Axmiol have his show trial. It will occupy everyone's attention and halt further investigation, at least for a while. I'm sure that's what you want."

"I - "

"Talk to me, Corython. Tell me who your friends are. Then we can go upstairs and put together a statement - and maybe leave out a few non-essential things. Quickly, Corython. For Pannyra's sake."

Corython, in abject despair, named Tralvar, Jarras, Rillan, Idenion and Laura. But he omitted Kyrin, and still referred to Laura as Lisset.

"Thank you," Myrig said gravely. "Now your wife will be safe - and so will your son, who was born three ilden ago."

Corython wept, a sudden storm of tears which cascaded down his cheeks and fell into the dust. "I shall never see him!" he sobbed.

Myrig placed a sympathetic hand on his shoulder. "I will enter a plea for clemency as you've been so obliging. Now get up and come with me. We have a statement to prepare."

***

415

The arrests began at dawn. Tralvar, of course, had been expecting it. The Narvellans hadn't exhibited any behavioural shift, and both Corython and Jarras seemed to have vanished off the face of the planet.

He'd managed to keep his worst fears from Dena. She'd assumed there had been a miscalculation but didn't suspect that the secret might be out. Tralvar fervently wished he knew what *had* gone wrong, but told himself he'd find out soon enough. At first light he left Dena sleeping, donned his freshly-laundered uniform and waited calmly in the study. When the street door was flung open to admit three Moderators, it was almost a relief.

He'd hoped that if he surrendered quietly they wouldn't search the house, but they were in no mood for half measures. "See who he's got with him," directed the senior official, and one of his younger colleagues went thundering upstairs. He soon located Dena who, despite the rude awakening, haughtily despatched him to wait on the landing while she dressed. Then, under an iron-grey sky, she and Tralvar were marched up to the akron.

"Be frank with them, Dena," Tralvar urged just before they were separated. "Don't shield. Don't give them an excuse to hurt you."

"But Tralvar, if - "

"Don't shield!" he repeated, and was gone.

The Narvellans had now detained the only two people who knew the next stage of the plan - Dena as a result of her unity with Tralvar - but the opportunity was allowed to slip by. Myrig was asleep, and apparently had shared his theory with no-one. Dena was questioned once, briefly, by her arresting officer, who believed she was simply Tralvar's companion for the night. His one clumsy attempt to read her told him nothing about the conspiracy, but everything about her pregnancy. Tralvar had hoped this would be so. With a fresh scandal to

416

occupy them, the elite weren't likely to give a thought to Quetri or his whereabouts...yet.

Narad, standing in for Myrig, was suitably intrigued. "This gets worse!" he remarked.

"Shall we apprehend Chisrin?" asked the Moderator who had made the discovery.

"Not now, lackwit. He'd miss a morning's work. We'll round him up later." Narad's strong, supple fingers toyed with a globe on his desk - a representation of Narvella Prime. "You may escort Tralvar in. And show him some respect. He may be under arrest but he is still First Citizen."

The young man blinked to signify his displeasure. "As my lord wishes," he answered, and strode away. Shortly afterward his two companions propelled Tralvar into the office, only to be summarily dismissed as soon as they had released him.

"If you want to extract a confession from me, you'd better call them back," Tralvar said laconically.

"That wouldn't be appropriate," returned Narad, continuing to twirl the globe. "So, let's make a brief study of this debacle. The only positive aspect is the fright it gave Axmiol. I've never seen him so rattled. Which will doubtless do him the world of good. Otherwise..." He made a gesture of negation. "I can't see you walking away from this one, Tralvar. I'm very disappointed in you."

"You'll get over it."

Narad smiled sourly. "To business, then. I'm supposed to get some kind of declaration from you - although I don't imagine for a moment that you'll be as vocal as your tame astronomer."

"I've no loved ones for you to threaten," Tralvar pointed out. "Feel free to strangle my estranged daughter if you want."

417

"Such a pity when families fall out," Narad remarked. "But what of Dena? Surely you care what happens to *her*?"

"You can't touch her," Tralvar declared scornfully. "She's going to be the star attraction at this so-called trial. The wicked seductress with the innocent face - isn't that how you'll present her? Unless, of course, you're going to arraign Chisrin as well."

"Chisrin ap Tuin might be a fool, but he isn't a traitor," retorted Narad. "You're a callous piece of work, Tralvar. After the way you treated your neph-khet I'm not surprised that you're prepared to sacrifice your woman."

"My neph-khet?" Tralvar forced himself not to look apprehensive. "What's the little telltale been saying?"

"I found him in tears at the spaceport," Narad related. "He said he couldn't endure you any longer - that you'd forced him to have unity with your drinking companions and watch while you entertained factory girls. Naturally I had to report this to the administration. It didn't endear you to them."

Tralvar told him, very graphically, what the administration could do. "I know what this trial's going to consist of," he went on. "It won't be to establish our innocence or guilt but to determine our punishment. You've already made up your minds about us and therefore I'm calling a halt to this interview."

"That's your prerogative," Narad conceded. "But first, there's just one thing that's been puzzling us. Every time you or anyone else tried to organise resistance in the past, it fizzled out through apathy. Now, suddenly, you have engineers and scientists falling over themselves to do your bidding. What's changed? How did you motivate them?"

"I said please," Tralvar answered mildly.

"And that's your final word." Narad sounded almost regretful. "Come: I'll show you to your quarters. We've allocated a guest suite to you and Corython. There'll be guards on the door but you should be comfortable enough."

"What about Dena?"

"Female prisoners are always held separately. But don't worry - she'll have some company soon."

The guest suite was not the most opulent of its type, having no balcony and only one entrance. Tralvar found Corython curled on one of the beds, staring at the wall. He didn't look as though he'd slept.

"Tralvar!" he exclaimed, leaping up. "Oh, chaos, I'm sorry. I'm sorry..."

"Shh." Tralvar went swiftly to the music console and set it in motion. An irritating Narvellan tune, all clanging chimes and droning reeds, filled the air.

"What are you *doing*?" protested Corython.

Tralvar pushed him into the washroom, set all the taps trickling noisily and turned on the drying unit. "They've put us together hoping we'll give more away," he said in a fierce whisper. "They'll have rigged the intercom system or hidden a microphone. Give me a few moments to look around and I'll find out."

"Can we turn it off?" Corython asked, peering fearfully about him.

"Of course - when it suits us. First we're going to use it to feed them disinformation."

Corython gazed at him in a mixture of admiration and perplexity. "How is it you know these things?"

"They made me read all their reports, remember?" Tralvar smirked. "I daresay they're wishing they hadn't."

"Tralvar...before we have to stop making this noise, there's something I must ask. Was Operation Ipsa your only plan? Did you really put all your trust in me?"

"No," Tralvar said after a pause. "No, I didn't."

"Oh, thank harmony! Myrig said - "

"And now I want you to go out there and ask that question again. Make it convincing!"

Corython obeyed, a little selfconsciously. "I've failed you, Tralvar. But Myrig told me not to be ashamed - that I was only part of your plan. Is that true?"

"He said it to trick you," Tralvar answered. "There was only one plan, and it didn't work. There's nothing else." As he spoke he explored the room, running his fingers under the tabletop and along the door frame. The akron's interiors were infinitely familiar to him; any incongruity, however small, wouldn't escape him for long. He motioned Corython to keep talking.

"I'm told I have a son," Corython went on. "What's Pannyra going to think when I don't visit her? Will they tell her where I am?"

Tralvar continued his search. The intercom, as he had surmised, was permanently on. "Hey, you lazy oafs - how about some breakfast?" he called before wrenching the wires out of its base. "Now what were you saying? Oh yes, Pannyra. I don't think our hosts will spoil the trial of the year by telling anyone in advance. They'll announce an important broadcast and suddenly you and I will be on air. Incidentally, I saw some cables being unspooled when they brought me up here - the heavy duty sort. I think they're trying to set up a transposal link as well as radio. Won't we be famous?"

"How can you joke about it?" Corython forgot he was supposed to be acting. "They're going to tell everyone a pack of lies and then they're going to kill us!"

"Ah." Tralvar removed a piece of wall panelling to reveal a dainty but badly assembled listening device. He tugged lightly at the plastic casing and the inexpert connections fell away. "Discords, they're no good at this - but their electricians doubtless have better things to

420

occupy them. Would you say this looks new, Corython my friend?"

"It's dusty."

"Which means it's been here quite some time. I do believe the elite have been spying on one another. Tsk tsk!"

"Can we talk privately now?" asked Corython.

Tralvar was still staring at the object he'd liberated. "What kind of telepath needs a thing like this?" he muttered. "There was something very wrong with Narvellan society *before* the Synectics got to them." He tossed the device away in contempt. "All right, Corython, talk to me. Tell me what happened at Ipsa."

Corython explained his findings - how something had been launched from the moon's surface to destroy the sphere. "At that speed, with no proximity wards, a small stone could have done it," he added. "It was so precise. They must have known what was coming."

"Oh, chaos!" Tralvar sat down heavily. "My dream! The one I didn't understand."

Corython waited for him to elaborate.

"Just after I'd been discussing the fly-by with Jarras and Rillan, I dreamt about the Synectics and the way they perceive everything as patterns. Lydion was taken and then cast out because he wasn't part of the pattern."

"So?"

"Don't you see? Lydion was the odd man out and they spotted him at once. The sphere that scanned them, the very act of the fly-by itself, didn't belong. Yes, they knew what we were doing. Yes, they were waiting. We warned them ourselves! All that work, all that preparation, wasted!" He buried his face in his hands. Corython impulsively offered his sympathy, but Tralvar suddenly uncoiled from his brooding stance and shook him. "Get your shields back up! Now!"

Corython looked hurt.

421

"Sorry, but you mustn't let your guard down. They'll have their most efficient telepaths ranged against us. Wait, I'll show you." He readied himself, then opened his mind to the not inconsiderable clamour around him.

+Dena? Dena, are you there?+

He caught just the hint of a reply before the contact was rudely blotted out.

+COMMUNICATION WITH THE FEMALE PRISONER IS FORBIDDEN+

Corython's perception shuddered away from the onslaught.

"You see?" said Tralvar. "We're pinned down. They'd just love the chance to get into our heads."

"Then why don't we just *let* them?"

"Listen, you coward. I've just had the most devastating news of my entire career - that Operation Ipsa failed because of an oversight on my part, when the truth was there in front of me. But I won't give up and neither must you. It's still down to you and me to make things as difficult for the Narvellans as we can, for as long as we can. And once you've answered a couple more of my questions I'll tell you why."

Corython stared morosely at the floor. "Did you sense all that commotion? They're getting ready for the trial, aren't they? Technicians demanding more cable, Axmiol yelling for his dress uniform..."

"They're aiming for noon, I imagine," Tralvar answered. "Now would you please tell me, without getting into apology mode, who else you named."

"Rillan, because they already knew about him," Corython began hesitantly. "Jarras - but I'd warned him earlier and I'm sure he got away."

"Thank you for that," Tralvar said softly. "Who else?"

"You, Idenion and...Lisset." He emphasised Laura's alias.

"Nothing they couldn't have deduced for themselves," Tralvar commented. "Now this is very important, Corython: did you mention Quetri?"

"The Narvellan who helped you? I couldn't even remember his name!"

"Good. Excellent. Of course, once Laura's here they'll see through her prill disguise. Our shields won't do us much good after that. But we'll have given Quetri all the time we could."

Corython stared. "*He's* your backup?"

"He is; and as soon as the Narvellans interrogate Laura they're going to find out we turned him. He's only had half a day to prepare. Let's hope it's enough."

***

Quetri witnessed the brief, brilliant explosion from his tiny apartment in Rhul, and heard the lies began to circulate. Sorrowful but resolute, he assembled a few possessions, checked the contents of the telescope case and made his way to the spaceport. On his arrival from Celestra he'd sought Navarian's contact in the government who, fortunately, was still in the same post and remembered how Tarysk had filched the bereaved neph-khet from the project. He'd welcomed him back and issued him with a set of co-ordinates and a high level security pass. Quetri handed these documents to the spaceport authorities and endured an excruciatingly tense wait while they searched for a pilot with the necessary clearance.

The short journey to Ipsa was, as usual, conducted in silence with the viewscreen off. "Suit up," said the pilot eventually - the first words he'd spoken since they'd left Rhul.

Quetri placed his belongings in a pressurised case and tested the seals, then donned a bioshell - all but the headgear. The pilot did the same, checking his air supply carefully.

"Do you intend coming with me?" Quetri inquired.

"I need to look in briefly to pick up personal correspondence. The project isn't allocated many flights and we have to make fullest use of each one."

Quetri remembered that the transposer was never used for anything remotely personal. It had never mattered much to him as he'd had no one to stay in touch with.

The sphere landed with a slight bump. The pilot closed a key with his padded glove and the cabin atmosphere began to filter out. "Helmet," he ordered, and Quetri locked the cumbersome headgear in place.

The hatch rippled open. Distant but piercingly bright sunlight beat down from a black sky, and Quetri was glad the photosensitive visor protected his eyes from the glare. Outside, the bleak boulder-strewn plain of Liapa extended to the horizon, each boulder casting an inky black shadow; and almost hidden in one such shadow was the mouth of a cave. The two men waded toward it in the weak gravity, negotiated the narrow aperture and waited for their visors to adjust. Ahead of them was a man-made tunnel with a gradual downward slope. Tiny luminous discs, embedded in the walls at regular intervals, guided them forward. Their night vision would have been no use in such absolute darkness.

Quetri's slow steady pace gave no hint of the turbulence in his mind. I can't do this, he thought in sudden panic. Someone will read me. Even if they don't find out what I'm planning, they'll discover I'm one of the Free. Or maybe the Synectics themselves will. How can I confront *them*?

At the end of the tunnel was an airlock with its outer door open. As they approached it Quetri began to feel the pull of the colony's artificial gravity. Navarian! his thoughts lamented. The last time he'd walked this route, his loving mentor had been on the other side of the airlock to greet him. Surprisingly, the thought restored his sense of purpose. I must stay focused, he told himself sternly. I'm here to avenge Navarian, to honour my promise to Tralvar - and to save my people, if I can.

The pressure normalised and the new arrivals were able to remove their helmets. Then the inner lock grated open, and Quetri hastened to slough off the rest of the clumsy suit. The pilot departed on his errands, leaving Quetri steeling himself for the next ordeal - reporting to the project leader's office.

It wasn't simply that he feared being read. The man who'd taken over from Navarian was named Clovath tyl Imlis - an administrator, not a scientist. He'd openly resented Quetri's privileged status and frequently complained to Navarian that a bondslave should not have been given such authority. Now the position was reversed, Quetri anticipated even more hostility.

As he was removing his belongings from the vacuum-sealed box, a worker appeared to escort him to his allocated room - a very cramped one, alive with vibration from the life support generators. Quetri didn't object. He wouldn't be there long. He locked the telescope case in a closet and removed the key.

"Lord Clovath is waiting," prompted the worker in some agitation. "Please hurry, Lord Quetri. He doesn't like delay."

Quetri began to explain that he was no lord, but something about his guide - the vacant gaze and tremulous mouth - made him pause. The man was a reducee! Quetri had never seen a Narvellan reducee before, and he certainly hadn't expected to see one here. Just what had gone on during his absence?

Project Leader Clovath had his back to the door when Quetri walked in. He spoke without turning round. "Let's get one thing clear, zyl Nyris. I didn't want you back but I was over-ruled. You'll defer to me in everything and remain in your quarters or the commonroom when not on duty. In particular, you will *not* go wandering in and out of the Synectics' chamber as you used to do. The Synectics no longer tolerate such attentions, and the chamber now has a security lock."

"What about the bio-monitors?" asked Quetri. "I assume we're allowed to study *them*?"

"Indeed, but they've been moved to an adjacent room. You'll find we do many things differently."

"May I - " Quetri's voice came out as a croak; he coughed and tried again. "May I see the monitors?"

"If you must." Clovath still hadn't so much as glanced at him. He led the way, though Quetri knew it perfectly well. They passed the commonroom, which seemed remarkably quiet - so quiet, in fact, that Quetri paused to look in. A moment later he'd planted himself furiously in front of Clovath and forced him to halt.

"They're *all* reducees!"

"Strictly speaking, they're not. Their conversion was carried out by our leading physicians, not a rabble of passers-by. Each man retains his technical skill and everything else he needs to carry out his duties. He can function in an emergency, hold a meaningful conversation - even write loving letters to his family."

And each and every one is terrified of you, Quetri felt like adding. Then, aloud: "Did the Synectics initiate this?"

"Of course. They want guaranteed loyalty. You, apparently, have already convinced them of yours." Clovath thrust Quetri to one side and continued down the corridor. Just before the entrance to the Synectics' domain a new observation point had been set up. Gone

426

were the column-mounted control systems, and in their place was a single huge screen displaying each Synectic's bio-signs on a rotating basis. Quetri drew in his breath sharply. The shrivelled beings in the stasis tubes were barely alive now, their sustenance cut to almost nothing - and yet their neural activity blazed from the screen with an intensity hitherto unmeasured.

"All that energy!" he whispered in awe.

"Impressive, isn't it, zyl Nyris? And all dedicated to one purpose!"

Quetri turned to face him, startled. "Which is?"

"You mean they didn't *tell* you?" Clovath's expression was one of religious fervour. "They're keeping the sun stable until we're all safe, even though the effort is killing them. It's their final act of self-sacrifice."

"They told you that?" Quetri's voice had sunk to a whisper again.

"They speak to me," Clovath intoned with pride. "*She* speaks to me."

The woman again, Quetri thought bleakly. No one else could invent such wicked lies.

Clovath gazed down indulgently from his superior height. "For all your fine airs I doubt if you ever received such confidences," he remarked.

"No," replied Quetri, trying to look humble, though he was secretly fraught with desperation. How was he to persuade this zealot to let him into the stasis chamber?

"Lord Clovath," he said eventually, "it may well be that the Synectics have evolved to the point where they find our proximity irksome. Nevertheless, they *are* still dependent on us. Out of my great love for this project, I entreat you to allow me into the chamber just once. The stasis units are not infallible and I'm well versed in detecting trouble before it happens."

Clovath deliberated for a while, observing the monitor. "Number Five's waste tube is partially blocked," he observed. "You may deal with that if you like. I'll grant you admittance for today only." He tapped briefly on a keyboard, then looked up with a cruel smile. "There. All done. Your password is 'slave'."

Before Quetri could think of a suitable reply, an extremely apologetic worker bustled in. "Forgive the interruption, my lords," he began, "but we've just decrypted a news update from Rhul. The Celestrians who tried to bomb our capital have been caught and their trial is to be relayed by transposer to our TV network."

"So soon?" murmured Quetri.

"Our people are efficient," Clovath told him airily. "I heard from my government contact this morning. Apparently they'd had their eye on someone for days, and he wasn't averse to betraying his associates." He suddenly rounded on the menial, who'd been hovering indecisively. "Are you still here?"

"Your...your pardon, lord," the man stammered. "I wanted to ask....that is, the others have been wondering..."

"Get to the point!"

"It's possible, isn't it, to tie in our transposer to the telecast? We....we all want to see this trial, Lord Clovath - please?" He looked as if he might cry.

"You see how his devotion to the Protectorate transcends his awe of me," Clovath remarked to Quetri. "To be honest, I wouldn't mind seeing those dissolute little vermin get their comeuppance - but the Synectics have strict rules governing the use of the transposer. It impinges on their thinking in some way. Still, for the sake of my workers' morale, I must ask. Come with me." He strode toward the chamber door, then looked round irritably when he realised Quetri was not following. "Well, what's keeping you? You couldn't wait to get in here a moment ago!"

Quetri had no choice but to go after him. Clovath would doubtless want to do all the communicating himself, but it was still a perilous situation. He had visions of babbling out his mission under the yellow scrutiny of the hag.

The stasis tubes' carapaces were shut. Clovath approached the tube on the far right and, striking an attitude, began his plea. We did it better, Navarian and I, Quetri reflected sombrely. We weren't so obsequious.

The metal shell around the unit opened with a clang and he nearly jumped out of his skin, but a moment later he saw that he would never again fear the hag's gaze. She no longer had any eyes. Her reply struck effortlessly through his shields:

+We will permit the use of the transposer. It is important that you should witness the fall of your adversaries, and we look forward to sharing your victory+

Clovath uttered his thanks. +I bring you Quetri zyl Nyris+ he added, much to Quetri's consternation.

+It is noted. We will converse with him later+ came the response, lacking the edge of the first. The Synectic mind was already preoccupied elsewhere. +We will meditate for the duration of the telecast. Make no further representation until it is over+

Quetri stood glued to the spot while Clovath performed more self-abasement. There had been a remote, almost numinous quality to the encounter which had never been there before. He felt as if he were balanced on the edge of a vast precipice. The Synectics had refined and strengthened their pattern almost to the point where they could detach it from their corporeal remains, and no doubt their meditation would advance that process still further. Then, just as Clovath was about to usher him from the chamber, he noticed something odd about the stasis units. There were only nine of them.

"Arbros died," Clovath said indifferently.

"Arbros? The founder?" echoed Quetri. "How could he die, with so many failsafes?"

"He died," Clovath repeated.

Quetri fell silent, suddenly realising what must have happened. Arbros was the oldest, and therefore the weakest. The other Synectics had discarded him, probably absorbing his energies in the process.

"Wake up!" advised Clovath, giving him a shove. "You'll be even less use than I thought if you keep daydreaming. Now, let's see if we can make space for ourselves in Communications. That transmission must be about to start."

Quetri lagged behind on the way back and, encountering the pilot about to re-enter the airlock, bade him a safe journey.

"Zyl Nyris."

Quetri halted, surprised to hear the taciturn individual speak his name. "What is it?"

"Now that you've seen them," said the other man ambiguously - it was not clear whether he meant the Synectics or the reducees - "are you sure you wish to stay?"

"I have to," Quetri replied staunchly. "It's my duty."

The pilot gave him an unfathomable stare. "Then I wish you joy of it," he said. The airlock thudded shut and Quetri was alone with his enemies.

***

"I still say you shouldn't have come with me," said Idenion, on the threshold of the lab. It was still very early, and a damp mist hung over the city. Laura pulled her cloak more tightly about her.

"Idenion, we waited all last night for something to happen. The Narvellans are just the same as ever, so the operation couldn't have succeeded. Maybe the sphere missed its target. And I'm not going to sit on my backside stitching overalls when all the answers are *here*, on this lateral!"

"All the danger, too," Idenion remarked as he eased open the lab door. "You can't sense it but there's Moderator spoor everywhere this morning."

"That doesn't mean I'd be safer at home." Laura walked briskly past him and vanished into the catering area. "Now, let's see if there's anything in the way of breakfast. I'm sorry I ran out of grain cakes - Dena always dealt with that."

Idenion made no reply, or none that she could hear.

"I've found some liman," Laura continued, opening and closing cupboards. "No food, though. I'll see if Drusa's got any to spare. And then I'd better go and find Tralvar."

"We'll take you to him," said a Moderator as she emerged from the kitchen.

"All part of the service," said another. They'd obviously been inside the lab all along. One of them had Idenion held fast, gauntleted fingers entwined in his hair. His hands had been tied, and a fading red blotch on his face indicated that he'd received a token slap.

"We've got to be careful with our favourite poet," remarked the second Moderator, laughing unpleasantly. "Lord Narad's orders. But we haven't had any orders about *you*, girl." And he pushed Laura roughly, sending her stumbling backwards. A moment later, her booted foot lashed out; the kick missed his groin and landed less painfully on his hip.

"Don't!" cried Idenion, trying to twist free of his captor's grasp. "You'll only make things worse!"

Laura ignored this advice. "If you want a fight, you've got one," she spat; but the Moderator did not retaliate. He was staring at her in alarm and astonishment.

"What *are* you?" he demanded.

And Laura knew, without meeting Idenion's despairing gaze, that her prill was dead. The Moderators, unsettled by this turn of events and anxious to hand responsibility to someone else, hurried their two prisoners outside.

Lydion, leaving Drusa's lodgings for his morning's work, was just in time to see the quartet disappearing up the hill toward the akron. In consternation he took off at a sprint toward Tralvar's house, not pausing for breath until he was inside. There was movement in the study. He flung himself at the half-open door, calling out before he reached it: "Tralvar, we've got to make a run for it! Everyone's being arrested - "

Too late, he realised the extent of his mistake. The two Moderators who had been ransacking the room let go their spoils and closed in on him.

"I'm delighted to see you here, Lydion of Atris," said a voice he knew. He just had time to recognise the man he'd humiliated at the retracer lab before a gloved fist smashed into his face.

He lay motionless where he'd fallen, despite an urge to writhe in pain. If they thought he was unconscious maybe they wouldn't hit him any more.

"What did you do that for?" asked the other Moderator irritably.

"He was resisting arrest," replied Lydion's attacker blandly.

"Oh, I get it!" said his friend. "He's the one who made you imbibe that pornography. Well, thanks to your grudge, we'll have to carry him to the akron. And

432

while we're doing that, you can decide what you're going to say to Axmiol about pre-empting the verdict."

Meanwhile, Idenion and Laura were halfway across the plaza in the company of their guards. It seemed to Laura that nothing else could possibly go wrong, but then a passer by - a scolia woman - halted and stared at her incredulously.

"First Singer!"

Laura frantically waved her away, but too late. Her cry had attracted the attention of two men delivering liman, and in no time there was a small knot of people keeping pace with them as they neared the akron.

"Who *are* you?" Laura's captor demanded. "Why do they follow you?"

She remained silent.

"Then you'll tell your story to Axmiol," he declared. Axmiol, however, was fully occupied with his outside broadcast team and would brook no interruption. So at length she found herself being offered breakfast by Myrig, urbane as always, although he looked as if he'd only had half a night's sleep.

"Well, Lisset - or should that be Laura? Or maybe even Clemoridys?" he inquired. "What have you to say?"

Laura had the distinct feeling that he'd known who she was all along. "What's the point in my saying anything? You must have all the answers by now."

"I wouldn't be too sure," Myrig smiled. "Neither I nor my men are familiar with the nonconversant mind. Your memory may contain all manner of treasures, but they're buried in a kaleidoscope of trivia. Humour me, if you will. If I keep my questions non-political, will you provide a little information? I'm curious about the way you simulated telepathy. Maybe we could start with that."

433

She took off her scieshanar, unsealed it and handed it to him. "A prill seed. The adult plant is used in the retracer."

"This shielded you?" Myrig nudged the dead seed gently.

"That was my second. They don't take kindly to my emotions, you see. I lost the first one through being miserable and that one because I was furious."

Myrig took his drink over to the window and looked out. The small knot of people hadn't dispersed. "As you love Idenion so much, why the long separation?"

"Tralvar didn't want me back."

"Oh?" He peered at her over his cup.

"He was in love with me too. And he knew I didn't love *him*."

Myrig chuckled. "So you spurned the First Citizen, did you? Wasn't that a trifle foolhardy in the light of what happened to your predecessor?"

Laura shrugged.

"Please - help yourself to more bread and cake. I'll see your friends are fed, if that's what's worrying you."

Laura hesitated before speaking. The Moderator had said that Narad would protect Idenion; she believed that, and adjusted her words accordingly. "I'm concerned about Dena. She genuinely didn't do anything except give me shelter. Please let her go."

Myrig pondered this for a moment. "It seems to me," he said at last, "that you've been keeping more secrets from eachother than you have from us. Finish your meal in peace - I won't question you further."

"Why not?" Laura suspected a trick.

"Axmiol instructed me to verify your identity, and nothing more. This I've now done. Interestingly, he asked me not to divulge it to anyone else. He believes it will make good television." He glanced outside again;

the group of people had doubled in size. "And I rather think he's right."

Elsewhere in the akron, Lydion was nursing a badly bruised cheekbone and listening to Tralvar berating him.

"What were you thinking of, you idiot? I'm grateful for your altruism, but what made you go charging in there like that? You were in the clear - Corython didn't know about you."

"But Laura did." Lydion seemed resigned to his lot. "I'd have been picked up sooner or later. Anyway, listen: when I was pretending to be stunned I heard something worth repeating. Jarras and Rillan still haven't been found, and Axmiol's livid at having to make do with us."

"Rillan's probably on Myrma," opined Tralvar. "He knows the co-ordinates by heart. And wherever Jarras went, I hope he avoids - "

He was interrupted by the arrival of a Narvellan - not a Moderator, but one of the technicians. "Lydion of Atris?"

Lydion looked up wearily. "What is it *now*?"

"We can't sustain the transposal link to Narvella. Axmiol requires your assistance."

Lydion was scandalised. "At my own trial?"

The young man cleared his throat. "I am empowered to say: help us and there may be a chance of a plea bargain."

"Do it, Lydion!" urged Idenion.

"No chance," he answered ruefully. "I couldn't concentrate with my face like this. It hurts, you know!"

"Axmiol is aware that you require healing," said the technician. "And to that end I bring you Tarlatine, wife to Lord Besu." He stood aside and a young, nervous elite-wife entered the room. She wore the regulation grey gown, but still looked extremely lovely. Lydion immediately stopped scowling.

"But Besu's *ancient*!" Idenion murmured, and was hushed by Tralvar.

"Tarlatine is an accomplished healer," continued her escort. "Permit her to treat your injury, Lydion of Atris, and then we will re-examine Axmiol's request."

Tarlatine came forward and placed her exquisitely manicured fingers on Lydion's damaged cheek. Commendably, he kept his hands to himself as she leant over him.

"Isn't that just typical of his luck?" Idenion remarked to Tralvar. "He gets a beautiful elite-wife as healer, and I get Narad!"

"You'll be glad of that soon," Tralvar whispered back.

Lydion's bruise didn't fade, but the pain from it obviously did. "Ah, that feels marvellous, golden girl!" he said when she'd finished. "Are you doing anything later?"

She skittered away, then looked back with a shy smile.

"Are you ready to accompany us, Lydion?" asked the technician patiently.

"I suppose so," he conceded. "While you're about it, why don't you ask the First Poet to provide a radio commentary? He's good at that."

"We have engaged the actor Forlane," the youth replied.

Lydion shot Idenion an apologetic glance. "Well, it was worth a try. I'd better go, people. I'll be back with you if I don't get this right - or even if I do!"

The door slammed on the three remaining prisoners.

"This is farcical!" Tralvar declared. "It's all about usefulness, not justice. I'm sure they won't have arrested Drusa - she's too good at steering relayists and Directresses through their identity crises. And where's

Kyrin? They must know of his involvement by now, but they don't want to deprive themselves of his services."

"Then we'll just have to persuade them that *we're* indispensable," Idenion said philosophically. "Corython, you've been very quiet. Please don't give up hope - we're going to get through this!"

Corython gave him a sorrowful stare. "You, maybe; and Tralvar. But neither of you were actively involved with Operation Ipsa. Lydion says Jarras and Rillan have evaded capture - so who does that leave? Me. The only saboteur to stand trial. Admit it, Idenion - I'm as good as dead."

For once, Idenion could think of nothing to reassure him.

The trial began shortly after mid-day. The prisoners were collected from their rooms by silent, grim-faced Moderators and escorted downstairs to the largest stateroom. Near its entrance, all was chaos and clutter: arc lamps, cables, a portable generator, and a huge banqueting table which had been dragged into the corridor. But once through the doors, order prevailed. Banners displaying the logo of the officiating TV network, green letters on gold, adorned the otherwise bare walls. A dais with a central staircase had been erected for Axmiol and the other dignitaries. Rows of chairs, occupied by surly Narvellan men, faced it. Stun-cannon, presently unattended, had been placed at either end of the central aisle.

Under the merciless artificial light, Laura, Dena, Idenion, Tralvar and Corython walked in single file toward the front of the hall, passing a cluster of prying lenses. "Fixed cameras," Laura remarked to her companions. "How quaint!" There was no sign of Lydion or Forlane. She assumed they were upstairs in the radio room. She continued walking, selfconscious rather than fearful, trying not to imagine how many eyes must be upon her.

To either side of the judges an attendant in green livery stood motionless. One held a ceremonial mace, the other an open scroll bearing the Protectorate's motto: "Moderation in All Things." On the floor at a right angle to the dais was a series of chalk marks and a handrail. In the rush to equip the room, there had not been time to install anything more permanent. The prisoners were ordered to step onto the markings and wait. A large microphone shaped like a teardrop hung poised above them, ready to convey their every utterance to the waiting worlds.

We're a sorry-looking lot, Laura thought. Tralvar's uniform doesn't fit him anymore, Idenion's still wearing that horrid ylur overall, and Corython looks as if he's slept in that tunic. And what about me? I wasn't even allowed to comb my hair. Dena's the only one who looks presentable.

Axmiol, in a knee-length coat of plain silver, rose to address them. There was no preamble, no concession to the Narvellan viewers: presumably the station presenters on Narvella Prime had taken care of that, along with some means of translation.

"I always suspected you Celestrians were not the pacifists you claimed to be," Axmiol began, "but this act of breathtaking barbarity - launching a missile against our homeworld - shows an aspect of you which appals me. My main regret is that we failed to capture two of your henchmen." He consulted some papers in front of him. "Jarras of Kest and Rillan of Treva, assembly workers, are hereby sentenced to death in their absence. As for the rest of you, the law dictates that you be given a chance to speak in your own defence. You may now do so - but be warned that any spurious or hostile comments may have an adverse effect on your

438

sentencing. You may not use your perception or discuss your statements amongst yourselves."

"Lord Axmiol," said Idenion instantly, "may I enter a plea for leniency on behalf of my sister? She only knew of the conspiracy because she shares a dwelling with me. She's done nothing."

"Done nothing, you say?" queried Axmiol with a certain malicious amusement. "Let me bring you up to date. Your overseer, Chisrin ap Tuin, became suspicious of your mysterious flitter journeys and clandestine meetings. To buy his silence, Dena seduced him; and furthermore, she is now with child by him."

"Dena?" cried Idenion disbelievingly. "No, no, Axmiol - this is a lie. It has to be."

"When Chisrin realised his folly and threatened to go to the authorities," Axmiol continued inexorably, "your sister fled to the First Citizen. She now enjoys his protection - for what it's worth."

Idenion looked from Dena to Tralvar in utter bewilderment.

"Not so innocent, is she, First Poet?" Axmiol remarked. "How unobservant you've been. But of course, you've had other matters to occupy you." He turned to Dena with one of his famous icy stares. "Do you deny this is the truth?"

"That would be futile," she replied distinctly, her head high. "But allow me to correct one statement, if I may. I am under no-one's protection. Tralvar is my partner in unity."

Laura and Tralvar regarded her admiringly. Idenion merely stared, realising for the first time how she'd changed. She was no longer the unworldly custodian of the Lyricon, nor a timid virgin. She was the First Citizen's consort.

"One moment, cousin!" came a familiar voice, and Chisrin stepped forward. The accused had their backs to him and had failed to notice his presence in the hall.

Axmiol frowned, not wishing to be reminded of his family connection with the disgraced overseer. "You weren't supposed to speak unless she denied the charges."

"And *you* weren't supposed to infer I was weakwilled," Chisrin retorted. "She didn't seduce me - I blackmailed her into submission. And I couldn't have cared less about her secret. I just wanted to get across her."

Idenion, incensed, launched himself forward. More by luck than accuracy, his fist connected with Chisrin's jaw. It was only a glancing blow, but its sheer unexpectedness sent Chisrin staggering back against the dais.

"Enough!" roared Axmiol. "First Poet, must I tie you to that rail? This is a court of law, not a circus!"

Idenion grudgingly returned to his position, massaging his bruised knuckles. "He will pay!"

"That is not for you to decide," Axmiol pronounced.

During the brief conflict, an aide had beckoned Narad from his place among the judges. He now resumed it and murmured something to Axmiol, who looked mildly perturbed.

"Are they causing an affray?"

"No, quite the opposite. They're just - waiting."

"Then let them wait." Axmiol turned his piercing gaze on Laura. "Narad is concerned because you've attracted a crowd - quite a large one. Perhaps you'd care to explain to him, and anyone else who may be interested, why you're able to command such a following."

"She is the First Singer," Idenion answered for her. "She is Clemoridys."

440

"Really, Idenion!" Narad said reprovingly. "You do yourself no good by lying at a time like this. Clemoridys is an ideal. She doesn't exist."

Axmiol leant forward to address his colleague. "You're not well acquainted with Celestrian history, are you, Narad?"

"I'm afraid not, Lord Governor. It fell outside my line of study."

"Whereas poetry was more worthy of your attention," said Axmiol superciliously. "You may not, therefore, be familiar with the name Alendis."

"I know that he was First Citizen before Tralvar. I assume Tralvar did away with him."

"Not so. In order to rid themselves of a sybaritic and unpopular leader, the Celestrians acquired the services of one Laura of Gilcoyne, from the planet they call Symerid Three. The girl also possessed a unique singing voice and it was that which rallied the people to her - and inspired Idenion's verses. As for the woman known as Lisset: when the device hiding her nonconversant state failed earlier today, her true identity became obvious. She is the same assassin the Celestrians hired to kill Alendis."

"You mean - she's been working to destroy *us*?" exclaimed Narad.

"Without a doubt."

"*Now* I understand! Tralvar could never head a successful rebellion because the people wouldn't back him. But they'd follow her - *have* been following her!"

"Your guilt is proven, Laura of Gilcoyne," Axmiol declared.

"You haven't let me say anything yet," she objected.

"Best not to," Idenion whispered in her ear.

"Ah yes, First Poet. Now we come to *you*." Axmiol was positively purring.

441

"With respect, my lord," said Narad swiftly, "it's obvious that Idenion has only played a passive role in the conspiracy, and this solely because he has been traduced and deceived by that woman. If you will give him into my custody as..." He hesitated a moment - "as a house guest, I will stand surety for his good behaviour."

Tralvar caught Idenion's eye. The look said, "save yourself!"

"I recommend you make use of this opportunity," Axmiol advised. "You may not like the alternatives."

Idenion was under no illusion about the true meaning of house guest. "I accept," he replied sombrely, "but only if Narad will guarantee Laura's safety."

"Out of the question!" snapped Axmiol.

"You'd better negotiate it, Narad," pursued Idenion. "If Laura dies my life is meaningless, and you'll have gained nothing but my hatred."

"I could have you reduced," Narad warned.

"But that isn't what you want, is it?" said Idenion softly.

"Idenion!" Laura flung herself into his arms and clung to him frantically. Surprisingly, no one tried to separate them. "Don't do this. Please don't do this!"

"I've no choice, dearest," he replied, smoothing her tousled hair. "If I refuse they'll reduce me and then I'd go with him anyway."

Myrig whispered something to Axmiol, who grudgingly acquiesced. "Myrig believes we should send the girl back to her homeworld. He says that if we make a martyr of her, there will be prolonged insurrection."

"I won't go!" Laura shouted.

"Laura, enough!" Tralvar pleaded. The more she continued to make herself the centre of attention the more she risked being read - something he hoped to avert as long as possible.

442

"Ah, First Citizen." Axmiol regaled him with a cold smile. "I was wondering when you'd join in the discussion. You've presented us with a thorny problem. We don't wish to lose you as we of the elite have enjoyed a good working relationship with you over the years. On the other hand, you've given your tacit support to the activities of these rebels. I suppose you'll want to tell us you were duped or misled...?"

"Don't insult me, Axmiol. Without my instigation there would have been no plot. I'm only sorry that my civic duties prevented me from helping them further, but I offered my assistance whenever I could."

"Even while you were wenching, boozing or pounding the zirid?" Axmiol retaliated. "It's very noble of you to try and shoulder the blame, but it's obvious you were little more than a bystander. So, the Protectorate will give you the opportunity to redeem yourself. You'll be a different man from now on."

They're going to reduce me, Tralvar thought bleakly. He'd never considered they'd opt for that, not in his case. He bowed his head as if accepting the decision, but inwardly he was desperately defiant. I won't let them do it, he resolved. If all else fails I'll force them to kill me. I'd have to kill a few of *them* to accomplish that; I wonder how I might -

"And so to the last." Axmiol's incisive tones jolted him back to the present. He glanced sideways at Corython: the young mathematician looked terrified. And here, thought Tralvar, is where it all starts coming apart. He'll babble on about Ipsa and the Synectics, and then the game will be up. Quetri, my lad, are you out there? You'd better work fast!

"Corython of Alcine," Axmiol went on briskly, "since you have already admitted your guilt the verdict against you is foregone. I have the material evidence here: your calculations, which you tried to burn. You directed a missile against Narvella Prime - "

"I did no such thing!" protested Corython.

" - which, had it not malfunctioned, would have caused devastation on a global scale," Axmiol concluded, brandishing the folder he had in front of him.

"Let me see that," Corython demanded.

"Certainly," said Axmiol pleasantly. He signalled to the aide, who took the document and conveyed it disinterestedly to its author.

Corython leafed rapidly through the folder. "This isn't my work," he objected, holding up the last two pages.

"The original was badly burnt. We reconstructed it."

Corython scanned the substituted formulae. "This is nonsense!" he yelled, much to everyone's surprise. A slur on his work was possibly the only thing which could have made him forget his peril and lose his temper. "You've incorporated six deliberate errors here, just so you could make that arc go where you wanted it to." He flung the papers to the floor. "The target was Ipsa. And even if Ipsa hadn't been there, the sphere was travelling *away* from Narvella Prime!"

"Ipsa. A lifeless moon. Rather a strange target, wouldn't you say?"

"There's an underground laboratory on Ipsa, housing the Synectics. Does that mean anything to you, Axmiol? I doubt if it does. The Synectics control you and every other Narvellan in this room!"

"As a matter of fact, I *do* remember the Synectic project," Axmiol replied coolly. "If I may refresh everyone's memories: the Synectic group mind, or Pahl-drehinor in our language, was formed to help solve our ecological problems - to increase food production and enable us to cope with climate change. This they

444

did, very successfully. After the Celestrian treaty, the group did indeed transfer to Ipsa in secret. They went on to create the industrial crystals which power most of our spacecraft."

"Axmiol, may I speak?" An agitated Chisrin thrust his way forward.

"You may not," Axmiol replied without looking at him. "Well, Corython, that's an interesting piece of intelligence - but several years out of date. After a promising start with the crystals the group consistently failed to deliver anything useful, and an order was given to terminate its funding. After more than twenty years in cocoons I doubt if any individuals survived."

"The project was *not* terminated," insisted Corython.

"I endorsed the order myself." Axmiol was growing irritable.

"Axmiol," Chisrin persisted, "if he says they're still there, shouldn't someone at least go and look? My wife - "

"Silence!" thundered Axmiol. "One more interruption and I'll have you removed from this court. So, Corython, your idiosyncratic defence is that you set out to murder a harmless bunch of elderly scientists. I fail to see how that's supposed to win our sympathy. By the way, who told you about the Synectics?"

As he spoke, Axmiol shifted his focus to Laura. Before she or Idenion realised she was under scrutiny, the Lord Governor had his information.

"You retraced the bondservant Quetri - and induced the madness in him!" he breathed. "And then the First Citizen took him as his neph-khet. To groom him for - what?"

Tralvar felt Axmiol's icy consciousness beating at his shields. Besu joined in, followed by Narad. Tralvar held out against the deep probe, but the Narvellans merely transferred their efforts to Dena, who gave a despairing cry as the knowledge was torn from her.

"You faked that quarrel with the boy, Tralvar!" Narad bellowed. "Your doxy's somewhere in Rhul with a bomb!"

"Priority alert." Axmiol, calm again, gestured to the nearest cameraman, who trundled his unwieldy machine as close as he could. The five prisoners watched helplessly. Everyone waited.

"Citizens of the Protectorate," Axmiol continued in Narvellan, "I charge you with this task: find and execute Quetri zyl Nyris!"

Chapter Fourteen

Quetri didn't hear his death sentence pronounced. He had - foolishly perhaps - watched the telecast long enough to see Tralvar's measured confession ruined by inane subtitles; then, reluctantly, had slipped away from the other men and hurried to his room. Carefully, he unpacked Tralvar's devices and tucked the detonator into a back pocket while he carried the bomb to the Synectics.

The big screen idled, showing the occupants were in trance mode. Quetri approached them noiselessly and planted the bomb about six paces from the row of tubes, next to an old bio-monitor pedestal. He was just backing out of the chamber when someone seized him violently and slammed him against the rocky wall of the corridor. He heard something crack - a rib perhaps - and wondered why he wasn't in more pain. He rolled sideways, came to his feet and found himself confronting an enraged Clovath.

"Alien-lover! Dirty little spy! Axmiol says he wants you dead and it'll be a privilege to do my duty!"

"Reducees cannot form a Ten," Quetri said levelly.

Clovath smirked and bunched his fists. "Who needs one? The airlock will take care of you!"

For the first and only time, Quetri was grateful to Tarysk tyl Pellon. She'd forced him to service her in bed, made him wait hand and foot on her obnoxious friends, chastised and branded him. But she'd also made him learn unarmed combat, as it amused her to watch the household servants fight one another. Quetri had usually lost the bouts, but at that time he hadn't been fighting for his life. Now, as he faced a murderous foe, the correct moves came instinctively to him. And when Clovath was lying semi-conscious on the ground, he found a

447

loose chunk of rock and methodically beat his attacker's brains out.

Furtive figures hovered in the shadows: the reducees, summoned by Clovath as he struggled. It was their blind subservience which had sealed his fate.

"Get back, all of you!" snarled Quetri, waving the bloodstained rock.

They obeyed.

Quetri gave an inward sigh of relief. Not only were they incapable of forming a Ten, but now that their leader was dead they couldn't even fight. "This base is under new management," he announced. "In future you will take your orders from me - is that clear?"

"Yes, Lord Quetri," they chorused.

"Louder."

"Yes, Lord Quetri!"

"Good. My first order is, go back to the telecast. I've work to do."

They dispersed obediently. Suddenly nauseated, Quetri spat out a few mouthfuls of bile. He dropped the rock and used his overshirt to scrub most of the gore from his hands. As soon as everyone was well clear he positioned himself on the Synectics' threshold, reaching into his pocket for the detonator - but to his utter dismay found it in two pieces, the casing smashed open and the mechanism irreparably damaged. He remembered the crack he'd heard when Clovath had thrown him against the wall, and for a moment allowed despair to overwhelm him.

Then, reviving, he raised his head. I can still do this, he told himself. What was it Tralvar said? Therite exists to explode - it can't help it. So all I have to do is puncture the container somehow and let the mythol evaporate. It's only a form of glass - surely I can punch a hole in that?

But what he couldn't do was wander off and look for tools. Firstly there was no time - the trial was nearly over and his friends were counting on him. Secondly, he had no idea who else had access to the stasis chamber. The reducees might not have the courage to fight him but they were perfectly capable of moving the bomb.

He ventured down the corridor beyond the chamber, keeping the entrance in view. He was perturbed at how many minor rockfalls there had been. The Synectics were more than able to scan their environment, and if they hadn't insisted that the roof was made safe there could only be one reason. They didn't intend to stay under it much longer.

He began hunting for flints amongst the debris and small boulders, at first discovering only small useless pieces. Then, at last, he found one he thought would do: undersized, impure, but with a sharp chisel edge on one side.

The bomb sat innocuously where he'd left it. Almost selfconsciously, feeling as if he were his own primitive ancestor, Quetri struck down with the flint. It glanced off the curved surface. He tried again, harder; and again, half expecting the device to blow up in his face. On the fourth attempt a network of cracks suddenly appeared, accompanied by a scarcely audible hissing. Quetri caught the faint sickly scent of mythol. He raised the flint one last time to broaden the fissure - and to his horror found he couldn't lower his arm. Then he saw a golden light shining under and around the sealed chamber door, and knew that in the next room the bio-screen had resumed its full activity. The Synectics were awake. And even as he tried to break away and flee, he was lifted effortlessly off his feet and carried almost playfully to the nearest wall. There they held him, spreadeagled and immovably trapped, high above the cavern floor. The stasis units were almost directly below him, and to one side the bomb, with its tiny trickle of escaping mist. Nothing else moved. The carapaces of the units remained shut. But in his mind, the hateful voice of the hag crooned with benign reproof.

+Little Quetri, how foolish of you! Were you trying to emulate your beloved guardian? We'll just keep you out of harm's way for a while. Later you will provide energy for the loop+

Quetri tried vainly to shut her out. The pattern was everywhere about him, much as Lydion must have perceived it. It lay coiled, pulsing, powerful, waiting to unleash itself into the void. The still-active transposal beam tweaked irritatingly at its extremities. Quetri must have made some kind of protest, for the hag continued:

+But we *do* need you, little one; a poor substitute though you are for Clovath. All that fire and anger! He would have nourished us well+

+Sarune, there is danger+ The other Synectics' thoughts were as brittle as breaking twigs.

+I will neutralise the explosive+ she placated them. +And then, Quetri, you will assist the metamorphosis you tried so hard to prevent!+

***

"The evidence is concluded," said Axmiol. "Does anyone wish to speak before I pass sentence?"

"What good would that do?" Corython inquired wearily. "You won't change your mind."

"And is this the opinion of you all?"

Tralvar, although he wanted to prolong the hearing, could think of nothing else to add. No-one spoke.

"Very well," said Axmiol. A silver pen drifted through the air to his outstretched hand. Laura was disconcerted, it being the first time she'd seen Narvellan telekinesis. The others looked indifferent, and Tralvar yawned ostentatiously. Axmiol wrote steadily for a time, then set down the pen and folded his hands. "The sentence of this court is as follows. Idenion, First Poet, your punishment is reduction, commuted to house arrest under the auspices of Narad zyl Pereth. Should he have cause to doubt your contrition, the original sentence will be implemented. Dena, Custodian of the Lyricon and Celebrant of the Scolia, your punishment is death by the appointed Ten - "

Before Dena or anyone else could react, Chisrin spoke up. "Hold, Lord Governor!"

Axmiol gave him a murderous look, but did not dismiss him. "The court will hear your objection."

"I claim custody of my unborn child. Under the Rule of Khesa, Dena must remain unharmed until the child is delivered."

Tralvar had never heard of the Rule of Khesa, but it obviously held some significance. Axmiol reluctantly beckoned Chisrin forward and handed him one of the certificates he'd been writing. "Here. For the moment, her life is yours. But from the time she delivers or miscarries, she belongs to the Protectorate."

He did this to save her, Tralvar thought, and immediately resented Chisrin for doing what he could not. He heard Laura's banishment pronounced, and perceived her growing agitation. Then it was his turn.

"Tralvar." Axmiol's voice was at its most conciliatory - and its most deadly. "There's such anger in your mind, my friend - such passion and self-loathing. We shall take this burden from you and enable you to serve us diligently and cheerfully. I propose to lead your Five myself, after we've finished here. Sijek, the most gentle of beings, will assist; the remaining three will be chosen for their strength and sensitivity. Thus we will have done everything to ensure you retain your talents, musical and scientific."

"I'm surprised you think I'm worth the trouble," Tralvar retorted. Axmiol merely treated him to a superior smile before turning to Corython.

"Corython of Alcine, I sentence you to death for the attempted destruction of our homeworld. A crime of this magnitude must carry the maximum penalty, and the law directs me to summon the Ten here and now."

Corython stood his ground. "You robbed us of our freedom, our happiness. What right had you - " The sound boom and the teardrop-shaped microphone suddenly swung away, indicating that the prisoners no longer had a voice. At a sign from Axmiol, the men in the front row stood up and moved forward.

"Idenion, look!" gasped Laura. "They're not an audience - they're executioners!"

As she spoke there was a sudden commotion at the far end of the hall. Several Moderators were struggling with a very determined young man, and it was unclear whether they were trying to expel him or drag him forward. Eventually they opted for the latter.

Axmiol directed his best baleful glare at the leading Moderator. "Hapka? What is the meaning of this hullabaloo?"

"Your pardon, Lord Governor, for disrupting the trial. This madness victim insisted on breaking in here. We tried to head him off but you know what they're like."

Axmiol's irritation was supplanted by sudden anxiety. "Bring him to me at once. These proceedings will have to wait."

As the captive was led toward the dais Laura gave a cry of astonishment. "Quon!"

He turned a haunted gaze on her.

"Idenion, it's Quon - from the liman mill!"

452

Idenion had recognised him. "If he's truly free, what in chaos is he doing here?" he muttered. "He'll never get out alive."

Quon, though clearly in a state of distress, spoke up bravely. The overhead microphone came sidling back to eavesdrop. "Lord Axmiol, I am Quon zyl Apteris, overseer at Etys Point Mill. You may remember that I led the Ten in the hunt for Firessa lyr Raxel."

"I remember the incident," Axmiol replied indifferently.

"I delivered my annual report to the akron today," Quon continued. "When the broadcast began I stayed to listen." He hurried his words, knowing that Axmiol would soon lose patience. "Ever since Firessa's execution I've felt as if I were living a lie - and when I heard Corython speak of the Synectics it was as if someone had woken me from a long nightmare. He's telling the truth!"

"Axmiol, you cannot ignore this!" pleaded Chisrin.

"Chisrin ap Tuin." Axmiol's response was surprisingly restrained. "I've been tolerant with you because your wife - and, need I remind you, my cousin - sacrificed herself to the Synectic project. I too would like to believe she still lives. But can you not see what's happened here? Quon zyl Apteris was following the trial on the radio when he became delusional." Then, to Quon: "Unhappy youth, you should not regret having served in a Ten. Be proud you did your duty."

Besu plucked at Axmiol's sleeve and spoke plaintively in Narvellan. His reedy voice carried easily to Idenion's sharp ears: "In the name of decency, do away with him. He'll infect us all!"

Axmiol frowned. "Peace, old one: the boy knows what to expect. We can at least be humane about it. Quon, I commend you for submitting yourself to this court but there is nothing we can grant you except a swift and merciful death."

"You must listen to me," Quon entreated. "These are not criminals!"

"End the poor lad's life, relieve his suffering!" cried Narad, genuine compassion in his voice.

The Ten closed their circle.

"Wait!" Idenion left his place and broke recklessly into their midst - just as he'd tried to do at the shaming of Isylla. "You can't execute a defence witness. He's just verified our story!"

"Do we now give credence to the insane?" inquired Axmiol at his most patronising. He gestured to the Ten, who impatiently thrust Idenion aside and ranged themselves even closer to their victim.

"We should kill *all* the prisoners!" wheezed Besu. "They are obviously afflicted with the same malady - "

"No, these people are not mad," Axmiol replied testily. "They're merely trying to capitalise on this young man's plight. Fortunately he'll soon be beyond their reach."

Two of the Ten forced Quon to his knees. "Lady Clemoridys!" he cried.

Laura's eyes were bright with tears. "Yes, Quon?"

"I maligned you at our first meeting. Forgive me. Tralvar, Corython....I tried. Forgive - " He drew one last laboured breath, then toppled over gently and lay still. Everyone save Laura was nauseated by the Ten's death-bolt. Chisrin snatched a tumbler of water from the judges' table and took it to Dena.

"Remove the body," Axmiol ordered. "And bring the astronomer here." The Ten lifted Quon and filed out; the second row of men stepped smartly forward. Corython, his face ashen, was marched over to the group by two Moderators.

454

"Corython." Axmiol spoke calmly, with an air of solicitude. "Before you are executed, I offer you one last chance to confess the truth and die honourably. To that end, you may address our nations." The microphone swivelled to hover over the condemned man. "Now, will you not give up this pretence about the Synectics?"

"Chaos take you, Axmiol!" Corython responded with the courage of desperation. "I'll confess to nothing! And why the sudden concern? Is doubt starting to creep in? Are you wondering what happened to your free will?"

Axmiol's temporary calm vanished. "How foolish you are," he said icily, "to adhere to your ridiculous assertions. So be it. Men of the Protectorate, begin."

This is it, thought Tralvar. We're finished. Time to crack a few heads. He leapt at the official holding the mace, wrested it from him and dealt the nearest Moderator a savage blow on the temple. The man crumpled. Without pausing Tralvar swung the mace again, this time hitting one of the Ten just as he raised an arm to protect his head. His elbow broke with a sharp snap. People had begun running and shouting. Tralvar stood poised to defend himself, but everyone retreated from him, leaving him alone and exposed. At either end of the hall, gun crews in protective goggles were aligning the two stun-cannon.

"Tralvar, look out!" screamed Laura - but too late. Both cannon fired simultaneously, spitting lightning. The combined blast knocked Tralvar off his feet and sent him crashing into a row of chairs.

Dena would have run to him but Chisrin held her back. "Don't! The cannon may still have some residual firepower. Tralvar's only stunned. He'll soon revive."

"And *then* what?" Dena asked bitterly.

When the twin rays struck Tralvar he experienced a paralysing cold. The world slowed around him and it seemed he'd never stop falling. Suddenly he was a child again, being dragged by one hand across an endless snowscape. The woman who held him turned to look back at her pursuers, and his small mittened fingers slipped from her grasp. Instantly he was sinking in deep snow, hearing the woman's sobs and the distant voices calling her name:

"Mehedra! Mehedra!"

Then the snow closed over his head and only the cold remained.

***

The pattern pulsed uneasily. The Synectics were at variance with one another. No untrained Narvellan could have sensed their rapid interaction, but Quetri had years of experience. While he hung uselessly from the chamber wall he strained to follow their dispute; perhaps something in it would help him. They didn't trouble to prevent his efforts. They no longer considered him important.

Sarune was in a rage. +Not ready? Not ready? How many more times will you retreat from the brink? We should have made our push long ago!+

+The explosive...?+ came a collective plea.

+Let me finish!+ she shrilled. +Our location is compromised, our plans also. There will be more attempts to destroy us. We cannot remain here+

+If you'd done as I suggested+ answered a firm, resonant thought- pattern, +we would have given the people the solutions they wanted and operated the Pahl-drehinor project with their blessing. And we would not have been in danger now+

Sarune was scornful. +We had no time for their trivial concerns. Our own objectives had to take precedence+

+I'm not sure that yours was the right way+ responded the other Synectic.

456

+Nor I+ proclaimed another.

+Nor I+ echoed a third.

Quetri held his breath at this show of rebellion.

+Craven fools+ Sarune's reply was scathing. +Have we not ventured to the edge of the infinite? Have we not seen the wonders that await us? There is no place in this universe for the feeble. I will deal with the incendiary material, then the traitor - and then we will liberate ourselves!+

Quetri looked down at the bomb. It looked tiny and ineffectual. She'll deactivate it, he thought brokenly. Smother it somehow. Then she'll knock the dissenters into shape, and then.... He couldn't finish the thought.

Sarune poured her awareness into the therite cylinder, confident of success. She'd trained to be a Directress and she knew the ways of minerals at molecular level. Then Quetri sensed a surge of dismay. The mythol had all but vanished, allowing air into the damaged container. The weak chemical bonds of the therite were steadily unravelling, seeking a new and lethal combination with the intruding oxygen. Frantically she tried to reinforce the bonds, but they dissolved faster than she could repair them.

+Assist me!+ she peremptorily ordered the other Synectics.

+Is there a problem?+ they inquired.

+Of course not!+ Sarune's pride led her to be sparing with the truth. +It's a non-native substance and I'm not familiar with it+

But even their united strength was not enough to suppress the chemical change. Quetri felt he would choke on their fear.

+I can't control it!+ Sarune's thoughts wailed. +It's going to detonate. Make ready to ascend. It's our only chance of survival!+

+We are not prepared+ they chorused.

+Do as we rehearsed! Evolve - or die!+

They obeyed in a flurry.

+Good!+ Sermesy encouraged. +Remember, eight is the key. I will unite you. Do it! *Now!*+

Tyvian, thought Quetri sorrowfully. The rule of eight. He showed them the way.

And suddenly there were no more strident commands, no more querulous bickering. There was only a perfect lattice, just like the one which had overwhelmed him outside Tyvian's lab, but infinitely more splendid and powerful. An eight-point figure with Sarune somewhere at its centre.

But - and Quetri hardly dared realise it - not powerful enough. To refine their efforts they released the bomb from their control, and the contents immediately began to smoulder. Then they released *him*. He'd been expecting it, but to no advantage; there was no possible way to break his fall. He tried to roll, but his left side struck solid rock, smashing his arm and shoulder and crushing his hip. The lattice blazed in his mind, bright and terrible, golden as the light streaming under the chamber door. At any moment he expected his life-energy to drain into the Synectic loop.

He'd fallen very close to the bomb. Sobbing with pain, he dragged himself to it and, with his one good arm, seized the greenly glowing cylinder and hurled it straight at Sarune's stasis-unit.

"*Tralvar!*" he screamed.

The chamber erupted in flame.

***

Axmiol gave an impatient nod toward the third row of Ten, and the first in line came forward to replace the injured man. Corython stared straight ahead, his face expressionless.

Laura wept at his simple dignity. "Idenion, I feel so responsible! I got him into this."

458

Corython overheard. "No, Laura, it was my own decision," he said calmly. "Give my love to Pannyra and my son." The Ten laid hold of him but he shrugged them off. "I'll not kneel to you. Begin."

Idenion turned away as the Ten's concentration built, unable to watch Corython die. And then, abruptly, the death-bolt was cut short. A strange silence descended on the hall. His perception closed off, Idenion could only sense a sudden absence of something. A veil had been lifted, but the resulting clarity only brought shock and confusion. Laura gazed uncomprehendingly at the still figures around her - a tableau broken by a slight blur of movement as Corython fell quietly to the floor. Further off, a Moderator and one of the gun crew had also fallen, and Narad had collapsed at the edge of the dais. Axmiol seemed frozen to his chair. Next to him Besu, mouth agape, stared sightlessly at the ceiling. Myrig buried his face in his hands and sobbed.

"It's over! It's over!"

In the radio room, the Narvellan technicians either sat immobile or had wandered off. The monitor had gone blank. Lydion, singlehandedly in charge, punched the panel and uttered an oath borrowed from Laura.

"The transposer's active and we still have sound, but the cameramen must be as pixilated as *this* bunch. Forlane - get down there, grab a microphone and carry on describing what you see. I'll try to keep the transmission going. Everyone must be told how this ended!"

Forlane hurried away. Two of the technicians, emulating normality, ambled in his wake. The remaining one began stumbling about the room, until Lydion seized him and bundled him outside.

"That's better," he muttered. "This lash-up's more likely to stay on the air if no-one collides with it!"

459

The door clicked open again and he wheeled round, assuming one of the workers had returned. Instead he saw Tarlatine, her lovely face streaked with tears.

"My husband is dead," she whispered. "I've been so afraid..."

He surveyed her, enlightened. "You were never part of the Synectic net, were you?"

"No." Her voice trembled. "And I was terrified Besu would find out. Elite-wives don't practice unity, as you know - but he was jealous. He wanted proof that I was faithful."

"But you didn't consent."

"I wouldn't be alive now if I had." She gave another of her nervous smiles. "I must give you more healing. They told me the previous treatment needn't last, because you...wouldn't survive."

"So much for my plea bargain," Lydion remarked. "I appreciate your offer, Tarlatine, but don't your own people need you now?"

"They do," she replied. "But dealing with such trauma - when I'm still so unsure of my way - will not be easy. I want to begin with you. Your good humour will give me confidence for the task ahead." She moved close to him and again placed her hand on his cheekbone. This time it seemed only natural that he should put his arms around her.

As Forlane neared the stateroom he heard someone screaming. It was Chisrin, on his knees, tearing with bloody fingernails at the gold cuff welded to his arm. "Get this off me!" he howled. "Get this off me!"

Forlane looked about for inspiration and singled out Hapka, who was unsuccessfully trying to resuscitate his stricken colleague. "Your friend is dead, Moderator. Would you kindly deal with that noisy individual while he still has a left arm?"

Hapka blinked, shook himself and seemed to recover. He went over to Chisrin and delivered an efficient chop to the back of his neck. The howling ceased.

"Now perhaps I can get a word in," Forlane said caustically - and indeed, the hall was now overly quiet. Laura and Dena were ministering to Tralvar; Idenion, prompted by innate sympathy, had seen Narad move feebly and gone to see if anything could be done for him.

Narad sensed his approach and made another futile attempt to sit up. His hazy eyes held infinite longing - and infinite regret. "Idenion," he whispered. "Idenion...Idenion..." With one final loving look, he died. Idenion stared down in blank dismay. Several dazed, disoriented Narvellans shuffled past, but he didn't raise his head. Then he felt Forlane's brief reassuring touch on his shoulder, and heard the actor's sonorous voice as he took up one of the desk microphones and began the closing speech.

"This is Forlane, speaking once again from the akron. You doubtless heard the lamentation of Chisrin ap Tuin as he struggled to remove his marriage band. His wife was Sarune, leader of the Synectics. For years he has sought her; today he has learnt the extent of her betrayal.

"The great stateroom slowly empties. The governors and administrators, security men, Moderators, weapons experts and conscripts into the Ten - all are dispersing slowly, singly, scarcely able to think for themselves after seven years of the Synectic rule. They stumble away from the scene of this ignominious trial, not even pausing to tend their dead. The Synectics, in their bid to cast off their physical bodies, intended to drain every Narvellan's life energy. I believe I have just seen that process interrupted at a very early stage.

461

"And what of the five people on trial this day, whose selfless actions freed the Narvellans from possession? Corython lies dead, slain by the Ten; Tralvar is unconscious after a stun-blast but, we trust, otherwise unharmed. Dena, his partner in unity, waits for him to revive. Beside me, First Poet Idenion keeps vigil by the body of the Narvellan who desired him. Finally there is Laura - and that, listeners, is surely the end of one story and the beginning of another."

Forlane added a farewell, then switched off the microphone and turned to Idenion. "I hope I wasn't too inaccurate. Lydion told me a few bits and pieces while we were on air, but there's still a great deal I don't understand."

"Accurate or not, I imagine the Narvellan translators will have made nonsense of it." Myrig, weary but rational, came forward to join them. "Don't look so startled! I was never in the Synectics' mind-trap."

"I should have guessed," Idenion said musingly. "Laura was convinced you knew who she was."

"She was right. I didn't know what you were up to but I thought I'd better let you get on with it." Myrig knelt respectfully by Narad, murmured a few ritual phrases and closed the lifeless eyes. "And now, I'd better seek out the rest of the Free. I've a fairly good idea who they are. We'll be needed to pick up the pieces."

"Would you do something else?" asked Idenion. "Call Narvella Prime and have them send a deputation to Ipsa."

"I certainly will. I need to speak with the homeworlds anyway." Myrig hastened off.

"I think I'll disappear too, since my work's done," said Forlane. "I was brought in somewhat peremptorily this morning, and I'd like to finish my bath. Give my regards to Laura."

"Of course." Idenion watched him forge his way through the last of the milling Narvellans, then turned and crossed the aisle to Laura's side. She'd pulled down two of the wall hangings, thrown one over Corython and wrapped Tralvar in the other.

"He's so cold," she explained.

"Where's Dena?"

"She went to instruct Kyrin. We have to get the medics over here."

Kyrin was already relaying Dena's information to the hospital, difficult though it was to circumvent the pall of misery generated by the Narvellans. +Several dead, four injured+ he reported. +Please send Drusa. We need her experience with stun-cannon victims+

At that moment Drusa herself walked into the stateroom, her face like thunder. "I saw Lydion being dragged off by two Moderators," she explained to Laura, "so I followed and hid in the laundry room all morning until it was safe to look for him. I needn't have worried. He's found a little elite-wife to cheer him up."

"Trust Lydion," Laura said wryly. "I'm sorry, I shouldn't find it amusing, but - "

"Don't mistake me," Drusa said briskly. "I never deluded myself that he'd stay once the campaign was over. I just thought he'd give it a day or two, that's all." She examined Tralvar, frowning. "Something isn't right. Stun victims always recover more quickly than this. We'd better keep him under observation."

The medical team hurtled in and carried off the injured and walking wounded to waiting flitters. Dena and Drusa took charge of Tralvar. Then the stateroom was quiet again except for two orderlies who had stayed to remove the corpses.

"Laura, Kyrin's asking to see you," Idenion said.

"Me? Why?"

"He says the whole square's full of people and they won't go away until they've seen the First Singer."

Just then one of the orderlies gave a shout. "Didn't anyone examine this man?" he demanded, pointing to Corython. "He's still alive!"

Idenion and Laura watched, hardly daring to hope, until the stretcher-bearers had left. Then alone in the empty hall, amid the torn banners and overturned chairs, they hugged one another like a couple of tired children.

"Come on," Laura said at last. "Let's go and find Kyrin."

***

Despite Laura's hopes, it was soon apparent that Corython would not recover. The healers reported that no higher brain activity remained, only the merest of autonomic functions. Interrupting the Ten had only turned a swift death into a slow but painless one.

Pannyra appeared with her baby boy, refusing to accept the inevitable. "Look, Corython, here's your son," she crooned. "His name's Nimion. Would you like to hold him?" And she laid the baby's tiny hand on Corython's palm. After a moment the slack fingers twitched, then curled briefly.

"Did you see?" cried Pannyra in delight. "He held Nimion's hand. I told you he'd come out of this!"

"It was just a reflex," one of the healers murmured to Laura. "There's nothing left."

And as night fell Corython finally slipped away, his quiet death as self-effacing as his life.

Pannyra became a shining example of Celestrian grief management. "I shall devote myself to my son's upbringing," she declared. "He'll be encouraged to emulate his father and to honour his sacrifice." Laura, although she admired her fortitude, didn't think her plans for Nimion were entirely sensible.

Meanwhile, in an adjacent room, Tralvar's condition was perplexing everyone. He appeared to be in no danger, and therefore should have woken up. But he remained unconscious. Moves were made to contact any Narvellans who knew about the stun-cannon's properties. In Treva, for instance, there was a small factory - staffed entirely by Narvellans - where replacement lenses were milled. It remained to be seen whether anyone would be fit to respond. Dena opted to remain with Tralvar; Laura and Idenion, physically and mentally exhausted, decided to sleep at Tralvar's house and return early in the morning.

The new day brought both good and bad news. A group of the Free in Rhul, including the pilot who'd most recently visited the Synectic base, mounted a hasty expedition to Ipsa. When they arrived they found the reducees cowering in the communications room, too disoriented to explain what had happened. But Clovath's body and the broken detonator told their own story, and when the rescuers forced open the door to the stasis chamber they found that Tralvar's bomb had done its work only too well.

Myrig listened soberly to the report. "And Quetri?"

"I'm sorry, Myrig, he's dead. The explosion brought the cavern roof down. There was a rift in the base's eco-shield and air was being vented, so we had to leave him there and save the living. We'll go back for him if you wish."

"Do so." This was Axmiol, in control of himself again, taking Myrig's place in front of the transposer. "Let him be buried as befits an elite noble and a hero of the people."

"How are we to accord him such a privilege, Lord Axmiol?" asked the expedition leader. "He was a bondslave."

"He won his freedom," declared Axmiol. "The zyl Nyris' debt to the tyl Pellons is cancelled. Contact me again when the funeral arrangements are complete."

"And what about *our* debt to the Celestrians?" Myrig asked his superior.

"We must make whatever restitution they demand," Axmiol replied. "Terms will have to be discussed when Tralvar is well enough. Will you continue to deputise for me, Myrig? Sijek is still very distressed and so are many of my colleagues."

"Very well," said Myrig, although he would have preferred to look in on Tralvar. He supposed Kyrin could inform him how things were.

Laura, keeping vigil alone while Idenion conferred with the healers, was much cheered by the whirlwind arrival of Jarras. "I've been at Ilonna," he explained. "I was just about in range of the Alcine satellite, so, thanks to Forlane's excellent commentary, I knew exactly what was going on. I delayed my return until it was daylight here because, after all that's happened, I didn't want to walk into any situation where the Narvellans had the advantage. Call me paranoid if you like."

"Just sensible, as ever," smiled Laura. "I still can't quite believe the Synectics are finished."

"I heard about Tralvar, of course," Jarras went on, "so I gave the spaceport a miss and came straight here."

"I'm glad the healers let you through. We had so many callers at the villa that I had to post a bulletin on the door."

"Are you sure it wasn't *you* they came to see?"

"Not this time. I talked with the people yesterday - or rather, Kyrin did - and they know there won't be any singing just yet. Tralvar's the centre of attention now, and quite right too. He's done so much for us all."

"I feel such a coward for running away," Jarras sighed. "I know it's what he wanted, but – "

"If you'd stayed you'd be dead," said Laura bluntly. "Rillan as well. Is there any sign of him, by the way?"

"Not so far." Jarras seemed unconcerned about his friend. "I checked with the spaceport and he hasn't called in, but if he's on Myrma he won't know it's safe to come home. Perhaps someone should - " He paused suddenly and peered closely at Tralvar. "Did I imagine it, or did he just move?"

Laura followed his gaze hopefully. "He looks the same to me."

"There! His eyes!" Jarras exclaimed. They both watched intently, and after a moment Tralvar's eyelids fluttered again. Laura called his name quietly, but was ill prepared for what followed. Tralvar opened his eyes, drew a deep breath and began to scream.

The healers rushed in and ejected Laura and Jarras from the room. Persistent enquiries only yielded the fact that Tralvar was in agony and no-one knew why. Painkillers appeared to have no effect and in the end it was necessary to sedate him. Laura, pale with worry, recalled a tale she'd heard long ago - how Tralvar as a child had borne serious injury in silence. And Jarras had seen him shrug off numerous industrial mishaps without pausing to see what damage he'd done to himself. Which meant he was now experiencing the worst pain imaginable. Laura wondered if he'd been emitting thoughts to rival his screams, but Jarras assured her he wasn't. The required focus simply wasn't there.

Idenion, banned from the sickroom also, asked Jarras if he knew which factory made the stun-cannon lenses.

"I know the place," Jarras replied. "And they've been approached already, you say? Right. I'll go over to Treva immediately and see who I can bring back. I'll get some sense out of them even if I have to knock their heads together."

"I've just remembered something," Laura said dolefully when he'd gone.

"What?" Idenion asked. And then, since the urgency of the situation demanded that he read her: "Oh. Are you sure?"

"Yes, the Synectics devised the stun-cannon. Quetri told us himself, the morning after the retrace. You'd gone back to work."

"So," said Idenion with a worried frown, "you think these lens engineers will have been following specifications without any real understanding."

"Precisely. Just like *our* engineers and the stardrive."

"We have our experts," Idenion reminded her. "Let's hope the Narvellans do too."

Jarras returned with the foreman, Gryc, who was composed enough to answer questions sensibly. A swift conference was held in the corridor. "The cannon was never intended for use against Celestrians," Gryc explained. "It was for riot control at home. And as Laura supposed, we don't know much about the science behind it. I've brought a few of the lenses we make; nothing unusual about them, as you can see. However, before it strikes the lens, the photon stream is diffracted through a crystal like this one. We don't make them on Celestra but we did have a couple of spares from discarded weapons."

"Did the Synectics create this?" asked Drusa, handling the curiously dense crystal with distaste.

"Yes. But unlike their version of aldacite, there's no natural counterpart."

Lydion arrived with Tarlatine. Drusa gave her a resentful look, but due to the current emergency refrained from anything more acrimonious. Tarlatine, without seeking permission, disappeared into Tralvar's room. Drusa followed, leaving the door open.

"There's some form of adverse resonance affecting his nervous system," Tarlatine reported from the bedside, "but the chemical you've given him masks it. In order for any Narvellan to treat him he must be free of sedation."

"I don't see how that's possible," frowned Drusa.

"May I hold the crystal?" continued Tarlatine, taking it from her. After a moment she shuddered and put it down. "To me it suggests splinters, icicles. Intuitively, I've no doubt that Tralvar's affliction is linked to it, or one like it. I suggest you send for a Directress. Their abilities are more in keeping with the analysis required."

"I've another suggestion," said Jarras from the doorway. "Let's re-create the accident. The original venue and the original weapons - which, I assume, are still in position."

"You mean - someone's got to set themselves up as a target?" exclaimed Laura.

"No, we just fire both cannon and have the Directresses standing by to read the signature."

"I concur," said Gryc. "Synchronous firing in an enclosed space could well have been to blame. The dissipation would have been compromised, and the beams may even have touched."

"Is that bad?"

"We were told not to let it happen."

"They *did* touch," said Laura.

"Why don't you people obey your own rules?" Jarras snapped, rounding on the Narvellan in exasperation.

"They panicked, Jarras." Idenion laid a calming hand on his arm. "Tralvar had half killed one of them with that mace."

469

Jarras simmered down. "I suppose we're a little closer to a solution," he muttered. "Come on, Gryc - let's find a Directress or two and conduct this experiment."

Gryc, somewhat piqued, followed him out. Tarlatine, after one more look at Tralvar, went to give whatever help she could to the men he had injured. Lydion watched with bemused affection as she drifted down the corridor; Drusa, after a moment's hesitation, touched his shoulder.

"I realise that anything I say will sound like jealousy, but I'm concerned for you. She's an elite-wife, and the Narvellans guard their highborn women so closely. That's one aspect of their behaviour that *isn't* going to change."

"She's an elite-*widow*," Lydion reminded her. "In the absence of male heirs, she inherits Besu's title. She outranks most of the elite, believe it or not."

"And you're attracted to power, are you?" Drusa couldn't resist one pointed remark.

"You know me better than that," said Lydion reproachfully. "I couldn't care less - although it *should* keep the Governors out of our hair! Tarly doesn't value her status. All she ever wanted was to be a healer. And if the Narvellans are allowed to keep their spheres, she wants to join the search for a new world. She's already put her name down."

"A brave woman," Drusa said with sincerity.

Lydion seemed far from happy. "Don't begrudge me my time with her, Drusa. I shan't have much of it. The irony is, I think I'm falling in love with her."

"What, you?" inquired Drusa gently.

"Stupid, isn't it? Well, tell me it serves me right."

But Drusa said nothing at all.

Idenion, with Laura, had returned to Tralvar's side. "We'd better stay here till Dena comes back," he said. "I doubt if she'll sleep much longer."

470

Laura gazed down at Tralvar's drawn, pallid face. For the first time she could see the burden of years on him, and it suddenly occurred to her that she had no idea how old he was.

"I don't think *he* knows either," Idenion mused. "Not with any accuracy."

"Wouldn't it be nice if someone could fill in that missing chunk of his past," Laura said wistfully. "He'd be so pleased." Then, impulsively: "Oh, Idenion - we're not going to lose him too, are we?"

"Not if Jarras has anything to do with it," said Idenion, suppressing his own fears. "He'll be back soon with some answers."

Jarras, meanwhile, was striding into the akron with Gryc in tow. All was hushed; there was no-one on the duty desk and the galleries were empty. He approached the stateroom to find a notice on the doors: "Sealed by Order of the Protectorate." A slender chain looped through the ornate handles served to reinforce this message. Jarras tore down the notice, broke the chain and shouldered one of the doors open.

"Check the weapons status," he ordered, and Gryc scurried over to the nearest cannon.

"This one is sufficiently charged."

"Good. Show me how to fire it, then go and inspect the other one while I organise some help." Then, inconsiderately: +Kyrin. *Kyrin*!+

+I am here+ responded the relayist sleepily. +What is it, Jarras?+

+Where are the Directresses? I need one or more in the stateroom, now!+

+Wait+ replied Kyrin, and began a search for the girls' distinctive mindset. +They're not in the akron+ he told Jarras at last. +I'm informed they've gone into the country to meditate+

"Chaos! They just would!" muttered Jarras in frustration.

"This cannon is also ready to fire," called Gryc from the far end of the hall.

"Fine! Stay there!" Jarras called back, despite having had his plan forestalled. There had to be another approach to the problem, if he could just be objective enough to think of one.

+Might I make a suggestion?+ Kyrin inquired. As befitted his expertise, he'd known from the outset why Jarras needed the Directresses' talents.

+Go ahead+ replied Jarras. +Anything's welcome at this stage+

Kyrin outlined his idea.

+You know,+ remarked Jarras, +that's a positive masterstroke!+

Kyrin accepted his thanks modestly. +I'll send him to you+ he promised, and was gone. Presently the heavy door opened a fraction to admit a very subdued Sijek.

"I'm told you require my skills," he said shyly. "I'm happy to oblige, but would remind you I've had no formal training."

Jarras explained, in very few words, what he wanted him to do. Sijek obediently but nervously positioned himself to one side of the aisle, halfway down the hall.

"He'll need a pair of goggles before we start," Gryc warned.

"That won't be necessary," replied Sijek. "Sight is irrelevant to this task. My eyes will be closed."

Gryc was perplexed, being unfamiliar with Sijek's unique abilities.

"I shall read the weapons-fire as Jarras requested," Sijek declared. "Please commence."

"You heard him," Jarras said. "Get ready, Gryc. Firing...*now*!"

The crackle of the discharge was daunting in the silence. Dainty lightnings lanced across the divide, touched, flared and vanished. Sijek winced but stood his ground.

"As you anticipated, there was an anomaly where the beams made contact," he told Jarras. "I perceived it as a dissonance but I divined it as...." His mind depicted a globe of needle-sharp diffraction spikes.

"Almost like a virus," said Gryc.

Jarras didn't know what a virus looked like but assumed Gryc did. Not that it *was* one; it would be a complex crystal emanation, like an aldacite backlash but many times worse.

"Do you think you can help Tralvar?" he asked Sijek anxiously.

"I don't know. I'd have to be in his presence before I could answer that."

"Then come with me!" urged Jarras.

Sijek hesitated. "I shall have to tell Axmiol."

"Do so, then - but please hurry!"

Sijek seemed merely to drift away, and Jarras resisted the urge to go after him and shake him. A well-trained neph-khet never ran anywhere, and Sijek had known no other way of life. But speed *was* of the essence. Celestrian anaesthetics were crude, and protracted use of them would be fatal to Tralvar. Yet if he were conscious he'd probably scream himself to death in the course of an afternoon.

"Jarras?" Gryc approached respectfully. "I've disabled these weapons so they cannot be accidentally fired. May I now return to Treva? I'm concerned about my workforce; they're terrified of retribution."

"There won't be any." Myrig had appeared in the doorway. "If you knew the Celestrians as I do, you wouldn't worry. There will be some high spirits, no doubt - some ceremonial wrecking of factory machinery

473

- but nothing more. I'll be making a broadcast later today. When you reach Treva perhaps you'd ask the local relayists to announce it? It concerns a special arrival at Alda Mexa spaceport."

"What are you talking about, Myrig?" asked Jarras with barely concealed impatience.

"You'll see. Oh, you'd better tell the hospital to stand by. They're going to be busy!"

"If you don't mind, I'm more concerned with Tralvar at the moment," Jarras said curtly.

"Then perhaps you'd take us to him." Axmiol, regal as ever, entered the stateroom with Sijek on his arm. "I consider myself responsible for Tralvar's condition. I shall assist Sijek in any way I can."

The hospital staff were suitably taken aback when Jarras arrived with the Lord Governor and his neph-khet. After scrutinising Tralvar minutely the pair went into a huddle with Tarlatine and some of the other healers.

"The crystal resonance has changed his natural pattern, which is now at war with itself," said Tarlatine. "That much is obvious. But none of us can perceive how it's happening."

"But *I* can!" insisted Sijek. "I saw a barbed globe when the cannon fired, and I saw a proliferation of them in miniature when I studied Tralvar. I *can* remove them! I've already destroyed two."

"But these anomalies don't really exist," said a senior healer.

"Sijek knows that," answered Tarlatine. "Does it matter what he sees as long as he can effect a cure?"

"One thing that we all agree on," pursued Sijek, "is that the sedation must cease. Its signature dazzles me."

"How long will it take you to remove all these barbs?" asked another healer.

"Several ilden. There are so many."

"Then how in harmony's name are we supposed to ease Tralvar's pain?"

"I'll do that," said Axmiol. "I shall take the pain to myself, enabling him to sleep naturally while Sijek works."

"Are you sure you can tolerate it?"

"I am. I inherited this particular talent via my father's line and used it during my mother's last illness. I will, however, have someone standing by in case the treatment takes longer than Sijek expects."

"I volunteer," said Tarlatine.

Just then, Dena appeared and reported that Tralvar was fighting off the anaesthetic. Axmiol and Sijek looked gravely at each other, then turned as one and paced into the sickroom.

Lydion, who had eavesdropped shamelessly on the discussion, accosted Tarlatine as she was about to follow. "I can't fathom Sijek," he said worriedly. "What will he do? What will *you* do? Is it risky?"

"Do not fear for us," she answered, to Lydion's dismay. She'd inadvertently placed a barrier between her race and his. "Axmiol has exceptional strength. The house of tyl Thuuvin has produced our best psychokinetic healers."

"I still don't know how this healing works."

"My love," she said patiently, "it's all to do with counterbalance. For every dissonance there is a consonance, for every pattern an opposing pattern. Tralvar, as a musician, will understand this subliminally and hopefully will allow Sijek to work unhindered. He has to re-impose Tralvar's basic pattern - to create an imprint and sustain it."

Lydion managed to stammer out some kind of reply before she turned away. Patterns, imprints - it all sounded very Synectic. He wanted, chauvinistically perhaps, to think of Tarlatine as a normal pretty girl who happened to heal bruises rather well. The truth was demonstrably different. Would the Narvellans, through their psychokinesis, one day evolve into something akin to Sarune and her tribe?

"A sobering thought," said Idenion, who'd been waiting nearby for the lovers to finish their conversation.

"She's out of my league, Idenion," Lydion said mournfully. "Why do I always give myself these problems?"

"What you need," Idenion suggested, "is a distraction. We've a world to set straight, don't forget. This healing's going to take the rest of the day, and I've finally persuaded Dena it's pointless to wait around. She wants to start sprucing up the Lyricon, and needs help."

"Meaning me?"

"Meaning you, to give the weathershield the once-over. Jarras is keen to get back to Treva because of something Myrig said to him earlier. He doesn't want exuberant workers to wreck anything they might later need."

"And what are *you* going to do?"

"Offer my services to Myrig. There's a lot of confusion and indecision out there, and if anyone's going to broadcast instructions it should be me. People may not recognise Myrig's voice, but they'll certainly know mine."

And so it was that only Laura, out of all the conspirators, saw a motley bunch of Celestrians arrive at the hospital. Some walked in, others were being carried. Some were badly sunburnt, others bright-eyed with fever, and all looked dehydrated and exhausted. Most were barefoot, and their clothes - what remained of them - were made of skins and grasses. Although Laura had never seen these people before, she knew she was looking at newly-returned deportees - and from their appearance, deportees who had never been near the Narvellan homeworlds.

Idenion learnt the full story from Myrig. The sympathetic administrator, knowing there was little chance the prisoners would ever leave Narvella Four, had - with the connivance of overseer Quodos and another Narvellan at Treva spaceport - sent them to Myrma.

"I gave them the choice," he added. "They were aware of the risks from exposure to that planet's microbes. But they all chose to go there."

"But," began Idenion, puzzled, "your government was expecting them. There must have been questions."

"Of course. But that's the beauty of having *two* homeworlds - Narvella Four was told there had been a change of plan and that the prisoners were now on Narvella Prime, whereas Narvella Prime simply assumed they were safely on Four. That young hothead Ibri nearly ruined everything by insisting they were dead. If anyone had taken him seriously I would in all probability have been discovered.

"The most difficult aspect was the lack of flight programmes. Every consignment of aldacite was carefully logged - every single crystal had to be accounted for. One or two, such as Jarras needed, could have been listed as damaged or defective - but not a whole batch."

"You stole that box from the monorail!" Idenion exclaimed.

"Quodos did. Unfortunately, and quite unwittingly, he chose *real* crystals, and there was quite a furore. I owe you and Dena an apology for what followed."

"Spending the evening in a locked train was the least of my worries," Idenion assured him. "It was Dena who suffered."

"That reprobate Chisrin!" Myrig muttered. "Fortunately we're now in a position to put things right. Dena can have a safe and swift abortion as soon as it can be arranged. Now let's draft out this broadcast material. I want to initiate some sensible, orderly factory demolition."

For the remainder of that day, Laura helped Drusa and her team with the new arrivals. She prepared beds, collected hospital robes from the storeroom, and handed out beakers of liman and palliatives for the fever. The critically ill were being cared for elsewhere - with the majority it was simply a case of making them comfortable until the protections kicked in. Laura was recognised, of course, but none of her charges was surprised to see her there.

"We should have known it was *you* who saved us, First Singer," they said, more than once.

"It was Tralvar, not me," she protested. They seemed unconvinced.

Every so often she stole back to Tralvar's room, only to meet with the same scene: Sijek in a trance, Tarlatine waiting quietly by, Axmiol seated at the bedside looking more worn and ill than Tralvar himself. As night fell she checked on them again, and this time Tarlatine indicated that she should stay.

"The treatment is almost finished," she confided, "but I fear Axmiol has reached the limit of his endurance. If I have to take over from him, would you see him safely restored? Encourage him to drink some water, but don't allow him any more Breath of Corayn. He's already had the maximum permitted dose."

"There's no scent of it in here."

"I prepared it as a sublingual spray - three doses in one. I warned him there'd be none left for later, but he insisted."

478

Axmiol suddenly groaned and crumpled sideways in his chair. Tarlatine moved swiftly to Sijek's side, gasping and wincing as she took up the burden of pain. Laura sponged the perspiration from Axmiol's brow, then raised him to a sitting position and offered him the drink Tarlatine had suggested. After a few sips he turned his head away.

"Thank you, First Singer," he murmured hoarsely. "Now get me some Breath of Corayn. Quickly, girl."

"Tarlatine says you can't have it."

"Chaos take you, I've just been saving your First Citizen's life! Now do as you're told!"

"You can't have it, Axmiol!" repeated Laura.

Drusa put her head round the door. "Problem?"

Axmiol's bluster faded. "Confounded women. Just find me a bed for the night, will you? I have to sleep...to channel off this pain..."

Drusa took charge. "There's a vacant room in the next wing," she said. "Some of the Myrmian party insisted on going home. Laura, would you fetch a nightflower sleeping draught from the dispensary? Bring it to room seven."

Laura obeyed, glad to be out of Axmiol's way. Even when on the verge of collapse, he was intimidation personified. When she returned from her errand she was surprised to see Sijek on his feet - or more precisely, barefoot on the cold floor.

"Cramp," he explained with a smile. The smile startled her; he seemed to have suffered no ill effects at all. Tarlatine, hollow-eyed, looked up from her chair.

"Isn't he unbelievable? I only assisted him for two astallen and I'm like a limp rag!"

"You and Axmiol had the worst of the task," Sijek replied. "All I did was tidy up."

"Is Tralvar cured?" asked Laura eagerly.

"Almost," said Sijek after a pause.

"And what might *that* mean?"

"At the last, some remnants of his affliction kept eluding me. I'd like to think I dealt with them all, but I fear not. He's neglected his health, and that could allow the false pattern to retain a hold." He paused apologetically. "But this is only my opinion, and I'm an amateur in these matters. I hope I'm wrong."

Laura crossed to the bedside. "He looks very peaceful."

"I've placed him in a healing sleep," said Tarlatine. "If you'll go with him, I think we should send him home now. I'd like him to be in familiar surroundings when he wakes."

Laura welcomed the idea. "Of course I'll go!"

"And make sure you have some rest yourself," Tarlatine added.

Sijek chose that moment to take his leave, saying his place was now with Axmiol. Tarlatine stared thoughtfully at the door as it swung shut.

"What Axmiol did was phenomenal. If I hadn't witnessed it I'd never have thought it possible. He was driven by his conscience, of course."

"If you say so," replied Laura, unconvinced.

The next morning, Tarlatine was proved correct when Axmiol appeared at the villa. "Is Tralvar awake yet?" he asked, almost humbly.

"Not yet," replied Idenion coolly. "We're taking turns to sit with him. Laura's with him now."

"May I participate?"

"That's up to Dena." Idenion left him in no doubt of what *his* decision would have been.

Dena was about to refuse, but a closer look at Axmiol's haggard features made her relent. She'd never dreamt she'd see the Lord Governor looking contrite. "Go up," she said quietly.

480

"I'm much obliged." Axmiol went noiselessly upstairs and peeped round the door of the master bedroom. Laura, mildly surprised to see him, beckoned him in. He seated himself deferentially at the far side of the room. No words were exchanged.

One ild later, Laura was about to take a meal break when Tralvar suddenly stirred and drew a deep breath. Before she could summon anyone he was awake and staring straight past her at Axmiol.

"What are *you* doing here?"

"I'm glad you are yourself again, First Citizen," Axmiol replied laconically. "It would appear my duty is now discharged. Please call on me when you're fully rested - there is much to discuss." He made as if to leave, then added less formally: "I'll ask Kyrin to circulate the news of your recovery. Did you know the entire world is holding its breath? It's amazing that a rascal like you can inspire such affection. Goodbye!"

"Laura...? What was all that about?" Tralvar asked blurrily.

"Don't you remember anything?"

"I remember someone making an appalling noise - yelling and raving..."

"That was you."

"Oh. Was I drunk?"

"You got in the way of two stun-cannon," Laura explained. "You've been very ill."

He considered that for a moment. "Wasn't there...a trial?"

"Two days ago."

He thought about that also. "Did our mission succeed?"

"Yes, Tralvar, it did. I'll tell you all about it when you're properly awake."

"There's something I have to remember," he persisted. "Something important. It was cold...and there were voices..."

"That was probably us trying to bring you round. Forget it."

"It wasn't you."

"You don't need to worry about a thing," Laura insisted. "We're free now. No more Synectics, no rules, no factories. I can sing whenever I want, wherever I want."

He closed his eyes. "Then sing. I'd like that."

"All right. Anything to stop you fretting." Laura searched her memory for something soothing and chose "Nana" by Manuel de Falla. When she'd finished the short, gentle piece she looked up to see Idenion and Dena standing in the doorway. She'd no idea how long they'd been there.

Tralvar was asleep again, so she accompanied the others back to the study. They'd been attempting to clear it up, but it was hard to differentiate between the Moderators' damage and Tralvar's untidiness.

"That was an affectionate little song," Dena commented.

"Oh, look, I'm sorry," Laura began awkwardly. "I should have called you."

"It was you he wanted to see," Dena said calmly. "I'll have plenty of time with him later."

"He wasn't trying to read me, was he?"

"He's still too unfocused," said Idenion.

"That's a relief. I didn't want him to know about Quetri just yet. And of course, I was lying to him."

"Were you? Why?"

"Oh, Idenion, think! I told him there was nothing to worry about and there most certainly still is. When everyone's stopped being so euphoric they'll realise the original problem hasn't gone away. I don't know how much time's left before the Narvellan solar system gets fried, but I suspect there's very little. And what then? What are we supposed to do with two planetfuls of homeless Narvellans?"

Chapter Fifteen

High on a hill outside Rhul, beneath a sky of yellow-white, Quetri lay in state within a transparent catafalque. The embalmers had restored his ruined body and clothed him in the silver robe of a highborn, but had spoilt the effect by adding too much artificial colour to his face. To either side of the tomb were two blazons: the first displaying a stylised version of Quetri's genetic profile, the second the zyl Nyris family tree. Quetri's female cousins, in full mourning white, scattered a trail of petals as they retreated from the memorial.

Their departure marked the culmination of a ceremony which had lasted all afternoon. As the sun touched the horizon the walls of the catafalque retracted, exposing its still occupant to the sky. Jets of flame sprang up, encircling the corpse, and in moments a consuming fire was raging.

Tralvar watched the recorded telecast impassively, grateful that the Narvellan tele-transcriptions were as restricted in length as the music globes. There was, he supposed, a certain grandeur in giving Quetri's remains back to the elements - but reconstructing the body only to destroy it again seemed particularly pointless. However, he kept his observations to himself. Axmiol was making a rare attempt at solicitude, and diplomacy would not be served by being critical.

"You may keep the player if you wish," Axmiol said, sounding almost kind.

"Thank you, but no," Tralvar replied. "I'll remember him in my own way. And now I'd better start reading these new reports."

"I'll see myself out," said Axmiol, but didn't leave immediately. "It doesn't seem...correct... that you're still in this house. Have you not considered moving back to the akron?"

"I like it here," Tralvar declared. "Would you really prefer me to lay waste to your tidy, efficiently run akron and keep everyone awake at night with my zirid practice? I don't imagine Dena would care to live there either."

"Ah, Dena. Has anyone spoken to her about her condition?"

"Myrig offered her an abortion. She's thinking about it."

Axmiol looked faintly surprised. "I see no reason for any delay. It's for her own wellbeing. And you, First Citizen, guard your health also. You look weary."

"Too many visitors, perhaps," Tralvar rejoined; and Axmiol, aware that he had outstayed his welcome, made a decorous departure.

Sighing, Tralvar gathered up the reports. There were a great many. His tiredness was more akin to world-weariness - an inevitable consequence of having lived on his nerves for so long. With the danger abruptly removed, he wondered how he'd ever coped.

Scarcely three octals had elapsed since the stun-cannon incident, and he'd done little save sit at conference tables and try to thrash out a sensible strategy for reorganising Celestra and safeguarding the Protectorate's future. To give them their due, the Narvellans had vowed to return Celestra to its pre-Synectic state as rapidly as possible, and their actions were already taking effect. Many of the theridolyte processing centres had been closed, and those which maintained production were manned by the Narvellans themselves.

Laura and Idenion had, of course, moved into the First Singer's apartment at the Lyricon, where Laura had immediately started work on her voice. A provisional date, a further three octals away, had been set for her return concert, and she was hoping to be back in training by then. Dena, after admitting the impossibility of fitting all Tralvar's paraphernalia into the custodian's quarters, had been commuting between the Lyricon and the villa. Although nothing had been said on the subject, Tralvar knew she was no longer at ease in the role of custodian - and he suspected it was to do with her changed psyche and its effect on the scolia.

Idenion, in conjunction with Forlane, continued to broadcast bulletins to the citizens. There was - despite popular demand - no prospect of a general holiday. Most people had returned to their previous occupations. The exceptions were the power workers and water supply engineers, most of whom, like Lydion, were conscripts. The breakdowns and shortages were almost as bad as before, and a slow improvement was the best that could be hoped for. The textile factories had remained open too, busily weaving ytil and firi instead of the drab ylur. In Alda Mexa the shanty town had virtually been abandoned, and demolition was about to begin. In its place there was to be a pleasure garden; the elite-wives, including Tarlatine, had offered to create it. It was now the middle of winter, the ideal time to be planting for next spring.

Concurrently, and with difficulty, a scheme for the Narvellan homeworlds had been drawn up. Tralvar thumbed through the documents to see what the latest findings were. Statistics, statistics. How the Narvellans loved them! One in twenty-five people killed by the Synectics' interrupted push; a high suicide rate among the Moderators; a train derailment south of Rhul caused by the linesmen shirking their duties. Tralvar made a scribbled note to check who was walking the Celestrian monorail line.

No longer impelled to leave their homeworlds, a substantial number of Narvellans had decided that the space initiative was doomed to failure, preferring to rely on bunkers and caves to protect themselves from the solar flares. Little attempt was being made to convince them otherwise, since it would be impossible to save everyone.

After lengthy debate it was decided that the existing space fleet should be split three ways: a third to search for a new home, using Celestra's admittedly out of date star charts, and a third to transfer people to Tegna Nine, an arid planet some two hundred light years from Narvella. It would be no use as a colony as it could never be self-sustaining, but it would serve for the present. As yet no one had been transferred, as a base similar to those on Narvella Four had to be built. A shortage of materials, including steel, had put the project behind schedule. The report gave precise details of the shortfall, but offered no speedy solutions.

The remaining portion of the fleet would start bringing more Narvellans to Celestra. They were to be given Ilonna as a temporary home - this had been Jarras' suggestion - and there was talk of setting up a base on Alda Four. Much trouble was being taken to ensure that all spheres received the same amount of use, to avoid unequal wear and tear.

Tralvar suddenly lurched back to wakefulness, having nodded off over the papers. He thought he'd heard a tap at the door and an eager young voice calling "First Citizen!" But of course, he'd been dreaming. Quetri was gone.

Tralvar had not lied about remembering him in his own way. As well as the original dossier - complete with photograph - obtained by Kyrin, he'd acquired an unexpected and poignant souvenir when Myrig had presented him with two music globes. The Moderators had trashed the recording studio, but Myrig had found the newly-processed globes in Narad's effects. One was of Corython playing Hymorel's Dance, the other of Quetri singing Isylla's Eyes. Tralvar had given Hymorel's Dance to Pannyra. He hadn't yet had the courage to play Quetri's song.

The knock at the door was repeated. So it hadn't been a dream after all; but the voice which called to him was female and peremptory.

"First Citizen! I know you're in there. Stop hiding and answer me!"

He dragged himself to his feet and went to release the spring-latch. He'd hated resorting to locks but it was the only way to deter the constant stream of well-wishers and casual callers. He wasn't used to being popular.

"Remember me?" said his visitor. There was just enough daylight left for him to recognise her without turning on the portico lamps.

"Well, if it isn't my bold Ninfi. If you're hoping for another torrid night I'm afraid I must turn you away. I've taken a partner in unity."

"I know. But she isn't here now," Ninfi returned calmly. "Could I have just a few moments of your time? Inside? It's important!"

She looked uncharacteristically serious and wasn't carrying any alcohol, so after a brief deliberation he let her in. As soon as she entered the study her eye fell on the picture of Quetri.

"That's *him*, isn't it? Your spy? You know, right up until the trial my friends were teasing me about your affair with him, and I was just longing to say that he was working with you to destroy the Narvellan overmind. But it was a secret, so I couldn't."

Tralvar stared at her, aghast.

"And what about your bomb factory?" she continued. "The one with the strange door. Is it still there or did the Moderators find it?"

"It's still there," he said lamely.

Ninfi took off her cloak, revealing a diaphanous dress of pale blue firi. "I made this," she informed him. "Do you like it?"

"Very becoming."

"It was an honour to share your secrets," she went on. "I felt privileged and special. So - in view of that - why did you lose your temper when I went looking for a scieshanar?"

So there's still something she doesn't know, Tralvar thought grimly. I told her enough to blow the conspiracy wide open but I drew the line at my dubious ancestry. I swear I'll never touch wine again!

Ninfi waited patiently for his answer.

"There was music in my study," Tralvar said at last. "Songs for Laura. Her presence was one secret I *didn't* trust you with." And I hope to chaos she believes that, he added to himself.

Ninfi looked relieved. "Oh, I see. I knew there had to be a really important reason for all that rage." She composed herself, folding her hands. "So I'm here to ask you again, very respectfully, if I may have a scieshanar. I'm carrying your child, First Citizen, and if it goes to term I'd like to notify you in the proper way."

Tralvar was momentarily lost for words.

"Are you pleased?" asked Ninfi with a tiny break in her voice.

"Astounded. But - yes, I'm pleased." Tralvar ventured a smile. Then, ever practical: "Did you wish me to make some kind of restitution or adoptive arrangement?"

She hugged him, a loving and spontaneous gesture. "Oh, Tralvar, you've got it all wrong! I'm delighted to be pregnant and I'm thrilled the baby's yours. And I'm going to raise it myself. Now, about that scieshanar...?"

"I don't have one at the moment," he said gravely, disentangling her. "But I'll see to it, I promise."

She thanked him with another of her broad smiles, and it belatedly dawned on him that despite her sexual expertise she was still very much an innocent. She simply didn't realise that she could have been in deadly danger as a result of his drunken indiscretions. As he led her, still prattling brightly, to the door, he had an accurate glimpse of the contented little earth-mother she would become; yet he felt no condescension. The entire campaign had been about regaining the planet for people like her. Maybe, he thought whimsically, in one of the parallel realities Laura believed in, scolia-master Tralvar would set up home with his Ninfi and set about producing a vast family. But in this life, they would go their separate ways.

As he closed the door a gust of cold wind made him shiver, evoking more memories of snow, lost childhood, flight and pursuit. And tantalisingly distant voices. He tried to focus on the words, but the impression was gone.

When Dena returned she found him at the zirid, playing a melancholy piece by the Symerid Three composer Chopin.

"Tralvar - " she began. He looked up with a resigned sigh.

"Dena, my treasure, haven't I asked you *never* to interrupt me when I'm practising?"

"I think you'll be glad I did," she replied quietly. "I've brought someone to see you."

"Dena, it's late and I'm tired. Tell whoever it is that I can't..." Then he halted incredulously as a tall, thin girl, arms crossed defensively over her chest, sidled nervously into the study. "*Nefyrra?*"

"Hello, father."

"Go on," Dena prompted. "Tell him what you told me."

Nefyrra suddenly rushed forward and fell to her knees by the zirid stool. "Tralvar - father - I'm so very sorry. Sorry for what happened to you and sorry I said those vile things. Can you ever forgive me?"

He put out a tentative hand and touched her unruly hair, so like his own. "I can't believe you're really here."

"I checked the archives," explained Dena, "and found all Alendis' partners were alive and well. I even found a couple of Strephin's. So it's as Quetri surmised - unity with a killer may be foolhardy but not fatal." She gave Tralvar a knowing smile. "As it happened, Nefyrra had begun to change her mind about you before I could present my findings."

"It's true, father," Nefyrra said earnestly. "When everyone thought you'd die, all I could think of was how much you'd done for us and how lovingly Floren had always spoken of you. I so wanted you to get well - I needed to tell you how wrong I'd been. So here I am."

Tralvar tried to speak, but the words dried in his throat. It had been a day of emotional extremes: first a guilt-laden farewell to Quetri via an impersonal recording medium, then sudden joy at Ninfi's news - and now his penitent daughter was kneeling at his feet. Overwhelmed, he wept, and Nefyrra put her sinewy arms around him and cried too. Dena looked on fondly.

"I don't want to stay in Tivenne," Nefyrra said at last, sniffing. "Can I live here with you and Dena? I'd be at the Lyricon a lot and I'd try not to be any trouble."

"Of course. Stay. Why not?" replied Tralvar, flinging out his arms as if to welcome a thousand Nefyrras. "Let's have a drink to celebrate. I hope you like resnay, girl, because I won't allow any more wine in the house!"

When everyone was calmer, Dena said: "Shall we tell him the rest now?"

Tralvar raised an eyebrow. "I think I've had enough shocks for one day."

"This won't be a shock," Dena assured him. "You've already guessed that I'm not happy with my custodianship. I've decided to resign and concentrate on dance - and on my life with you. What you *don't* know, although you won't find it a surprise, is that Nefyrra has left the Tivenne scolia. She's always had difficulty with the lattice and felt she was holding the others back."

"My gift to her," Tralvar said ironically.

"She'll still continue as a solo player," Dena went on. "At the same time I shall train her to take over my work at the Lyricon. I think she'll be perfect for it."

Tralvar frowned. "Isn't she a little young?"

"I was only her age when I succeeded Floren," Dena reminded him.

"Dena won't rush my training," Nefyrra added. "Please say you agree."

Tralvar didn't need much persuasion. Everything seemed to be falling into place - everything except the half-memories that had been plaguing him for days.

"Now, I'm sure you and Nefyrra have a lot to talk about," Dena said briskly, "so I'll make supper."

"Don't tire yourself," Tralvar said automatically. "By the way, Axmiol was here earlier. He wanted to know why you hadn't contacted Myrig."

Dena paused at the door. "Oh, Tralvar," she said softly, "please don't spoil today."

That night he was troubled by dreams, and several times Dena heard him call someone's name. Concerned, she wrote the name down: Mehedra. She'd ask him about it in the morning.

But an explanation was not forthcoming. Tralvar merely grabbed the piece of paper, gave her a hasty hug and said, "That's *it*! That's what I've been trying to remember. Dena, you're a gem!" Then he was out of the house like a whirlwind, leaving Dena and Nefyrra staring after him in bewilderment.

He reached Drusa's apartment just before she left for work. "I need you to come with me to Tafret," he said without preamble. "I want to be retraced."

"Just like that?" inquired Drusa. "You always said you'd never submit to it. What's changed your mind? Something to do with Laura, I suppose."

"No, *not* Laura," he contradicted with some small satisfaction. "This is to do with my infancy. I've always remembered falling into a snowdrift, but nothing else - nothing to explain where I came from or why my parents disowned me. Then, when I was hit by the stun-beams, the intense cold triggered the rest of that memory. I've had flashbacks ever since, and last night called out a name in my sleep. This name." He handed her Dena's note. "Drusa - I think Mehedra may be my mother!"

A flitter, with several medical staff already on board, came to an impatient halt outside.

"You'd better come to the hospital with me," Drusa suggested. "We can radio Tafret from there."

On the way, Tralvar turned his attention to another problem. "Have you spoken to Dena about terminating her pregnancy? She seems to be putting it off."

"You can't blame her," said Drusa. "It goes against everything our society holds dear."

"What about Chisrin? Surely *he* doesn't want her to have it?"

"He's gone on a retreat, like the Directresses do. There's not much chance of tracking him down."

"Typical!" sneered Tralvar. "Abnegating his responsibilities. In that case we'll just have to redouble our arguments. We both know that Dena isn't strong enough to bear that child!"

493

***

Tafret Academy's portals were normally closed to everyone save trainee relayists and their mentors, but an exception was made for Tralvar and his party. He had, after all, just saved the world. Together with Drusa and Lydion, he entered the low, graceful building and proceeded along colonnaded walkways until he reached the retracer room - which, in content at least, looked remarkably like Tyvian's lab. To promote relaxation there were flowers, indoor trees and a softly plashing fountain.

To protect the operator, the technical team had been experimenting with a feedback loop that would direct most of the aldacite emissions back into the computer. The remaining field was weak and unlikely to have addictive properties. They had conducted several test runs but Tralvar's was to be the first complete retrace under the new system. Nohal, a senior lecturer, would operate the machine, and Drusa would invigilate. Lydion's task would be to configure the results, as he'd already proved his expertise in this area.

Tralvar fidgeted about on the couch. "When's he going to start?"

"We're waiting for you to relax," said Drusa.

"I'm trying," Tralvar apologised. "Can't you give me something? Resnay, for instance?"

"No food or drink," Drusa told him. "Here, inhale this flower essence. Slowly!"

Tralvar obeyed, then lay back in the darkened room and tried to arrest his racing thoughts. Out of the corner of his eye he glimpsed a faint silvery light emanating from the top of the prill tank, and heard the sweet high note of the activated crystals. A warm numbness began to steal over him.

He fought it. With every shred of mental strength he had, he tried to stay awake. If he succumbed to that sound, all his wrong decisions and failed relationships would march across the screen at Nohal's command. Elanir - the scolia - Alendis - Tristell - Laura - Ninfi. Oh, chaos - Ninfi. He imagined how hurt she'd be when he sent her a blank scieshanar. If only he could remember a little more about the snow. Whirling snow, bitter wind, tiny chips of ice stinging his face...

"At last!" breathed Nohal. "He's under. We'd better dispense with the usual triggers and get straight to his childhood. I don't know how long we'll have."

Drusa leant towards Tralvar and spoke softly. "Is Mehedra with you? Who *is* Mehedra? Why are you outside in a storm? Show us, Tralvar. Quickly now. Show us Mehedra..."

"Hurry, Kalyx. Hurry!"

Kalyx tried to obey his mother but his little feet couldn't move as fast as she wanted. He was miserable and very cold. It had been exciting at first, sneaking through the city before anyone was awake. And he'd been intrigued when the big door had rolled open. But the fun had ended there. He'd never been outside the dome before, and he didn't like it. Everything looked one colour in the dim dawn. The relentless wind struck through his furs and his chest hurt when he breathed. And why was all this white icy stuff flying about? He looked up and suddenly realised there was no roof. There was nothing! He set up a thin wail of fear.

His mother embraced him clumsily and brushed some of the damp flakes from his collar and hat. "Remember the picture I showed you, Kalyx? The long straight road and the little house at the other end? This is the road."

Kalyx was doubtful.

"It *is*, dearest, but the snow's covered it up. Your father's waiting for us in the house. Don't you want to see him?"

Never having met him, Kalyx was indifferent to the prospect. His very noisy misery continued as they struggled on. From afar they heard the dull rasp of the door and, turning, saw a circle of yellow light appear in the gloomy bulk of the dome. Silhouetted figures darted about. And Kalyx sensed, with a child's unshielded perception, their self-righteous rage.

+Mehedra! Mehedra!+

"No, father," the woman muttered fiercely. "This time I *won't* obey you." Then, urgently: "Be brave, Kalyx. We're going to run very fast."

+Mehedra?+ This thought, light and loving, was from a different quarter. +Are you discovered?+

+Discovered but not caught+ she replied. +Bide there, my love. All will be well+ Then she seized Kalyx and began to drag him along. The snow swirled and the wind whistled, temporarily halting their ill-equipped pursuers. Once Mehedra stumbled, letting go the child's hand; he tottered blindly to the edge of the causeway and instantly vanished into a deep drift. Mehedra hauled him out. "Idiot boy!" she shrieked, more in relief than anger. He'd stopped crying, shocked into silence; with difficulty she lifted him in her arms and trudged on. The boy's damp face was pressed against coarse synthetic fur. He could no longer try to see where he was being taken. It all seemed part of some dreadful punishment.

Then, suddenly, another fur-clad figure appeared and lifted him from Mehedra's faltering grasp.

"Lykalion!" she cried thankfully.

"Let's get to the trading post!" he shouted back.

And in just a few loping steps the newcomer had carried him into warmth and light.

At this point Nohal began to lose the track - indicative, perhaps, of some impending shock that Tralvar didn't want to re-live. Drusa, who'd helped retrace many relayists through their childhoods, went to assist Nohal at the monitor. Lydion put on a prill seed necklet and took her place by the couch. Tralvar was breathing stertorously and there was a film of sweat on his brow.

"He isn't a good subject," Drusa commented. "Watch his respiration. I didn't want him to attempt this so soon after his stun-cannon injury, but he refused to wait." Then, to Nohal: "Now that his parents are together, shall we set up a cognitive loop? I know the procedure. It's what Tyvian normally did when working with such early memories."

"And this will help Tralvar understand what was said in front of him as a child?"

"If it works, yes."

"Very well, let's try it. *You'll* have to tie it in, since he's resisting everything I prompt him with. If you're successful I'll try and pick up the track where I left it. Ready?"

"When you are."

Kalyx, stripped of his furs and wrapped in a blanket, was warm again. But he fought off sleep, gazing intently at the adults as they talked and embraced.

"Why didn't you take a sled, my best girl?" asked Lykalion, holding his partner close and smoothing some stray tendrils of hair from her forehead.

"None of them were charged. We don't use them at this time of year." Mehedra allowed herself a few more moments in his arms, then reluctantly disengaged herself. "We mustn't delay. It will only take my father's party three more astallen to get here. Is your sphere close by?"

"Out back."

"Then do as we agreed. Take your son to freedom."

Lykalion glanced at the boy, who stared unblinkingly back at him. "I can't leave you here,

Mehedra. How can I abandon you to that martinet? Come with me!"

"Lykalion," she said patiently, "I can't leave. I'm First Tech Designate. I've spent twelve years being schooled for my position and I shall study for six more before I take over the running of the dome. My father is ageing and there's no time to train anyone else. But although it's too late for me, I will not impose this duty on our son. Take him!"

"Mehedra, please!"

"My only love." With one gentle hand she traced the laughter lines on his face. "I couldn't live in the outside world any more than you could live penned up in a dome. But I'll always remember our special time, our nights here in this lodge, when the skies were clear and you taught me the names of the stars." She turned to Kalyx and hugged his unyielding little body. "Don't forget, you must ensure no-one can trace him. Change his name, keep moving him between foster-parents."

"Do you really think your people would come after him?"

"How can I tell? Scapirion has never lost a First Tech before."

"He's only half Scapirian."

"He's my firstborn, and the law is the law. Promise you'll follow my instructions!"

"If I must."

"I can have no more children," Mehedra added. "The rank of First Tech will pass from my family."

"No wonder your father's so livid!" Lykalion remarked.

"Did you think it was all because of you?" Mehedra countered with the hint of a smile. They clung to eachother one last time, then retrieved their heavy coats from the drying chamber. Lykalion disappeared outside; Mehedra dressed a very uncooperative Kalyx and went after him, propelling the boy in front of her. The sphere nestled, white on white, a dozen paces from the rear wall of the lodge.

"Mehedra!" The cry was vocalised. The blizzard had lessened and her father and his men were almost at the end of the causeway.

"Go, Lykalion! *Now!*" she ordered harshly, and tried to hand Kalyx over, but he held fast to the hem of her coat. It took the efforts of both his parents to prise him off. Then Lykalion dragged him kicking and screaming toward the sphere, while Mehedra returned quietly to her waiting captors.

For the first time in his young life, Kalyx found his voice. In a thin high treble he called after her: "I hate you! I hate you!" There followed a storm of sorrow to equal anything the south polar weather could produce, and the prill promptly withdrew from their subject. Nohal was obliged to take the system offline.

"Are you in any distress, Nohal?" asked Drusa.

Nohal took off the diagnostic sensor and stretched thankfully. "No, the distress was all his."

"He's waking up!" called Lydion.

Drusa hurried to the couch, expecting to confront a disoriented and traumatised First Citizen. Instead, Tralvar sat up and said:

"Can I have that resnay now?"

Lydion produced a flask from his pocket.

"I'm sorry I brought you two here for nothing," Tralvar continued. "I really thought it would work."

Lydion was vastly amused. "Can you believe it? He *still* doesn't remember!"

Tralvar regarded him quizzically, suspecting a prank. "You traced something?"

"Quite a lot, or so it appeared from looking over Nohal's shoulder. Unfortunately, just as it was getting interesting, Drusa re-assigned me. I've just spent three astallen watching you snoring."

"I don't snore!" Tralvar said indignantly.

"Oh yes you do."

"Boys!" Drusa held up a restraining hand.

"If he's fooling, I'll smack him round the head a lot harder than that Moderator did," Tralvar promised darkly.

"Lydion's perfectly serious." Nohal approached the group. "As soon as he's processed the results you'll have the answers you seek. I don't know how linear it is, nor if the conversations were fully realised; I was too busy keeping the track steady to pay more than cursory attention."

"Then would you kindly get on with it, Lydion?" Tralvar requested with exaggerated patience.

"My pleasure." Lydion stood up with irritating slowness. "Just as a taster, I could name the one thing I recognised."

"*Well*?"

"The Scapirion dome."

Tralvar was taken aback. "Chaos! I'm from *Scapirion*?"

"Now don't jump to conclusions," Drusa advised. "We need to see the whole sequence. While Lydion's working on it, why don't we pay Rinyi a visit? Nohal says he's making wonderful progress."

Tralvar brightened. "Yes. Yes, I'd like to see him and thank him properly. If it hadn't been for his chance meeting with Quetri in the plaza, everything might have turned out very differently."

***

Chisrin paused halfway up a rock face and considered his next move. He was an expert mountaineer and scaling the highest peak in Celestra's northern hemisphere had seemed an excellent way to purge himself of the spiritual damage Sarune had wrought on him. The ascent had not been too difficult, but challenging enough, and at last he was beginning to recover from the shock of having his lifebond sundered. But nothing could assuage his guilt over the way he'd mistreated Dena. Everywhere - on lowland pastures, isolated plateaus and even barren rocks - white eprys flowers bloomed, a continual reminder of his crime against her.

He reached the summit of the mountain just as night was falling, set up a primitive camp and sat contemplating an amazing sunset of gold and green. The following day he was calmer and finally able to see a way forward. He now knew how he would make atonement to Dena. It would be a departure from convention and his people would either be scandalised or scornful, but he'd made up his mind. Because of his misdeeds he had been pronounced a social outcast or "ksil"; now he would further humble himself by placing his life in Dena's hands.

***

The day after the retrace Tralvar called a small gathering to discuss the findings and what effect, if any, they would have on his future. Nefyrra offered to cook for his guests. In addition to Dena and herself there were Laura, Idenion, Lydion and Tarlatine. Jarras had also been invited, but at the end of the meal there was still no sign of him. Matters in Treva were not fully resolved and he'd probably been delayed there.

"How does it feel to have parents, Tralvar?" asked Laura, mopping up the remains of a delicious sauce.

"I don't feel any different, to be honest," he confessed.

"So you won't be calling yourself Kalyx?"

"What's the point? Everyone would go on calling me Tralvar. And besides, Tralvar's what I grew up with.

I grew into it, you might say. I suppose you know it means foundling or orphan?"

"I remember you telling me once."

"Colloquial Atrisian," Idenion put in.

"Oh, I'd forgotten we had a philologist among us," remarked Lydion. "Are you going to write a poem about Tralvar's new identity?"

"He'd better not," Tralvar said, glaring at them both.

Nefyrra diplomatically handed him a drink and started clearing the plates. Idenion stood up to help.

"That was lovely, Nefyrra," said Dena approvingly.

"So, Tralvar," said Tarlatine, "discovering your line hasn't made you any happier?"

"Well - in one or two small ways," he conceded. "For instance, I always thought my succession of foster parents was due to my bad behaviour, but now it turns out that Lykalion was responsible. He never came near me, though."

"If he had, he wouldn't have been keeping his promise," Dena said softly.

"Don't you think there's an element of pre-destiny in all this?" asked Laura. "You avoided becoming First Tech and ended up as First Scientist!"

"The irony hadn't escaped me," Tralvar said with one of his humourless grins. "I wonder if Mehedra ever realised who I was?"

"Are you going to contact her?" inquired Tarlatine.

"I might talk to the Scapirians. Maybe I could use my origin as leverage to re-open trade. But I don't feel I've anything to say to Mehedra herself. Later, perhaps. Not now."

"What was the second thing that pleased you?" Laura wanted to know. "Being able to register your line?"

"Knowing why it hadn't *been* registered. I'd thought of all the bad reasons - spite, neglect, rejection - but I never imagined that someone was trying to give me a better life."

"I had quite a surprise too," Lydion said nonchalantly. "Lykalion's *my* father!"

Everyone stared at him, including Idenion, who had returned just in time to hear the announcement.

"He wasn't my father then, of course," Lydion continued airily. "Not for another six years or so." Then, seeing Tralvar's scepticism: "Tarlatine, my love, lend him the scieshanar I gave you the day after the trial."

She took off the small medallion and handed it over. Its mute message was indisputable. Tralvar studied it a little longer than necessary, then gave it back to her and rounded on Lydion.

"Why in chaos didn't you say something yesterday?"

"I wasn't sure how you'd take to having me as a half-brother," Lydion replied equably. "You'd just threatened to smack me round the head."

"Oh, take no notice of that," Dena advised him. "Tralvar's very fond of you."

Laura was less surprised than she might have been. She'd always thought the two men were alike in terms of appearance. "Isn't anyone going to ask Lydion for *his* reactions?" she inquired.

"Oh, I'm pleased," he assured everyone. "I've always wanted a family, as Laura well knows. Now, suddenly, I'm an uncle twice over - if we include Ninfi's child, that is."

"It's early days for that."

"Nonsense. Have you *seen* that girl? She's breeding material if ever I saw it. She - " Lydion's graphic comment was halted by the slam of the front door. Jarras hastened in, profusely apologetic.

"I'm forever being sidetracked these days. I'm so sorry. I had something to finish at the spaceport, Tralvar. I'll talk to you about it when you have a moment."

"I'll see if Nefyrra's saved anything for you," Tralvar said, and alerted her to the latecomer's presence. Jarras took off his cloak and exchanged a few words with Laura; then Nefyrra appeared in the doorway and he stepped forward to introduce himself.

What followed was so extraordinary that none of those present ever forgot it. Idenion firmly believed that two people could form a life-bond at first sight, although he'd never witnessed such an event. Laura certainly thought it could happen, and had even quoted a song about it. Dena, out of sentiment, hoped it was possible. Tralvar doubted it. Lydion thought it was a myth, as did Tarlatine. But henceforth, all would affirm that such a bond could be forged. Nefyrra and Jarras, as they held one another's gaze in rapt silence, were living proof. For an instant Tralvar saw his daughter as Jarras saw her - tall, regal, beautiful. There was a haunting inevitability about it all. He'd only just been reconciled with Nefyrra, yet he would now have to share her. And Jarras, who had so often seemed like a son to him, would step into the role he'd been destined for.

The young couple, oblivious to everyone, sat down in a corner. The rest of the company turned to Tralvar in expectation of some wise utterance.

"Well!" he said at length. "Isn't this nice?"

"We should have a party," Lydion declared, saving him from having to make a speech. "The youngsters have found each other, Tralvar and I are long-lost siblings - what other excuse do we need? Funny: I always thought my old man couldn't keep a secret! We'll invite him too if we can find him."

"Isn't it a pity," said Tralvar contemplatively, "that I was the only one to inherit his sunny temperament?"

Lydion stared. "Tralvar! Did you just make a joke?"

"I think I might have done."

"In that case we'll have an even *bigger* party!"

There was a chorus of laughter. Laura was delighted to see Tralvar joining in unreservedly.

Later, when the guests had gone and Nefyrra and Dena were asleep, Jarras quietly entered the study where Tralvar was still working.

"I....hope you didn't think I was being too precipitate with Nefyrra," he ventured.

"There was no reason to wait," Tralvar answered, faintly surprised. "I trust she went to sleep happy?"

"Yes. Yes, she did."

"Then to make sure she stays that way I'm insisting on one thing. You will *not* take her back to Treva, not even for a short time. She'd hate it. You can live here, or at the Lyricon if you think I might cramp your style, or anywhere else in the city."

"I still have duties in Treva."

"No you don't. I've been intending to make you First Scientist for years, and your appointment starts tomorrow. You'll be answerable directly to the First Citizen and that means you'll report to me every day. Now, what was this spaceport matter you wanted to see me about?"

"It concerns Rillan. You do realise his protections will have failed by now?"

"Yes, it had occurred to me."

"Four days ago I sent one of the drone spheres to Myrma, to map every part of the planet and search for a theridolyte signature. It didn't find one."

"So Rillan isn't there?"

"The result's fairly conclusive. I've also had a report from the convoy leader who was one of the last people to speak with him. He says Rillan was having trouble with his spacecraft just before the Liapa explosion. And Myrig says the data crystal he took from Corython's computer registered a transposer malfunction at the end of the download."

"Meaning?"

"I believe he tried to return here and didn't make it. Some kind of systems failure."

"It would have to be a complete systems collapse, otherwise he'd have repaired it."

"I know. I can't begin to guess what might have happened. But I don't think we'll see him again, Tralvar." Jarras moved in the direction of the front door.

"You're not leaving?"

"I have to, I'm afraid. I need to report back to Communications - I left the mapping programme running."

"You said you'd finished the sweep."

"I had. This is a second one. I know what it will say, but I had to be sure."

"I understand." Tralvar stood up to see him out. "You'd worked with Rillan a long time, hadn't you?"

"Over seven years. I shall miss him. But I'll also bear in mind that he was doing what he wanted to do. He was making that delivery run before the occupation even started." Jarras paused at the threshold. "I'll be back early tomorrow. I hope Nefyrra doesn't change her mind about me."

"She won't."

"Oh, one last thing. The factories on the south side have all been flattened, but that siren's still standing. There was a story going round the maintenance crews that you had plans to shoot it down."

"I always said I'd like to," Tralvar admitted. "But it's too risky in a crowd. Where would the therite bolt go if I missed?"

"I'll quash that rumour, then."

"No, wait. Get Wemm or one of the quarrymen to set up a controlled explosion, and I'll come and throw the switch. How does that sound?"

"Like a good compromise."

"And it'll get me into the open. I've been holed up in here for too long - people will begin to think I'm on the bottle again. But make it the day after tomorrow, Jarras - you've a pairbond to register first!"

***

The following day was cold but sunny. The registry was dealing with several newly bonded couples and a group of volunteers was clearing foliage from the archive garden. The Narvellans' census office was closed. When his daughter and Jarras had inscribed their signatures and emerged flushed and smiling into the bright morning, Tralvar reaffirmed his commitment to Dena by adding his full ancestry to the record of their union. He then had a scieshanar struck for dispatch to Ninfi. Afterwards, Dena and Nefyrra decided to spend some time at the Lyricon - only a short walk from the registry - and Jarras elected to make a lightning visit to Treva in order to delegate his duties and bring back Wemm. Tralvar would have been happy to accompany the women, but he was expecting Myrig to call at the villa.

"Would you do me a favour?" he asked Jarras before their ways diverged. "I want to see the Narvellan from the stun-cannon factory."

"Gryc? Why?"

"It's just occurred to me that he might be able to upgrade the weathershield. He'll know about prismatic effects, refraction and the like."

"I suppose he does, but - "

"Just think how pleased Laura would be if we could use the full range of colours at her concert. Not a word to her, mind!"

"You've been trying to get the full spectrum back for about ten years."

"Well, maybe it needs a fresh eye. There's no harm in trying, is there? Oh, and see if Wemm can put some fireworks together. I'm sorry to leave you with all the running around but I can't ignore the Ilonna settlement plans. This time, nothing's going to happen without my knowledge!"

Myrig duly arrived with full details of the colonists - a long list of names, ages and skills. "These people have been selected from all social levels," he was at pains to point out. "In fact, I made the final choice."

"I'm glad to hear it," said Tralvar, in genuine relief. "I know you'll have been fair. I'll study the list later, but you have my provisional approval."

"There are two other matters I want to bring to your attention," Myrig continued. "Firstly, Tarysk tyl Pellon has made a personal representation to me. She wants a place on the colonial fleet."

"I don't have the authority to refuse outright," Tralvar said slowly, "but you can tell her that if she dares set foot on Celestra I shall personally ensure she never leaves. What else?"

"Chisrin wishes to make atonement to Dena. He didn't care to approach you himself."

"Very wise."

"I recommend that you consider his proposal," Myrig went on. "In effect, he's offering to place his life in Dena's hands - to become her vassal. The ritual he wishes to perform, the Sekhu, is normally restricted to matters of honour between men. It would earn Dena much respect among my people."

"Ritual? Why can't he just say he's sorry?"

"That isn't the way we do things, Tralvar, as you're well aware. I've written down an outline of the Sekhu and what Dena needs to know. If she agrees, send word and I'll organise it. It would be at the akron, of course."

"I'll see what she says," answered Tralvar impassively.

But he delayed passing on the request. Dena was in a buoyant mood that evening and he had no wish to spoil it by mentioning Chisrin. When the next day dawned he still hadn't told her.

In the afternoon Laura, Idenion and Dena made a pilgrimage to the site of their former home. Then, in the company of many ex-labourers, they watched indulgently as Tralvar set off the demolition charges around the siren - that most hated symbol of the Synectics' tyranny. For a moment the device hung in mid-air above a column of green fire; then it toppled with a clang. Everyone cheered, and Tralvar was promptly mobbed by young girls hoping for the chance to emulate Ninfi. Idenion looked on with amusement.

"Ah, the fickleness of women! I haven't done anything heroic just lately, so they desert me in their hundreds."

Laura responded with a watery smile. Yesterday she'd refused to visit the registry with the others; Idenion was still upset about it, though he hid it well. She'd tried to explain to him, not very successfully, that she wasn't having second thoughts about her future on Celestra. Neither was she averse to being on a database. She was quite certain that as soon as her true identity had been discovered, a Narvellan clerk had scurried off to delete Lisset of Treva and add Laura of Gilcoyne to the Protectorate's exhaustive list. But she simply wasn't ready to commit her name to a system concerned solely with offspring and genealogy. At least, not yet. "Just let the dust settle," she had pleaded.

Tralvar was still trying to shake off his admirers. Lydion sauntered by, grinning.

"Isn't he hopeless?" he remarked to Laura. "He's no idea how to handle girls. If I were a free agent I might invoke the family connection and take a few of them off his hands. As it is, I think I'd better round up Tarlatine and make for safety."

Idenion turned to elicit Dena's comments, only to find she had wandered off. She was standing some distance away, near the ruins of Chisrin's house. The eprys bush still bloomed in what remained of the garden. She bent to pick something from the ground, then once more stood lost in thought. Her pregnancy wasn't yet visible, but in some indefinable way she radiated expectant motherhood.

"She looks beautiful," Laura said wistfully.

"You *would* say that," Idenion answered, his tone reflective rather than critical. "I think she's been more damaged than any of us. She's suffered notoriety, her health's at risk, and she's giving up the custodianship without having had time to enjoy it."

"But she's happy enough now, isn't she?" ventured Laura. "Tralvar dotes on her."

"Tralvar wasn't exactly what I had in mind for my sister," Idenion said candidly. "He's so destructive. Look at her, Laura. She's shielded, but isn't it obvious what she's thinking?"

The truth dawned on Laura. "She's going to keep the baby!"

"Well done. And what do you imagine Tralvar will say when she tells him?"

"He'll be furious."

"Quite. He can't over-rule her but he'll find some way to make trouble. He won't be able to help it."

510

An outbreak of rain brought the street party to a sudden halt. As soon as she and Tralvar were home, Dena nerved herself to acquaint him with her decision. But Tralvar, contrary to Laura's prediction, showed surprisingly little anger. Dena was too trusting to be suspicious and gently allayed his concerns about the birth. "I've spoken to Tarlatine and the other healers and they're going to induce labour four octals prematurely, while the baby's still a size I can cope with. I won't be in any danger."

"There's always danger," he contradicted. His expression denoted weary acceptance. "Won't you tell me what the deciding factor was? I assume there *was* one."

"Two, actually. Tarlatine said that when the Trevan exiles came home, every woman of childbearing age was pregnant. Yet as soon as the protections took hold, they all miscarried. The gift of life is so often taken from us - what right have I to destroy *this* life? And then there's Laura, still pining for a child by Idenion. Would she not cleave to the child of his twin? How could I face her if I let it be killed?"

"You've been rehearsing that," Tralvar observed. "Don't worry, I'm not going to yell at you. Not for upholding Celestrian principles."

And in truth, he was grudgingly proud of her. But his malice toward Chisrin burned unabated. Until today he'd assumed the Narvellan was beyond his reach, having been handed some silly designation by the Protectorate and allowed to walk free. Now, thanks to Myrig, there was a chance for Dena to get even. She wouldn't want to, of course, but that could be taken care of by a couple of judicious lies. It would be worth it.

***

511

Two days later, in one of the akron's audience chambers, Dena sat uneasily in the presiding administrator's chair and waited for the ritual to begin.

"I'm not eligible to hold an audience," she said to Tralvar in a small, worried voice.

"It's only a charade," Tralvar said irritably. "And if that lout doesn't soon show his face, I'm taking you home."

The ceremony required Dena to appoint two independent witnesses, but the rules had been adjusted slightly as she'd refused to attend unless Tralvar was with her. Nefyrra was the second witness. The chair was the only piece of furniture in the long, narrow room. The floor was of polished wood and a long strip of carpet led to a door at the far end.

"Perhaps he's changed his mind," suggested Nefyrra.

Tralvar scratched the back of his neck vigorously. "This is positively the last time I'm wearing this stupid uniform," he announced to no-one in particular.

At last they heard footsteps approaching and the door opened to admit Chisrin and two Moderators. They marched forward in unison and came to a halt in front of the waiting Celestrians. The Moderators no longer seemed threatening - just two arrogant young Narvellans in ostentatious black. Chisrin's hair was neatly braided and he wore only an ylur tunic and rope sandals. The skin around his left wrist was pink and wrinkled where the Mark of Netsamet had been.

"Well, get on with it," said Tralvar impatiently. Chisrin cleared his throat, then began in High Narvellan:

"To Dena of Celestra, companion of Tralvar - thus speaks Chisrin of Narvella, your servant. Hail to you, your house, your family, your world. I have come to make atonement for my crime against you. Whatever you desire of me, name it and I shall comply. The task

512

you set me will be carried out with zeal, no matter what it might be."

He paused. No-one spoke.

"If you accept my homage, then set me a task," he repeated.

Dena said nothing. One Moderator looked bored, the other amused. Chisrin repeated his request a third time. Dena's face was expressionless but her tension was palpable. Her knuckles gleamed whitely as she gripped the arms of the chair.

"Dena, please!" cried Chisrin.

"That's enough," said one of the Moderators. "She isn't going to speak. End this."

Chisrin, eyes filled with anguish, knelt before Dena and bowed his head. Then he rose, turned on his heel and almost ran from the chamber.

"He looked so desperate," said Dena when they were alone again. "Are you sure it was right to stay silent?"

"Of course," Tralvar assured her. "If you'd set him something to do he'd have been your slave in Narvella's eyes. By saying nothing, you've freed him. And by the way, you won't have to put up with him skulking around Alda Mexa much longer. He's being sent to Alda Four Base as soon as it's up and running."

"He asked Laura if he might attend her concert," Nefyrra announced.

"Oh? When was this?"

"Yesterday. He sent a message via Kyrin. Laura said it was all right as long as he stayed at the back and didn't bother anyone."

Tralvar frowned. "If Laura's given her permission, I suppose I'll have to go along with it. But don't forget I'll be on stage most of the time - I won't be able to eject him if he decides to be a nuisance."

But inwardly he knew this wouldn't happen. Chisrin had been firmly put in his place. Of course, Dena was bound to find out eventually - but not, Tralvar hoped, before the disgraced Narvellan had been packed off to Alda Four. Keeping her in ignorance might mean avoiding unity for a while, but that probably wouldn't be too difficult. They'd both be very busy in the days ahead.

***

During the octal leading up to Laura's concert, Tralvar and Gryc - and Lydion, when he could be spared from maintaining the city's power supply - worked ceaselessly on the weathershield. After five days they'd only achieved sputters and thunderclaps, partial shield collapse, projector overload and a circuit blow-out. Then, on the sixth day, after Gryc had reconfigured the energy field, they were rewarded with a beautiful green sky-effect. After some furious trimming of the projectors this was followed by red, orange and indigo.

"Well done!" Dena enthused as the trio emerged from the generator room to admire their handiwork. "Now go home, Tralvar, and have a long hot bath. You're treading grease all over the stage!"

"Did Laura see any of the display?" asked Lydion.

"No - she's at the library with Idenion, translating lyrics."

"Great. Then we can surprise her!"

"How's her voice?" Tralvar inquired. "Have the exercises paid off?"

"Not exactly. She was right to opt for the - what does she call them? - torch songs. She says the more ambitious pieces will have to wait until the Peisistrata."

"That seems aeons away. So does spring."

"It'll be here before we know it," Lydion prophesied. "Gryc, many thanks for your invaluable help. Will you be returning to Treva?"

"Maybe. I'm still waiting for reassignment. It could be Treva, it could be Ilonna."

According to Myrig, Ilonna would be populated in six phases over ten days. The first migrants were due that very evening. Tralvar had wondered at the rapid turnaround, so punishing for the spacecraft, but Myrig had assured him it was nothing to do with solar flare activity. Rather, he had dedicated as many spheres as possible to exploration, leaving comparitively few to transfer the colonists.

The elite and their entourage were also planning a move to Ilonna, leaving only a token few staff to maintain contact with the Celestrian administration. Myrig and Axmiol would remain. Also - despite the disapproval of her peers - Tarlatine. At Myrig's behest, Tralvar signed various documents giving his official blessing to the changes, and put out an edict stating that Ilonna was out of bounds to all Celestrians unless invited. Then, having done his duty, he thankfully turned his attention to the concert rehearsals. He'd scarcely one day left to hone his keyboard skills - and for this occasion, only the best would do.

It was, as Dena remarked, as if Laura had only just returned. Joyous citizens crammed into the Lyricon until every terrace, aisle and balcony was full. The rain held off, the sun set in a blaze of golden glory and one or two chilly stars began to appear. Wemm's fireworks flared in brief emerald splendour above the colonnades. Then, suddenly, the weathershield pulsed into life and summer held sway. The concert was preceded as usual with dances; one solitary girl in a company of youths.

Chisrin had secured a place on the mezzanine level, in blatant disregard of Laura's instructions. He didn't recognise the dancer until one or two boys in the audience shouted "Ailsi!" He knew her then, the spirited little waif who'd remained loyal to him no matter what he did to drive her away. He'd never thanked her for nursing him through his therite blindness. He'd wanted to tell her how, during his trance, her sheer love of life had shone out and sustained him. But she was only Ailsi, and he'd still been too proud.

The stage emptied. A sense of anticipation began to build. Then Forlane appeared and began to reiterate the closing speech from Vanity O'erthrown: "I hope, as do we all, that a way can be found to bring Laura back - to lead us through these troubled times - " A roar from the audience drowned the rest of his words. Laura, barefoot, strolled onto the stage behind him. She wore a clinging, off-the-shoulder dress which sparkled with a myriad points of pink light: fragments of the flawed aldacite crystals which Ailsi had kept.

Laura waited until the thunderous applause had died away. "I'm back where I belong," she announced at last. "What would you have me do?"

"Sing!" came the reply. "*Sing*! Sing for us!"

Forlane left the stage. Tralvar appeared and settled himself at the zirid. The blue sky darkened to indigo. Laura glanced up in surprise. Then she moved across to Tralvar's side and the performance began.

"Have you room for two more?" called Lydion, bounding into the custodian's suite with Tarlatine at his side.

"Just about," Dena replied from the balcony. With her were Nefyrra, Jarras, Idenion and several of the scolia; they obligingly moved over.

"If you're up here, Lydion, who's running the shield?" asked Jarras. "Not Tonor, surely?"

"No, it's Gryc. He took pity on me when I said I was always stuck in the basement whenever Laura gave a concert. When I knew I was actually going to *see* one, I asked her to dedicate something to my golden girl and me." He gave Tarlatine a squeeze. "I told her it had to be really special."

"Then it *will* be," pronounced Dena.

Chisrin watched attentively. To him, the voice was unremarkable; he'd somehow expected that. But the songs! The lyric bards of Symerid Three had written some wondrous pieces. And Idenion's translations, considering the haste in which they'd been done, were masterly. Laura's songs were of love. Love betrayed, love regained, ennui, triumph, regret, fulfilment, heartbreak. There was such a rapport between her and Tralvar that Chisrin found it hard to believe they weren't lovers.

But he couldn't enjoy what he was hearing. Each line, with its bittersweet, double-edged truths, seemed to be aimed specifically at him. Presently he got up and pushed his way out.

Overhead as Laura sang, the artificial sky moved through its new spectrum: pink, red, orange, green, blue, indigo. She tried to ignore it. At the end of her sixth number she paused to drink some water, and three strelsis players moved unobtrusively to join her.

Dena looked surprised. "What are *they* doing on stage? Tralvar said he didn't need anyone else."

"Slight change of plan," Idenion said airily. "As Tralvar's so fond of telling us, the zirid isn't a concert instrument. Laura wants to put everything into this last song and she was worried she'd drown him out. And by the way, Lydion, this one's for you."

The scolia played an introduction and Laura began Jacques Brel's "Ne Me Quitte Pas." She and Idenion had translated it directly from French into Celestrian, and had successfully retained all its raw passion. In moments, she'd drawn the entire audience into the mood of the song. Lydion had his arms very tightly around Tarlatine, whose eyes were bright with unshed tears.

The last tremulous notes died away. Laura, poised and smiling, gratefully acknowledged the applause. She beckoned Tralvar forward and the noise redoubled. While they were side by side, Laura said without dislodging her smile:

"Chaos, Tralvar, what have you done to the shield? The orange takes the colour out of everything and the green makes everyone look dead. What were you thinking of?"

"I thought you'd like it!" he retorted, not bothering to look pleasant.

As they left the stage they ran into Forlane. "Splendid concert, First Singer!" he said, embracing her. "But Tralvar, what in discord's name is wrong with that weathershield? Garish in the extreme, wouldn't you say?"

"All those colours give me a headache!" This was Ailsi. "Can't you put the blue back?"

"Yes," chorused the other dancers. "We liked the blue sky. Why did you change it?"

Tralvar parried a few more comments of this nature, looking more and more disconsolate. Presently Lydion appeared, grinning from ear to ear.

"I needed something to cheer me up after that harrowing song," he remarked, "and you've just provided it, dear brother. You should see your face! *How* long were you trying to fix that shield? Ten years?"

Tralvar scowled and said nothing.

"Well, since no-one topside liked it either, I suppose I'd better change it back. I assume you want me to?"

"If you can do it without my help," Tralvar said resignedly. "I'm fit for nothing at the moment."

Lydion patted him soothingly on the shoulder. "Don't worry, master musician. I'll talk nicely to Gryc and I'm sure he'll lend a hand. We'll have that blue sky back before you can say ingratitude." He began to hurry off, then paused again in merriment. "Ten years...!" he repeated.

They could hear him chortling all the way to the generator room.

***

Tralvar was glad to fall asleep that night, but moments later - or so it seemed - Dena was shaking him awake. It was daylight, but only just.

"I'm sorry to wake you so early," she said, "but the Narvellans have an emergency and you're wanted at Communications. Jarras is there already. He's coming back for you."

Tralvar crawled out of bed. "Is it the solar flares?"

"No, but Jarras says it's serious." Dena rounded up his scattered clothes. "Shall I bring you some liman?"

"Resnay would be better."

"Would it?"

Tralvar sighed. "Just fetch it, Dena, please. I need something to sharpen my wits. Otherwise I might as well stay at home."

He was reasonably alert and presentable by the time Jarras arrived, though the damp morning air made him cough. To his surprise, Laura was waiting in the flitter.

"Myrig's idea," explained Jarras. "She has an original way of looking at things, as he put it."

Tralvar settled himself into the cabin. "Hello again, First Singer. My perception's a little delicate at present so why don't you tell me what's been happening? Slowly!"

"The Synectics had one more dirty trick up their sleeves," she replied. "All the synthetic crystals are failing. Last night the Ilonna spheres were on their way here with a second contingent of migrants. They went into transposal and were lost."

"One or two didn't achieve transposal," Jarras elaborated. "They reported massive systems failures just

519

before they went silent. But they're the lucky ones - we know where they are, and they can be picked up. The rest could have fallen out of transposal anywhere between here and Narvella. With no way to communicate, we'll never find them."

"All those people...!" Tralvar breathed.

"It's worse than that. The Narvellans have lost a third of their fleet! How many colonists won't now be saved, thanks to this final betrayal?"

"So you think it was deliberate," mused Tralvar. "I'm not so sure."

Jarras looked startled. "It had to be! Why else would all the crystals fail at once?"

"Because of the Narvellans' mania for order. I've seen the paperwork, remember? All the spacecraft that disappeared will have logged the same amount of flight time. It was supposed to equalise stress. Rillan, on the other hand, thrashed that sphere of his. Back and forth, back and forth on the Narvella run..."

Realisation hit Jarras with sickening clarity. "Oh, chaos, *no*!"

"He was the first casualty," Tralvar concluded sombrely. "We just didn't know it until today."

Jarras swung the flitter in a viciously tight arc. It thudded to the ground next to the Communications tower. "He was out there, stranded and alone, until his air was gone," he said bitterly. "And nobody guessed. We thought he was on Myrma enjoying himself!"

"Come on," Tralvar said gently. "Let's try and do something constructive."

"Tralvar has a point about the Synectics' motives," said Laura as they entered the elevator. "Industrial aldacite was their best achievement. Why would they deliberately incorporate a limitation? A few premature breakdowns would have destroyed their credibility."

"Then you think they didn't know?" asked Jarras.

"Oh, I'm sure they *knew*. But it wasn't a trap left in the event of their destruction. They simply couldn't design a stable crystal."

Myrig and Axmiol were waiting in the observation lounge at the top of the tower. Another man, whom Laura recognised as Narad's aide at the trial, was with them. Breakfast had been set on a side table, but no one seemed to have eaten anything. Likewise, everyone ignored the panoramic view over the spacefield.

Tralvar wasted no time on formalities. "Ground every single sphere, if you haven't already done so," he ordered.

"We have," answered Myrig. "Axmiol has spoken to the homeworlds and I've alerted all the spaceports here. This - " he indicated the third man - is Bydlor, Narad's secretary. Narad's department was in charge of all records pertaining to the fleet - completion dates, serial numbers, port of origin."

"I've instituted a search of all files," Bydlor said. "A team has been at work for several ilden. Unfortunately, it appears that crystal segregation was seldom practised once the consignments reached the workplace. There's no evidence that the assembly crews noted which spheres received genuine crystals."

"The emphasis was on maintaining quotas, if you recall," Tralvar said pointedly.

Bydlor accepted the rebuke with a slight bow. "We will continue to search."

"There has to be someone who can divine real crystals," Axmiol said. "I was hoping you'd know, First Citizen."

"I don't know of anyone," Tralvar answered after a pause.

"Rillan could," said Jarras. "Not that it's any use to us now."

"There must be others. Think! Laura, have you any suggestions?"

Laura was about to admit that she hadn't when a worried technician looked in from Communications Control. "My lords, Rhul has just reported that they're unable to make contact with the expeditionary fleet. It's believed they must be in transposal."

Axmiol's face grew a shade greyer. "Tell Rhul to keep trying."

"Yes, my Lord Governor."

"And stop calling me that. I'm no longer in charge here."

"Your pardon, lord." The technician scuttled back to the transposer.

The exchange had given Laura time to assemble her thoughts. "Didn't any of the fleet carry reserve crystals? Is there no chance that some of the missing spheres might make repairs and turn up?"

It was Jarras who replied. "You're forgetting how our spacecraft are constructed. Remember the time I almost lost the thruster array and got chased by your jets? I used circuitry from the drinks cooler to fix the array, because all circuits can be interchanged. But every component, with the exception of the Drive itself, has crystals in it - and if they'd *all* failed, I'd have been helpless. Spheres normally carry a surplus of a dozen or so. No use at all when you need hundreds."

"There are reserve stockpiles at Treva," Myrig added, "set aside for our final departure. At least we know which of *those* are real!"

"Have the Directresses been consulted?" asked Laura.

"Not yet."

"But isn't Passik the leading authority on crystals?"

Myrig sighed. "Passik, and most of the other Directresses, can detect a vein of aldacite in the ground.

522

And once it's been mined, she can tell us whether or not it has flaws. What she and the others *cannot* do is identify synthetics."

Both Jarras and Tralvar looked surprised.

"The reason," explained Bydlor, "is in the synthesis itself. A grain of real aldacite is used as a base, and new material is literally grown on. A crystal created in the laboratory has the same signature, same appearance and same refractive properties as an original. So the Directresses say."

"What about Sijek?" asked Jarras.

"Ah," said Axmiol fondly. "The wild talent. He says every single crystal, genuine or not, is different. Which doesn't help us much."

"Chisrin said he knew which ones were real," Laura said suddenly.

"Chisrin is ksil and his word would not be accepted," stated Axmiol.

Tralvar was incensed. "I can't believe I'm hearing this! Your spacefleet's landlocked and the solar flares are imminent. What's more important - tradition, or saving yourselves?"

"Law-abiding Narvellans will not accept the word of a ksil," Axmiol repeated.

Tralvar bit back his anger, but still looked as if he might walk out.

"I've just remembered," said Laura, changing the subject and thereby saving the conference. "When Idenion was bringing me from Earth, I thought the crystal resonance was off-key."

"Did you now!" Axmiol was intrigued. "It's as I was saying earlier, Myrig - the fault must be in the resonance."

"But if it happens in transposal, how can you investigate it?" Myrig asked.

"We can simulate transposal in the laboratory," said Axmiol.

"It would take forever!" Myrig objected. "Not only that, but Laura's sense of pitch may be unique to her species. There has to be another way!"

"There's nothing else we can suggest," said Tralvar, still intent on winding up the proceedings. "We don't have any crystal experts. Even Tyvian, with his aldacite dependence, couldn't tell real from fake."

"That's *it*!" Laura exclaimed. "The prill. I'd forgotten!"

The three Narvellans turned hopefully toward her.

"Tyvian said the prill - the retracer plants - would only bond with natural aldacite," she elaborated.

Myrig exhaled slowly. "Thank you, Laura."

"I'll contact Tafret Academy and ask for their fullest co-operation," said Tralvar, relieved that they had a plan of sorts. "You, or whoever takes charge, will have to be taught how to liaise with the prill."

Now they had something positive to do, the atmosphere became more relaxed. Everyone save Tralvar ate a portion of the neglected breakfast, and a work strategy began to take shape.

Almost two ilden later, the technician returned apologetically. "My lords, citizens, Lady Laura," he began, "there is bad news from Rhul. The expeditionary fleet has also fallen prey to crystal malfunction. However, several of the craft lost transposal near a barren planet, and were able to co-ordinate a landfall using their solar batteries. With the few functioning crystals that remained they repaired a single transposer. We have their position. And hopefully we should be able to find others."

"No one goes anywhere until we have authenticated enough crystals," declared Myrig. "I'll speak to Rhul myself and explain the procedure we're adopting." He left his place at the conference table and went into the adjacent room.

Bydlor wandered away from the group and stood staring out of the window. His attention was not on the view.

"Bydlor, what's wrong?" asked Laura after a few moments. He turned round with a sigh.

"Forgive me. My brother is with the fleet and I fear for him. The last time we spoke he said that he and the rest of the crew were being targeted by propagandists - nihilists, he called them - who said we shouldn't go, that we'd forfeited the right to survive. Perhaps we have."

With swift, decisive steps, Axmiol crossed the room and seized him by the shoulders. "We have *every* right to survive. We could give up now - we could slink back to Narvella Prime and die like cowards in shelters and caves. But I happen to think we're worth more than that. We're going to surmount this problem - we're going to reassemble our fleet and live with the losses - and we're going to find a new, safe world. Will you follow your brother's fine example, or shall I take you home and find you a hole to crawl into?"

Bydlor raised his head and met the challenge of Axmiol's gaze. "I want to live," he said.

Axmiol released him, smiled, and went to join Myrig.

"He'll pull everything together, won't he?" Laura murmured to Tralvar.

"Axmiol? Oh yes. He'll rally his people if anyone can. But he has a lot of hard work ahead of him!"

Chapter Sixteen

"So you've finally decided to come back, have you?" said Dena, looking up accusingly from her writing table. "Where have you been?"

"On tour," replied Ailsi, twining her small lissome frame round a nearby chair. It was noisy in the custodian's suite; sounds of repair work were rising from the auditorium and someone was tuning a strelsis in the next apartment.

"You mean, dancing?"

"Of course! In the southern city-states, mostly. They all wanted to see the dance I did for Laura. And Vanity O'erthrown's still very popular, though we had to change the ending."

"Well," said Dena severely, "There are just two octals before the Peisistrata. If you can't learn the new choreography in that time I'll have to use your understudy. I'll find you a copy of the notation."

"I'll be ready. I always am," said Ailsi, then gasped as Dena stood up. "Chaos! I'd no idea you were so...gravid! I haven't been away *that* long, surely?"

"My baby isn't due for another five octals, believe it or not, but the birth will have to be induced before then."

"Does Chisrin know you kept it?"

"I don't suppose so. I didn't tell him." Dena located the scroll containing her new composition and handed it to Ailsi.

"I heard about your little spat with Tralvar," the dancer went on. "The ritual he sabotaged?"

"Oh dear. Does that mean my private life is the talk of all the cities?"

"The First Citizen's consort doesn't *have* a private life," Ailsi returned. "Tralvar's quite a celebrity now. What did he do exactly? Why were you so put out?"

"I won't have my mind made up for me." Dena regained her chair and settled into it thankfully. "Tralvar knew I'd forgiven Chisrin but he cheated me out of showing it."

"And I suppose you didn't tell Chisrin that either."

"I tried, but he's on Alda Four Base and they wouldn't bring him to the radio. The strange thing is, he's spoken to Tralvar a couple of times since and hasn't even mentioned me. He thinks the base isn't safe, that there's going to be a landslip or something, and of course no-one will listen to him because he's in disgrace. Tralvar tried having a word with Myrig but I don't think it helped."

Ailsi cast a casual glance over the chart and tried a few experimental steps. "I noticed there were hardly any Narvellans left in the city. Isn't it good? No more shielding your thoughts or looking to see if there's a Moderator on your tail. We've got our planet back!"

"Not quite, but it won't be long now. I've seen some of the fleet's requisitions - medical supplies, seeds, tools and so on. Tralvar's just leaving them to it. And now, if you'll excuse me, I've some requisitions of my own to complete. The music's all organised but the catering's in a total mess."

"Why don't you let Nefyrra take care of that?" suggested Ailsi. "You must be tired. Go home and let Tralvar fuss over you!"

"I'd be tempted, but he isn't there. He's on his way to open the pleasure gardens to the public - although I can't think why he decided to open them just *before* the Peisistrata. If there's sciesha, there could be some damage done."

"Oh, there'll be sciesha," Ailsi said softly. "It's in the air, even now."

Forlane, as he surveyed the boisterous crowd which had gathered for the opening ceremony, was of the same opinion - but unlike Dena, knew exactly why Tralvar was dedicating the garden ahead of schedule. The novelty would channel off the urge for sciesha until a more appropriate moment. Not that he, Forlane, was averse to sciesha. He hoped it would be all the better for the delay.

"I'm glad I brought you!" Tralvar shouted from close by. "I'd never have made myself heard. And I'm glad Laura's not here - I didn't want her bawling at this lot and straining her voice. But why didn't I think to bring Kyrin? He'd have settled them down!"

"Calmly now, First Citizen!" beamed Forlane. "This mob's less vociferous than many I've faced in the Lyricon. Observe!" Then, in his best stage accents: "People! Attend! Forlane, your humble servant of the theatre, wishes to make a speech on this auspicious occasion."

Whoops and yells ensued, along with a few cries of "Let's hear it!" Forlane merely waited. And gradually, responding to his charismatic presence, the crowd grew quiet.

"That's more like it," said the actor almost conversationally. He sauntered across to the garden's entrance - a graceful archway set in a trellised wall of pale stone. A grass rope was suspended across its width. "Through this arch we have a realm of mystery. Pathways and pergolas! Fountains and frolics! Sequestered arbours where tired lovers may rest - and recuperate!"

"Just what I need!" called Lydion. Tarlatine laughed and clung to his arm.

"All this," continued Forlane, "has been created by the charming and incomparable elite-wives - although I'm sure their menfolk lent a hand with the bricklaying. Step forward, ladies!" He beckoned to a group of soberly dressed Narvellan women, who smiled and huddled together nervously. Tarlatine, who had long since abandoned her cumbersome grey attire for the freedom of a Celestrian tunic, replied for them.

"We did all of it ourselves! We're telekinetic, remember? We hope you'll enjoy the fruits of our labours for many years to come!"

A shadow crossed Lydion's face.

"Tarlatine wants me to remind you," Forlane went on, "that the trees won't look their best for a few more seasons. But we'll be able to see their promise today, and admire the flowers and plants assembled from every region of our world. In short, if it'll grow here, it's here. Laura, our First Singer - who can't be with us today as she's rehearsing for the Peisistrata - suggested we name this unique place the Tyvian Gardens. Are we agreed?"

There was a chorus of approval.

"In that case, it only remains for our First Citizen to do the honours."

Tralvar casually unhooked the grass rope and tossed it aside. "The Tyvian Gardens are now open. Anyone not having a good time will answer to me!"

Amid laughter, the crowd streamed through the arch. Tarlatine stayed to talk with the elite-wives and temporarily lost sight of Lydion. Her break with tradition was never more marked, and for a moment she felt slightly selfconscious in her revealing dress. Then she realised why. Myrig was standing at a distance, watching her. Excusing herself, she made her way over to him.

"We should talk," he said.

"Why choose today?" she challenged. "You've known where to find me ever since I started work here."

"Hitherto, our preparations were incomplete," he returned.

"You're...ready to leave?"

"Whenever Axmiol gives the word. We've selected new colonists following the loss of the Ilonna migrants, and hopefully made more informed choices than before. Your recommendations were followed: there will be twice as many women as men, and all males over twenty-five will already have sired at least one child. The exception to that is, of course, Axmiol - but I'm sure you'd be the first to agree that we need his leadership."

"Indeed we do," affirmed Tarlatine. "And what of your son? Did you persuade him to leave Narvella Prime?"

"He wishes to remain there," Myrig answered remotely. "I'll not speak of him further. Instead, let's talk about *you*. Your affair with Lydion of Atris continues to concern me. Will you not give him up now?"

"I will not," Tarlatine said emphatically. "But neither will I forget my duty. Let me know the time and place of departure and I will be there. Until then I shall cleave to Lydion, and when I'm summoned he'll know I loved him to the last. I'll take the husband you assign to me and I'll bear his children - but always I shall think of Lydion and these very precious days."

"You're an honourable woman, Tarlatine nyl Besu lyr Scibor," Myrig said quietly.

"Forget about my title," she advised. "The old order will soon be gone: we start again as equals. May it always remain so." Then she hurried away, almost colliding with Tralvar. He gazed after her narrowly.

"Making trouble, Myrig? I really must insist that you leave her alone. I regard her as family."

Myrig gave him a world-weary stare. "So do I. And I hardly need remind you, First Citizen, that in the old days she would have been publicly shamed and your incorrigible brother flogged. We allowed them their passion. But they're almost out of time."

"I see."

"Axmiol would like you to call on him at noon tomorrow. There are a few final matters to tidy up. Kyrin was to have notified you, but since I'm here I'll save him the trouble."

"Which audience room should I attend?"

"None of them. Axmiol will see you in his quarters."

"I'm flattered," Tralvar remarked, but despite his flippancy knew that Axmiol would have a sound reason for his choice. Myrig's parting words, however, did surprise him.

"And you're to bring Laura with you."

Tralvar didn't ask why, knowing he wouldn't have received an answer. Nor was an explanation immediately forthcoming when, on the morrow, he and Laura were shown into Axmiol's study by the ever-present Sijek. The room was not, as they had expected, austere, but comfortably furnished along Celestrian lines. Axmiol was seated at a small desk, on which stood a photograph of a Narvellan family group.

"Sit. Be welcome," he greeted them. His manner was as formal as ever, but tempered now with sadness. "As Myrig has intimated, the crystal replacement programme is complete, and tomorrow Sijek and I will relocate to Ilonna. No one else will be arriving from the homeworlds; the colonial fleet has a full complement of passengers. At your suggestion, Tralvar, we have included the two zyl Nyris girls."

"How many spheres are in the fleet?" asked Laura.

"Two thousand and six," Axmiol replied unhesitatingly.

"Is that all?" Tralvar was taken aback. "I'd no idea you'd lost so many! What happened to the ones based at Rhul?"

"Their logic systems were corrupted by nihilists, who also waylaid the steel consignment intended for Tegna Nine."

"Why didn't you tell me?" Tralvar asked peevishly.

"It was our problem, First Citizen. What could you have done?"

"Couldn't you have repaired the spheres?"

"Given time. There wasn't enough."

"Shouldn't you have anticipated something like this?" Laura asked, sounding more critical than she'd intended.

"I wasn't there," Axmiol answered drily. "The Lord Protector is in his dotage - he thought the agitators would be content with making noise."

"Why don't they want the colony to survive? Do they think if they can't go then no-one must?"

"Not exactly. Remember what Bydlor said? They don't want *anyone* to survive. They think we, as a species, acted dishonourably in allowing the Synectics to be destroyed. They believe that incorporeal group minds are the next stage in our evolution, and a few even hope that if they meditate sufficiently they can liberate their minds from their bodies." He gave a tired but cold smile. "They will not succeed."

"I hope you've managed to keep them away from Ilonna," Tralvar remarked.

"Do you not recall," Axmiol said haughtily, "that our ruling elite has never been overthrown? It would have been a sorry day indeed if we'd failed to suppress this final rebellion. The nihilists' first move was also their last; we have them all, and I'm sure you'd rather not hear how we achieved that. They will live just long enough to abjure their foolish beliefs. And now, shall we return to the business of the day? I have two reports to hand over. The first is a list, compiled by our Directresses, of newly located aldacite deposits. It will save your people digging at random when they need more. The second file contains Firessa lyr Raxel's research into Celestra's falling birthrate: the discovery of the virus which inhibits fertility, the missing co-factor, and a few more items besides." He turned to Laura. "First Singer, you have made Celestra your own, and will doubtless be at the forefront of its recovery. Thus, I'm delivering Firessa's work into your hands."

"Why me? I really think Tralvar should have it."

"Tralvar will go on doing what he does best - defending his planet. But the preservation of documents isn't a talent I associate with him. I've seen the state of his house, don't forget. Take the dossier, Laura. I know how much this project means to you."

"Who's going to finish it?" she asked, half to herself.

"Trust me, you'll find that person." He handed Tralvar and Laura a folder each.

"So this is our final leavetaking," Tralvar observed.

"Don't pretend you're sorry," Axmiol returned.

"Axmiol," ventured Laura, "surely you aren't removing your chosen ones from Celestra until..."

"You don't usually mince your words, First Singer."

"Until after the solar flares," she continued, a little ruffled. "They may be delayed, or not as bad as you fear."

"Sadly, there will be no such reprieve," Axmiol replied sombrely.

"Is there something else you haven't told us?" inquired Tralvar, more gently this time.

Axmiol bowed his head. "The first coronal mass ejection struck Narvella Prime the day before last, destroying what remained of the ozone layer and irradiating a third of the globe. Communications are out worldwide, but the transposers are still operating, and the news reached me almost at once. As yet, I haven't informed the majority of my people, nor even decided how much to tell them. I had hoped for something more swift. What I've seen is..." He paused, overcome.

"Please go now," urged Sijek.

Tralvar seemed reluctant, but Laura gave him a push toward the door.

"Wait." Axmiol partially regained his composure. "We have positioned two drones near our outer planets to independently monitor the condition of the sun. I will make this data available to you. Be assured we will not leave until the cycle of flares is complete."

"Will you look for survivors?" Laura asked.

"We cannot," Axmiol said expressionlessly. "I won't risk losing any more spheres. The build-up of plasma in the region of the homeworlds would cause onboard circuitry to fail."

"We may have a chance to go back one day," Sijek said softly. "But for now, the future lies with our colony."

Tralvar paused halfway out of the study. "Am I allowed to know if you have a destination in mind?"

"Yes," Sijek replied positively. "Yes, we do. But I'm instructed not to disclose its whereabouts. Ours was an uneasy alliance at best, and now honour demands that we make a clean break. Once we're on our way, Celestra will not hear from us again."

***

" - and then he said they'd live just long enough to abjure their foolish beliefs," Laura related over lunch the following day. "I hope he didn't see me shudder. I suddenly realised what the elite had been obliged to do in order to stay in power. Bureaucrats? They're more like the Borgias!"

"What are they?" asked Dena.

"Assassins, just like our friendly elite. And I'm not talking state execution in the Ten style - this is strictly

534

back-alley stuff. We didn't see any of it happening because their enemies didn't get leave to come here!"

"I suspected as much," Idenion admitted. "They all thought it was perfectly natural that Tralvar should be a murderer. Narad actually admired him for it."

"Do you think Axmiol's a killer?" Dena inquired uneasily.

"Normally these things get delegated," Laura explained. "It would be such a contradiction if he *has* murdered anyone. He's such a fine healer."

"So was Alendis," remarked Idenion.

Laura diplomatically changed the subject. "Shouldn't we tell Tralvar to hurry up? His food's getting cold."

"Someone always comes to the door at mealtimes," Dena said. "Give him a moment longer. I want to know how Nefyrra's dealing with the caterers. And did that consignment of strelsis strings arrive from Atris?"

Laura had just begun to reassure her when Tralvar appeared with his visitor. It was Myrig. Tralvar's face was an unreadable mask.

"You'd better tell Dena what you've just told me," he suggested. Myrig needed no further prompting.

"We've had an urgent message from Alda Four Base," he began. "There's been an accident - subsidence - "

"Exactly what Chisrin tried to warn you about!" exclaimed Laura.

"Quite so," Myrig conceded. "A schoolroom took the worst damage and a number of children were trapped by debris. Almost singlehandedly Chisrin got them out, but there was a further cave-in and he was badly injured."

"How badly?" asked Dena in a very small voice.

"He's dying," Myrig said quietly. "He has another few ilden at best. In response to his heroism we have rescinded his state of ksil, so he may now make his wishes known. He begs you, Dena, to go to him and complete the Sekhu ritual."

"She isn't going," said Tralvar.

"I entreat you on his behalf," Myrig persisted.

"Discords, Myrig, look at her! She's about to give birth - she can't go gallivanting offworld. Especially not there, when the whole place is liable to fall down!"

"The damaged habitat has been sealed off. The others are unaffected," stated Myrig.

"For the last time, she's going nowhere!" Tralvar snapped.

"Will you two stop discussing me as if I weren't here?" shouted Dena. They both stared at her in surprise.

"You took a decision for me once before, Tralvar," she went on. "You had no right to do so then, and you haven't now. I won't let Chisrin die believing I slighted him. I'm going to complete the ritual."

"Have some sense, Dena!" This was Idenion. She rounded on him angrily.

"Are *you* going to oppose me too? I *have* to do this. I don't understand why the Sekhu's so important - I just know that it is. Do you think Myrig's got nothing better to do than chase around the city at the whim of a dying man? He's here because it means something!"

"I believe Tralvar understands, otherwise he would have turned me away at the door," Myrig said softly.

"I was hoping Dena would turn you away herself," Tralvar retorted. "Well, wife, what's your final word? Do you still intend rushing to the bedside of a man who's done you nothing but harm?"

"Yes," she replied calmly.

Tralvar flinched very slightly. "Very well, do what you must. But I'll have no part in it whatever." And he slammed out of the room.

536

"We'll have to go with her," Idenion said to Laura.

"I'm afraid only one of you can go," said Myrig. "I've already checked with the spaceport and your spheres are all absent on freight duties. But I've reserved two places on a Narvellan craft which is transferring some of our citizens to the base. The departure time is noon-plus-two, so we must hurry. Quickly, now - who's coming with Dena?"

"It had better be me," Laura decided. "Chisrin won't want Idenion near him after that scene at the trial!"

Dena went in search of a cloak and shoes. While she was absent, Idenion spoke earnestly to Myrig.

"I'm not at all happy about this, Administrator. I take it you're not going with the girls?"

"Only as far as the spaceport. But the staff at the base hospital are dedicated and responsible, and the sphere will be standing by to bring them swiftly home."

Idenion had to be satisfied with that. "Take care of her," he begged Laura in sudden anxiety. "Chisrin could be trouble, even now."

"I'll stay next to her the whole time," Laura promised. Then Dena returned and Myrig ushered them out to the flitter.

On the way to the spaceport he schooled Dena in the conclusion to the Sekhu - the part that Tralvar had withheld from her. "She will have to be severe," he warned Laura. "And you, First Singer, must stand by and allow her to do it. In matters of honour there is no room for sentiment."

Laura was glad the journey only lasted two astallen. The cabin was crowded and she had to stand, while Dena perched on a corner of a bunk. The Narvellan passengers did not speak. They seemed distant and strange, as if they were already light-years away. Laura, close to the viewscreen, thought she'd at least see something of Alda Four; but they were approaching the planet's night side, and she saw nothing except a hexagonal pattern of lights as they neared the base. They landed in a maintenance bay similar to the one at Alda Mexa, and waited a further astal while it was pressurised. Then, at last, the sphere's hatch rippled open and everyone was free to leave.

The outpost was minimally equipped. A female healer arrived and escorted the two women down bare, prefabricated corridors toward the infirmary. The lighting was sparse but adequate. Most of the base personnel were in their quarters, exhausted after the rigours of the landslip, but in the communications room several young Narvellans were clustered round the transposer. The image was not visible from the corridor, but from the sonorous narration Laura assumed an inspirational lecture was in progress.

Dena, short of breath, struggled on without complaint. Laura was just about to object on her behalf when they reached the infirmary. Here, the facilities were even more makeshift. There were no walls between the wards, just heavy synthetic sheeting. In the distance the telecast droned on. Some of the children whom Chisrin had rescued lay on rough pallets, asleep or sedated. Finally, the nurse paused in front of a screened-off area.

"Before you see Chisrin, a brief word. He has few visible injuries but has suffered severe internal bleeding which we were unable to arrest. He made light of his condition and insisted that we save the children first." She turned to Dena. "To sustain himself until you arrived, he's been using the Breath of Corayn. He's taken seven times the lethal dose. Since he was dying anyway we saw no reason to withhold it. I shall now call him out of his trance, and I suggest you conclude your business swiftly."

She moved the screen aside, and after a moment beckoned them through. Chisrin lay on a narrow bed beneath a single blanket. His luxuriant hair had been trimmed short and his muscular arms rested limply at his sides. His skin was a sickly yellow. When he saw Dena's very pregnant state his eyes widened momentarily.

"You silly girl," he whispered.

Dena appeared to ignore him. "I am present at your behest to hear the words of the Sekhu," she intoned. Laura found her a chair; she sat down at Chisrin's right hand. "Say the words," she repeated.

He began to recite the opening stanza, pausing frequently to regain his breath.

"I must continue my rounds," the nurse murmured to Laura, and discreetly quit the alcove. Laura darted after her.

"You can't leave! We're witnesses!"

"Laura of Gilcoyne," said the woman with an indulgent smile, "legality isn't an issue. He won't live long enough for it to matter. He seeks only to make his peace with her."

Laura, slightly abashed, returned to Chisrin's bedside. Exactly how was Dena going to authenticate the proceedings? She had to set him a task, didn't she? What could he possibly do?

She soon found out. As Chisrin finished speaking, Dena drew a small transparent disc from her pocket. He regarded it in dismay.

"Where did you get that?"

"From the ruins of your house," she replied. "You now know what your task is: to make Sarune appear. Well, Chisrin, why do you hesitate? Do you refuse? Should I go now?"

"You are cruel, Dena." Chisrin closed his eyes briefly, wondering if she realised just *how* cruel. By ordering him to run the impress, she was compelling him to divert the psychokinetic control he had over his injuries. Without that, his life expectancy could be measured in moments. "I accept. It is a fitting penance," he said at last. "Help me to hold the disc."

Dena obeyed, placing her hand over his. Laura drew closer and watched, fascinated, as the clear surface began to glow and sparkle. For almost half an astal she could see nothing except the dancing motes of Chisrin's waning mental energy; then suddenly, as he made one last effort, an image appeared. For the first and only time, Laura looked on the pre-Synectic Sarune. There was no Narvellan landscape, no lithe athletic girl - just a fleeting close-up of a cool imperious face and an infinitely superior smile.

The picture wavered, vanished. Chisrin made several fruitless attempts to speak, and Dena feared he'd be unable to complete the ritual. Then he rallied and choked out the final phrases. "Lady, I have discharged my task as ordered. Do you release me from my debt?"

"I release you," she said sombrely.

A look of tired gratitude rewarded her. "Then goodbye, my little nemesis," he murmured. "Take care of her, First Singer." He lapsed into unconsciousness, and less than an astal later his tortured breathing ceased. The impress disc slid from beneath his hand and rolled onto the floor. Dena didn't trouble to pick it up. It would never show anything again.

Laura turned aside and shed a few tears. Despite his lack of scruple she'd always liked Chisrin, preferring his blunt directness to the deviousness of the elite. She wished he could have had his chance on the new world.

After a very short interval indeed, Dena tapped her on the shoulder. "Come, Laura," she said calmly. "He's dead now. We needn't stay here any longer."

Laura, through tear-reddened eyes, gazed dolefully at her composed little face. Celestrian attitudes to death were still very difficult to fathom. "No, we needn't," she conceded. "Let's go." It felt disrespectful to walk off and leave Chisrin untended. But, she reminded herself, the elite had restored his honour. His people would grant him a decent funeral.

It was only when they started back toward the landing bay that they noticed how quiet everything was. There was no sign of the nurse, no monologue from the transposer, nothing. Laura, leading the way, hesitated a moment before turning left into the main axial corridor.

"I think I've got this right - " she began, when Dena gave a sudden agonised cry and fell to her knees. Laura rushed back to her.

"What is it? Is it the baby?"

"Something...punched...me," Dena gasped. Then she toppled sideways and lay clutching her swollen belly. A watery bloodstain began seeping through her dress.

Laura looked wildly about for assistance, then made a dash for the communications room. The transposer screen was blank save for a sprinkle of static. Before it, staring at nothing, were the same Narvellans she'd noticed earlier.

"Help me!" she cried. "Dena's having her baby!" When there was no reaction she shook each of the youths in turn. "Answer me! What's the matter with you?" Then, in a panic, she ran back to Dena. She had some vain hope that the stricken girl could summon help telepathically, but one look at her pain-wracked form showed how impossible this was. And would it have done any good? What if all the personnel were in the same trance-like state as those she'd just seen? Their whole demeanour smacked of group mind activity, and she was suddenly very scared. But scared or not, she had to go back in there. She moved Dena to a slightly more comfortable position against the wall, then, steeling herself, returned to the communications room and scurried past the clustered figures. The transposer, her only link to sanity, lay before her - and she had absolutely no idea how to use it. She tried to remember what she'd seen Idenion do, but couldn't. Angry with herself, she jabbed and swatted at the controls until - miraculously - the screen lit. A startled Celestrian operator looked out at her.

"First Singer! How may I - "

"Where are you?" she interrupted. "Alda Mexa?"

"No, Treva," he replied, bewildered.

"Then would you radio Alda Mexa for me? I don't dare meddle with this transposer again. Tell them to get Tralvar out here. It's an emergency." Laura briefly described what had happened. "And the Narvellans have gone weird," she concluded. "Catatonic. I'm sure our sphere's still in the bay, but there's no-one to fly it."

"My colleague is already calling the akron," the young man reassured her. "Keep this channel open and we'll patch you through." But even as he spoke, his image began to break up.

"We need Tarlatine!" Laura shouted just before the link collapsed. She didn't try to restore it. Secure in the knowledge that Tralvar would rescue them, she hurried back to Dena with news of her success.

The message reached Tralvar, via Kyrin, precisely one astal later. There were still no spheres available. Celestra's emergency procedures worked well enough planetside, but there were no contingency plans for off-world. Tralvar felt sick with guilt, but remained calm. He instructed Kyrin to alert Tarlatine, but decided not to take her with him as she could well be susceptible to whatever ailed the Alda Four colonists. So, for that

542

matter, could he. Laura was the only one with guaranteed immunity.

At least, with most of the Narvellans gone, there were plenty of flitters about. In less time than it had taken for the message to reach him, he was at the spaceport. He stormed into the maintenance bay, elbowed some technicians aside and made a swift study of the service manifest. Then, having selected one of the two spheres under repair, he ordered the engineering team to disembark and leave the area. They didn't refuse, but the team leader had the good sense to send for Jarras - who, fortuitously, had just arrived at Communications on a Peisistrata-related errand.

Tralvar was carrying out some perfunctory systems checks and didn't pause or look up as Jarras entered the sphere. "Sent you to talk some sense into me, did they? Don't try."

Jarras decided to be casual. "Undiagnosed power loss," he read from an unfinished report. "Do you really think it's safe to let Dena ride in this thing?"

"She doesn't have to. Once I'm there I can abandon it. Now will you either help me or get lost?"

"I'm here to help. Have you a flight programme?"

"I know the co-ordinates. And don't worry, I won't be stranded halfway. This sphere won't transpose but there's more than enough power to reach Alda Four. Now *move*! You're hindering me."

"Tralvar..." Jarras ventured. "Let *me* go. Your space phobia - "

"I have to do this," Tralvar insisted. "I owe it to Dena. It's only due to my stupid pride that she's out there at all." His hands were shaking.

"I think I'd better go with you," Jarras said quietly.

Tralvar sighed in equal amounts of resignation and relief. "Yes, Jarras. I think you had."

543

Despite the incipient power drain Jarras managed to coax some extra speed from the auxiliaries, and they reached Alda Four in one and a half astallen. Out of courtesy, they radioed in. No one replied. During the last unavoidable wait while the landing bay automatically re-pressurised, Tralvar turned very calmly to Jarras and said: "I'm going to use my perception on whatever's out there. If I get drawn into it, hit me."

"But surely if we both -"

"No, Jarras. Only one of us, and that's an order." He concentrated, and at once some of the tension left him. "Of course! We should have guessed. It's all right, you can read them if you want. I doubt if they'll notice."

Jarras obeyed gingerly, and encountered grief: profound, desolate, unremitting. The entire base was afflicted, and the young people in the communications section had bonded for mutual support. Narvella Prime was no more. A newscast, transposed from Narvella Four to Ilonna and thence to the base, had shown their homeworld's last moments: a vast, gaseous halo encircling the planet, boiling away its atmosphere and oceans, baking the land masses. The flares were not yet at their peak. Everyone knew Narvella Four would be next.

"It's what Axmiol wanted them to see," Tralvar said sombrely. "Swift, total destruction. No more looking to the past."

Through the miasma of sorrow, Laura's unruly thought patterns drew them like a beacon. When they were able to open the hatch they hastened straight to her side, and found her sitting on the floor with Dena cradled in her arms. Tenderly, Tralvar lifted the unconscious girl and carried her back to the sphere she and Laura had arrived in. Jarras helped Laura up, aware that she was close to tears.

544

"Just a moment. Pins and needles," she apologised, leaning on him. "I thought you'd never get here. I've been so afraid!"

"You kept your head, and that's what matters," he said appreciatively.

"But - what's *wrong* with the Narvellans?"

"They're in mourning for their homeworld." Jarras didn't feel like elaborating. "Can you walk yet? Then come on, we must hurry."

As they followed Tralvar, Laura heard the wail of a child and had a brief glimpse of someone - the nurse, perhaps - moving swiftly in response. The Narvellans were beginning to deal with their loss.

Tralvar didn't speak until the spacecraft had cleared Alda Four. Then he suddenly blazed at Laura: "What in chaos happened? You were supposed to be taking care of Dena!"

"No, *you* were," she countered. "Don't start accusing me - I don't know anything about childbirth, remember? Her waters broke, she had one or two strong contractions, and then everything just stopped."

Jarras studied Dena intently. "I'm no healer, but I can't sense *anything* from her. Nor the child."

"Can you land next to the hospital?" Tralvar asked.

"Certainly," Jarras replied promptly. "I've done it before, not long ago."

Tralvar focused all his attention on Dena and tried not to think about the vast, uncaring universe beyond the sphere's white shell. Isylla and her un-named child, Grevin, Tarit, Shann, the sultry Eluthia and the detestable Tarysk tyl Pellon: it was so difficult to believe they were dead along with countless others. A small but evil knot of pain burned in his right side. He tried to ignore that too.

***

Dena's baby, a girl, was stillborn. Tarlatine, coolly professional despite the tragedy which had befallen her people, spoke sensibly to Tralvar.

"The child was already dead when Laura sent her message. Arriving here any earlier wouldn't have saved it. Dena's still very weak, but we've dealt with the afterbirth and stabilised her, and either Drusa or myself will be watching while she rests."

"But has she regained consciousness?" persisted Tralvar.

"Yes; she woke and asked for water. Now *please*, Tralvar, go home and come back tomorrow. You can't expect to be given charge of her if you've had no sleep."

"Laura went home ilden ago. *She* trusts us," Drusa added pointedly.

At last, Tralvar agreed to leave. "If there's any change, send for me at once," he ordered.

Drusa gave a sigh of relief. "I thought he'd never go. Do you still want to deep-read her?"

"I think I should try. She just isn't responding as she should. Something's dragging her down."

"Tarly?" Lydion put an inquiring head round the door. "How is she?"

"Not good."

"I've just seen Tralvar on his way out. I take it you've spun him a line?"

"Tralvar's not the best person to have around a sickroom," said Drusa. "Dena needs calm, and so do we."

"You know her better than we do," Tarlatine added. "Do you sense anything at the surface level that would cause her to reject healing? I was just about to move in deeper."

"I don't read sleeping minds too well, but I'll give it a try," said Lydion amiably. Dena's dainty, lively thoughts, as she directed her dancers or instructed the scolia, had for years been part of his life at the Lyricon. Unsuspectingly he focused his perception - then suddenly winced and took a step back from the bed. Dena hadn't moved.

"Lydion?" said Tarlatine anxiously. "What is it?"

"I was kicked out. Forcibly. I don't think she's asleep, not in the accepted sense." Lydion kneaded his temples, frowning. "Something bad happened at that base, Tarly. Something very bad indeed."

In the middle of the night Tarlatine admitted defeat and sent one of the hospital flitters for Tralvar.

"We've done all we can," she informed him, struggling with exhaustion. "She's gone very far away from us. We're hoping that you, her partner in unity, may be able to call her back."

Tralvar was distraught. "You told me she was recovering!"

"We told you she'd been conscious - and so she was, briefly."

"And now?"

"Now I can only confess that I've failed her. I can't even read her any more."

Tralvar touched Dena's pallid little face. It was cold. Trembling with anxiety he centred his thoughts on her, confirming that her gentle mindset was simply not present. He braced himself for rejection, but it didn't happen. A shifting, featureless greyness met his increasingly frantic efforts to find something coherent. Finally, when it seemed that he might harm himself, Tarlatine pulled him back.

"There's nothing!" he choked. "She's - like Corython!"

"No, *not* like Corython," Drusa said firmly. "All of Dena is still there but she's hiding from us. How or why, we don't know."

"Then she'll die," said Tralvar brokenly.

"Perhaps not," said Tarlatine. "There's still one person who could reach her. Idenion, her twin. They evolved together in darkness, and he's possibly the only one she would allow into her present darkness."

"Then get him over here!"

"He's already been sent for. But be warned, he may not consent to the procedure - and may not be able to accomplish anything even if he does. Unless..."

"Unless what?"

"Forgive me, I'm thinking aloud. Let's wait until Idenion arrives and then I'll explain what I had in mind. Watch her for me, would you, Tralvar? And keep calling her. Drusa and I have some preparations to make."

Tarlatine ushered Drusa into the dispensary. They could still see Tralvar through the partition window, but could not be heard.

"Do you really think Idenion will be able to help?" Drusa asked.

"Amongst my people, the bond between twins transcends the normal boundaries of perception. I'm hoping that will be the case with Idenion, although to be perfectly frank I haven't seen much evidence of it.'"

"Me neither. He and Dena worry about each other, as any brother and sister would, but Idenion sensed nothing when she was raped and *she* didn't have a clue he was in danger at Scapirion."

"So he's going to need some help of the chemical variety. I want you to do two things for me, Drusa. First, find me some starfire - "

"Starfire? That's a proscribed substance!"

"I know. I also know that you and Lydion used it to enhance unity. And I imagine you kept your supply here rather than at home."

Drusa stared at the floor, embarrassed.

"Bring me whatever you have. Then I want you to consult the Narvellan census database and locate Idenion's and Dena's mother. Ask her which of them was born first. It's very important that we know this."

Idenion came in while Drusa was still about her errands. He knew what he was expected to do, and the risks it entailed. He was pale, calm and resolute.

Laura, unable to stay behind, was with him. "He's had no rest!" she lamented. "He kept having nightmares about the time he was caught in some Ten activity near the generating station. The not-darkness, he called it."

Tarlatine was secretly glad to hear of his distress. It meant there was some empathy between the twins after all.

Laura went to have a quiet word with Tralvar, who was looking so tired and ill that she wondered if he should see a healer himself. "We aren't needed here," she told him. "Come on - I'm going to find you some hot liman. Then we can wait next door."

"Shouldn't we get started?" Idenion asked Tarlatine.

"I was waiting for Drusa to bring the starfire," she replied, "but I suppose there's just a chance you won't need it. Can you find your twin, Idenion? Can you save her?"

Idenion tried, bravely casting his mind into the grey not-darkness. He sensed defeat, but not - as he'd feared - the vertiginous enticements of non-being. Dena hadn't quite given up. With his perception at its most sensitive he began to detect hints and glimpses of her, fleeting and elusive, emanating from the most secret recesses of her inner self. And it was this, in the end, which thwarted him. His consciousness snapped back into the reality of the dimly lit ward, with Tarlatine hovering tensely at his side. He drew several deep breaths, succumbed to a coughing spell, then gasped:

"I can't do it. She's my sister. We're told when so very young that we can't have unity with our siblings - and this is *more* than unity. I can't override the law - it's too much a part of me...."

"Give him this," said Drusa, somewhere to his right. Her hand appeared holding a phial of green liquid. "It will break down his inhibitions."

"It's your decision, Idenion," said Tarlatine.

"I'll take it," he replied instantly. They sprinkled the contents of the phial onto a cloth and gave it to him.

"It's virtually instantaneous," Drusa warned. "Prepare yourself. And when you find her, remember - *you* were the firstborn."

The exotic yet acrid scent stung his nostrils. He inhaled a second time, then a third - and suddenly his perception opened onto a vast echoing plain where the intricate traceries of relayists' thoughts crossed and enmeshed. It was beautiful and he wanted to explore it, but his sense of purpose prevailed. Close at hand was the beloved, imperilled mind of his little sister. And he was going to rescue her.

His expanded consciousness sailed effortlessly through the shifting grey, searching, foraging, brightly positive. +No more secrets, Dena! I know where you are!+

+You are mistaken+

Idenion halted, every mote of his enhanced psyche pulsing with alarm. It was unthinkable, impossible - yet the terrifying truth was before him. This entity was not Dena. And although he'd never encountered the trespasser before, he knew her.

+Sarune+

A scorch of contempt smote him – contempt for all things Celestrian. He kept his nerve.

+Sarune, release my sister+

+Upstart!+ she responded. +Remove yourself, twin, or you will not live to be sorry+

His intuition had grown exponentially with the rest of his faculties. +You killed them!+ he accused. +The other Synectics. The bomb interrupted your collective push so you killed the others to get away!+

+Their energy was sufficient+ she agreed. +My destiny was more important than their survival. And I will not be hindered by the likes of you!+

+Why do you hate us so?+ he asked, genuinely puzzled. +Our attempts to defeat you had no effect. You were bested by one of your own kind+

+How little you know!+ she retorted. +It was your fly-by that caused us to fail. Why didn't you strike at once? It's what I would have done. But no, you waited. And we had to scour space incessantly, wasting time and energy which should have been spent perfecting our lattice. And then you sent Quetri, whose obsessive love for your duplicitous leader defied anything we could throw at him. He died crying Tralvar's name. Oh, yes, the Celestrians have a lot to answer for!+

Elsewhere, Laura stared through the glass partition in an agony of suspense. Idenion was slumped next to Dena, with Tarlatine supporting his head. His eyes were half open, his limbs peculiarly rigid.

"Oh, Tralvar, what's taking so long? Did they *have* to give him starfire? It's going wrong, isn't it?"

"I don't know, Laura. I don't know."

She cried on his shoulder and he put both arms around her comfortingly. To think there was a time, he thought, when I would have committed mass murder just to hold her. And now that I have my wish, I can only think of my poor little Dena. It's my fault she's like this. I've tainted her and now she can't fight this malaise.

They clung to each other, wordless, waiting.

+Let Dena go, Sarune+ Idenion commanded. +You have everything you sought. Freedom, immortality - +

+What a romantic you are!+ Sarune's thoughts dripped sarcasm. +Incorporeal is not the same as immortal. The universe is perilous: I must sustain my pattern against pitiless odds. As for freedom - do you think I'm here from choice? Always something has impeded my escape. First the fool who called himself my husband, then his brat, and now your sister. She will not relinquish me, so she must perish+

+Dena is not holding you. Neither were Chisrin and the baby. Your own fear is to blame. The entire universe awaits you, but you cannot detach yourself from the memory of what you were+

+Lies! All lies!+

+I once heard+ Idenion continued reflectively, +of a dimension consisting of pure thought. It's out there somewhere, waiting for you. But you won't find it or any of the wonders you dreamt of, because you fear to let go!+

Sarune's mind was poised like a fist, either to eject him as she had Lydion, or to obliterate him. +Yes, destroy me+ he continued recklessly. +And Dena, and anyone else you think has snared you. It will avail you nothing. You have failed, Sarune. Your mind will wither, diminish and die, like your physical body. Your fear has triumphed+

A barrage of denial slammed against his increasingly dazed perception. +I fear nothing!+ Sarune shrieked - and was gone. Idenion cast about very gently in his grey surroundings, but there was no hint of her malign presence. And slowly, to his wonderment, he realised the greyness had ceased to resemble the not-darkness. It was now more like a pre-dawn light.

And at last he found Dena where she was hiding, sad and small and withdrawn.

+Dena, it's me. It's Idenion. I've come to take you on a journey+

+I'm so tired, Idenion+ she murmured, as on many a workday morning. +Has the siren sounded?+

+Yes, a long time ago+ Idenion replied. +Come on, little sister. We can't stay here+

+Where are we going?+ she asked, a little more wakeful.

+Out into the light. We did this once before, remember? I led, you followed+

+It's very dark+ she said dubiously.

+Not for long. Trust me! This way, Dena. This way....+

+He's bringing her+ Drusa informed Tralvar. He hurtled back into the ward, Laura following, just as the two figures began to stir.

"Tralvar...?" Dena whispered. "Why did you leave me so alone?"

The words stung him. But he didn't dispute the matter, merely imprisoned her hand until Drusa made him stand aside.

Idenion came awake slowly. Laura, overjoyed, hugged him and kissed his forehead. "Thank harmony! I'm so proud of you - but don't you ever scare me like that again!"

"I led her, Laura," he said dreamily. "Out of Hades, like Orpheus. I didn't look round. I wanted to. But then she'd have been lost forever...."

"I know, my best love. I know."

"Did she follow? Is she here?"

"Yes, Idenion, she's here."

He sat up to drink some water. "Sarune was to blame," he explained earnestly to the gathering. "I put her to flight. But you'll have heard that."

"We heard *you* well enough," said Drusa.

"You were hallucinating," Tarlatine informed him. "There was only Dena and yourself."

Tralvar said nothing. He was remembering a certain flitter ride with Chisrin. He'd been prattling to Sarune all the way home from the quarry, with no apparent response.

"*You* think she was there, don't you?" asked Laura. "Tralvar? Tralvar!"

He had doubled up in pain, holding his side. "It's nothing to worry about," he said when the spasm passed. "Sometimes when I'm tired and stressed, I get a little reminder of my bout with the stun-cannon. There, it's gone now."

Tarlatine knew better. "Do you want me to send for Sijek?"

"No. No, it's not that bad. I'll have to get used to doing without him, won't I?"

"Then try to lead a less stressful life."

Tralvar gave a conspiratorial smile. "As a matter of fact I've been having some thoughts about that. But I'm keeping them to myself until after the Peisistrata."

***

While Dena convalesced at Tralvar's house, the whole of Alda Mexa focused its energies on the long-awaited Peisistrata - the first in five years. There were eleven days before the start of the festival - eleven days to gather food for a citywide banquet, garland the streets, prepare the marina for an influx of river traffic and make sure every scolia player and dancer was rehearsed and ready. Nefyrra rose to the occasion magnificently, although the few people who incurred her wrath were left in no doubt as to her parentage.

The Peisistrata was a two-day event, the first consisting of outdoor music and street theatre, the second devoted to feasting. To conclude the second day there was a midnight concert at the Lyricon - not for the inhabitants of Alda Mexa but the many visitors who habitually crowded into the city from Tivenne, Treva and even further afield. Laura would be performing last; just two songs were scheduled, as there were several other acts before her. She would, of course, sing "L'Invitation au Voyage", then, daringly, the Bell Song from Lakme. She hoped her voice wouldn't let her down.

Day One dawned fine and bright. Lydion and Tarlatine went to Lateral Four in the mid-morning to see Forlane announce the start of the festivities. The street was a riot of colour, from the floral decorations on every house to the bright costumes of the celebrants. Everyone waited in an impatient hush as Forlane, in resplendent purple, stepped forward.

"It seems appropriate that Laura should provide us with some opening lines," he began, "and thus I offer you this translation from the poet Byron of Symerid Three. Laura assures me that Byron knew how to enjoy himself!" He paused, then declaimed in tones easily heard by all:

"On with the dance! Let joy be unconfined;
No sleep till morn, when Youth and Pleasure meet
To chase the glowing hours with flying feet!"

With a clash of cymbals and bells, the lateral erupted into movement. Tarlatine opened her mind to the sheer hedonism of the gathering and laughed a little too wildly.

"Like it?" Lydion shouted in her ear.

"Love it!" she shouted back.

The highlight of the morning was the pageant of Hymorel and his wives. "The legend is," Lydion explained, "that after the meteor strike which devastated Celestra - oh yes, it happened, there's geological evidence - the survival of the species depended on one man and seven women."

"So this is a fertility rite?"

"More of a match-making exercise. It's a good way for our girls and the visitors to get acquainted."

The performance began; seven nubile girls in white weaving an intricate dance around a young man clad only in gold net. This year's Hymorel was none other than Ibri, the young radical who had outsmarted his Narvellan interrogators. He strutted, smirked and postured. And when, as part of the proceedings, girls along the route called out to him, he drew each one into a lascivious embrace before announcing her name to the crowd.

"Vulgarian!" remarked Forlane, nearby. "Things were done more artistically in my day."

"*You* were Hymorel?" inquired Tarlatine.

"Yes, indeed I was." He chuckled reminiscently. "I'm glad to see you enjoying yourself, dear lady. I feel a little guilty that we're partying so crazily when your homeworld lies in ruins."

"But according to Lydion, the legend's based on a disaster that befell *this* world."

"That's correct."

"Then why shouldn't you celebrate? I certainly don't begrudge it. Perhaps one day my people will commemorate *our* survival with feasting and music."

Forlane couldn't quite see that happening, but found her attitude refreshing.

The afternoon saw the long-anticipated return of the Zarf Dance. The reptilian zarf puppet, rescued from the Lyricon basement and newly repaired, was carried by seven slender young men whose near-naked bodies shone with oil. The dance circled the entire lateral, with the zarf snapping its jaws and chasing anything female. Tarlatine gripped Lydion's arm tightly and shivered at the eerie music that accompanied the spectacle. Toward evening, when the celebrations began to flag, they made their way back to Lydion's little house beside the outer colonnade of the Lyricon.

Supper that night was a frugal affair, in preparation for the following day's feast. Lydion had brought in a generous supply of pastries, exotic fruits and wine. But in fact they ate very little as they spent most of the day making love. Shortly before midnight, Lydion led Tarlatine outside to watch a lantern-lit procession wending its way up to the Lyricon. Most of the street lamps were already extinguished, leaving only the coloured motes of light moving far below.

"Oh, Lydion, it's beautiful," she whispered. "I'm so glad I saw all of this."

They waited, in a night suddenly grown overcast, until half the lantern-bearers had passed by. Then Lydion said:

"Well, duty calls. This is Nefyrra's big moment so I can't leave anyone else to run the weathershield. Why don't you go up to the custodian's suite and see the concert? I'm sure no-one would mind."

"I think I'll just stay here and wait for you," Tarlatine replied.

He gave one of his ready smiles. "That sounds delightful. Shan't be long - a couple of ilden at the most."

Tarlatine remained where she was, still as a statue, until rain drove her indoors.

The concert proceeded without a hitch. Ailsi and the other dancers were faultless. The scolia had the audience clapping and stamping to their lively rhythms, and would doubtless have had them dancing too if there had been room. Tralvar and Nefyrra played a duet, to appreciative applause. And Laura put so much sensuality into "L'Invitation au Voyage" that Nefyrra quite expected sciesha to break out on the terraces.

Then it was time for the Bell Song. Laura sang the first unaccompanied lines strongly, her voice at the peak of its form after days of endless practice. Nefyrra held her breath as the high note - the one Laura always seemed to founder on - approached, but it emerged piercingly perfect. The scolia came in with the accompaniment, and Nefyrra relaxed. Now she could enjoy the rest of the song.

She wasn't surprised when the crowd demanded an encore. Laura had prepared one in advance - "Les Filles de Cadiz". But afterward, the audience demanded yet another song. And another.

In the generator room, Lydion continued his solitary task. It was taking all his expertise to keep the shield running smoothly for so long, but he was determined not to let a breakdown spoil the finale. At last, faint echoes of Nefyrra's closing speech wafted down from the stage, and there came the sussuration of many feet leaving the amphitheatre. Grimy but happy with a job well done, he shut off the projectors, turned off the lights and walked the short distance to his home.

"Tarly!" he called softly as he went in. "Tarlatine!" And stopped, stricken. Her brightly coloured tunic lay crumpled on the bedroom floor. A wardrobe door stood open, displaying a gap where her Narvellan garments had been. A box of personal effects was gone from a shelf.

"No," Lydion breathed. "Oh, chaos, no. Not now. Not tonight!" Then he was out of the house and running along the darkened street, reaching the flitter park just ahead of some revellers. As he'd hoped, most of the machines were fully charged - no-one had used them during the feast. He flew straight to the spaceport with some half-formed idea of taking a sphere to Ilonna, but thought better of it and went to the communications tower instead.

When the lift doors whisked apart, admitting him to the upper level, his gaze was inescapably drawn to the deep space scanner. An iridescent cloud was moving across the giant screen: two thousand tiny points of light, accelerating beyond the orbits of the outer planets. With a bitter exclamation, he stumbled forward in the direction of the transposer.

"They won't answer," said someone. "Leave well alone."

Lydion turned sharply and peered across the ill-lit control centre. "Jarras? What are *you* doing here?"

"I'm on watch. Nefyrra wanted me out from underfoot, so I swapped duties. I mean it, Lydion - stay away from that panel. You know what was decided. No further communication."

"But they've got Tarly!"

"That infers they dragged her off," Jarras said acidly. "She chose to go. Walked straight past me, as it happens. Poised and calm, no tears, two brawny bodyguards in tow."

Lydion slumped into a chair. "If the concert hadn't run late I'd have been at home," he lamented.

"Just as well you weren't. You'd have tried to interfere and got yourself beaten up again."

"I suppose." Lydion stared bleakly at the receding traces.

"You always knew this day would come," Jarras added more gently.

"Do you think she was looking back at Alda Mexa?" Lydion asked wretchedly. "Would they have had their viewscreen on during take-off?"

"On a sub-orbital flight to Ilonna, they might well have done. Why?"

"Because she'd have seen the weathershield - a tiny blue glow in the darkness. And she'd have known I was

559

there, thinking of her. I'd like to believe she *did* see it, Jarras."

At that moment the cloud disappeared from the scanner. The fleet was in transposal. Numbly, Lydion returned home; and once there, found the note he'd overlooked in his haste.

"My Lydion: forgive me for not saying goodbye. Goodbye implies an ending, and my love for you is as constant as ever. I shall never forget the man who brought me joy and merriment after years of dullness and duty. I've absorbed so much of your fun-loving nature that my future children must surely absorb these traits from me, and in them I'll again see you. Promise me you won't mope or become cynical, but go on being your irrepressible self. Live, love, take sciesha, celebrate our love with more love. See how Celestrian I've become? I owe you so much. Now you owe it to me to be happy. Ever your Tarlatine."

He read the note about sixteen times, then realised Drusa was standing at his elbow. "We heard they'd left," she said. "Are you going to do as she says?"

He leant tiredly against her, seeking her hand, all the laughter gone from his eyes. "One day, Drusa. One day. But not yet."

***

"Hey, sleepy head!" A well-aimed pillow hit Idenion on the shoulder. "Wake up! It's after midday!"

Idenion sat up and yawned. "Must you shout so, Jarras? I was up very late."

"We all were."

"Not as late as me. I was writing a poem."

"What about?"

"Need you ask, after what you told me last night? Lydion, of course. I can empathise with his despair."

"Despair? Lydion? He'll be off chasing skirt in a few days."

560

"I wonder!"

"A few octals, then. Anyway, as far as today's concerned, I just wanted to let you know you'll be in charge of the Lyricon for a while - not that anyone's going to be thinking about music!"

Idenion then knew that his sensitised state was not due to over-indulgence. The air was thick with languorous, erotic promptings. Sciesha! He closed his mind to it determinedly.

"It's going to start any moment," Jarras confirmed. "Most of the visitors are still in town - I think they were expecting it." Then, searchingly: "Don't you *ever* take sciesha?"

Idenion struggled out of bed. "It makes me act like a barbarian, so I avoid it for everyone's sake. Where are Laura and Nefyrra? Indoors, I hope?"

"At Tralvar's, with Dena. I've just come from there. I warned them they'd be stranded but they said they couldn't disappoint her - they'd promised her an expert rundown on the concert. Aside from that, she's a bit low because Ninfi's just sent back her scieshanar."

"Oh?"

"Yes, Tralvar has a son. Ninfi says he was about four octals premature, but healthy and well. She wants to call him Kalyx."

"Does Tralvar approve of that?"

"Absolutely; why shouldn't he? Discords, you're looking rough. Don't you have any liman?"

"We ran out."

"I'll fetch you some of Nefyrra's. And then I must get going - Tralvar wants me to take a team to Ilonna and find out what state the Narvellans have left it in."

"Neat as a pin, I daresay."

"I'm curious to find out. But if I'm still in Alda Mexa when that sciesha starts, I won't *have* a team!" Jarras disappeared into the custodian's quarters, returned just long enough to thrust a cup of liman into Idenion's hand, and was gone.

Idenion finished his drink, showered and dressed, ate some fruit and went back to inspect his poem. It didn't have the passion of Clemoridys, but it wasn't bad. At least, he didn't *think* it was bad; it was difficult to concentrate with the clamour of sciesha all around. He wondered if Jarras had got clear. Shouts and shrieks came from the square, and from the auditorium itself. Looking out, he saw two dancers playing tag across the empty terraces. Eventually the girl allowed herself to be caught and, in the insufficient shadow of a pillar, she and her lover began an energetic coupling.

"Makes you want to join in, doesn't it?" said an impudent little voice. It was Ailsi, in an unusually demure white dress. Tiny white ribbons adorned her curls.

"*You* didn't start this off, I hope," Idenion accused.

Ailsi laughed. "On *this* scale? That's a bit beyond little me."

"I'm very glad to hear it. Now, since I'm apparently in charge this afternoon, what can I do for you?" His tone was discouraging.

"I want to talk to you about Laura," Ailsi said.

He frowned, but she went on determinedly:

"She told me a long time ago how sad she was that she couldn't have your children, and how you'd refused to sire a sciesha child for her to adopt."

"She'd be jealous," Idenion said for what seemed the hundredth time.

"Your stock reply. That's why she hasn't mentioned it lately. Did you know she wanted to adopt Dena's baby?"

"No!" Idenion was taken aback.

"It made sense, didn't it? A half-alien child? Tralvar wouldn't have wanted it around as a constant

562

reminder of Chisrin. That's what she was counting on, anyway."

"She never said a word to me," Idenion mused, half to himself. "How in chaos did she manage to keep it from me?"

"Maybe you should try reading her a little more," Ailsi suggested. "She'd even thought of a name. Desrina. So imagine how she must have felt when the baby died. And now there's Ninfi's child - another slap in the face. *And* - " she paused dramatically - "Nefyrra's expecting. It's early days - she hasn't even told Jarras yet - but she's sure. Laura's going to feel even more left out."

"Nobody ever asks me how *I* feel," Idenion pointed out with some emotion.

"Inadequate, I should think," Ailsi said cuttingly. "So, I'm here to offer you a favour. Take sciesha with me."

"So *that's* your game!" Idenion was furious. "Why must you always try to make mischief? Can't you see when to stop?"

She stood her ground. "I'm not here out of mischief. Call it altruism, if you like. It's something I felt I had to do."

"Just go, Ailsi."

"Don't be so self-righteous!" she snapped. "Do you think I *want* to proposition you? I don't even find you attractive!"

He was perturbed at her brutal honesty. "If you're trying to seduce me, you've a strange way of going about it."

"I believe in being frank. I'll follow it up with a confession, shall I? While I was on tour, I saw the bloom on me twice. And I didn't do anything about it."

On Celestra, that was tantamount to a sin. "Why?" Idenion asked faintly.

563

"Because I didn't want to be pregnant. I wanted to dance. So here I am, guilty and penitent, ready to do the right thing." Then, when he didn't move: "Well, at least *read* me. I want you to know I'm sincere. Then, if you like, I'll go away."

"I...I don't..."

"*Please*?"

He read her. Truth, earnestness and a surprising amount of maturity.

"Thank you *very* much, Idenion," she said softly. And then - and he would never know how she did it - she seized his mind and turned it outward, to the sciesha. Sheer primal energy hit him like a physical blow, and he cried out. Mating fever took swift hold of him, and all reason - even his identity - fled beyond his reach. Two stark facts remained: he craved sex, and there was a willing woman before him. In a fury of lust, he threw her down.

Several astallen later, he crawled off the ruin of his bed and stood gazing ashamedly at his sciesha partner. Ailsi was trying not to cry. He could see the marks of his fingers on her upper arms. There was an angry scratch across her left breast and the beginnings of a bruise under one eye.

"I shall have to revise my opinion of you," she said shakily. "You're quite a man."

"Well, I hope you're pleased with yourself, you little minx," he responded angrily. "I've hurt you and I've betrayed Laura. It was all just as I said, wasn't it? Selfish mischief! How am I ever going to justify - " Then he stopped in something akin to awe. On her face, breasts and taut little stomach, unmistakable red whorls had begun to appear.

"You were saying?" she inquired.

"Ailsi! How did you *know*?"

564

"I'm a dancer. I'm very much in tune with my own body, and I knew the signs." She stood up and began to dress, wincing a little. "Right, to practicalities. Do you have a scieshanar?"

"Er...er...no."

"Then I'll find something to use instead." She rifled through a couple of drawers and found Laura's Greek medallion. "Here's a pendant with the Lyricon on it. I'll take this, shall I?"

"I suppose so. Laura doesn't wear it any more."

Ailsi paused at the bedroom door. "Oh, by the way - I'm opening a little dance studio in Tivenne. I'm going to teach. So I won't be around to annoy you." With one last impish smile, she vanished. Drained and bemused, Idenion subsided onto the bed.

When the sciesha had burnt itself out, Laura returned to find him still lying there in a post-coital stupor. She also found two of Ailsi's hair ribbons and discovered her pendant was missing. But she merely smiled to herself and said nothing.

Later, at supper, she did have something to tell him. "Tralvar wants to give up being First Citizen," she announced.

"That doesn't surprise me," Idenion said. "He needs a rest."

"He's going to phase out his activities, giving himself more time to enjoy his music. He'll create a new post, that of deputy First Citizen, and train someone to eventually take his place."

"Good idea." Idenion seemed more interested in his soup.

"Would you care to know who he wants as deputy?" pursued Laura.

"Jarras, I suppose." Idenion poured himself some more wine.

"No. You."

"*Me*?" Idenion nearly dropped the wine bottle. "Me, First Citizen?"

"He says you're a good communicator and you're fast learning some commonsense," Laura said proudly.

He should have been here this afternoon, Idenion thought. "All right, I'll let him try me out. He'll soon change his mind."

"I'm hoping he doesn't," Laura declared. "It's about time you had a good solid career." She deliberated a moment, then added: "Especially if you're going to be a family man."

"There's a very good chance of that," he admitted.

Delighted, Laura held out her wine glass. "Here's to the future," she said. "And a little less excitement."

Epilogue

An early autumn chill was in the air when a courier delivered a small package from Tivenne. Idenion opened it to find Laura's medallion and a few words in Ailsi's neat handwriting: "Come and collect your daughter."

In a daze the prospective parents made the arrangements, travelling by flitter rather than the more public monorail. Ailsi met them at the flitter park and carefully handed Laura a tiny bundle cocooned in a huge shawl. Very gently, Laura uncovered the baby's head to reveal straight, silky blonde hair like Idenion's. A pair of quizzical grey eyes peered up at her.

"I was going to call her Clemoridys," said Ailsi, "but that's a bit of a mouthful so I shortened it to Clemis. You don't have to stick with that, of course - she isn't registered yet."

"When was she born?"

"Four octals ago."

"She's so little," Laura breathed. "Are you sure it isn't too soon for us to take her?"

"Hey, look, I've done my bit for the planet," Ailsi declared. "I've lost my milk so there's no point in my hanging onto her, is there? I want to concentrate on getting back into shape." She still looked as skinny as ever.

"May I hold her?" asked Idenion, and Laura gingerly passed the infant to him.

"Look at her eyes, Idenion! I swear she's reading my mind already."

"Of course she is," Idenion said cheerfully. "Don't you remember what I told you about the very young? They absorb everything. Later on, she'll be more

567

selective - but not till she's able to send thoughts herself."

"I can't thank you enough, Ailsi," said Laura humbly.

"Don't mention it."

"And I *will* call her Clemis. It's a lovely name."

"Good! That's all right then. I'm off." She stuffed a piece of paper into Idenion's pocket. "That has her full birth details, my lineage and so on. And here - " she slipped an ylur bag from her shoulder and handed it to Laura - "are her spare clothes and some brushed ytil nappies. They're the best, you know."

"Er...yes." Laura tried to look knowledgeable.

"You'll need a carrying sling," Ailsi added. "I never bothered with one. Well, let me know how she goes on." Then she left them, her walk a little too jaunty.

"She...won't want to take her back, will she?" quavered Laura.

"No," Idenion said reassuringly. "I just asked her."

"And what did she say?"

"She said, a promise is a promise. By the way, Clemis means star-child."

"Oh, Idenion!" Laura was suddenly apprehensive. "I'm so clueless about babies. How often do I feed her? What on? Where's she going to sleep?"

"All you need do," said Idenion soothingly, "is speak to Nefyrra. She's been steeped in baby lore all year. And if it's medical advice you want, there's always Drusa."

"Of course. I'm panicking." Laura smiled apologetically. "Well, I suppose I'd better sign that marriage register now, hadn't I? Just to make everything legal."

"I was hoping you'd say that." Idenion gazed fondly down at his baby daughter who, surrounded by loving thoughts, was now almost asleep. "And we'll have to

568

think about a trip to see Nathaniel. You'll want to show off our little girl, won't you?"

"Not until she's older!" Laura protested. "And maybe not even then. It's too dangerous. Besides, Nathaniel thinks I've gone for good. It would be cruel to make him lose me a second time. And *you'll* have to stay put too. No more gadding off to Earth now you're First Citizen Elect!"

"An awesome responsibility," Idenion murmured. He was still looking at Clemis as he said it.

"We'll cope. No, we'll thrive," Laura declared. "*This* is our future now: this world, each other, and the new generation."

Together they walked back to the flitter.

THE END

GLOSSARY

CAST OF CHARACTERS

Celestrians:

Ailsi	young factory worker/dancer
Alkesta	pregnant girl
Corython	astronomer, mathematician
Cyphos	factory worker /stonemason
Dena	Idenion's twin sister
Drusa	Tyvian's assistant, a healer
Forlane	an actor
Ibri	militant factory worker
Idenion	First Poet, in love with Laura
Jarras	a scientist, Tralvar's colleague
Jedak	political pamphleteer based in Ninka
Kalyx	Tralvar's childhood name
Kyrin	a professional relayist
Lydion	weathershield operator
Lykalion	Lydion's father
Malcor	Ailsi's lover
Mahra	a midwife
Mehedra	Tralvar's mother
Nefyrra	Tralvar's daughter
Ninfi	girl who seduces Tralvar
Nohal	senior relayist at Tafret Academy
Rillan	young technician, friend of Jarras
Rinyi	relayist, lover of Isylla
Tatra	Cyphos' wife
Thala	Rillan's partner, co-emissary to Narvella
Tralvar	First Scientist, later First Citizen
Tristell	Celestra's last singer (deceased)
Tyvian	botanist, creator of the retracer

Narvellans:

Axmiol tyl Thuuvin	Governor of Celestra
Besu	an elderly administrator
Bydlor	aide to Administrator Narad
Chisrin ap Tuin	geologist, overseer at aldacite factory, Dena's lover
Clovath zyl Imlis	head of maintenance at the Synectic base
Eluthia	Lydion's Narvellan girlfriend
Grevin tal Prelix	Ex-Governor of Celestra
Firessa lyr Raxel	biologist, victim of the Ten
Hapka	a Moderator
Hysek tyl Pellon	Narvellan who refuses to adopt Quetri
Isylla	Grevin's wife (disgraced)
Myrig tyl Plessit	Administrator, organiser of Celestrian workforce
Narad zyl Pereth	Administrator, enamoured of Idenion
Navarian tyl Pellon	Quetri's patron (deceased)
Passik	a Directress
Quetri zyl Nyris	young Narvellan bondservant who assists the Celestrian cause
Quodos	overseer at sphere assembly works
Quon zyl Apteris	overseer at liman processing plant
Salvi	a Directress, suspected of "impurity"
Sarune	leader of the Synectics, wife to Chisrin
Sijek tyl Thuuvin	Axmiol's favoured one
Tarlatine	elite-wife, married to Besu, later loved by Lydion
Tarysk tyl Pellon	Quetri's present owner

Earthers:

Gus	owner of the Firelight jazz club
Laura Meredith, nee Gilcoyne	the heroine, a singer
Nathaniel Gilcoyne (retired)	Laura's uncle, stockbroker
Peter Meredith	Laura's husband
Margaret Moffatt	Nathaniel's housekeeper
Caitlin Stretton	Laura's nosy neighbour
Chris / Darren	UFO hunters

PLACE NAMES

Celestra and Narvella:

Akron	administration centre and ruler's home
Alda	Celestra's sun
Alda Mexa	Celestra's capital, City of the Sun
Alda Nima	town where famous bell of same name was created
Atris	city to the north
Corayn	centre for herbs and medicines
Etys	river, tributary of the Lisir
Etys Point	location of a liman refinery
Etys South	another industrial complex on the river
Ilonna	a ghost town
Ipsa	a moon of Narvella Five
Kassi	a town in Celestra's southern hemisphere
Lake Holpen	beauty spot near Alda Mexa
Liapa	plain on Ipsa, site of the Synectics' base

572

Lisir Mexa	river which runs through Alda
Lyricon Mexa	cherished theatre, situated in Alda
Myrma	a pleasure planet near Celestra
Narvella	a distant star with two inhabited planets
Narvella Prime	main planet of Narvella System
Scapirion	town on Celestra's south polar continent, with reclusive inhabitants
Symerid	Sol
Symerid Three	Earth
Tafret	town where young relayists are sent for training
Tivenne	village near Alda Mexa
Treva	town to north-east of Alda Mexa, industrial heart of Celestra
Virda	fishing village, home to Kyrin

Earth/England:

Cheveney	Laura's village
Wickens Clump	wood where UFO's have been sighted
Windbourne	Nathaniel's house

ALIEN TERMS

Aldacite	versatile crystal used in logic systems etc.
Astal/Astallen	unit of time, equivalent to six minutes
Biosphere/Sphere	Celestrian spacecraft
Directresses	Narvellan women who dowse for minerals

Firi	filmy material worn by dancers
Hrilffa	thorny plant
Ild/Ilden	unit of time equivalent to just under 50 minutes or eight astallen: There are 30 ilden in one day
Isk	unit of time equivalent to a second.
Ksil	dishonoured (Narvellan)
Kyffu	waterfowl
Liman	a milky drink native to Celestra
Mark of Netsamet	Narvellan man's wedding band
Neph-khet	"favoured one," a Narvellan youth beloved of an older man
Octal	a period of eight days
Peisistrata	Celestrian festival
Pilif	small succulent yellow fruit
Prill	telepathic plant
Pyxis	musical instrument like a flute
Relayists	telepaths who circulate news and conduct commerce
Resnay	strong alcoholic drink
Retracer	a device for recording peoples' memories
Rule of Khesa	obscure Narvellan legislation
Scolia	Celestrian orchestra
Sekhu	Narvellan ritual of atonement
Sciesha	mating fever
Scieshanar	medallion, Celestrian, denoting one's ancestry
Silmos/Silmi	a measurement of distance, equal to one-third of a mile
Span	Celestrian month
Sphere	see biosphere
Starfire	powerful stimulant (proscribed substance)

Strelsis	stringed instrument in various sizes
Theridolyte	a strengthened and stabilised version of therite
Therite	a mineral, unstable when processed, used for quarrying & weapons
Total Unity	the telepathic part of the sex act
Transposal	the Celestrian hyperdrive
Transposer	hyperspace transmitter/receiver
Ylur	coarse material from which overalls are made
Ytil	material normally used for garments
Zarf	a mythical Celestrian beast with a voracious sexual appetite
Zirid	keyboard instrument